THE FROZEN LAKE

Elizabeth Edmondson lives in Italy and England. Her English roots are in the Lake District, where her father's family comes from. She is married with two grown-up children.

The Frozen Lake was inspired by an old snapshot of an eccentric great-aunt out on the ice, and a rich fund of family memories and stories of life in the Lakes in the nineteen-thirties have made a big contribution to the book.

For automatic updates on Elizabeth Edmondson, visit HarperCollins.co.uk and register for AuthorTracker.

ELIZABETH EDMONDSON

The Frozen Lake

HarperCollins*Publishers*

HarperCollins*Publishers*
77–85 Fulham Palace Road,
Hammersmith, London W6 8JB

www.harpercollins.co.uk

A Paperback Original 2005
1 3 5 7 9 8 6 4 2

A catalogue record for this book
is available from the British Library

ISBN 0 00 718486 7

Typeset in Sabon by Palimpsest Book Production Limited,
Polmont, Stirlingshire

Printed and bound in Great Britain by
Clays Ltd, St Ives plc

For Tio, who was there

This book is dedicated with love to my uncle,
James Edmondson, whose memories of Westmoreland
winters of long ago and stories of life in the
nineteen-thirties have been a delight and an inspiration.

Manchester Guardian

APRIL 1921

STOP PRESS

Westmoreland man killed in mountaineering accident

Neville Richardson, eldest son of Sir Henry and Lady Richardson of Wyncrag, fell to his death earlier this month, while climbing in the Andes. Aged forty-one, he leaves a wife, Helena, a son and two daughters. Sir Henry's youngest son, Jack Richardson MC, died in France in 1917.

Never does the scenery appear to more advantage as when the lake is covered with transparent ice from end to end, and the glint of sunshine, investing its surface with bright and changeful colours, makes it appear like an opal set in a wreath of virgin white. Towards sunset the snow-clad fells assume every tint the sun can create, from deepest crimson to palest gold. Frost fringes becks and rivers, and the ice patterns windows with its chilly fingers, weaving ethereal cobwebs across hedges and fells. Breath freezes on the air and the black coats of Fell ponies on the hillside are dusted white, manes and eyelashes touched with ice, and icicles tangle the shaggy fleeces of the hardy native sheep while they forage for food beneath the snow.

There has not been a frost such as this since the winter of 1920/1921, and the news that the great lakes of the north are freezing over has reached not merely our local papers, but the columns of the great London newspapers, sending accounts of the icy weather around the globe. As northerners sharpen their skates and watch the clear blue skies and starry nights for any sign of an unwelcome break in the weather, exiles in England and abroad are remembering frozen days of long ago, closing their eyes to grey town streets as they dream of dazzling winter skies, of air unsullied by smoke and soot and fumes. In their minds, they are once again skating from one end of the lake to the other beneath the towering fells, sharp blades hissing on dazzling ice, ears and fingers tingling, spirits filled with a wild joy.

Homecomings

ONE

London, Chelsea

Why didn't she go north for Christmas?

Alix Richardson broke two eggs into a bowl and stirred them with a fork. Cecy Grindley's words hadn't been critical or nosy, she had just asked a simple and natural question. Even though her childhood friend was aware of Alix's sentiments towards her grandmother, she didn't see that as a good reason for staying away from Wyncrag.

Cecy was probably right. Alix stared down at the yellow mixture without enthusiasm. She didn't care much for omelettes, but seemed to be eating a lot of them.

Food for a solitary life.

Other people spent Christmas with their families. It was customary, even if they regretted it every time, and every year swore, never again. Those who had no real family life always imagined such gatherings as the acme of happiness and warmth, although the truth was that they were just as likely to turn out disastrously: family rows, old grudges dug up to fuel resentment and animosity, lost tempers and frayed nerves exposed over roast meats and bumpers of brandy.

Alix lit the gas under the omelette pan and watched the

knob of butter dissolve and sizzle. Christmas at Wyncrag wasn't like that. Grandmama's eyebrows might be raised, but never voices. Temper, anger and arguments had no place in that household. Nursery scenes were kept to the nursery; once outside those protective doors, good manners and fear of Grandmama kept the house serene and orderly. On the surface, at any rate.

She poured the beaten eggs into the butter and tilted the pan as the omelette began to cook. There had been a time, once, when noise and laughter and happy voices had been heard at Wyncrag. When she and Edwin and Isabel and their parents had been together as a family.

In her mind's eye, Alix could see her sister coming home to Wyncrag from a day's shooting, before the frost had set in and the snow had swept down from the fells. Even at four-teen, Isabel had been a first-rate shot, unlike the rest of her family, who might take out a gun from time to time, but shared none of their neighbours' passion for the sport.

She could remember being on the ice with Edwin, her twin, that December, sliding and skating and tobogganing.

The holiday had begun with the house ringing to children's excited shrieks and the sound of their running feet – and had ended with cold, half-overheard words. Their last Christmas together.

She slid the omelette on to a plate taken from the rack over the stove and carried it to the table in the other room. She poured herself a glass of wine and put a forkful of omelette into her mouth, quite unaware of its taste.

There had been those conversations that ended abruptly when she or Edwin entered a room. She remembered, with sudden unnerving clarity, her mother for once raising her voice to Grandmama and Grandmama's vicious, indecipher-able replies, delivered in a hissing undertone.

She drank some of the wine – it could have been vinegar or orangeade. Isabel was ill, the twins were told. They didn't say what was wrong with her, something infectious, so that she had been shut away in a distant corner of the house. Alix recalled quite vividly, looking through the eyes of forgotten childhood, coming into the hall to find Rokeby distractedly taking down the Christmas decorations. Aunt Trudie was there, too, tearing the candles and ornaments from the tree and piling them higgledy-piggledy in a cracker box, instead of wrapping each one in tissue paper and laying it in the wooden chest kept for the purpose.

Alix pushed the rest of her omelette to one side of her plate. Hotpot, it was a long time since she'd eaten hotpot. People in London knew nothing about hotpots. Or porridge at breakfast, with brown sugar and thick cream from the farm. Grandpapa ate his in the Scots way, with salt, but for her it was sugar and cream every time. Chocolate pudding. If she went home, Cook would make her one of her ambrosial chocolate puddings with the hot chocolate sauce that was famous throughout the lakes, the recipe for which was kept under lock and key.

Alix got up and carried plate and glass into the kitchen. She put them by the sink; her char would do the washing-up in the morning. She made coffee, watching with unseeing eyes as the hot liquid bubbled to the top of the pot.

She had cut her ties with Wyncrag, gone off to make a life of her own. Did the traditions mean anything to her? Did she yearn for carols and plum pudding and parcels under the tree?

No.

But she did yearn for the lake and the hills and for the feel of icy air on glowing cheeks, and she longed once again to be flying over the ice under pure, cold blue skies. And for hotpot and chocolate pudding. Not to mention the delicious game there always was at this time of the year. Bread, too, you couldn't seem to buy proper bread in London. At Wyncrag, the baker's boy still delivered the bread every morning, a basket of loaves wrapped in a cloth, miraculously warm.

Was there a risk of Grandmama dragging her back under her thumb if she went back? Surely not, not now.

If she went to Wyncrag for Christmas – it was only a few days, after all – she could spend hours and hours with Edwin. Talking and walking and skating and laughing, just as they used to. She'd avoided him since she came south, although she knew he came several times a year to London. She missed him, but their very closeness made her wary of seeing much of him. He knew her too well, and she felt that his under-standing touched raw nerves that were best left alone. She had chosen to leave the north and her family, while his deci-sion had been to remain. It was easier for him. Grandmama didn't rule him with the ferocity that she applied to her female descendants, and so he could have his own place in Lowfell and keep a small flat in London, privileges that would never be granted to her.

Yet now, suddenly, she longed to see him again. And there was Perdita – what a difference between twelve and fifteen; did she want her sister to grow up a stranger to her?

She saw Grandpapa, when he came to London, two or three times a year. Strong-minded she might have become, but she wasn't heartless. He would write, giving her plenty of notice, and then take her to dinner at one of his favourite restaurants, dark, peaceful places, where the waiters moved at a gentle pace and the food was substantial, beautifully cooked and comforting.

In the spring, they had gone to Germany for a week together. He had spent a good deal of time in Germany as a young man and had studied there. He wanted his children and his grandchildren to speak the language, and had employed German governesses and tutors to teach them. He shook his head over the new Germany, the sour fruit of Versailles, he called it. Alix had enjoyed herself, tasting the bizarre delights of Berlin in the company of young relations of Grandpapa's friends. She hoped he had no notion of how different her contemporaries were from the serious, responsible citizens he knew so well, although Grandpapa had always had the knack of ignoring what he couldn't change. She loved him, but knew that her world and its ways were a closed book to him – thank God for it. He would be so pleased to see her if she went back to Wyncrag this year. She had quickly read and torn up the wistful letter that came from him, as it did towards the end of every year, enclosing a handsome cheque and saying how much he missed seeing her at Christmas.

It was stupid. It was the time of year, the tinsel tiresomeness of it all, the catchy sentimentality of the season.

Of course she wouldn't go north. It was a stupid idea.

And an idea that would never have occurred to her if she hadn't run into Cecy while Christmas shopping in Harrods. Cecy, a Grindley of Grindley Hall, their nearest neighbours in Westmoreland, and one of her oldest friends.

She had been more pleased to see Cecy than she would have believed possible, her familiar smile, eyes merry behind round spectacles, a weight of fair hair trying to escape from a bun. Cecy belonged to the time before she'd plunged into the restless, messy life of her recent past. Then, she'd scorned friendship; now, she was grateful that there was any aspect of human relationship left that she hadn't mocked and trampled on.

These last weeks, she thought, looking back over the bleak days, had made her long for the warmth of simple, genuine friendship. Friendship, not the mindless desire not to be alone for a moment, day or night. Her address book, her one-time bible, crammed full of names and telephone numbers of people she never wanted to see or hear from again, was shut up in her desk.

She still had no idea why she had woken up one morning, earlier than usual, hung-over, hot, uncomfortable, and had conceived an instant, blinding hatred for the man sprawled beside her, one masculine leg hanging over the side of the bed. He was no worse than the others, less so perhaps; inoffensive, with some charm about him, able to take away the loneliness for a few moments of passion and rob the night of its desolation.

She suddenly wanted none of him. She had yanked at his leg, thrown his clothes at him, driven him from the flat. Home from work that evening, she had taken the telephone off the hook, unwired the door bell, and spent the whole evening soaking in the bath and reading the children's books she had bought at lunchtime: *The Phoenix and the Carpet* and *Alice's Adventures in Wonderland* and *What Katy Did*.

She had expected the mood to pass, that in a little while she would want to be back among her set – but it hadn't happened. The liveliness seemed brittle, their vivacity aimless and empty, the round of parties and nightclubs pointless, the sophistication superficial and unsatisfactory. She was like a snake that had sloughed its skin, and was waiting to see what new patterns it might find its scales forming themselves into. She bathed a lot, drank very little, refused all invitations, fled round corners or hid in shop doorways to avoid the acquaintances who'd been her companions for months past.

And now there was Cecy, smiling at her in the old way. She felt guilty at how she had let her old friends drop. All very well to cut herself off from her family, but Cecy wasn't family. Alix had known she was in London, a medical student at one of the big hospitals, but had made no effort to meet up with her.

She suggested a film.

'There's the new Cary Grant at the Odeon. With Bettina Brand. Queues round the block, I should think.'

'Never mind,' Cecy said. 'Let's brave the queue, and go.'

It was a good programme, with a cartoon before the Pathé News and the main feature. They found the cartoon very

10

funny, although the light-hearted mood was rather dispelled by the grainy news pictures of a rally in Berlin.

'Good marchers, you've got to say that for them,' said a woman in the row behind.

'Some of that discipline would do all the layabouts in this country a bit of good.'

'That Hitler's barking: shouting and yelling and shooting his arm into the air all the time. And his moustache, did you ever see anything so silly?'

'He makes my flesh creep, him and those others going about in uniforms all the time.'

'Sssh.'

The scenes of Herr Hitler addressing a rally gave way to ranks of German beauties, bursting with health at a Strength Through Joy camp, waving scarves in synchronised patterns, and then to a shot of members of Hitler Youth relaxing with outsize tankards of beer on benches at a heavily timbered country inn, with snow-capped mountains as a backdrop.

'At last,' Cecy said, settling herself more comfortably in her seat as the strains of organ music faded away, and the curtains swished open again to show MGM's roaring lion.

Late to bed, and cursed with wakefulness, Alix finally fell into a restless sleep in the early hours of the morning. As a result, she overslept and only just got to her office on time, signing her name in the book at one minute to nine. The man on duty at the reception desk scowled at her, he'd hoped to catch her out for once. 'Thank you, Mr Milsom,' she said brightly. Avoiding the minute and ancient lift in the centre of the stairwell, she started up the three flights of stairs to her office in the copywriting department.

Although office was a generous word for a cubby-hole carved out of a box room, with barely enough room for a small desk, a chair and a wobbly bookshelf containing out of date directories (cunningly dumped there by other members

11

of staff), a thesaurus (essential, always tracked down and recovered within a short time of it being purloined from the shelf), a dictionary (1912 edition, the more modern one having been borrowed by the copy department and never returned), an aged copy of *Gray's Anatomy* (invaluable for pharmaceutical clients and for the dull but profitable remedies-for-all-ailments products), last year's *Wisden* (a mystery, that one), dictionaries of quotations and proverbs (almost as closely guarded as the Roget) and several discarded trashy novels, borrowed by members of the typing pool on dull days and kept there as being the only available shelf space.

A brisk morning's work with the EasiTums account – *For the liverish feeling that takes the zest out of life* – saw her desk clear of immediate tasks, and at ten to one, she was in the telephone box on the corner of the street.

She'd try Edwin at his studio number first, she might be lucky and she'd rather telephone him there than risk ringing Wyncrag. She picked up the receiver, dialled the operator, and asked for a long distance number. There was a long pause, clicking sounds, the operator told her to put in her coins, and she was through.

Her twin's voice came down the line, blessedly familiar. 'Alix?'

'Oh, Edwin, yes, it's me. Look, I wonder . . .' Now she didn't really know what to say. 'Is it true, is the lake freezing?'

'Coming along nicely. Give it a few more days of this frost and we'll be skating on it. They all swear there's no sign of the weather changing. Come up, do, or can't you bear to drag yourself away from the bright lights of London?'

'If only you knew. I was thinking of it, but Grandmama . . .'

'She'll be pleased.'

'It's been more than three years.'

'No time at all, and besides, it is your home. Come up as soon as you can get away. Don't bring the man in your life with you, however.'

12

'There isn't one.'

The silence at the other end spoke volumes.

'Edwin? Are you still there?'

'Let me know what train, so that you can be met, Lexy,' he said.

His use of her nursery name from long ago made her blink. 'I'd better telephone Grandmama.'

'I'll tell her. I'll say I rang you and persuaded you to come north. And I'll look out your skates for you, take them to the blacksmith if the blades need sharpening.'

The operator cut in, her voice indifferent. 'Your three minutes are up, caller.'

TWO

London, Whitehall

Saul Richardson looked down from the tall window. Beneath him, the traffic in Whitehall buzzed to and fro, the cars and taxis so many black beetles, the red livery of the double-decker buses a flash of brightness in the rainy gloom. A troop of Horseguards trotted past, hooves ringing on the Tarmac, the riders' uniforms and the gleam of their breastplates adding another dash of colour to the scene. Black horses shook heads and manes, snatched at bridles, eager to get back to their stalls, out of the sleeting rain.

He turned and looked in the other direction, out over Parliament Square. Westminster Abbey and squat St Margaret's, both blackened by soot, looked ancient, cold and unwelcoming. The great Gothic edifice of the Houses of Parliament did nothing to enliven the scene. A solitary constable in a cape stood on duty at the gates to the House of Commons. No flag fluttered above St Stephen's Tower; the House had risen for the Christmas break, and MPs were away in constituencies, gadding abroad on fact-finding or government missions, or packing for holidays in warmer climes. Only MPs like Saul, a junior member of His Majesty's Government, were still in town, serving king and country.

The door opened and a young man, smooth as to clothes, hair and expression, came into the room.

'The morning newspapers, sir. I've marked one or two items for you to look at.'

'Thank you, Charles,' Saul said, still gazing out of the window.

Charles coughed, Saul looked around at him. 'What is it?'

'The lakes are freezing, so it says in *The Times*.'

'The lakes? Which lakes? What are you talking about? Canada? The United States?'

'Your lake, sir. I thought you would be interested.'

'My lake?'

'In Westmoreland.'

'I'll have a look at the papers in a minute.'

'These letters are for you to attend to.'

'Leave them on the desk.'

'Will there be anything else?'

'No, no . . . Why?'

'Because if you don't need me for a while, I'll go to Downing Street and collect those papers from the Cabinet Office.'

'Can't they send a messenger? Oh, very well.' Saul waited for the door to shut completely, and then bounded to his desk and took up the newspaper. Ignoring trouble in Turkey – dammit, there was always trouble in Turkey – alarming news in from the Far East and the tense situation in Spain, Charles, impudent young ass, had folded the newspaper back to an aerial photograph of snow-covered fells towering over that oh-so-familiar sheet of water, gleaming in icy splendour.

Saul read the caption and the piece that accompanied the photograph. Then he threw the paper down on the desk and went back to the window, his arms folded. He had the odd sensation of being two men, one clad in the black jacket and grey striped trousers of the official world, pale faced, not a sleek hair out of place; the other existing three hundred miles

15

away, wearing tweeds, brown boots and skates on his feet, hair ruffled by the wind, cheeks glowing from the cold.

He reached out for the telephone on his desk and picked up the receiver. 'Get me Mrs Richardson, please.'

A minute later, the telephone bell shrilled out. 'Jane? I'm cancelling the Christmas visit to the constituency. We'll go north. Ring Mama and tell her we're coming. After the weekend, I think. We'll drive. I leave all the arrangements to you.'

He replaced the receiver, strode across the room, unhooked his overcoat from the coatstand, put it on, wrapped his sombre scarf into the neck of the coat and, bowler hat in hand, left the room. He travelled swiftly through the outer office. 'I'll be back at about, oh, say four,' he said in passing to the bun-faced woman lodged behind an enormous typewriter. 'Tell Charles to deal with those papers, no, I can't be contacted.'

Then he was out in the corridor and walking quickly towards the lifts. He didn't want to leave London without seeing Mavis.

THREE

London, Knightsbridge

The phone rang and rang. Jane Richardson could see, as clearly as though she were there, the telephones sounding their shrill alerts: in the Great Hall, in Rokeby's pantry, in Henry's study, in Caroline's dressing room.

Finally, the phone was picked up in mid-ring, and Jane heard a harsh, French-accented voice say, 'Hello?'

'Who is this?' Jane said, her own voice tart now.

'Lipp.'

'Lipp. I might have known. Why are you answering the phone?'

'There's no one else to answer it. Is that Mrs Saul?'

How she hated to be called Mrs Saul. 'Lipp, after all these years you surely know that when you answer the telephone, if you must do so, please respond with the number. Don't just say, Hello. It's most unhelpful. One could have been connected to anyone, and I don't see why you have to answer the telephone. Where is Rokeby? You must know.' Of course Lipp knew, she always knew where everyone was.

'Rokeby's helping Sir Henry with the generator.'

'Oh, really, it's too bad.' Why a man of her father-in-law's

17

years and dignity, who moreover kept a full staff, felt he had to attend to the generator was beyond her understanding. 'Go and tell Lady Richardson I would like to speak to her, please.'

There was a clunk as Lipp laid the receiver down; far away in London, Jane could hear the click-clack of Lipp's heels receding into the distance as her mother-in-law's maid went upstairs.

Lipp must have left the receiver too close to the edge of the table, for there was a rustling sound and a thump, then more bangs. The receiver dangling on its cord, no doubt, swinging to and fro, and banging against the table leg as it did so. There was a harsh crackle down the line, further bumps and bangs, and then she heard Caroline's voice.

'Jane?'

'Shall I put this one down now, my lady?' cut in Lipp's voice.

'Yes,' said Jane and Caroline together.

Crash.

'That terrible woman,' Jane said, under her breath.

'What did you say? Nothing? I distinctly heard you speak. Never mind. How is Saul?'

'Perfectly well. He wants us to come to Wyncrag for Christmas.'

Caroline's crystalline tones came down the line, as clear as though she were standing beside her; Caroline's voice was like that on the telephone. 'I was expecting you. When are you coming?'

'Saul hasn't decided. He intends to drive down, so he'll be anxious to get away from London in good time before the Christmas exodus starts. One day next week, I'll let you know. Perdita breaks up this week, I suppose. Who else will be there?'

'Edwin wants to persuade Alix to come.'

'Alix! Good heavens, after all this time? Have you heard from her?'

18

'I've heard of her, which is quite enough. It seems that she's fallen into unsuitable company.'

'Alix is old enough to decide what company is or isn't suitable for her, Caroline. She's no longer a child. If you set into her the moment she steps into Wyncrag, you may find she turns straight around and leaves. I would.'

'I hardly think your opinion on this subject is of any importance.'

Nor was her opinion on anything else, not as far as Caroline was concerned.

'Besides, I have no expectation of her coming.'

The sound of the receiver being put down, a pause, and then another voice quacked at her. 'You have upset Madame.'

Lipp again.

'Madame's upset me.'

'She is no longer young, you should have consideration.'

'Thank you, Lipp. Is there anything else you want to say?'

'Madame wishes you to go to Bond Street and collect some linen she has ordered. You may bring it up with you in the car.'

'Goodbye,' Jane said firmly. She replaced the receiver with deliberate care, and then sat absolutely still, hands folded in her lap. Not a hair was out of place; from her elegant grey shoes through her pale grey skirt and cashmere grey twinset, worn with a restrained diamond brooch, to her faultless face and sleek jaw-length hair, she was a picture of perfection.

Outside, all was calm. Within, she seethed. She longed to hurl the telephone across the room, to bang her hands on the table, to yell and stamp. Wyncrag. How she hated Wyncrag. Almost as much as she hated the Surrey house with its ridiculous half-timbering and pompous attempt to look like a real country house. Almost as much as she hated this flat, with its spindly French furniture, its valuable rugs and pictures and mirrors. Perfect. Sterile. Appropriate. Just as she was the perfect, most appropriate wife imaginable for an up-and-coming politician.

19

She flipped open the cigarette box and jammed a cigarette between her lips. She lit it with the heavy silver table lighter, shaped like a tureen, loathsome thing, and flipped open a copy of *Country Life*, jerking through the pages filled with photographs of desirable properties for sale.

Her eyes fell on a small, black and white picture. *Impey Manor*, she read. *Fifteenth-century manor house with many original features, in need of modernisation and improvements. Gardens, garaging, stabling, maze, small lake, paddocks, nine acres in all.*

In your dreams, she thought. In those dreams where she lived in shabby comfort in the country, in a mellow old house, full of twisting passages and unexpected stairs. Dogs. Ponies. Doves fluttering around a dovecote. Winter mud and ice; sudden spring; the deep smells of summer, newly cut grass, hay, roses; autumn trees in a blaze of colour. Children in gumboots swishing through the fallen leaves.

That was the knife twisting in the wound. To linger in such dreams was unendurable. She dragged herself back into the actual world of here and now. Forget manor houses and the country and roses, she told herself.

Children.

The children Saul wouldn't let her have. Or, rather, the children Saul's mother didn't want her to have, since she and her husband were cousins, and the dangers of inbreeding, as Caroline so charmingly put it, not worth risking.

She slammed the magazine shut, got up, drawing ferociously on her cigarette, making mental lists. Saul first: his man would see to his clothes. His skates, were they here or at Wyncrag? Binoculars. Books, presents, she would have to finish her shopping in a hurry. Her mind skittered from thing to thing. The evening dress that needed altering. Her engagement diary, day after day over Christmas and New Year filled with cocktails and dinners and dances; every one to be cancelled, apologies to be made, ruffled feathers smoothed,

20

every word watched. Any carelessness could mean a vote lost.

Time spent in Saul's constituency was always time spent walking on eggshells. Dammit, she'd have to lie and deceive. 'Sir Henry, Mr Richardson's father, not too well.' How ridiculous, his father was always as fit as a flea, with the energy of three ordinary men. Saul's constituents weren't to know that, thank God he sat for a southern seat.

His mother then? Lady Richardson? They'd picture a fragile beauty, walking with a stick, silvery hair, a faded rose. Let them picture, provided they never set eyes on the short, powerful woman with her hooded, hawk's eyes and hair still showing the traces of the rich chestnut colour of her youth. What would bring Saul more sympathy, rushing to his mother's or his father's side?

How tired she was of the whole wretched business; to think how pleased she'd felt when he'd been elected, when his delight in it had been so open, more like the thrill of a little boy given just the present he wanted than a grown man embarking on a political career.

She stubbed out her cigarette with restrained violence, then rang for her maid.

FOUR

SS Gloriana, *at sea, the Bay of Biscay*

The waves were long and deep, and dark beneath the foamy carpet of spray. Hal Grindley's mackintosh was bunched tightly around him, its collar up, its deep pockets a refuge for his icy hands. He wore no hat; the wind would have whipped it off in a second.

He was standing at the same place at the rail on the third deck where he had stood every night of the voyage since the first day out from Bombay. From there he had watched an enormous moon rise over a gleaming dark sea, and had seen the southern stars give way to the more familiar northern constellations shining with pinpoint brilliance in icy December skies. There, evening after evening, he had felt in its full intensity the strange suspension of reality belonging to a sea voyage. There he had thought about Margo, night after night, trying to order his feelings, to lessen the hurt, to regain a sense of proportion.

She had been with him in his mind all those months since his departure from San Francisco; she was beside him in his dreams as he crisscrossed Australia, as he tossed and turned in the sweltering heat of summer, as he sat outside on veran-

22

dahs in India, listening to the eerie night sounds of the east. Finally, as the seas grew more grey and rough, he had reached the state of indifference he had longed for. A door slammed behind him, shutting away all the years he had spent with her, reducing her betrayal to no more than the hissing breaking of a wave, spray tossed into the air and vanishing in the mass of water.

Tonight, as the SS *Gloriana* forged her way through the heaving seas of the Bay of Biscay, there were no stars to be seen.

A door opened further along the deck, and he caught the vanishing sounds of chimes summoning passengers to dinner. With a last look out into the blackness of the night, he went back in to warmth and light and the steady hum of the ship's engines. He made his way to his cabin to shed his coat; he was already dressed for dinner, although he had disarranged his black tie by fastening the collar of his mackintosh close about his neck. He twitched the tie back into place and set off once more to make his way along the swaying corridor, not at all bothered by the plunging motion of the vessel.

The vast dining room was sparsely filled. A steward at his elbow deferentially whispered in his ear that normal seating arrangements had been set aside for the present, as so few passengers were dining. He allowed himself to be escorted to a table where a handful of people were already seated; they gave him the confiding smiles of those immune to seasickness.

The little wooden guards, designed to stop the silver and china sliding to the floor, were up on all the tables, and as the waiter pushed his seat in and he reached for his napkin, the glasses at his place rattled into each other. The waiter deftly set them to rights. Hal spread the thick linen napkin across his knees and turned his attention to his table companions.

It was inevitable that one of those seated at the table was

23

Lady Gutteridge. She was the wife of the Governor of the Central Provinces, bringing her girls back to prepare for the Season next year. Nothing short of an Act of God could subdue her immense vitality, and certainly she would stand no nonsense from mere waves. He wondered if her two daughters were glad of the chance to stay in their cabins, shut away for a few hours from the relentless supervision and chivvying of their demanding mother.

Both girls had paid Hal some attention in the sly snatches of time when no watchful maternal eye was upon them. One of the girls had judged him too old to be interesting, he was too sure of himself, had too hard a core to be played with. The other was fascinated, drawn to him by the very qualities that repelled her sister, delighted with his lean, dark looks. His sardonic expression made her shiver, and when he was amused, with his almost black eyes gleaming and that mobile mouth set in a slanting smile, she found him deeply disturbing.

Was he going to be in London for the Season? she wanted to know when she cornered him during a game of deck quoits.

Wasting her time, her sister told her. Hal Grindley, whoever he was, certainly wasn't going to figure on Mummy's List, why, they knew nothing at all about him or who his people were. He was reticent on the subjects of school and regiment and university, those pillars of status, and his clothes defied classification, though his well-cut evening clothes could only have come from the hands of a London tailor – but what about those yellow socks?

Rumour had it that he came from the north of England, that he had been living in America and travelling about all over Australia and God knew where; definite signs of not being any kind of an eligible partner, neither for a dance nor for life.

It was all too true, but the damage was done, and for all

the next year she would be the despair of her mother, rejecting as soppy and stupid all the desirable young men paraded for her approval and finally making a most inappropriate match with a rising but none-too-young Labour politician – 'of all dreadful people, my dear!' – who had something of the same quicksilver mind and natural ease of authority that she had fallen for in the enigmatic Mr Grindley.

The colonial bishop seated opposite asked Hal where he would be going when they landed in England.

'To Westmoreland,' he replied without any hesitation. Where the lakes were freezing, and where he had family.

He didn't add that visiting his family hadn't been any part of his original plan, but the story in the newspapers brought on board when the ship called at Gibraltar had brought back a longing for his native hills that overwhelmed him. He had sent telegrams and retired to his cabin with a head suddenly alive with memories of childhood winters beside the lake and among the great fells, of skating in clear bright air, of toboggans and yachts and hot pies eaten with cold fingers on the ice, and Nanny scolding when he came in freezing and hungry and exhausted, ready to sleep for twelve hours and then to be back on the ice, sliding and tumbling among his friends.

He could see Grindley Hall in his mind's eye; would Peter have made many changes? What about Peter's new wife? She sounded uninteresting, certainly a comedown after funny, vital Delia whom he had adored, and who had run away from Peter one summer's night with a Scottish poet. She had paid a high price for her new life in a Highland castle, since Peter had vented his hurt rage in a refusal to allow her any contact with her children. She kept in touch with them, he knew, only by clandestine means, writing to Nanny at a separate address from the Hall.

Hal didn't blame her. He'd run away himself, to all intents and purposes. Less scandalously, but almost as effectively. Like Delia, Hal had sought refuge from his family among

25

Bohemians and artists, only in his case, he knew that those he had abandoned felt nothing but relief at his absence. He was a changeling among the Grindleys, sharing neither of the family's absorbing interests of killing things and making money.

After a dinner that had run to its usual five courses, despite the raging sea, he and the bishop took refuge from her ladyship in the Smoking Room, a place too masculine for even one of her assurance to enter. There, amid the satisfactory aroma of good cigars and leather chairs, they sat companionably enough, the bishop drinking whisky and Hal with a glass of bourbon at his elbow.

Talk of the frozen north led the bishop to turn the subject to the one great passion of his life: fishing. Fly fishing in particular, and he settled down to indulge in a long drone about casts and flies and pools in obscure places and long-lost fishy prey that had got away.

Hal found listening to this saga quite restful, having grown up surrounded by guns and rods, and by material evidence of the Grindley obsession in the shape of such delights as an enormous salmon mounted in a glass case, set among bright green reeds, with a placard beneath it announcing that it had been caught by Gertrude Grindley in 1898.

This particular trophy had for some reason ended up in his bedroom, where it at first gave him nightmares and then simply joined the list of things he disliked about his home. He marginally preferred the fish to the antlered heads with their sad eyes, and the stuffed stoats, weasels and foxes that some taxidermy-mad ancestor had collected so avidly and which stood around on side-tables and on shelves in every room of the house.

His attention was jerked back to what the bishop was saying by the alarming words, 'and of course, I used to go fishing there with your uncle, Robert Grindley. Dead now, I heard.'

26

'Uncle?'

'You're old Nicholas Grindley's boy, aren't you? He's dead, too, of course, none of that generation left except a sister, that'll be your Aunt Daphne. You must be Peter's youngest brother. I was at school with Peter, he fagged for me one year. We called him Jakes. On account of the family business, you know.'

'Ah, yes.' Hal could remember all too well his own school soubriquets of Jeyes, and Clean-round-the-bend. Roger had been called Flush, he recalled, which never seemed to bother him.

'How is Peter? Keeping well? I heard about his wife; shocking business, shocking. He's married again, though.'

'Yes. I rarely see him, living abroad as I do.'

'Yes, yes, you always were the odd one out.'

Hal was feeling some alarm. 'I'd rather you didn't mention that you know my family. To Lady Gutteridge. I mean . . .'

The bishop shook with laughter. 'No, no, I saw right from the start that it would never do, and I have no desire to make mischief. Mind you, Grindley Hall is all very well, but I should think she has ambitions beyond the younger son of a northern squire, if you don't mind my saying so.'

'Oh, just so. However, with that kind of woman, one can't be too careful.'

'No, indeed, indeed. You can rely on me. Yes, Peter Grindley, how that takes me back. I remember one year, we'd taken a couple of rods up Loweswater way . . .'

Hal was beginning to regret that the bishop had caught whatever tropical disease it was that left him so thin and yellow and apparently unable to continue with his ministry overseas. Not that the bishop seemed to mind. As he turned his episcopal thoughts from past fish to watery pleasures yet to come, the sense of boredom that Hal had so often experienced when with his family and their friends began to get the better of his good nature and manners. He rose to his feet. 'I think I'll turn in,' he said, stretching out a hand to steady himself as the ship hurtled down into an extra deep wave.

'Quite so,' said the colonial bishop, his mind full of whisky fumes and fishy foes.

It was bitterly cold, the day the ship docked at Tilbury, and he bid the bishop goodbye at the Customs Shed. The bishop was heading for a cathedral town in the West Country; Hal was spending the night in his club in London. He would devote the next day to professional and business affairs, and then catch the night sleeper to the north, and the frozen lake.

FIVE

Yorkshire

Perdita Richardson hadn't expected a letter from her best friend Ursula Grindley, not so near the end of term. Yet there it was, tucked into a tattered old copy of the Couperin *Suites* by an obliging and well-bribed school maid.

Letters at Yorkshire Ladies College, where Perdita was a boarder, were considered dangerous items and reading an illicit letter was almost as much of a problem as receiving it, for the young ladies were constantly watched. Twenty seconds in a practice room without playing a note and a teacher would be at the door wanting to know why you were slacking. Hawk eyes bored into you in the library, as you went along the corridor, in the dining room; spies were everywhere in dormitories and common room. The lavatory was a possibility, but there were set times for that, and usually a queue outside the door.

Perdita broke into a ripple of arpeggios with her left hand while she tucked the letter into her liberty bodice with her right hand. Later, she would contrive to slip it inside her sock, and then, in the afternoon, she would work the frayed lace trick.

'I don't know what it is with you and bootlaces, Perdita Richardson. Yours are always breaking.' The brick-faced games mistress suspected a ruse, but couldn't deny that there was the lace in two pieces, and, on inspection, it had suffered what appeared to be a natural breakage with appropriate fraying.

'I think it's because my hockey boots are too small for me,' said Perdita helpfully. 'It must put a strain on the laces.'

'See you are supplied with a new pair of boots for next term. Go and put in a spare lace. Be back in five minutes.'

She could stretch that to seven or eight, Perdita thought as she jogged back to the changing rooms. Once there, she tugged off the offending boot, one she'd taken from the lost property box, and pulled on her own boot with its perfectly good lace. Then she sat down on the wooden lockers, plucked the letter from its hiding place in her sock and began to read.

It started without any preamble – a precaution in case it should fall into hostile hands.

Very near the end of term, I know, but I had to write to tell you all the news as there's a terrific to-do going on here. The chief reason is that the family Black Sheep will shortly be with us – in case you don't know who that is, it's my Uncle Hal. You never met him – nor did I, or if I did I was a mere puling infant & don't remember it – because he went off years and years ago, to America! Yes, that one!

Well, the fuss, you'd think some arch-criminal was on his way. And the point is, I can't find out that he ever actually did anything very terrible, except to take up acting when he was at Cambridge and then head for London to Go On The Stage! That was before he went to America. I mean, what's so shocking about an actor, only you know what Daddy's like, he shouts and rants about 'Those Sort of People'? He says actors are a bunch of Pansies and then goes red if he thinks I've heard – he imagines I don't know what he means. Musicians and painters are Pansies, too, of course – if they're men. If they're women, they're badly brought up with no allure and probably thick ankles who should have been controlled by their fathers. He doesn't get any less Victorian as he gets older. He should control his temper, never mind his daughter – all that going red can't be doing him any good at all.

I asked Nanny to tell me about Hal. She has a soft spot for him, you can tell that at once. She let out that his brothers called him the Afterthought, because he's so much younger than they are. He's thirty-eight, she says, and Pa's fifty-five, and Uncle Roger fifty-two, so it's quite a gap, I do see. Grandma must have been awfully old to have a baby when he was born. One thing is, he didn't come back from America when Grandma died, and that's held against him, BUT, Nanny says that Daddy didn't send the cablegram until he knew it was too late for him to get here for the funeral.

It isn't only the acting that's causing all the agitation. It's money. Isn't that always the way with my family? Hal got a third of the business when Grandpa died, and that still rankles with Daddy – considering he got the house as well as shares and so on, I don't think he's being very fair. Anyhow, they reckoned that being an actor and no good at it – well, no one's ever heard of him, have they? – he'd have sold his shares, spent the money and be living in penury. Only he hasn't, they're all still in his name. There's some deal brewing, and they need his shares to put it all through. Hence the flap – will he be difficult about it?

The Grindleys are gathering. Uncle Roger and Aunt Angela have arrived, with Cecy. Uncle Roger's still being beastly about her training to be a doctor. Aunt Angela

31

says Hal is a nice man, only not in the least interested in sport and shooting and all that. He was clever, too, and you know how suspicious Daddy is of anyone clever, books and plays and things all being a waste of time and not in the real world, meaning lav. pans and baths. You don't know how lucky you are that your family's money comes from dull old engineering works and not from sanitary chinaware. Nicky knocked a boy down this term because he got so fed up with remarks about things going down the pan. He's at home, therefore, in disgrace, but he doesn't care a bit; he hates school.

Anyhow, that's not all. Exquisite Eve (my new name for my awful stepmother, don't you like it?) has set her mind against Hal, don't ask me why, and says he shouldn't have just announced he was coming but should have waited to be invited. He'd have had to wait a jolly long time in that case. Aunt Angela says, 'Rot, it's his home,' or words to that effect, but Eve isn't pleased. Then a cable came from Lisbon mentioning the name of his ship, the SS Gloriana. When Uncle Roger heard that, he cried out, 'That's not on the Atlantic run, it's a P&O vessel and goes to and from India and Australia.' So that's got them even more worked up, did he get the letters about the shares that they sent to New York, and what on earth could he be doing in Australia and India? As if no one ever went there before, which of course they do, all the time.

My stepsister Rosalind will be turning up from her finishing school in Munich. You haven't met her, but I've told you how ghastly she is – well, she would be, with exquisite Eve for a mother. Daddy thinks she's wonderful, he goes on and on about her poise and beautiful manners and grooming – you'd think she was a horse. Only she isn't, she's frightfully pretty in a boring, brittle sort of way, and very affected. She behaves as though the Hall is a leftover from the Middle Ages (she's got a point there), and treats me like I was some kind of a peasant. Simon can't take his eyes off her, I never saw anything so soppy, and he won't hear a word against her. He's home from Cambridge, and gloomy as usual, he knows that Daddy won't hear of him joining the army after university; the eldest son has to go into the business, and that's that. Honestly, my brothers, what a pair, but at least Nicky isn't at all struck by the fair Rosalind. Just wait till you see her.

Must finish, or there'll be so many pages you won't be able to flush them down the lav, hope it's a Jowetts, we need to keep the money coming in to pay for Rosalind's expensive clothes and Eve's beauty treatments. Oh, and guess what, we're going to have a dance over Christmas, hooray, but it's in honour of Rosalind's seventeenth birthday. It makes me sick. Catch Daddy ever giving a dance in my honour.

Can't wait to see you and have a really good talk about it all,

xxx

PS Cecy says she's been trying to persuade E's twin (better not mention her name) to come back for Christmas. I hope she does.

SIX

London, Bloomsbury

Edwin had met Lidia on the steps of the Photographic Institute in London. To be exact, he had tripped over her; she had been on her knees, scrubbing, and he hadn't been looking where he was going.

'*Blöder Idiot,*' she exclaimed.

'*Oh, Entschuldigung, ich habe Sie nicht gesehen,*' he replied, startled. 'I've knocked over your bucket,' he continued in English.

'It is nothing,' she muttered, getting to her feet and wiping her hands on her worn crossover apron. Why was the man staring at her like that?

'I am sorry,' he said again. 'May I take the bucket in for you?'

She clutched the bucket to her chest, and backed away. 'No, no. It would be most unsuitable.'

Edwin didn't give a fig about what was or wasn't suitable. He took the bucket firmly from her and followed her down the basement steps to deposit it in the area. Then he went back up to the pavement, and, lighting a cigarette, took up a position by the railings.

He didn't have long to wait before she came up the steps, dressed now in a shabby, dark coat and a nondescript hat. 'Oh,' she said, when she saw him. 'Why are you still here?'

'I'm waiting for you. Have you finished your work for now? Then I shall buy you a cup of coffee. No, don't protest, it's the least I can do after sending your bucket flying.'

He walked her quite a way, to a place he knew of near Harrods. A Hungarian pastry chef had opened a hugely successful tea room, where his exquisite cakes and pastries were bought and sampled by appreciative members of the upper classes.

She didn't hang back at the door, despite her poor clothes, but lifted her chin and went in. The proprietor eyed her with momentary disapproval, then took in the well-cut, if casual, clothes of her companion and ushered them to a table.

Edwin ordered coffee and pastries. 'I don't have to ask a Viennese if she likes these,' he said with a smile.

'How do you know I come from Vienna?'

'Your accent. I studied in Vienna for a while.'

'You don't have a Viennese accent.'

'No, I learnt my German as a child, from a German governess.'

'Do you always stare at people? Isn't this rude, for an Englishman?'

He wasn't at all abashed. 'I'm a photographer. I always stare when I see something or someone I want to take photographs of.'

The light died out of her face, and her big dark eyes became wary. 'Photographs?'

'Not the kind you're thinking of,' he said quickly. 'Nothing distasteful or dishonourable.'

That was what she was thinking, of course. You didn't arrive as a penniless but attractive refugee to any country without certain suggestions being made to you. Had she chosen that route, she would never have had to scrub a step,

35

and she wouldn't be wearing these clothes. She said no more, but took a bite of her *Marillenkuchen* and with that delicious apricot mouthful, all her memories of Vienna, pushed so resolutely out of her mind, came flooding back.

She smiled.

She couldn't help it, and she couldn't have dreamt of the effect it would have on Edwin, who sat transfixed, gazing at her with blank astonishment.

He had thought she had an interesting face. The arrangement of cheekbones and nose and mouth appealed to him, as an artist, not as a man. Now he was overwhelmed.

She didn't want to meet him again, didn't want to be photographed, wanted to be left alone. She didn't notice him following her through dingy streets to a house in Bloomsbury. As she put her key in the lock of the front door, which badly needed a coat of paint, she looked around and up and down the street, as though she sensed his eyes upon her; he had ducked behind a parked van, and she didn't see him.

He sauntered around the corner and went into a shop that announced itself as a newsagent and tobacconist. A small man with a moustache stood behind the counter, and he greeted Edwin in a voice that held a trace of a foreign accent. Edwin bought a paper and a packet of cigarettes.

There were no other customers in the shop, and it wasn't hard to fall into conversation with the man. Edwin's relaxed, unassertive ways encouraged people to talk to him, and in no time at all, he had the rundown on everyone in Cranmer Street, including the inhabitants of number sixteen. The owners of the house were an elderly couple, who let out rooms to add to a meagre pension. Their only lodgers at present were a young married couple. The man was English, his wife from Austria. Also staying there for some weeks now was the wife's sister, recently arrived from Vienna.

'A musician,' the little man said, his eyes gleaming with pleasure. 'She plays the piano. For hours. Bach, mostly, and

Scarlatti. Beautiful, beautiful.' Then the eyes became watchful. 'You are from the authorities, perhaps?'

'Good heavens, no,' Edwin said, taken aback. 'Do I look like a policeman?'

'It is not only the police, but there are Home Office officials, who come and ask unpleasant questions in areas like this. There are a lot of foreigners here. But Mrs Jenkins, the musician's sister, is married to an Englishman, she has a British passport, I have seen it, I know what it looks like. I was once a German, but now I, too, have a British passport.'

'Does the sister have a passport?'

'Only an Austrian one, if that. She has come as a refugee, her brother-in-law arranged it. It wasn't easy, because he's a writer, and has little money. However, Mrs Jenkins works, and earns some money, and so they managed it. Mrs Jenkins was very worried about her sister, for they are Jews, like me. It isn't safe to be Jewish these days.'

'No, I suppose not,' Edwin said inadequately. 'I'm aware that Mrs Jenkins's sister – I don't recall her name . . .?' He looked expectantly at the newsagent.

'Weiss. Lidia Weiss.'

'Miss Weiss has a cleaning job. Surely, if she is a musician she shouldn't be scrubbing floors?'

The man shook his head, making clucking noises. 'No, no, of course not. It is terrible for her hands. Musicians have to be careful of their hands, and the water, and the cold, it isn't good for bones and muscles. Only what work is there for a musician, newly arrived in this country? They are two a penny. I myself know a cellist of international reputation who stays alive by washing up at a restaurant. A violinist, a wonderful artist, is a lavatory attendant – and the stories he tells about what goes on in such a place, it makes your hair stand on end, the English are a strange people. A friend of mine who is a horn player is more fortunate, he is a big, strong fellow, and he is employed by a nightclub. On the door.' The little man spread his hands in a despairing gesture. 'Lidia Weiss is lucky, she is well-educated, she speaks good English. If she didn't, it would be difficult for her even to get a cleaning job.'

'I see,' Edwin said.

It took him two days to scrape an acquaintance with Richard Jenkins, a thin, likeable young man engaged in writing a long novel set in mediaeval Wales. This work was to make his fortune; Edwin doubted it, and when he went back with Richard to take potluck at the evening meal, he saw that Lidia doubted it too, but was too kind to say so. He had handed the food he had thoughtfully brought with him to a relieved Anna Jenkins, who had been wondering how she could make an already watery tomato soup and a tin of sardines feed four people, and then turned around to be introduced to Lidia. She looked at him as though she had seen a ghost.

Although they hadn't met before, Richard moved in much the same London circle as Edwin, and they had friends in common among the Bohemian group of writers, artists and musicians endeavouring to live by their various talents. By the end of the evening, Lidia seemed to have shed her mistrust of Edwin. She sat down at the battered old piano after supper and played for them. Edwin didn't take his eyes off her, his gaze moving from her rapt face to her reddened, swollen hands.

She visited him in the rooms he kept in London, one of which was rigged up as a small studio. The first time she came, she brought her sister Anna with her. Then, finally, after further tea-time outings to sample Viennese pastries, a recital at the Queen's Hall, 'A friend asked me to use the tickets, such a shame to waste them,' he lied, and an evening at the cinema, she came to his rooms alone.

She refused to marry him.

'Why, why?' he would ask her in despair as they lay side by side on his narrow bed. 'What's wrong with me? I'm so much in love with you, don't you feel anything for me?'

'Nothing is wrong with you, but everything is wrong with me. I am foreign, and Jewish, and Richard tells me that you come from an important, rich family. They would hate me. Then, I'm older than you, and men should be older than the women they marry.'

'Four years! It's hardly a generation. One of my aunts is married to a man fifteen years her junior, and they are very happy.'

'Even so. And besides . . .' It was hard to tell him that she slept with him for the release and comfort it gave her, not because she was in love with him. She craved human warmth and company, desperate to drown her grief at her parents' death in a railway accident, to forget for a short while the loss of her first lover, a Berliner who had vanished into one of the KZ camps for some minor act of disobedience to the State, and had died there in mysterious circumstances. After making love she wept on Edwin's shoulder, for the people who were gone, for the country she had loved, for the Jews who were left.

Edwin had never in his life been exposed to such raw emotion, he wanted to detach himself from it, yet ended by finding himself even more deeply in love with his brown-haired Viennese refugee.

She was a harpsichordist, not a pianist, he learnt. Which was not a good thing to be, because if good pianos were hard to come by, harpsichords of any kind were impossible. Edwin pleaded with her to give up her cleaning job, to come and live with him if she wouldn't marry him, but she refused, and twice a week went to classes, paid for out of her slender earnings, to learn shorthand and typing.

Edwin had to return to the north. He begged her to come with him. His studio there wasn't in his parents' house, he told her, but on the ground floor of a house in the local town. 'I own the whole house, there are bedrooms, a bathroom, a kitchen. It's a small town, but friendly. The air is good, there are hills,' he added helplessly.

She shook her head, and got out of bed to dress in her worn clothes and go off to attend to the steps of the Photographic Institute. Edwin went around to Cranmer Street, and railed at her sister, Anna, who looked at him with pity in her eyes.

'It will be better for her when she has another job. It will be better for her when she can work indoors, and use her mind, and not have her hands in water all day. Then she can play properly, and remember what she is.'

Like you, thought Edwin, although he was too kind to say so. Like Anna, who had a degree in chemistry, and was grateful for the job of laboratory assistant at a girls' school.

'Please persuade her. None of this is because I feel sorry for her, you do understand that?'

'I know. It is because you love her. Sadly, love comes at no one's bidding, and so . . .' She shrugged.

The scrubbing got no easier, when Edwin had gone, and the piano playing became more and more painful and difficult. Edwin wrote to her every day, passionate letters, and sent her photographs, of fells and lakes and ruined chapels.

'What an artist!' Richard said, when he saw them.

Lidia agreed, as she put them silently away in the bottom of the tatty suitcase where she kept all her worldly possessions. She cooked supper; Anna was feeling unwell. She often felt sick these days, she said the smell of the chemicals at school was upsetting her. She knew this wasn't the reason, and so did Lidia, but neither of them spoke about it.

More letters, more photographs, this time of snow scenes, sunlit and moonlit, an enchanted world, it seemed to Lidia. *Do you skate?* he wrote. *I know, that's like asking a duck if it quacks. I remember you telling me about Christmas in the mountains. They will soon be skating on the lake here.*

Then Anna told Richard her news, and he was ecstatic, brushing aside her worry about her job – they thought she was unmarried; where was the money to come from? Richard's thin face took on a determined look, and three days later he announced that he had accepted a job. Teaching at a preparatory school for boys in Sussex, a live-in job with a small house provided. No, she wasn't to exclaim about his writing. Schoolmasters had long holidays, he'd been a fool not to find such a job long ago. Yes, he would miss London, but country air and food were what his Anna needed at a time like this. He was to take up his post at the beginning of the Lent term, but might move into the house whenever he wished.

Of course, Lidia must come too, he said.

Lidia looked at her sister's tired but radiant face. 'Later perhaps,' she said, and arranged to work all the extra hours she could, to pay for the train fare to the north and to buy a pair of skates.

SEVEN

Sussex

The telephone rang in Hut 3 of the Gibson Aeronautical Company's premises, the shrill sound startling Michael Wrexham. He blinked, looking up from the measurements he was checking, and stretched out his hand to answer the call.

'Michael?' said the caller. 'Freddie here. Can we talk?'

'Go ahead.' Michael Wrexham balanced the receiver on his shoulder, and put a tick on the sheet in front of him. He was sitting on a high stool at a drawing board. A strong light from an angular lamp clipped to the board cast a brilliant pool on his work. Outside the steamed-up windows of the wooden building, snow pattered down in the darkness, unnoticed. A stove at the other end of the hut kept it warm, if stuffy. There were three drawing boards, and a desk with a typewriter on it. He was the only occupant; the others had long since gone home, and the typewriter had had its cover tucked over it on the dot of five-thirty.

'Have you noticed the weather, or are you so wrapped up in your blasted aeroplanes that snow passes you by?'

Michael shifted his gaze to the nearest window. 'It is snowing here, now you come to mention it.'

'It's snowing almost everywhere. Especially in the north. What are you doing for Christmas? Any chance of your getting a few days' leave?'

'Difficult at the moment, Freddie. There's a bit of a flap on.'

'That's what you always say. Now listen, I feel a terrific urge to get in a bit of skating. I know I won't be able to entice you to Switzerland, but how about a trip to the Lake District? You must have read that the great lakes are all freezing. We could put up at an inn, I telephoned around and there are two rooms going spare at an inn called the Pheasant, in Westmoreland – a cancellation. A family had booked, but the father's gone down with measles of all things, poor chap. I feel sorry for them, missing all the fun. A colleague at the hospital says they look after you well there, and the food's good. The innkeeper, Mr Dixon, is holding the rooms for me, until tomorrow morning. Do say you'll come. We can walk and skate, it's a wonderful chance to get those muscles working and breathe a bit of fresh air. You're no use to anyone cooped up in your office all the hours God gives.'

Michael laughed. 'I must say, I don't feel very fit. But I don't think I can get away.' He hesitated. 'It's tricky just now, you know how things are. Look, leave it with me. I'll get back to you first thing, one way or the other.'

'Right-oh. Speak to you then.'

'Bye, Freddie.'

He put the receiver down and pushed the telephone away. He sat straight on his stool, musing. Westmoreland. He closed his eyes for a minute, seeing the fells, the frozen lake, the craggy landscape of so many childhood holidays. He hadn't been back for years. Sixteen years, his exact mind told him, when he'd been twelve years old.

He bent over his drawing board once more, slide rule in hand, muttering to himself. The door opened, and a blast of cold air hit the back of his neck. 'Shut that door,' he

43

yelled, then turned to see a tall, bearded man standing at the door, the shoulders of his jacket covered in snow. Giles Gibson stamped his feet, leaving a puddle of melting snow about his brogues. 'Sorry, sir,' Michael said. 'Didn't realize it was you.'

'It's late. You should have gone home.'

'I wanted to get these figures finished.'

'For the Pegasus?'

'That's right.'

'Are you nearly through?'

He straightened, running a hand through his hair. 'Another hour should see it done.'

'Finish it, and then come across to my office, would you?'

'Yes,' Michael said, already mentally back with his work.

'An hour, no more. I'm going out to dinner tonight. I can't be late, or Marjorie will be annoyed.'

'Yes. I mean, no. I'll be there.'

Giles Gibson's office was in another wooden hut, on the other side of the airstrip. Michael felt his breath taken away by the cold, and set off at a steady jog across the windy spaces. Snow blew into his face, making him blink as fat flakes settled on his eyelashes. He swung up the three steps to Gibson's hut, knocking at the door as he went in.

'Snowing hard,' he said, giving himself a shake.

Gibson was already in his overcoat, sitting behind his desk and shovelling some papers into a drawer before locking it and pocketing the key. 'Come on, I'll give you a lift to your digs, you can't cycle home in this weather.'

'It's not as bad as that,' he protested. 'Still, I'd be glad of the ride.'

'We'll talk on the way.' Gibson switched off the light over his desk, and followed him out of the door, locking the door and giving it a push to make sure it was secure. Then the two of them hurried, heads down, towards the main buildings, skirting around the edge to the potholed area where Gibson parked his car.

'Get in,' Gibson said, going around to the driver's side. 'Let's hope she starts.'

The engine made some dispirited noises, groaned and coughed, and then subsided into silence.

'I'll do it,' Michael said, taking the crank handle from Gibson.

'Careful, she's got the devil of a kick,' Gibson called to him as he went to the front of the car.

'You're right about the kick,' Michael said as he climbed into the car, rubbing his shoulder. He gave the door a tug to close it.

They spluttered down the rutted lane, Gibson peering through the windscreen, where the wipers were fighting a losing battle with the snow.

'A pal of mine telephoned today,' Michael said. 'He wants me to go to Westmoreland for a few days. They say the lakes will freeze over, so one could get some skating in. He's very keen on winter sports.'

Gibson was hearty in his approval. 'Excellent. Just the ticket. Fresh air and a bit of exercise. Do you the world of good.'

'I told him I didn't think I'd be able to get away.'

'You did, did you?'

'If you drop me here at the bottom, I can walk the rest of the way. Then you can take a right turn there and be back on the main road.'

Gibson pulled the car into the side of the road. 'Ring up your friend, or send him a telegram saying you'll join him.' He raised a gloved hand as Michael opened his mouth to protest. 'No, that's an order. Finish what you've got to do on Pegasus, and then I don't want to see you again until January.'

Michael got out of the car, thanked Gibson for the lift,

and crunched across pristine snow to the small terraced house where he lodged. The hall had a light burning, but the rest of the house was in darkness. His landlady had left him a note. *Supper keeping hot in oven, have gone over to be with Mrs Knight, she's nervous of the snow.*

Mrs Knight was nervous of everything. No doubt she thought a vagrant snowman was going to come tapping on her door, all set for a spot of icy rapine and ravaging. He screwed up the note and threw it into the embers of the fire in the kitchen. He put some more coal on the fire, and took out the plate of food from the oven. Congealed meatloaf and lumpy mashed potato. Hadn't Freddie said the food at the Pheasant was good?

He ate his supper and sat looking into the flames as he drank a cup of tea. He was tired, he had to admit it. Bone tired, after months of long hours and no breaks. Was fatigue affecting his work? Even the simplest calculations seemed to take longer than they used to. Perhaps Gibson was right, and he needed to get away.

He shut his eyes, his mind drifting away to the frozen north. Sixteen years since he'd been there; sixteen years since he'd nearly died of pneumonia. He had been found wandering in a wood, had caught a severe chill, they told him when he was out of danger, and he came around from the lost days of fever to find all memory of the winter holiday wiped from his mind.

His chin fell to his chest, the landlady's tabby cat jumped on to his lap, running all her claws into his legs; he stirred, and then slept.

His landlady found him there when she came back hours later. 'Look at him, sleeping like a baby,' she said to the cat. 'I'll make him a nice cup of cocoa and then wake him up so's he can take himself off to bed.' She looked at his face, interesting even in sleep; she liked a proper man, and his sort made you remember what it was like to be young. Pity he spent so much time at his precious work, what chance had he to meet a nice young lady when he worked all the time?

She poured the gooey brew into a cup, and shook him gently by the shoulder. 'Wake up, Mr Wrexham, it's bedtime, and I made you a nice cup of cocoa.'

He blinked and shook himself awake. 'I must have dropped off. Good heavens, is that the time? Oh, thank you, how kind.' He looked doubtfully into the cup, he loathed cocoa. 'I'll take it upstairs with me, if that's all right.'

Where he took it with him into the bathroom, and tipped it down the basin.

EIGHT

York

Where was Perdita?

There were so many girls in the vast nave of York Minster, rows and rows of grey flannel overcoats, a sea of grey hats, each with its purple band. True, they weren't identical, they came in many different heights and sizes, but then, at that age, girls shot up so, his sister could be inches taller by now.

Craning his neck in his efforts to scan the congregation, he lost his place in the hymn sheet, earning a scornful look from the tall woman in a sensible felt hat who was sitting in the seat next to him as he came in several 'Noels' too late. Lord, these were the same carols he'd sung at his school a thousand years ago, did nothing ever change? The carol ended, an invisible choir sang some incomprehensible verses in mediaeval English, a woman with rigid grey hair and a tight mouth, wearing a Cambridge MA gown, ascended the pulpit and began to read the story of the Annunciation.

The service wound to a close, the jolly-looking bishop in gold and pink raised his crook to give the blessing, the organist crashed into the opening chords of *Adeste fideles*, and the stately procession of senior and lesser clergy, headmistress, servers and choir made its way down the central aisle.

There was Perdita. One of the choir, wearing a white surplice that looked too short for her, her dark brown hair scraped back from her face in a pair of straggling plaits, her face pale and unrevealing as she sang the soaring final descant. He turned his head to watch the retreating backs of the choir. How quickly could he make a getaway? He stuffed the order of service into the rack at the back of the seat in front of him, beside the hymnal and the prayer book, and began to edge his way past his more devout neighbours who were kneeling or sitting with bowed heads in attitudes of prayer.

Dark-overcoated fathers looked at him with scorn, disapproval of his brown tweed overcoat and corduroy trousers written all over their faces. Their wives screwed up their mouths and made little mutterings of dismay at his unmannerly attempts to escape. Then he was at the end of the row and in the aisle, free to make a dash for the action end of the cathedral before he was completely swamped in the wave of schoolgirls pouring out of the front rows.

Polished brown shoes of every size trod on his feet, hockey-trained muscles shoved him out of the way, firm elbows dug into his sides; what a relief to reach a place of safety in front of the choir screen and tuck himself in beside a huge urn of festive greenery. He had kept an eye on the choir as it disappeared into the far reaches of the north aisle; surely all the girls from the choir would pass this way sooner or later.

They did, looking like chesspieces in their purple cassocks, with white surplices now draped over arms or shoulders.

'Edwin, oh, good, I am so pleased to see you. I wasn't sure if anyone was coming for me.' Perdita gestured to her cassock and surplice. 'I have to put these in the hamper and get my coat and hat. Will you wait here?'

'I shan't budge,' he said. 'I never saw so many girls in my life, they're terrifying.'

49

She smiled her wide smile at him and bounded away.

A giant grey crocodile was forming in the south aisle, with gowned mistresses running up and down like sheepdogs, lining the girls up in pairs and rounding up stragglers. 'Come along, girls, we have a train to catch. Fiona, put your hat straight. Mathilda, where are your gloves? Deirdre, how many times do I have to tell you not to stand on one leg?'

'My stockings make me itch,' said the unfortunate Deirdre, who had been rubbing her shin violently with the edge of her sensible brown leather shoe.

'Deirdre! Mentioning underwear in public, whatever are you thinking of?'

His breath was visible in the cold air; it hadn't seemed so very cold at first, but the chill had struck up through the ancient stones, and now his feet were growing numb. His nose was no doubt pink; the parents and girls milling around him nearly all had glowing noses and cheeks.

However warm the overcoats and furs, nothing could subdue the arctic chill of York Minster on a December day. The weather had been unusually bitter, even for the north of England, but he could never remember a time when he had been in the Minster and not felt cold.

Cold as charity. The words mocked him as he looked down the immense length of the nave to where the great west doors stood open and the congregation streamed out into the pale wintry sunlight. Then Perdita was beside him. 'I'm glad you came to collect me, it's a gruesome journey by train. Five hours in a stuffy compartment, or sitting on freezing platforms, and I hate having to change trains here, there and everywhere.'

Another of the iron-grey regiment of teachers – grey as to hair and expression rather than in what she wore – was bearing down on them. 'Perdita Richardson!'

Perdita hastily unwound her arm from his. 'This is my brother, Edwin, Miss Hartness.'

Eyes sharp with disbelief raked him from head to toe. 'He looks very old to be your brother.'

He was amused. 'I think my grandmother let you know I would be coming.'

'The headmistress received a telegram from Lady Richardson to that effect, I believe. We don't usually let our girls leave with their brothers. You girls without parents do make difficulties for the school.'

He turned to Perdita. 'Do you have any luggage?'

The mistress answered for her. 'The girls' trunks and boxes were sent by railway two days ago. Perdita has an overnight case.'

Miss Hartness still looked suspicious; did she think he was a fraudster planning to abduct the girl? He was fond of his sister, but the woman should realize that if he had such intentions, he'd pick a dazzler, not a gawky girl like Perdita. . . .'

The woman was still talking. 'Now, I really do think . . .'

He was spared her probably unflattering thoughts, since at that moment a bird-like figure, elegantly clad in a scarlet coat with a modish hat perched on her sleek head, darted out of the throng. 'Edwin, darling, are you here to pick up Perdita? This is my Grace, only a baby, her first term at the Ladies College, isn't it, darling?'

A diminutive girl with her fair hair tied in two tight plaits looked up at her mother with calm grey eyes. 'Oh, Mummy, don't call me a baby.'

Edwin kissed the woman, shook hands with the solemn child, who gave him a cool look and then skipped aside to talk to a friend.

'Hello, Lucy,' he said. 'Is Rollo with you?'

'He's gone to see where Watkins has got to, it's always such a mêlée here after the end of term service.' She leant up to peck him on the cheek. 'Lovely to see you, darling, they say the lake may freeze from shore to shore, if so, nothing will stop us coming over after New Year. Give my love to

Caroline and Henry, won't you? Goodbye, Perdita, have a wonderful Christmas, of course you will, Christmas is always heaven at Wyncrag.'

Miss Hartness's expression lost some of its suspicious edge, although her mouth was still set in a tight line. 'You know Mrs Lambert, I see.'

'She's a cousin.' He could tell that although the mistress was pleased to have a positive identification for him as the genuine article and not a brotherly impostor, she didn't altogether approve of the vivacious and elegant Lucy Lambert.

'Very well, Perdita,' said Miss Hartness. 'You may go.'

'Merry Christmas, Miss Hartness.'

He urged Perdita along, as she called out farewells and seasonal good wishes to friends and teachers. 'Buck up, old girl. We've a long drive back to Westmoreland.'

'Is it true?' she asked. 'Is the lake frozen?'

'Not yet, but Riggs says the frost will hold, and if it does, the lake should freeze from north to south and east to west.'

'Freeze over completely? I do hope it does, I long for it, every year, but it never happens. Will I be able to skate across to the island?'

'Certainly you will, and from one end to the other if it freezes as hard as it did last time.'

'When was that?'

'The winter before you were born.' He took her arm again. 'It seems a long time ago, and here you are, a young lady.'

'Just a schoolgirl. Not a young lady, sadly.'

'Why not a young lady?' They had reached the west door and were out in the cold air. There was the unmistakable smell of coal fires; the jumble of houses along Stonegate and Petergate each had a column of smoke rising into a cloudless sky.

'It's all right for schoolgirls to look like I do. For young ladies, it's hopeless.'

He caught the note of despair behind her even tones.

'You look very nice to me, old thing.'

'You're my brother, you're used to me. But anyone else would just think, awkward, overgrown schoolgirl.'

'Who else?'

'Oh, everyone,' said Perdita. She changed the subject. 'Where have you parked the car?'

'In St Helen's Square. Not far. Where's your overnight case?'

'Our suitcases are all lined up on the pavement beside the motor coaches, over there. Where shall we lunch?'

'I thought we'd stop at the Fox and Hounds. They do a decent meal there, and I expect you're hungry.'

They drove north through Boroughbridge and on to the Great North Road. It was cold inside Edwin's car, and white puffy clouds began to drift across the sky as the easterly wind strengthened.

'Plenty of snow on the ground already.' Perdita was glad of the rug that Edwin had tucked around her. She huffed on her fingers to warm them. 'Is the road clear?'

'It was yesterday, and it hasn't snowed seriously for two or three days.'

'Did you take any photographs on the way?'

'A few. The light was very strange in the early afternoon, just before dusk. Very clear, good contrasts.'

They sat at a table in front of a roaring log fire at the inn and ate hearty platefuls of ham and leek pie. They were the only customers apart from a couple of local shepherds, and the landlord, a burly man with bushy eyebrows, had time to chat. 'Blowing up for a bit of a storm, I reckon. Best not linger if you've far to go.'

'Westmoreland,' said Perdita, scraping the last spoonful of custard from her pudding plate.

Edwin got up from the table, pulling it out so that Perdita could get past. He settled the bill and they bid the landlord and his customers a cheerful goodbye before going out to face the blast of the wind, now blowing from the north-east. It sent flurries of snow dancing around the yard of the inn as Edwin opened the car door for Perdita. He wiped the settling flakes from the windscreen and the small rear window before getting in and coaxing the car back into life.

After a few miles, the skies lightened, and the snow petered out, leaving paths of smooth, unbroken whiteness among the boulders and rocky places. Where the snow lay sparsely, the tough moorland sheep, fleeces thick with ice and snow, searched for tufts to tear away and chew briskly as they eyed the car driving past on the narrow, winding road. There were few other vehicles. They passed a farm cart, the big shire horse placing his huge hooves with care on the uneven surface, his back protected from snow by an old blanket the carter had thrown over him. The driver sat under a battered felt hat, shoulders hunched against the cold, reins bunched in a mittened hand. He gave them a slow salute as he pulled to one side to let them through. A post van came the other way, acknowledging the presence of other people in this desolate place with a cheery hoot of his horn.

Perdita was stiff and very cold by the time they reached Sedburgh, and thankful when her brother suggested they might stop. 'We can stretch our legs a bit.'

'You mean you want to take some photographs,' she said. She scrambled out of the car and stood stamping her feet as she blew on numb fingers.

'Just the street here, with the dusk coming on, and lights showing in the windows.'

'A long exposure job,' said Perdita, who liked to help her brother with his work. 'Have you got a tripod in the car?'

'On the back seat.'

The locals went to and fro about their business with hardly a second glance at him as he set up his apparatus. One or two stopped to greet him, and the vicar halted his striding

54

steps for a few minutes' chat. 'You'll need chains further on,' he said as he went on his way.

Perdita didn't ask if Edwin had chains. Born and bred in the north, she took cold winters and blocked passes for granted; any driver who ventured out at this time of year without a set of chains tucked away inside the boot was asking for trouble. Edwin would have a shovel, too, and a powerful torch tucked into a pair of gumboots thrust down behind the driver's seat.

Perdita craned her neck to catch a view of the sky from the car window. It was clear now, and the first stars were out. The car's powerful lamps cast long beams on to the freezing surface of the road. As the road climbed again, the snow lay more thickly, and they stopped the car to put on chains. From then on it was a snail's pace journey, snow giving way to stretches of treacherous ice, other icy patches covered by a concealing cover of windblown snow.

'Grandmama will be cross,' said Perdita, peering at her wristwatch. 'We'll barely be home by eight o'clock.'

'Late running service in the Minster, heavy snow on the way,' Edwin said.

'And no stopping here and there to take photographs. Don't worry, I shan't say anything. She'll blame me, in any case, if we're late; she always does. Could we have had a puncture?'

'I did, on the way to York.'

'There you are, then.'

'And dinner on the dot or no dinner, I'm not doing anything until I've had a hot bath.'

'You'll have not to potter,' warned Perdita, as they finally turned in through the gates of the drive that wound up to the front of the house. She was never sure whether this was the way she liked the house best, a shadowy, gaunt shape, with its improbable crenellations and towers outlined against a starry sky, lights shining out from a few of the large stone windows. Mostly, they were dark, with heavy curtains within keeping the light in and the cold out. A daytime arrival had its own, different charm, revealing the vast array of arches and the ornate details of carving on door and window surrounds. Sir Henry's grandfather had built the house to his own design after a lengthy visit to the continent, where the Renaissance palaces and Bavarian castles had impressed him equally.

The front door was opening as they drew up, light spilled out on to the broad stone steps and Rokeby came down with stately tread to help Perdita out of the car.

Perdita greeted the butler with enthusiasm. 'Hello, Rokeby.'

'Welcome back, Miss Perdita.'

'I'll just take her around to the stables,' Edwin said. 'Get someone to come out for the suitcases and things, will you, Rokeby?'

The butler bowed, and escorted Perdita into the hall. A fire was lit at one end in an enormous fireplace, and the wall lamps, huge nineteenth-century mediaeval torches, threw light on to the upper part of the walls, where antlered heads twinkled with tinsel and tiny bells.

'Aunt Trudie's been at work,' said Perdita, looking around her. 'Cheers those gruesome old heads up a bit, don't you think?'

'Miss Trudie has achieved a very festive touch,' said Rokeby, his lips sealed on the subject of the chaos that eccentric lady had caused while touched by the Christmas spirit. Great branches of firs and prickly bundles of holly had been deposited in the Herb Room, a vast, stone-flagged room off the kitchen where the dogs were fed and any untidy work was done on the worn wooden table that ran down its centre. The gardener and his two assistants had been pressed into service; one of the maids, who had deft fingers, had been summoned from dusting duties to make paper flowers; Eckersley had been sent in the large car to buy all kinds of gaudy delights from the nearest Woolworth's, and even he, Rokeby, had been instructed to make good use of his unusual height and climb up and down ladders to affix garlands and streamers in various inaccessible places.

'Everyone has gone up to dress,' he told Perdita. 'Your trunk has not yet arrived, I dare say the weather has caused some delays.'

'Oh, I'll find something. I'd better get a move on, though, I don't want Grandmama in a temper on my first night home.'

'No,' agreed Rokeby, with feeling. 'Miss Alix is upstairs, she arrived a little while ago and went straight up.'

Perdita's face lit up. 'She's here?' She made for the stairs and started up them, two at a time.

NINE

Wyncrag, Westmoreland

Alix stood at the top of the second landing, watching Perdita's rapid ascent. As she reached the last few steps her sister hesitated, looking upwards, her face uncertain. 'Alix? Is that you?'

'Hello, Perdy.'

Perdita came slowly up to the top of the staircase, leaning against the wide polished banister rail as she eyed her sister up and down. 'You've changed. You look quite different.'

Her voice was brusque, but Alix knew that it was shyness. 'So do you, you're so tall, Perdy.' And then she gave a spurt of laughter, 'Lord, that's the school tweed suit you're wearing, gracious, I'd forgotten how awful it was.'

Perdita lost some of her shyness and grinned. 'Isn't it? In fact, this was yours. It's a bit tight on me.'

'You've got a bust, which is more than I had at your age. Do you still have to wear those vile green divided skirts for games?'

Perdita nodded.

'You'll have to change for dinner,' Alix said, suddenly practical. 'In about five minutes if we aren't to be late. I don't

58

suppose Grandmama is any less of a stickler for punctuality than she used to be.'

'No, she isn't. Oh, help!' Perdita flung herself through the door of her room.

Alix followed her in. 'I'll give you a hand with hooks, if you like.'

Perdita's room was large, as were most of the rooms at Wyncrag, and heavily panelled; their great-grandfather must have cut down half a forest to satisfy his love of panelling when he was building the house. Underfoot was a thick carpet. All the bedrooms were carpeted, for which the occupants were thankful during the long, cold winters. Winter curtains, velvet, lined and interlined until they could practically have stood up without support, hung across the big windows. The marble fireplace had a fire lit in its grate, but it hardly took the chill off the room.

Perdita bent down to take her shoes and stockings off, then stretched out her frozen feet towards the fire. 'The trouble is, one has almost to toast them before they feel warm, especially after being in Edwin's car.' She rubbed them for a few moments before padding over to the immense mahogany wardrobe. She flung open the doors and stood gazing at the clothes hanging within, each garment covered with tissue paper shawls and smelling of lavender from the little bags tied to each hanger.

'Lipp?' Alix asked. It had to be; lavender and Lipp went together at Wyncrag.

'Lipp,' Perdita said, as she dragged a dark blue frock off its hanger, and laid it on the bed, a hefty four-poster with a high mound of a mattress. She struggled out of her suit jacket, blouse, vest and liberty bodice, and took off her half slip and tweedy skirt. Then she rummaged in the top drawer of a chest of drawers and found a brassière.

'That's pretty,' Alix said. It seemed an unlikely item of underwear for Perdita to own; she could make a good guess at just how few pretty things her younger sister was likely to possess.

'It was a present from Aunt Dorothea, Grandmama doesn't know about it, although I suppose she will now if Lipp's been snooping in my drawers. I shall have to hide it.'

'You couldn't have taken it to school, of course.'

'Goodness, no; brassières are banned at school by Matron on grounds of immorality and frivolity.'

She hunted for a pair of stockings, not silk, Alix noticed, but at least not quite such a dreary colour as her depressing brown school ones. A long slip completed her underwear, and then she heaved the dress over her head.

Alix got up and went over to do up the back, as Perdita looked doubtfully at herself in the looking glass inside the wardrobe door.

'Oh, well,' was all she said before thrusting herself into a shapeless evening bolero, charcoal coloured, with metallic threads.

They were at the door just as the gong went and Rokeby's voice boomed up to them with his announcement of dinner.

The dining room at Wyncrag was long, high, and lit only by candlelight. Lady Richardson considered dining under electric lights vulgar. There were two fireplaces, each with a roaring fire. Alix knew those fires of old; if you sat near them you roasted, and your face went red; if you sat further away you froze and your arms developed goose pimples. Her grandfather gestured to her to come and sit beside him. His whole-hearted welcome to her earlier on had in itself made the journey worthwhile, she thought, as she gave Aunt Trudie an affectionate smile. He had been so very pleased to see her. Unlike his wife.

Alix had been thinking about her grandmother as she travelled northwards. When the other two passengers left the train at Crewe, wishing her a happy Christmas, she sat alone in the first-class compartment of the Lakeland Express, wondering whether Lady Richardson would show any pleasure in seeing her again.

No, she shouldn't expect a warm welcome, not from Grandmama. She released the blind at the window beside her seat and looked out at the darkening wintry scene. Snow-clad hills were illuminated by brilliant starlight; she heard the shrill whistle of the locomotive as it took a curve, its wailing sound floating out into the remote whiteness of the landscape. The train sped past a village, a square church tower visible for a moment before the train plunged into the darkness of a deep, rock-sided cutting.

The window blurred with smoke. She pulled the blind down again, and sat back in her wide, well-upholstered seat, reaching up to switch on the light over the empty place next to her. Half past five; nearly two hours to go. She shut her eyes, listening to the steady tuppence-three-farthings rhythm of the train. Her eyes stayed closed, the book on her lap slipped to the floor, and she sank into a dreamy half-awake, half-asleep state, her mind filled with images of hills and snow.

The sound of the compartment door opening roused her, and the cheery, 'Just coming in, Miss Richardson,' spoken in the familiar accent of the fells and lakes, told her she was home. 'It'll be a few minutes yet,' he added, as she jumped to her feet. 'No need to hurry.'

There was every need to hurry. She didn't want to miss a minute, no, not a second, of the ice-world lying outside. She gathered together her possessions, picked up the book from the floor, paused in front of the mirror to tidy her hair under her hat. As the train pulled into the curve of the platform she stood in the corridor and tugged at the thick leather strap to let down a window. The dark air rushed in at her, arctic cold, but so fresh and clean that she wanted to gulp great mouthfuls of it, to rid her lungs and head of the smoke and fret of London. The gloom and sour, smoky smell of Euston lay in another dimension, surely not inhabiting the same world as this.

Then through the murk of steam she saw a short, stocky, bow-legged figure in gaiters advancing along the dimly lit platform through the little throng of waiting people. Eckersley, in his gaiters, his chauffeur's hat slightly askew, his weathered face breaking into a smile at the sight of her.

'Eckersley, oh, it's been so long!'

'Too long, Miss Alix, and we're right glad to have you home. Is that all your luggage with the porter there? I've got the motor car just outside. Hand that suitcase to me.'

If only Grandmama's greeting had been half as friendly. She had dutifully gone up to Lady Richardson's room soon after her arrival, to be received with perfect, frigid courtesy. And Alix knew, without a word being spoken, that her grandmother wholly disapproved of her elegant new persona and what it said about her life in London.

It was now Perdita's turn to greet her grandparents, and Alix could see the stiffness in her young body as she clumped in her heavy shoes to Grandmama's end of the table.

'Good evening,' she said, bending her head to receive her grandmother's chilly kiss.

'You were extremely late back from Yorkshire, Perdita. I was concerned.'

'Here we go,' Edwin said under his breath as he slid into his seat and gave Aunt Trudie a conspiratorial smile. Then he turned and grinned at Alix.

How lovely it was to see him again, his dark hair falling across his forehead as it always had done, his long fingers crumbling his roll, his grey eyes, the mirror of hers, alight with pleasure at the sight of her.

Grandmama's attention had turned from Perdita to her

grandson, and it was clear to anyone who knew her that, although her voice was calm, she was, in fact, very angry with him.

'I can't say how distressing, Edwin. In the dark, and the snow, you and Perdita, with no older person there. It's most inappropriate.'

'What's inappropriate about it? We're brother and sister, not a couple out on a romantic tryst. And I am twenty-four, not some boy scout who'd panic at a bit of snow.'

'That's not the point.'

'Good evening, Edwin,' said Sir Henry, coming to his rescue. 'Rokeby, stop hovering about and pour Mr Edwin a glass of wine. Edwin, you look cold. I'm afraid the central heating's not working properly tonight,' he went on, clearly keen to distract his wife's attention from the iniquities of her errant grandchildren.

Wyncrag had central heating throughout the house, an extraordinary luxury that scandalized neighbours who used no form of heating except coal fires. Warm passages and bathrooms and bedrooms were considered soft and un-English. However, Sir Henry had travelled, and appreciated the warmth in some of the North American houses he had visited. It came as a welcome novelty to him to step into a hall or a bathroom and not find the temperature dropping by several degrees.

'Poor quality coal, playing the devil with the furnace,' he said. When the miles of piping he had had installed in every room and passage carried a stream of hot water as intended, the house was a haven of blissful warmth. But the advanced system battled against a temperamental furnace that produced water that was either too cold, or almost boiling hot. 'Hardens are delivering more coal tomorrow, and they can take the rest of this load away, I never saw such stuff. Can't think where it came from; it certainly isn't fit for household use.'

Soup was served. Trudie, looking particularly vague, began

an anecdote about the dogs, the tension eased. Then Lady Richardson noticed for the first time what Perdita was wearing. 'What have you got on, child? You look like something out of the orphanage.'

'Sorry, Grandmama,' said Perdita, concentrating on her plate. 'It doesn't seem to fit very well, and I didn't have time to look for anything else.' She reached out to flick at a candle that had a guttering flame, and there was a loud ripping sound.

'Oh, dear, I think the sleeve's coming off,' she said, lifting her arm to inspect the damage.

'Perdita!'

'I've grown rather a lot.'

'She has,' Edwin said. 'I hardly recognised her in the Minster.'

'My feet have grown, too,' said Perdita. 'My school shoes are awfully uncomfortable. I seem to be growing out of everything.'

Lady Richardson was disapproving. 'I think it's most unsuitable for you still to be growing at your age. I'd reached my full height by the time I was twelve. Tomorrow, we shall look through your things, Perdita, and decide what can be done about your frocks. Lipp may be able to lengthen them and let them out.'

'It doesn't matter much in the holidays, I shall be in jodhs most of the time.'

'You won't, however, wear jodhpurs in the evening, nor do I expect to see you in them for meals. I shall see if any of my old dresses could be made over for you, although I fear you're too tall.'

'No, Grandmama, really,' said Alix. 'That's too bad. You can't ask Perdita to wear hand-me-down frocks. She'd look a perfect fright, now she's fifteen and nearly grown-up.'

'Fifteen is very far from being grown-up.'

'Oh, I don't know,' said Perdita unwisely. 'Look at Juliet.

64

We've been doing *Romeo and Juliet* this term, and . . .'

'I can't think what your English mistress imagines she's doing; it's not a suitable play for girls of your age. Emotion is so bad for girls.'

'If Perdita's grown, then of course she must have new frocks,' said her grandfather. 'If the freeze continues, a lot of families will be up here for Christmas and into the new year, and that means parties. At least, it always did in my day. Perdita will need a long dress or two.'

'She's much too young for that,' Lady Richardson said.

'She's too tall for anything else,' said Sir Henry, inspecting his granddaughter with a critical eye.

Perdita was used to people talking about her as though she weren't there, so she tucked into her lamb and green peas and asked Edwin to pass the water. Then she gave Alix a wide smile. 'Have you got lots of blissful clothes with you? Edwin said you'd got fearfully smart last time he saw you, only I didn't believe him. It's ages since you were here, and then it was all tweeds bagging at the back and dull jumpers. I do love the colour of frock you're wearing, where do you buy heavenly things like that?'

'I'd offer to let you try all my clothes on, but you've grown so, they won't fit you.'

Perdita sighed. 'I'm too big all over, you mean. Don't spare my feelings, I know it.'

'It's fortunate that Alix is here,' said Aunt Trudie, chasing a pea around her plate. 'She must know all about the latest fashions, and can say just what we should be wearing.'

'Alix's clothes would be entirely unsuitable for Perdita.' Grandmama's voice was sharp and Alix felt the familiar twinge of alarm come over her. Only, this time, the severe words weren't directed at her. 'Don't put ideas into her head, please, Trudie. London fashions are all very well in their place, but not here.'

Grandmama hasn't changed, Alix thought, as she waited

for the maid to hand the pudding. Not a jot. Then her attention was centred on the plate placed in front of her. Chocolate pudding, wonderful Cook, serving her favourite on the first night she was back.

It was clear that Perdita liked chocolate pudding, too, but there was no need for Grandmama to be so quick with a sharp comment. 'Not so much, Perdita, please. Chocolate is too rich for you.'

Perdita swiftly took another spoonful. Kind Aunt Trudie distracted Grandmama with a query about flowers, and she was left to consume her pudding in peace.

When she was a girl, Grandmama must have enjoyed things like chocolate, Alix mused as she savoured her pudding. She couldn't always have been such a puritan. Family portraits hung on the walls of the dining room, and Grandmama was seated beneath a painting of herself when she was a girl, a vital beauty in a pink silk with a bustle, her hair artlessly up, her dress cut low over her white bosom, a fan in her hand. It had been painted by a French artist, and had, Grandpapa had told her, caused a scandal when it was first hung in the Academy summer exhibition.

'It wasn't considered at all a suitable picture of the daughter of a Master of a Cambridge college. It was a true likeness, though, that's just how she looked the night I met her. At a ball.'

It was strange that Grandmama had never taken down that portrait of herself. No one now would recognise the hawk-like woman sitting beneath it as being the girl in the painting. Life had emptied her of joy. She'd had tremendous charm, an ancient family friend had once told Alix, memory gleaming in his eyes. 'When she was a young married woman, she had so much charm she only had to smile at a man to bring him to her side.'

Alix had never been aware of any charm. Her eyes strayed to the picture hanging on the wall at the other end of the table, a three-quarters portrait of a young man in the uniform of an army officer: Jack Richardson, killed in action in 1917. 'You have his chin, Perdy,' she said, nodding her head at the painting.

The silence at the table was absolute. What on earth was there in that remark to make Grandmama look like that? Was she still grieving for her youngest son, after nearly twenty years? They all knew he'd been her favourite; perhaps she would never get over it.

Later, when Perdita had gone yawning to bed, Alix and Edwin found themselves alone at last. Grandpapa was in his study, Grandmama had gone to her room, Aunt Trudie was taking the dogs out for a last run. By unspoken agreement, they headed for the billiard room. It was an old haunt of theirs, not least because it was a difficult room for eavesdroppers, being next to the study and only having one door. It was felt to be off-limits to Lipp's snooping, although, as Edwin observed, one could be sure of nothing where she was concerned.

Alix had spent enough time in the world to know that Lipp wouldn't be tolerated in any normal household. 'Other people don't let themselves be bullied by their servants,' she told Edwin as he chalked a cue for her.

'Other people wouldn't employ Lipp as a maid. What a monster she's become.'

'Grandmama's eyes and ears and feet.'

It was peaceful in the billiard room with its deep, leather-covered armchairs and sofas, the prints and maps on the panelled walls, the soft carpet underfoot, the subdued lighting, and the green baize surface with the red and white balls gleaming beneath the lamp suspended above the table.

Their voices were low to match their quiet surroundings. Outside the curtained windows, in a white world lit only by the sliver of a crescent moon and the chilly sparkle of winter stars, the silence was absolute; within there was only the crackling of the fire and the click of cue against ball.

'Grandmama hates Perdy,' Alix said at last. 'You never told me.'

'When you're here most of the time, as I am, you don't notice it. Though I was a bit taken aback by the way she treated Perdy this evening, I will admit.'

'She's much worse than she was with me, and that was bad enough. We have to do something. It can't be good for Perdy to be the focus of so much dislike, she'll grow up warped if it goes on.'

'Perdy's tougher than you think, or at least she seems to be. I suppose she's developed a kind of carapace; well, you'd have to, wouldn't you? Thank God for boarding schools, that's all.'

'And to think that one would live to say that!'

Edwin took up a cue and leant over the green surface of the table.

'What is it about Jack and Grandmama?' Alix said. Returning after an absence of three years, three years that had taken her to independence and a sense of the strength of her own judgement, she was struck by how complex a woman her grandmother was. She was also struck by the ability Grandmama had to quell and diminish each member of her family. Each living member, that was. 'There's some mystery there; it's more than just years of grief.'

'I think it's much, much better not to open that particular can of worms, Lexy.'

'But don't you long to know?'

'Why she was attached to Jack above all her other children? Not really. He was her Benjamin, and for some reason he touched her heart in a way none of the others did. Then, also, he died young, too young to be a disappointment to her, one supposes. No unsatisfactory bride brought home, no making his own way, no setting up a family of his own to

68

take his affection away from his mother. From all I've ever heard, he was a wilful man, unpleasant even, judging by how disinclined the locals are to speak of him – those that remember him, that is. You must have noticed that Aunt Trudie never mentions him, and you just try talking about him to Rokeby and watch him clam up.'

'So he remains our mysterious Uncle Jack,' said Alix, giving a violent yawn and laying down her cue. 'Lord, how tired I am. Off to bed, I think; I'll leave you to turn the lights out.' She gave her brother an affectionate kiss on his lean cheek.

'Sleep tight, Lexy. And welcome home.'

TEN

The Great North Road

By arriving early at his office, and working without a break for lunch, Michael wrapped up the last details of the Pegasus designs by mid-afternoon. He wished a Merry Christmas to his colleagues and to Giles Gibson, cycled back to his digs in time to collect his gear and suitcase and caught the four thirty-five train to Waterloo. He took a taxi from the station to Freddie's flat off Marylebone High Street.

'Just in time for dinner,' announced his friend, stacking his cases beside his own suitcases which were already packed and waiting, together with a pile of books, in his small hallway. 'I thought of getting tickets for a show, but I didn't, just in case some demanding calculations made you miss your train.'

'Waste of money buying a seat for me, the way I feel,' Michael said, smothering a yawn. 'I'd sleep through any performance. Where shall we dine?'

They walked to Soho, and enjoyed a leisurely Italian meal at Bertorelli's. 'Up early tomorrow, old thing,' Freddie said when they got back to his flat. 'Long drive ahead of us, and I don't suppose the roads will be any too good when we get further north.'

So Michael was ruthlessly woken from a deep sleep at seven the next morning and sat down to a hearty breakfast of bacon and eggs cooked by Freddie's man, who came in on a daily basis.

'Do stop looking at your watch,' Michael complained, as Freddie checked the time yet again and refused to let him start on another piece of toast.

'We've got to get on, no point in spoiling the run by getting held up this end in the rush hour.'

Freddie was a car fiend, and his big touring Bentley was his pride and joy. Since he loathed driving in a closed car, they had the roof down, and, togged up in leather jackets and helmets, with scarves around their necks, gauntlets on their hands and stout goggles over their eyes, they drove through the heavy London traffic, heading for Potter's Bar and the Great North Road.

Despite the layers of protective clothing, they were chilled enough to be glad of a stop for coffee at Baldock. Michael had the big Thermos refilled and they were soon back in the car and on their way to Grantham.

'I dislike Lincolnshire,' said Freddie. 'I never drive through this landscape without wanting to be among the northern crags.'

'I don't much like the Fens myself,' he agreed. 'Never mind, we'll soon be in sight of hills, and tomorrow we'll be on the ice, or at least out tobogganing.'

'It's sixteen years since the lake froze completely, they say. I can't wait to see what it's like, and to be out there on my skates. I go to the rink in London, but there's nothing to touch skating out of doors.'

'I was there sixteen years ago.'

'What, in Westmoreland? That winter, when it last froze?'

'That winter.'

'How old were you?'

'Twelve. It wasn't much of a holiday for any of us, for I

caught a chill and got pneumonia. We never went back to the lakes after that. My mother didn't fancy going north again.'

'So it's sixteen years since you've been there. No wonder you didn't sound too keen when I rang and put the plan to you. Understandable, if you had a bad time there when you were a boy.'

'If I didn't jump at your offer straight away, it was because of worries about leaving my work, that's all. I'm glad my chief almost threw me out; I intend to spend all the hours of daylight on the ice or on the snow. I've been caged up in the office for too long, and I need to get fit.'

The last miles of the journey were slow and tedious, with an icy surface on the dark country roads and the great head-lamps lighting up the icy filigree of the roadside hedges, making eerie patterns out of branches and tree trunks. They were more than glad to reach the inn, where a solicitous Mrs Dixon showed them to low-beamed bedrooms with creaking wooden floors and panelled walls hung with faded prints and framed maps and assorted copper items. Fires flickered in the grates, and downstairs, while they waited for dinner to be served, a huge log fire burned in the wide, centuries-old stone fireplace.

The inn was full, and all the conversation was about the lake. 'Holding splendidly,' said a middle-aged man with a bushy moustache. 'Brought your skates, have you?'

'We certainly have,' replied Freddie. 'Out on the ice first thing, just the ticket, isn't it, Michael?'

Michael was more than half asleep in the warmth of the fire, but he nodded in agreement.

'Didn't I read that they had bonfires on the ice last time it froze?' Freddie said.

'No good asking me,' he said with a yawn. 'I don't remember much about that winter.'

'They did indeed,' the innkeeper said, coming in to summon

his guests to dinner. 'Braziers to roast chestnuts on and warm your hands, and a huge bonfire as well. There were some who skated holding great flaming torches, oh, that was a sight to see.'

'Sounds rather like the Inquisition on Ice,' murmured Freddie, as they went in to their soup.

They found themselves sitting at the same table as the man with the moustache, and two young women. He was a solicitor from Manchester, he told them. The young women smiled, and said they were teachers, PT teachers. One of them ventured that she loved winter sports, didn't he agree the frozen lake was topping?

Nice, ordinary people, thought Michael, as he drank his soup and let his gaze drift around the small dining room. A family sat at the next table, father, mother and two dark-haired sons of about fourteen and sixteen. A fair younger sister was busily making bread pellets and dropping them into her soup, despite her mother's protestations. An older man, tall and thin, sat at a small table by himself, a monocle in one eye, a book laid beside his plate. Peaceful people, enjoying a respite from work and duties, like himself.

Ordinary people who might soon be plunged into the furnace of war, if what Giles Gibson said were true. Michael wondered if the prospect of war was the cause of the slight feeling of unease that he couldn't otherwise explain. More likely it was simple weariness after a long, cold drive.

'They say there's a glamorous American woman who's taken a house here over Christmas and the new year,' announced the young woman next to him. 'Practically no one's seen her, but the woman at the Post Office is sure she's a film star.'

The solicitor laughed. 'To people in an out of the way place like this, any visiting American is immediately assumed to be a film star. What would a film star be doing here, I'd like to know?'

'Skating?'

'Plenty of winter sports in America, my dear. No need to cross the Atlantic for ice and snow. We get excited about it, because we don't often see weather as cold and frosty as this, but Americans would make nothing of it, take my word for it.'

She looked disappointed. 'I hope she is someone famous, I'd like to get her autograph if she is.'

'If she's famous and over here, I expect she's travelling incognito, and wouldn't thank you for asking her for an autograph,' Freddie said. 'We'll see her on the ice in dark glasses and with a scarf covering her hair and face, and shapeless clothes so that we shan't recognise her legs. All glamorous film stars have lovely legs, you know.'

The young women both giggled at that. 'She's got a companion with her, so the woman at the Post Office told me. Her husband, I suppose, but you never know with film people, do you?'

The woman at the next table cast a frowning glance towards them, her mouth pursed up in disapproval. Her sons were listening avidly to the discussion about the American visitor, and she gave them a quelling look before starting up a very dull conversation of her own about whether the scarf she had bought for Uncle Bobbie would prove to be warm enough for such bitter weather as they were having.

After dinner, the solicitor bore Freddie away to the tap for a game of shove ha'penny. 'I haven't played for years,' Freddie said.

'Good, then I'll beat you. Better than taking on the locals, they have a way with the ha'pennies.'

Michael wandered into the room that served as bar and sitting room, pipe in hand, and ordered a brandy. 'And something for yourself,' he added to the landlord.

He sat down in a settle by the fire, and the landlord joined him in a minute or two, a pewter mug of bitter ale in his hand. They sat in companionable silence while Michael lit his pipe, and then the landlord spoke. 'We're fair glad you and Dr Kerr were able to come, Mr Wrexham. We were in a way to being perplexed about those empty rooms. No trouble filling them, you'll say, in weather such as we're having, but we'd turned away two visitors, and it'ud look bad if you hadn't come, and we'd got the rooms spare after all, for they were insistent they'd have the rooms if they weren't taken, and I'd not be wanting them under my roof.'

'Why, what was wrong with them?' Michael asked idly, watching the smoke from the fire curling up the chimney.

'If you'd seen them . . .' The landlord pursed his lips, shook his head. 'The moment they came in here, looking for me, I thought, aye, now, here's summat to think about, and if these two men don't mean trouble, my name's not Robert Dixon. Very short hair one of them had. Nothing wrong with short hair, but there's no need to look like you might have taken your own razor to your scalp. Bristly, I'd call it. That was the bigger of the two men. Although it was the other that did the talking. He had short hair, too, but more gentlemanlike, if you take my meaning. And a smooth way of talking. I fancied, just for a moment, that I'd seen him somewhere before, but the wife says no, that was just my imagining.'

He paused to take a good draught of his beer, and Michael sipped his brandy, more than half-asleep now.

'The long and the short of it was, I said right out, polite, mind you, but definite, as how we were full up and likely to be so right to t'other side of the new year.'

Michael stirred himself, feeling that he was expected to express a proper interest. 'So what didn't you like about them, Mr Dixon?'

'I'll tell you what I didn't like, and then you tell me if you think I did wrong. They weren't wearing those uniforms that have been banned, but I reckon they might as well have been.'

'Uniforms?'

'Black shirts is what I'm talking about; they looked as though for two pennies they'd be dressed up in that uniform those Mosleyites like to wear.'

'Good Lord,' Michael said, waking up properly. 'You mean you think they were British Fascists?'

'I do that,' the landlord said, pleased with Michael's reaction. 'I've seen some of those folk, in Manchester, and they've got a look to them I don't care for. Now, you tell me this, Mr Wrexham, in my place, what would you have done?'

'Oh, I don't think I'd care to have a pair of fascists in black shirts under my roof, if that's what they were, and I dare say you're right. What on earth are they doing up here? It's a bit off their usual haunts, I should think.'

'They said they were up here for sport. Skating and that, the same as my other guests. "Toughening ourselves up," one said. "And a spot of business," said the other. Well, they didn't look like men who needed any further toughening, and that's a fact, and I shouldn't care to think about what their business might be.'

'So you turned them away?'

'I did that. Which is why, as I said, I was that pleased when Dr Kerr telephoned us again, saying he'd take the rooms for himself and for you.'

'I wonder where they went.'

'Now that I can tell you. They've got rooms at Mrs McKechnie's up at the top of the town. She's not so fussy, she'd let to Old Nick himself if he could pay. Being a Scot, you understand.'

'Well, well,' Michael said. 'Let's just hope they don't get up to any of their tricks up here.'

'You can trust young Jimmy Ogilvy for that. He's our policeman, and a right big fellow he is, too. I was thinking I'd step over to his house tomorrow and tell him about those two, he might like to let his superiors know what's what. Just in case.'

ELEVEN

London, Pimlico

Mrs Sacker knew at once that the man was a policeman. She also knew, before he showed her his card, that he wasn't from the local police station nor from the CID. Even the most respectable London landlady came into contact with the police; if not questions about her tenants, then there were routine enquiries about residents, temporary and permanent, in neighbouring houses and streets. Landladies are often at home. They watch. They sum people up quickly – and shrewdly, if they want the rent to be paid regularly.

'Two guineas a week my gentlemen pay,' she told the dark-overcoated man as she let him in through the front door. No point in keeping him on the doorstep for watchful eyes to take gleeful note. *One of your lodgers in trouble, is he, Mrs Sacker?*

The man removed his hat and followed her down the stairs to the big, high-ceilinged kitchen. There was welcome warmth and a seat close by the range, and the offer of a cup of tea.

'Only gentlemen?' he enquired.

Her mouth pursed. '*Only* gentlemen. Women, however respectable, are a trouble. I mean, you expect gentlemen to be in rooms, but a lady? No, if she's a lady, she's at home. With her parents if she isn't married, or living with a sister or an aunt. I don't hold with women going out to work, I never have.'

'Many women have to earn a living, Mrs Sacker, the same as the rest of us.'

'Taking the bread out of men's mouths. It's one thing for a widow like myself to let out rooms, and look after a few gentlemen, that's women's work and entirely right. Hoity-toitying into an office and being paid proper wages like a man is quite another matter.'

'I expect you're careful about who you take on. Have to be in your line of business, and with a high reputation to keep up. I dare say your rooms aren't ever empty for long.'

Mrs Sacker wasn't deceived. He was trying to flatter her into helpfulness. Well, she was as ready to help the police in their proper business as anyone else, but catching criminals was their proper business, not creeping around asking questions about her tenants who were most certainly not criminals.

'My gentlemen tend to stay. They're well looked after and why should they move on?'

'So how long has Mr Roberts been with you?'

Aha, Mr Jago was his target, was he? There was one person they wouldn't get any information on, and for why? Because he was a gentleman who kept himself to himself.

'Very respectable, Mr Roberts is,' she said. 'More than a year he's been here now. He's one that's been brought up properly, you can always tell a gentleman who's had a nanny and been to the right kind of schools. Everything in its place, that's Mr Roberts.'

'Doesn't the army teach a man neatness in his ways?' the policeman asked mildly.

'It does and it doesn't. Once they've been in the army, they'll be careful, most of them, about keeping their clothes in good order, they like their shoes polished, put on clean collars, that kind of thing. But someone like Mr Roberts, you can tell he was at a public school. Take his hairbrushes. He's got a pair of them, laid out on the dressing table just so. With his initials, JR, on the back, and a number below. Not an army number, only two figures, 44. That's a school number. They all have a number at those kind of schools. In nails on the soles of their shoes and printed on the name tapes. Although you'd know it as soon as you spoke to him, he speaks like the gentleman he is, and he has lovely manners, doesn't have to think about them, he's been taught those manners since he could sit up. Course he has.'

'So he's English?'

'Yes, he's English.' Her voice was indignant. 'As English as you and me sitting here now.'

David Pritchard was Welsh on both sides, but he knew better than to intrude any jot of his personality on the conversation. 'I had heard, from one or two people I've spoken to, who know him, that his English doesn't always sound up-to-date. That he uses some old-fashioned expressions.'

Mrs Sacker smiled. If that was all they had to go on . . . 'It's his way. It's what they call an affectation. "Hand in hand with a statelier past," he says to me. There's some of the old ways he prefers, and why not?'

'Not a foreigner then. Not French, nothing like that?'

'French! I wouldn't have a Frenchman in my house.'

'You have had visitors from abroad. A Dutchman used to stay here, our records show. And a Mr Schiller, from Vienna. And one or two Irishmen.'

That was Special Branch for you, suspecting every foreigner of being a danger, and letting these communists get away with murder under their very noses. Only, if it was Irishmen they were after, then Mr Roberts had nothing to worry about.

Inspector Pritchard saw the look of relief in her face. He said nothing, but took another drink of his tea.

'You've no business calling the Irish foreigners,' Mrs Sacker said. 'They speak the same language as we do, it's not right to say they're the same as Italians or Frenchies. And Mr van Hoek, he might have been English the way he spoke the language. He was in the cheese trade, over here to study our methods, he told me. I'm quite partial to a piece of Dutch cheese, myself, I like a cheese that always tastes the same.'

Inspector Pritchard nodded in agreement, although he would as soon eat a piece of India rubber as Edam. 'I take it you're sure Mr Roberts didn't come from Ireland.'

'Quite sure, and just to show you he's English, I've seen his passport, which he keeps in the top drawer in his room.'

'He's away at the moment, isn't he?'

'He is, visiting friends for Christmas, as are millions of other perfectly respectable English people.'

'Might I have a look at this drawer? See if this passport's there?'

'You might not. Not without you've got a warrant. But I can set your mind at rest, it's there all right, for I took up a pile of his laundry only this morning and put his handkerchiefs away in that very drawer, and his passport is there. So he hasn't done a flit.'

'Now, why should you think for a moment that we'd suspect him of leaving the country?'

She got up from the table and went to the range to move the large kettle an inch or so to one side. Her bearing was rigid, an effect enhanced by the straight grey dress she wore unfashionably long. Inspector Pritchard guessed that her corsets were inflexible and firmly fastened, although he didn't know why she bothered, bony types like her hardly needed to cage themselves in whalebone since they came ready stiffened.

'If you don't, why do you want to know if he's got his passport with him?'

'Do you have Mr Roberts's current address?'

'I do not.'

80

'You won't be forwarding any mail to him?'

'I shan't.' Her mouth snapped shut on the words.

Was that because she was keeping his post for him, or because he received no letters? 'We have information leading us to believe that Mr Roberts is involved with the fascist movement.'

'It's no crime to be a fascist, not that I ever heard.'

'A man's politics are his own business, I agree with that, but when politics spill over into violence, then it becomes a police affair.'

'Violence? Mr Roberts? Get along with you. I'd know if he'd been up to any violence, and he never has, and that's the truth.'

'I'm not accusing Mr Roberts of any violent act, but the movement he belongs to is happy to use any means, including violence, to achieve its ends.'

'So you say. I don't see your lot stepping in to stop the Reds getting up to mischief. And it's people like you going on about Spain and Hitler that stir up trouble. A citizen of any country that's keen to keep those Bolsheviks at bay deserves our support.'

Inspector Pritchard got up. 'You can't even help us by telling me whereabouts he's gone visiting? Would it be to the country or to another town?'

'He's gone to the south coast, I believe,' she said, her refined accents now firmly back in place. 'I'll show you out.'

His superior listened to the account of Inspector Pritchard's visit. 'It bears out what we've heard about Mrs Sacker's sympathies. Do we have anything on her?'

'Only that her late husband's name was Säckler, not Sacker, and that he was a naturalised Austrian.'

'Ah. Do you think Roberts bears further investigation?'

'I think we should still keep an eye on him.'

'Difficult, if we don't know where he's gone. Do you believe he's at the south coast?'

'Not for a moment. Not unless they've had a heavy snow-fall in Hastings that I haven't heard about. I saw a tin of wax in her kitchen, and it's the same kind my youngest son uses on his skating boots when he goes off on these winter sports trips of his. Now, sir, where can you skate without leaving the country? Barring ice rinks, which I don't feel is where he's spending his holiday.'

'This winter, almost anywhere in the north where there are lakes.'

'Exactly. It could be Scotland, it could be this side of the border. Only I did happen to see a postcard with a picture of Helvellyn sitting above Mrs Sacker's fireplace. It might be from him, it might not. But he's up north somewhere, I feel sure of it.'

'He couldn't have gone abroad, could he? He may have two passports.'

Inspector Pritchard shook his head. 'No, I reckon he's keeping his nose clean. I'd expect all his papers to be in perfect order, without any funny business. We're dealing with a real professional here, no question about it.'

'I'll leave it in your hands, then. Keep me informed.'

Westmoreland

TWELVE

'Well!' said Lady Richardson, as Perdita hurtled into the dining room. 'Is there a fire?'

'Sorry, Grandmama,' Perdita said as she eyed the sideboard. 'I'm hungry, and I didn't want to be late.'

Lady Richardson looked at her over a silver teapot. 'You are late. I don't know why, since you can't have taken long to dress. You're in breeches, I see.'

'I'm going to the stables as soon as I've had breakfast.'

'They seem very generously cut.'

Perdita pulled at the waistband. It was held in by a canvas belt, a necessary addition as the breeches were clearly several inches too large for her. 'They're Aunt Trudie's. I can't get into any of my jodhs. They're all too small. These are long enough, only a bit big around the middle.'

Alix came into the room, kissed both her grandparents and joined Perdita at the sideboard. 'Good heavens, Perdy, what are you wearing? You look a perfect scarecrow.'

'Oh, thanks,' Perdita said, going bright red.

Alix could have bitten her tongue off, as she remembered suddenly what it was like to be fifteen, when any adverse remark seemed like a monstrous criticism.

'I didn't put that very well. The breeches look as if they

85

belonged on a scarecrow. You don't look like a scarecrow.'

The damage was done. Perdita kept her head down as she dug a big silver ladle into the dish of porridge.

'They are Trudie's,' Grandmama said. 'Apparently the girl no longer fits into her jodhpurs.'

Grandpapa looked up from *The Times*. 'It seems to me that Perdita needs more than the new frock or two we were talking about. Where does Trudie get her riding clothes?'

'She has them made. Harold Simpkins, I think,' Alix said, when Grandmama made no reply.

'Very well. Get him to come and measure Perdita for whatever she needs. Can't have her careering about the country in breeches that are far too big for her. People will talk.'

That was an old saying of Grandpapa's, amusing because he had never given a damn what anyone thought about him or his family. Grandmama, now, she did mind about people talking. Not that she cared a fig for their opinion, but because to draw attention to yourself in any way was ill-bred, a failure of manners.

'Lots of people get breeches from Partridges,' Perdita said, glancing up from her porridge. 'I could, too. It'd be quicker.'

'Ready-made?' said Grandmama. 'I hardly think so.'

'They mightn't fit so well,' said Alix. 'They need to be comfortable for riding.'

'I know that. I just don't want anybody to make a fuss about it, that's all.'

'We've already established that your wardrobe needs an overhaul,' Grandpapa said. 'Go somewhere smart and get whatever you want. Tell them to send the bills to me.'

'Perdita, go shopping for herself? It's out of the question.'

'I'm not suggesting she goes on her own. Alix can go with her.'

Grandmama's face was a mask, her mouth inflexible. 'Alix has no idea what is suitable.'

Alix bit back a rejoinder and kept her voice indifferent. 'If we're talking about buying off the peg, I don't suppose it will be a matter of what's suitable, more a matter of what one can find that's the right length, Perdita's so tall now. Lucky girl,' she added, wanting to make amends for the unfortunate scarecrow remark. 'There are so many clothes that look better if you're tall.'

'Just so,' said her grandfather. 'I expect it'll mean a fair bit of traipsing around from one shop to another. Manchester's the place to go, you won't find anything suitable nearer than that. You won't want to go to Manchester, Caroline, not at this time of year.'

He had her there. Grandmama hated crowds, and a busy city thronged with Christmas shoppers was her idea of hell. Alix turned her back on the table, and stalked along the sideboard, lifting the covers on the usual delicious Wyncrag breakfast. What a fuss about a schoolgirl growing out of her clothes. She piled her plate with bacon, eggs, sausages, tomatoes and mushrooms. She hadn't, she realized, felt hungry like this for a very long time.

'Surely a rather large helping,' commented her grandmother as Alix sat down at the table and shook out a napkin.

'Tea or coffee, Miss Alix?' asked the maid, standing beside her with a heavy silver pot in each hand.

'Coffee please, Phoebe, and lots of cream, if Perdita's left any.'

Perdita finished pouring cream on to her porridge and licked the drop from the lip with her finger before passing it to Alix. 'I'll have it back when you've finished with it.'

'You've had quite enough cream, Perdita,' her grandmother said at once. 'It's bad for your complexion.'

'Not that I've got any complexion to speak of,' said Perdita. 'Didn't our mother used to be terribly sleek and smart? Nanny told me once that she looked like a picture in *Vogue*.'

'Helena was a most elegant woman,' Grandpapa said from behind his paper. 'She paid for good dressing, and Neville loved to see her looking her best. "Buy yourself something pretty," he would say, and so she did. Clothes, and jewels, too. He bought her some very good pieces, and it was a pleasure to see her wearing them.'

'Helena was a married woman,' Grandmama said coldly. 'And an American.'

Married, good; American, bad, Alix said to herself.

'Please pass the marmalade, Alix, and Perdita, do you really want toast as well?'

'Yes,' said Perdita, spreading a slice with a thick layer of butter. 'I've got to keep up my strength for being out in the snow. Otherwise I might expire from frostbite and exposure, and be found a pale and interesting corpse in the ice.'

Booted, jacketed and with woolly hats on their heads, Alix and Edwin set out with the large sledge in tow. It was an old one that had belonged to their grandfather when he was a boy, and it had the extravagantly curved runners of its time.

'What about the lower orchard?' Alix said. 'The bit where it slopes down almost to the edge of the lake, you always get a good run there.'

'When we've put in a bit of practice,' said Edwin. 'We'll be rusty to start with, when did you last go on a sledge? We'd be bound to have trouble with the trees. Besides, the fun there is shooting out on to the ice, and if we did that, we might get a soaking, it's where the beck runs into the lake.'

'Pagan's Field, then.' Alix put her arm through his, and they tramped across the snow in companionable silence, the sledge running smoothly behind them on the ice-crusted snow.

'What's up, Lexy?' Edwin asked presently, giving her a perceptive look. 'I heard you'd broken up with John. Is that true? You never wrote, and I didn't like to pry. You're such a prickly old thing.'

She gave his arm an affectionate squeeze. 'Love's the devil, isn't it, Edwin? One longs for it so, and then when it goes wrong, it's the bitterest taste on earth.'

'Did it go so wrong?'

'He upped and left me, you know. He was never happy about our having an affair, it affronted his conscience. He felt the purity of his soul was sullied.'

'Oh, Lord. Why ever didn't you marry?'

'We nearly did, we were unofficially engaged, only he kept on saying that marriage was a sacrament and for life, binding body and soul now and in the next world. All pretty hairy stuff. He just couldn't bring himself to take the plunge, not when he saw a wedding as a sacrament, not just an announcement in *The Times* and a morning coat and top hat and Mr and Mrs from then on and making the best of it, as people do. So, naturally, he was nervous about what would happen to his immortal soul if it all went wrong, as marriages often seem to. It's all for the best, I know; we'd have been miserable together, the three of us.'

'Three of you?' Edwin stopped in his tracks and looked down at his twin in surprise. 'Alix, what do you mean?'

'It would have been a threesome, that's all. Him, me, and his conscience. Not really room for us all in the marriage bed, you know.'

'And his conscience pricked him so much that he left you.'

'Yes, for a virginal creature of great perfection; no contest, you see.'

'Anyone we know?'

Her laugh held no mirth. 'The Blessed Virgin Mary, idiot. He's gone into the church, become a monk.'

'Good Lord,' said Edwin, completely taken aback. 'I don't think I ever knew anyone who wanted to become a monk. A Catholic monk? Good thing you kept him away from Grandmama, you know how she is about RCs. Well, let's hope poring over his conscience makes him really miserable. He wasn't good enough for you. I'm glad to see the back of your dowdy old clothes, too. Was that a reaction to his going off for higher things?'

'It was rather. I went a bit wild, generally. Don't let's talk about it, it still makes me feel dreadful. Talk about you. How's your love life?'

'Hellish, since you ask.' Edwin stooped and gathered two fistfuls of snow, which he shaped and pressed into a ball.

Alix made another snowball and then began to roll it. 'You do the body, and I'll make a head.'

Edwin heaped up a pile of snow and patted it into a semblance of human form. Alix fixed on the head and gave the snowman a bulbous nose.

They stood back and regarded the stout white figure.

'Not bad,' said Edwin. 'We'll have to find him a hat.'

Alix cleared a patch of snow and prised up two black stones for eyes. 'And a carrot from Cook.'

Edwin wound his muffler around the snowman's neck.

'You'll be cold without it.'

'No, I'll be glowing with exercise, while this poor chap has to stand in chilly stillness. I'll collect it on the way back, and we'll see if there's an old one lying about.'

'He does look lonely. Should we give him a mate?'

Edwin laughed. 'Why should he have all the luck? Besides, he mightn't take to her. Tomorrow we'll come and build him a twin, that'll be better company for him.'

What a pair we are, thought Alix, as they took a short-cut, clambering over a dry-stone wall, passing the sledge over and sending it sliding on ahead of them. 'Is your love life hellish because she's walked out of your life, or because she's a shrew, or because she's already married to someone else, such as your best friend?'

'You're my best friend, Lexy. No, she isn't married, nor a shrew, nor has she walked. She just doesn't feel about me the way I feel about her.'

The one who kisses and the one who turns the cheek, just

as it had been between her and John. 'Have I met her? Do I know her?'

He shook his head.

'No.'

'Would I like her?'

He made an impatient gesture. 'I dare say. How can I possibly tell? I'd like you to meet her. I've asked her up here, told her she can have the rooms above my studio for as long as she wants. Only she won't come.'

'Tell me about her. What's her name?'

'Lidia.'

'Is she pretty?'

'Beautiful, not pretty. She has the kind of timeless face you see in pictures, hers aren't at all modern looks. She smiled, after we'd met. It went straight to my heart and that was that. Pierced, and bleeding, just like in the songs.'

'Where did you meet her?'

'At the Photographic Institute.'

Alix felt a spurt of jealousy; lucky Edwin to find a woman who shared his love of photography. 'Is she a photographer?'

'No, she was scrubbing steps.'

'Edwin!'

'She's not a charlady, she's a refugee,' he said impatiently. 'A musician, as it happens. Only think what having her hands in a pail of water all day does for a harpsichordist.'

'A harpsichordist? That's unusual,' Alix said, not wanting to let Edwin see that there was anything amiss with her, although she already loathed this foreign intruder; who cared about her hands?

They had reached Pagan's Field, a sloping expanse of virgin snow that squeaked and scrunched underfoot. The sledge was long enough for both of them to sit on it, and time and again they toiled and slipped up the hill, dragging the sledge behind them, and then flew down the slope. The run ended with a stretch of flat ground, through which one of the rivers from

91

the fells meandered towards the lake. The rough grass there brought the sledge to a bumpy halt well before the frozen edges of the river, little more than a stream at present, that ran sparkling between undercut miniature cliffs of snow.

Sometimes one of them took the ride alone, lying flat, face only inches above the flying snow. Alix tumbled off after one such trip, and lay laughing in the snow, Lidia forgotten, feeling cold and wet and happier than she could remember being since . . . since goodness knew when; she couldn't remember when she last felt like this.

Edwin hauled her to her feet. 'If you lie there, you'll catch cold, and you know how much Grandmama hates anyone sneezing.'

Alix brushed the snow off. 'Why is she never ill?'

'She has migraines.'

'Hardly ever. Only when she's severely vexed, and since she makes sure everyone does precisely what she wants, she rarely is.'

Edwin paused in the act of creating a large snowball in his gloved hands. 'Do you know, that never occurred to me, about her migraines coming on when someone has crossed her? I must say that as soon as Lipp starts pursing her mouth and muttering about m'lady's twinges, I run for cover.'

'You can, of course, to Lowfell. And I suppose Grandpapa just shuts himself away in his study as he always has done. One thing you have to say for Grandmama, she doesn't look for sympathy when she's laid up with a headache.'

'They say migraines are devastatingly painful.'

'And admitting pain is a sign of weakness.'

Edwin gave her a direct look. 'You should know about that. You've inherited exactly the same stoicism, only with you it's anguish of the spirit you won't own up to.'

Startled, Alix ducked his snowball and began to gather one of her own. Was that true? She didn't care to think she might be like Grandmama in any way. Did she refuse to admit that she hurt? Yes, she supposed she did, preferring to lick her wounds in private and to draw down the shutters between herself and any well-wishers, however kindly their intentions.

She chucked the snowball at Edwin with unusual force, leaving him protesting and laughing and shaking the snow off his shoulders. 'You wretch, it's gone down my neck. Hold on there, and I'll give you a taste of your own medicine.'

'You have to catch me first,' said Alix, sliding and slipping down the hillside to escape his long arms.

Eyes and cheeks glowing from their exertions, they went in through the back of the house, leaving their boots in the flagstoned passage. 'I'll come up and collect your wet things, Miss Alix,' Phoebe called out as they padded past the kitchen in damp socks, leaving a trail of fat footprints.

Rokeby was hovering in the hall. 'There's a letter for you, Mr Edwin, sent up from Lowfell.'

'Thank you,' said Edwin, more concerned with his cold feet than a letter. He had no expectation of it being from Lidia, and nothing else could stir any great interest.

Perdita came thumping into the hall, her face pink with the cold air and indignation. 'Golly,' she said. 'Grandpapa was going on about the Grindleys, for Rokeby says Roger and Angela are there, and I said I wondered if they'd taken that terrifying stuffed ferret out of the downstairs lav, because Angela made a row about it last time she was at the Hall, and Grandmama heard me and really laid into me. I mean, what's so awful about mentioning a stuffed ferret?'

Alix wasn't paying much attention to Perdita; she was too busy watching Edwin's face as he read his letter.

'She treats me like a baby; I don't see why she should. Alix, you aren't listening to a word I'm saying.'

'You're the last of the brood,' said Alix. 'Children, grand-children, all living here, all under her thumb. It won't last into another generation, we shan't bring up our children here, so she's making the most of her crumbling power.'

'Edwin might live here. When Grandpapa dies, although I bet he'll go on for ever, and I hope he does.'

'Can you see Edwin living at Wyncrag without Grandpapa, if Grandmama were still alive? Not if he had a grain of sense. It isn't bad news, is it Edwin, you look stunned?'

'No, no, not bad news at all.' Edwin stuffed the letter back in its envelope and turned to the waiting Rokeby.

His eyes were alight with joy; what was there in the letter to make him look like that? Alix asked herself.

'I need to send a telegram. Urgently.'

'What's he so excited about?' Perdita asked Alix, as Edwin rushed towards the library. 'He's gone quite pale. Do you know who that letter was from? You look a bit pale yourself.'

'Do I? A trick of the light. Ask Edwin later, I don't think he wants to be bothered now.' It must show, she thought, the sharp face of jealousy, the knowledge that whoever wrote that letter – Lidia, sure to be – was close to Edwin in a way that she, his twin, never could be. And that, with this new relationship, there would be a distance between her and her brother. Quite hard to accept that, after nearly twenty-five years. She'd come to think it wouldn't ever happen, as girlfriends came and went out of Edwin's life, and none of them made any real difference.

Had she considered for a second how excluded Edwin might have felt over the last few years when she'd been so wrapped up in her own love affair? She didn't think he'd minded, he'd had his work, his own interests, and perhaps with their strange gift of knowing how each other felt, he'd known, even before she had, that John would leave her, that he wasn't going to become part of her life on any permanent basis.

It was that strange link between them that made her realize now that Lidia was not the same as his other girlfriends. He'd had flirtations and friendships, and even one more serious affair, but none of them had got under his skin the way this woman had. In which case, his falling in love with her would make a tremendous difference to Edwin and therefore to herself.

A refugee. What kind of a refugee? She thought of those blank faces staring out from blurred newspaper photographs of dishevelled ship- and train-loads. Faces blank because beyond despair. What had Lidia gone through, what might have happened to her family, friends? Was she grieving for a lost life in another country, was that why she wouldn't have Edwin, had she worn out any capacity for new feelings?

And why had Edwin fallen so much in love with her, and why did she reject him? It was a tease's trick to refuse to marry him and then to write letters that brought brilliance to his eyes and sent him rushing to despatch telegrams. Perhaps Lidia was coming north, after all. And wouldn't that just spoil Christmas and the frozen lake, for all of them. For her, because she'd been longing to have Edwin to herself. For the whole household, if Lidia turned out to be as unsuitable as she sounded. No one more fierce in her intolerance than Grandmama, no one less happy to accept an outsider as a husband or wife for any of her family.

Edwin flew back across the hall, his shoes ringing out on the tiles. 'Just off to the Post Office.'

'We'll come,' said Perdita quickly. 'Won't we, Alix? I want to see what the ice is like over on that side of the lake.'

'Be quick then,' said Edwin. 'There's not a moment to lose.'

Alix sat beside him in the front, and Perdita squeezed herself into the tiny space behind the seats. 'Jolly uncomfortable in the back here, you ought to get a bigger car.'

Edwin concentrated on getting his car safely over the ice lurking at the entrance to the drive, and out on to the narrow, twisting country road that led to the ferry. 'I was going to ask if you both wanted to come to Manchester tomorrow. I've got some business there, and you've got shopping to do. But if you're going to be rude about my car, Perdy, then the invitation's withdrawn.'

'I long to go to Manchester, and Ursula breaks up on Friday, so tomorrow would be perfect,' said Perdita. 'But can we take a proper car, please? I'd be bent double for good if I went all the way to Manchester like this, fit for nothing but the freak show.'

A carter coming the other way stopped his horse to tell Edwin that the ferry wasn't running.

'Frozen solid, no point in breaking the ice and heaving her out, not any more. You'll have to go around the head of the lake, Mr Edwin.'

Edwin thanked him, cursed, and backed carefully into a gateway thickly rutted with frozen mud.

Half an hour later, they drove over the humpbacked bridge and drew up outside the Post Office. Her brother and sister dragged Perdita from her wedged position, and she stood beside the car shaking herself like a horse.

Edwin vanished into the Post Office. Alix and Perdita walked down to the lakeside. A few intrepid skaters were on the ice, not venturing beyond the rope barriers with their signs saying DANGER THIN ICE. A troop of children were sliding ecstatically over the frozen surface, under the watchful eye of PC Ogilvy. Perdita waved to him, and he slithered in a stately fashion towards them.

'Hello, Jimmy. How's the ice bearing?'

'Coming along nicely, Miss Perdita.'

'Can we skate all across the lake?'

'Wherever you like, so long as you watch out for the soft patches where the Wyn flows out, it doesn't ever freeze right over there. I'll be taking those signs down come tomorrow morning. And I reckon now it's holding, it'll be solid for a good while, no one's forecasting a thaw for the foreseeable future.'

Edwin came out of the Post Office. 'That's done,' he said with great satisfaction. He caught sight of Alix's face. 'Feeling the cold, old thing? You've gone soft spending all that time in London.'

THIRTEEN

Hal didn't recognise the chauffeur.

He hadn't expected the motor car to be the same one, but who was the man standing beside the gleaming Delage? What had become of Wilbur? He was a young man still, Hal's contemporary, a partner in first boyish and then youthful forays up fells and into the old lead mines and out on the lake. And the uniform, no Grindley chauffeur had ever worn a uniform like this one except on the most formal occasions. Was Hal's arrival at the railway station a formal occasion? He thought not. Yet here was this dark-jowled man with guileless brown eyes touching his hat and asking him in an accent that owed nothing to the north of England if he were Mr Henry Grindley.

And that gave him a jolt. No one had called him Henry for more than fifteen years, and not often before that; only headmasters and strangers. He had been Hal to everyone since he was a baby.

The chauffeur helped the porter load Hal's luggage into the boot of the car. Then he opened the rear door for Hal, saluted, and took his place behind the steering wheel.

It felt odd, to be in these familiar surroundings but sitting in the back of a car behind straight grey-uniformed shoulders, instead of sitting beside Jerry Wilbur, or even pushing him over to take the wheel himself.

He leant forward. 'What's your name?'

'Parsons, sir.'

It seemed unlikely, but Hal let it pass. 'Where's Wilbur?'

'I don't know, sir.'

'You do know who Wilbur is.'

Or was, had something happened to him and no one had bothered to say? Nanny would have written to him about it, she wrote him regular if indecipherable missives in a spidery hand. Recent letters, now he came to think of it, had mentioned Changes at the Hall. These Changes, he gathered, were not for the better, at least not according to Nanny. Since she was pure conservative from the starch on her cap to the tips of her sensible shoes, he hadn't taken much notice of her grumbles. Peter's new wife would be bound to make changes, new wives always did. He had had plenty of experience of new wives in America, where his friends of both sexes dipped in and out of marriages with astonishing ease.

'I heard of Wilbur, yes. He drove cars before me.'

So Wilbur had left. Hal felt a moment of dismay; how many others of his friends would still be there? It hadn't occurred to him, but fifteen odd years was a long time to expect everything to be the same. He had changed out of all recognition, so he couldn't seriously think that at Grindley Hall everything would be just as it was. How childish, and how childish was his disappointment at not being greeted by Wilbur.

'Where are you from?' he asked the chauffeur.

'Spain. I am from Spain.'

Best not to enquire further. The fellow might be a republican or a follower of General Franco, and Hal had no wish to pry or offend. Strange that he hadn't opted to stay and fight for whichever side he favoured.

'I have no sides in Spain,' the man said, as though he had

98

read Hal's thoughts. 'I have family, uncles, brothers fighting on both sides, this one hates priests, that one is all for Franco. So I leave. Is better, then at least my mother has one son left alive to bury her when she grows old and dies, one son who is not crazy in his head and fighting for crazy men.'

'So now you work at Grindley Hall.'

The man gave an expressive shrug. 'One is lucky to have any work.' He was silent for a moment and then burst out in an unexpected and infectious guffaw. 'I feel at home. In Spain, my family fight each other. Here, in cold England, I find also that families fight each other.'

Hal didn't want to know. He sat back in his seat, looking out into the dusk, and the Spaniard, probably regretting his outburst, stayed silent as he drove expertly along the wintry roads. It was a half-hour journey from the station, but it only seemed minutes before they were driving through the sweep gate to the Hall, the stone Grindley griffins perched on either side atop the gateposts. Hal had once suggested that a pair of lavatory seats would be a better emblem for the family; they hadn't found this amusing. Grindleys as a whole resented any humour directed at the source of their wealth.

The drive was neater than he remembered, the gravel swept clear of snow and crunching loudly under the wide tyres. Hal looked up at the familiar façade of the house where he had been born, not sure if he felt pleasure or misery at seeing it again. The huge front door swung open as the car drew up, and a maid in formal black dress and starched pinny and cap came out to stand at the top of the steps.

Hal didn't recognise her either, nor the smart uniform. Hall maids in his day were a comfortable lot, duly clad in morning or afternoon uniform, but never looking as pressed and trim as this young lady. She looked straight through Hal and told the driver to take the car around to the back and unload the gentleman's luggage straight away.

'Mrs Grindley is upstairs resting before dinner,' she told

Hal as she followed him into the black-and-white chequered hall. 'Mr Grindley will be home at half past six. Tea has been served in the drawing room, Mr and Mrs Roger Grindley are there, they have just arrived. It is this way.'

'Thank you, I know where it is,' Hal said. He crossed the hall and opened the fine white panelled door into the drawing room. He stopped inside the doorway, looking around in surprise. There had been something different about the hall, although he hadn't been able to put his finger on it. Now it came to him, where were all the stuffed animals?

The drawing room ran from the front to the back of one side of the house, a long, wide room with windows leading on to a terrace. Gone were the heavy damasks, the patterned carpet, the heavy armchairs and sofas; gone most noticeably were the stuffed bear with a tray in its paws, several noble stags' heads, the pair of stoats glaring at each other from two branches, a bewildered owl, and the fox with his head turned as though politely surprised to find the hounds upon him.

The parquet floor gleamed at his feet. Fine Persian rugs were placed here and there. Two deep sofas with plain dark pink covers faced each other across the fireplace, other chairs were in lighter shades of raspberry and looked thoroughly uncomfortable.

'Good God,' he said before he could stop himself. 'Interior design comes to Grindley Hall? I don't believe it.'

His remark was greeted by a peal of laughter and he looked over to the sofa, where a tall, fair woman, still laughing, was standing up and holding out her hands. 'Hal, my dear! How distinguished you look, I don't think I would have recognised you.'

'Angela,' he said, kissing her warmly on both cheeks. He was shocked to see the lines around her eyes. How old was she? Late forties, must be, but it wasn't merely years that had added a strained look to eyes and mouth. If he were any judge, that was tension, not age. Well, being married to Roger would hardly be a bed of roses.

'Good to see you, Hal,' said his brother.

Roger hadn't changed, Hal thought as they shook hands. He was heavier, but had the height to carry it off, so didn't yet look portly. The main difference was in his air of success and prosperity; that was what advancement in the law had done for him. He dimly remembered a line in one of Nanny's letters.

'Aren't you a KC now, Roger?'

Roger nodded, a satisfied look on his wide, handsome face. 'I took silk more than five years ago. I thought Peter would have told you.'

'I travel about so much,' said Hal apologetically. He should have written, of course he should, only he never did write to his brothers. And of course becoming a KC was a great step for a lawyer, but it had seemed of no great importance in his theatrical world far across the Atlantic.

A much younger woman than Angela, but with the same fair complexion, had been standing by the window.

'You can't be Cecy!'

'I am. Hello, Uncle Hal.'

'Good heavens, Cecy. You were all legs and pigtails last time I saw you.'

There was a silence. Angela broke it with a polite enquiry about his voyage – what a time of year to brave the Bay of Biscay – had it been very rough – had he been staying in London, Peter had said his ship was due two days ago – had anyone shown him to his room?

'I didn't give the maid a chance to,' Hal said. 'What happened to Wilbur, Roger?'

'Wilbur? Oh, the chauffeur. He went into the army, I believe. Eve found this present man, he's some sort of foreigner, I shouldn't care to have him in my employ, he looks rather a ruffian. However, Eve says he's cheap and drives very well.

101

Peter leaves all the staff side to her. You'll find quite a few changes. Bound to, after so long.'

Silence again. It occurred to Hal that the stiffness of the atmosphere was not caused by his arrival. The tea tray stood untouched on a low table beside the fireplace. Whatever Roger's family had been doing, it wasn't taking a welcome cup of tea after a long drive. He could see that Cecy was eager to leave the room, she was sliding unobtrusively round behind the sofas towards the door.

'Where are you going, Cecy?' her father asked in a cold voice.

'Upstairs. To dress. My frock needs pressing, I'll have to ask the maid to do it for me. She won't know which one I'm wearing tonight.' With that she made a positive dash for the door and was gone.

'Children,' Roger said grumpily. 'You never married, I suppose, Hal.'

'No,' Hal said.

'They're the very devil. One minute all dimples and not much of a nuisance to anyone, and the next causing no end of trouble. I'll see you at dinner, then,' he added, making for the door.

'What's Cecy up to?' Hal asked Angela, who had sat down again. She picked up a glossy magazine and began to flick through the pages. 'Has my niece taken up with some undesirable man?'

'That would be simple,' Angela said. 'Unsuitable boyfriends are child's play compared to a career as far as Roger is concerned.'

'Career?'

'Don't ask. Medicine, I'm afraid.'

'Cecy's doing medical training? Training to be a doctor, not a nurse? Sorry, no need to ask, not with her being your daughter. Good for her.'

'I agree with you, but Roger never liked the idea, and he

knows that Peter will have a go at him about it, he thinks it's rather lax.'

'This is Peter as head of the family, I take it?'

'It's a role he plays more and more.' She put the magazine back on the table and stood up. 'I really do have to go and dress.'

'Tell me one thing,' said Hal. 'What happened to the menagerie?'

'The menagerie?'

'The stuffed creatures.'

'Oh, the stoats and those poor, sad-eyed deer. Eve doesn't care to have dead animals around her. So down they came and out they went. I couldn't approve more. There was a wicked-looking ferret that had come to roost in the downstairs cloakroom. When I told Peter it was playing havoc with his bowels, he wouldn't speak to me for a week. I was quite right, however. He used to disappear in there for hours with a pipe and the paper. No longer, and he's lost that costive look he had.'

Hal held the door open for her. As they crossed the hall, the front door flew open and a red-faced schoolgirl in a thick navy overcoat stumped in, a satchel hanging off her shoulder, a hockey stick in one hand and a bicycle pump in the other. She was yelling as she came in, shouting out to Simon to jolly well come down right now and apologize for swiping her pump, the one that worked, and replacing it with his duff one, a foul trick to play on her, she finished with a triumphant roar.

She stopped, drew breath, saw them standing there and bounded towards them. 'Aunt Angela, you're here. Has Cecy come with you? I'm so late, all because I had a flat tyre and rotten Simon switched the pumps.' She stared at Hal with undisguised interest.

'This is your Uncle Hal, Ursula.'

Hal looked at the girl with more attention. So this was

Peter's youngest. Of course she was, he thought with a sudden pang. Of course she was: now that the redness of her face was fading, he could see the likeness. 'You're very like Delia,' he said.

A blast of icy air at his back as the front door opened and shut again, and he turned to see his oldest brother regarding him with cold eyes as he pulled off his leather gloves.

'That's a name we don't ever mention in this house,' Peter said curtly. 'Ursula, what are you doing hanging around in your school clothes? Go upstairs and change at once.' He turned to Angela. 'Ha. Roger's here, I take it?'

'Aren't you going to say hello to Hal? You haven't seen him for nearly sixteen years.'

From Peter's expression, he could quite happily have gone another sixteen years without seeing his youngest brother.

'You're looking very well,' he said, smoothing back his fast-retreating hair with his hand as he eyed Hal's hair, short but undeniably thick.

'So are you, Peter. I'm glad to see you again.' Which Hal was, despite his brother's aura of barely controlled ferocity.

'I've made it an absolute rule,' Peter was saying in a loud voice, 'that we do not under any circumstances talk about Delia, especially not in front of the children. As far as they are concerned, she might as well be dead. She is forbidden to have any contact with them, with the full consent of the court, I may add. They know how wicked she has been and have no wish at all to have anything to do with her. It shouldn't be necessary for me to explain this to you, anyone with a modicum of tact . . . Well, I dare say it's all very different in America.'

'There's a lot more divorce over there, certainly.'

Peter winced at the word. 'That will lead to their downfall. It's monstrous what women get away with these days, it goes against nature and against every finer feeling. These so-called modern women are no more nor less than whores.

104

Excuse me, Angela, it's not a word I should use in front of you.'

'It's not a word you should use of your ex-wife,' Angela said under her breath as she stepped past Peter and made for the stairs.

Hal wasn't too sure about Peter's finer feelings, and he was deeply shocked to hear his former sister-in-law spoken of in such harsh terms. He held his tongue. He was here because of the frozen lake, nothing more, and he would avoid quarrelling with either of his brothers if he could help it.

He thought about his two brothers as he followed the maid up the elegant staircase. Why had Angela, with her intelligence and caustic wit, ever married Roger? He had been good-looking, that had had something to do with it, and perhaps the growing career at the bar had seemed to promise brains and a certain worldliness. More astonishing was that ultra-conventional Roger should have fallen in love with a woman doctor, of all people. Roger as a young man, and no doubt to this day, resented women having the vote. He had never made any secret of his views.

Perhaps Angela had thought it would be possible to continue practising as a doctor once she was married, and perhaps it had gone against the grain to give up her medical work, even though she had all the help she needed in the house and nursery. She must have known that after those years away, it would be next to impossible to pick up the threads of a medical career. Let alone deal with Roger's hostility.

Hal knew all about how Roger got his way, not through forcefulness like Peter, but through persistent nastiness. Faced with her husband's bad temper and rudeness about her place in society, home, and likely incompetence if she went back into her profession, Angela had no doubt chosen the quieter course.

Only Cecy had then broken out; that was certainly one in the eye for Roger and he would naturally look upon it as a betrayal.

'One of the maids will look after you, sir, since you haven't brought a man with you,' said the maid as she showed him into the Red Room. 'Dinner is at eight-thirty, drinks are served in the drawing room from eight o'clock.'

He had half hoped they would put him in his old room, up on the attic floor with windows looking out behind the parapet, but the maid led the way to the Red Room, on the first floor. It had always been a guest room, but, when he was last here, a guest room with the patina of age and wear upon it. Now the paintwork gleamed, and the room had a spick and span, chintzy appearance. Rose-patterned wallpaper matched coverlet and chairs and cushions and the rug beside the bed. He pulled a face, remembering the higgledy-piggledy arrangement of old furniture and faded red damask curtains, and the assortment of china animals above the fireplace.

He picked up one of the thick towels on the washstand, one cream, one green, and went out to find an empty bathroom.

'I was wondering when you'd find time to pop up and see me,' said Nanny.

Hal, who liked to soak in a tub, had rushed his bath and dressed in a great hurry before springing up the stairs two at a time to reach Nanny's domain. 'You wouldn't want me to come up here covered in smuts from the train,' he said, bending down to give her a hug. She wasn't a small woman, but he felt now as though he towered over her, surely she hadn't been as bent as that when he went away?

'Fifteen years and more, it's been, and that's a long time at my age, and my bones aren't as strong as they should be,' she told him. 'I tell the doctor my bones can do what they want as long as I keep my wits, and so far I have. And you'll have been leaning out of the train window to have smuts on you, how often have I told you not to do that? There was a man lost his head going into a tunnel, who's to say it won't happen again? Now sit down, there's ten minutes before you have to be downstairs, and it won't do to be late, for Mrs Grindley, as we must call her, although it sticks in my throat, gets in a temper if people are late. She gets into a temper about almost everything, you'll notice that for yourself soon enough. Don't be taken in, she's got a will of iron, all the prettiness is like the army lads who go about with twigs in their helmets.'

'Camouflage.'

'I know what it's called, Master Smart,' she said swiftly.

He had to smile at the old nursery nickname. Peter had been Master Temper and Roger, Master Nastytongue whenever Nanny was displeased with them.

'Which of them have you seen?' Her knuckles might look too big for her hands and her hair might be grey and wispy, but her voice was low and sure – and those pale blue eyes were as keen as ever.

'Angela, and two rather delightful nieces.'

'Cecy and Ursula. She's a little minx, that one.'

'Ursula? She does resemble her mother, doesn't she?'

'More's the pity. It doesn't make her life any easier, let me tell you. What about your brothers?'

'Oh, I've seen both of them, and left Peter in a rage because I mentioned Delia's name, and Roger fretting over having a clever daughter.'

'Fancy Cecy going to be a doctor.'

'She, too, takes after her mother.'

'I don't hold with lady doctors. Never have and never will. Still, there are those who prefer it, and who's to say they're not entitled to their choice the same as I am?'

'Well, Nanny, if there's a war they'll need all the doctors they can get.'

'There isn't going to be another war. And don't go suggesting there will be one, or Mr Peter will be in even more of a rage. He won't have any warmongering talk at the Hall, those are his very words.'

It was typical of Peter to issue an edict like that. Would he be taking the same line at work? Hal doubted it. War brought fat contracts, and Peter wouldn't be last in line for those.

'Mr Peter says he trusts the Germans to keep the Bolshies under control,' said Nanny, clear approval in her voice; she detested Those Reds, as she called them.

'Daddy's got it all wrong,' said a clear young voice from the door. 'Hello, Nanny. Can you do my frock up for me?'

Ursula came into the room, one hand behind her holding a rather shapeless green dress together. 'Hello again, Uncle Hal. I thought you'd be here, reporting to Nanny. She'll want to know every single thing you've done since you last saw her.'

'That could take some time, I suppose,' Hal said.

'You mind your tongue, Ursula.' Nanny fastened the last of the buttons and Ursula straightened herself.

'Five minutes to tell me the news,' Nanny said. And then, to Hal, 'I don't get about so much these days. Ursula acts as my eyes and ears.'

'Well, Nanny, the ice is bearing,' said Ursula, sitting down on a pouffe that gave out a whistling sound as she sank into it. 'That's the most important thing. There'll be skating all across the lake before the weekend's out, that's what they say.'

Hal propped himself against a tallboy, too big for the room, an item of furniture that he guessed Nanny had appropriated from some other part of the house. Ursula had Delia's colouring as well as her mother's features and voice: hair the colour of a copper scuttle, intense blue eyes in a pale face. She even had Delia's hands, he noticed, as she tucked a lock of her straight hair behind an ear.

He couldn't keep up with her flow of news. The people

she was talking about were strangers for the most part. Until she told Nanny the news from Wyncrag. 'Perdy's back, she got back from school last night. Late for dinner, and Lady Richardson ripping her up, saying she shouldn't be out in a car with Edwin. Her brother, I ask you, why not?'

'Lady Richardson has her reasons,' Nanny said. 'Has Alix arrived yet?'

'Oh, yes, she came by train, the same train you must have come on today, Uncle Hal. If she'd waited a day, you could have travelled up together. Although you might not have recognised her after all this time. She's looking fearfully smart, apparently, Nanny. Lady R's as stiff as a poker with her, and Perdy's already in trouble.'

'What has Perdy done?' Nanny asked.

'Grown.'

'Do enlighten me,' he said. 'Who is Perdy?'

'Perdita Richardson,' Nanny said. 'Since your time. You should remember, I told you all about her in my letters. Helena's youngest, born just before Helena and Isabel were killed in America. In a car smash, such a terrible tragedy. You do remember that, surely? It wasn't long after you'd gone away.'

'Yes.' He had written to Lady Richardson, and had received a brief, terse letter thanking him for his condolences. 'She must have been shattered, losing her son so soon before, and then her daughter-in-law.'

Nanny's face took on a tight, thin-lipped look, one he remembered so well from his childhood, the face that said, 'So far and no further; not another word do I have to say upon this subject.'

FOURTEEN

'Another foul evening,' Ursula wrote in her journal that night. 'No one except Aunt Angela is pleased to see Uncle Hal, it must be horrid for him to come home and find he's about as welcome as a stray dog. I knew Eve was going to be at her sniffiest with him, she was moaning on to Daddy about what a nuisance it was Hal deciding to pay a visit just now, with Rosalind on the verge of her coming out and not needing to be associated with any doubtful characters. Any more doubtful characters, she means, since she feels that Mummy casts a cloud of unrespectability over the household and that it's hard on Rosalind to be in any way connected with such a person. I don't think Uncle Hal has any idea why Daddy wanted him to come to the Hall. I think he's only come because of the frozen lake, otherwise he'd have stayed away. He'll wish he had once Daddy and Roger start on him about those shares. They don't think I know anything about it, in which case they shouldn't talk so jolly loud. And Eve's awfully cross that they need Hal's agreement to make the sale, she's so snobby about him being an actor. How old-fashioned can you be? Some actors are awfully grand. I don't suppose Uncle Hal is or we'd have heard about him, but he doesn't look like a down-and-out to me, which is how Eve seems to regard him. He looks jolly successful in my opinion, like someone who doesn't give a button what people like Eve say about him. And he's got a mocking look in his eye, I think he finds the whole situation amusing. I wish I did.'

FIFTEEN

Hal walked to Wyncrag after lunch, accompanied part of the way by Angela and Cecy who were going into the village, where Cecy wanted to buy a new pair of skates. It was slow walking on the icy snow, but Hal's spirits rose as he breathed the cold pure air and looked up at the brilliant peaks set against a winter blue sky. Every stone wall, each field and tree was familiar to him; the years rolled away and he was back in the days of his youth, eager and brimful of expectation and ambition.

He had been set on becoming a great actor, one of the thespians of his generation, he would stun audiences with his interpretations of classic roles, his Hamlet and Macbeth and Benedict would be the talk of London and he would introduce intelligent and appreciative audiences to the complexities of modern works.

It hadn't turned out like that. How many of the dreams we have at twenty do come true? he asked himself, as he followed the well-known path that led to the Wyncrag drive. He wasn't walking on virgin snow so the two houses obviously kept up their steady relationship, many other feet had trodden this path since the last snowfall. He was looking down at the gritty frozen whiteness out of a reluctance to look up and see in reality what he could see in his mind's eye: the extraordinary façade of Wyncrag. When he did look up, he surprised himself. It was as he remembered it, but it looked less real than the images he carried in his head. More like a film set than a massive northern pile. A film set for what? A fairy tale, maybe, with all those snowy turrets. Or possibly *Hamlet*, with a blond prince prowling the battlements of Elsinore, an enclosed world of darkness and secrets.

'Come inside, come inside,' Sir Henry said, greeting him as though he'd been away for a fortnight rather than fifteen years. 'We'll get them to rustle up some coffee for us. I was just wondering whether to put some more grit down on the drive,' he went on, as they walked together towards the house. 'You've missed my young folk, the twins and Perdita have gone to Manchester. The wheels of the car were slipping when they drove off, that's why I came out to have a look. Of course, I think of them as your contemporaries and they aren't, they were no more than children last time you saw them, and you'll never have seen young Perdy at all.'

'I was extremely sorry to hear about your tragedy,' Hal said.

'You wrote a very kind letter, that was good of you.'

'I liked Neville and Helena, and to lose both of them in one year . . . Isabel, too. It was hard.'

Hard? Was that little thump of a word all he could find to say about such a loss? Sir Henry's great loss had been Neville, his son, not Helena of course. Helena had never made her father-in-law's heart sing at the sight of her, had never turned a grey day into a glorious one, had never sent him on his way on winged feet merely by a look, a smile, a turn of the head.

'It was, it was hard,' Sir Henry was saying. 'But it's in the past now, it all happened a good while ago and I don't think about them much. I wish Neville could have been spared, but

113

it wasn't to be, and no good comes of repining, he was careless, and you can't be careless on a precipice.'

Hal had to search for words to talk about Sir Henry's eldest son. Why was it so difficult? He'd liked Neville, dammit. Admired him. 'He was a skilful mountaineer. It's a dangerous activity, but I should have thought he was the last person to take a risk.'

'Mountains are unforgiving, and I dare say if he had to go, he was happy to die among his beloved mountains. He was lucky to survive the war, but his luck ran out when he went off to the Andes. He'd always wanted to climb there. Well, we all have to live our own lives.' He was silent as he led Hal around to a side door. 'We'll go to my study, you'll want to see Caroline and Trudie, but they can wait until you've warmed yourself and told me what you've been up to. Friendly welcome at the Hall, huh?' he said with a shrewd look. 'Lot of changes there, you'll find. Your brother's a fool to have married that woman, but I dare say you've already worked that out for yourself.'

Hal laughed, glad that they weren't going into the drawing room. He wanted time to adjust to being in a Wyncrag without Helena. He cursed himself for a fool, he must concentrate on the here and now, not let memories from all those years ago sneak back into his life. Lord, he'd been so young. That was what accounted for the intensity of feeling that had struck him as he once again came to Wyncrag. A pale reflection of the feelings he had revelled in at the age of twenty, lost in the throes of first love, the not untypical love of a very young man for an older and very attractive woman.

He walked around the panelled walls looking at the familiar architectural prints hanging there. 'I've hardly exchanged more than a few civil nothings with Eve, but no doubt she means well.'

Sir Henry gave him a sceptical look, but said no more as Rokeby came in with the coffee, and greeted Hal with stately

114

courtesy. Hal was delighted to see him again, and impressed by how the years had turned him into the very model of a perfect butler.

'Sit down, take one of the chairs by the fire,' Sir Henry said, gesturing to one of a pair of shabby leather armchairs set in front of the burning fire. 'Stir that fire up a bit, Rokeby,' he went on. 'Put another log on, must keep Hal warm, he'll not be used to our northern chill any more.'

'I'm not such a poor creature as you think,' Hal protested. 'New York can be bitter in the winter, and I go to Vermont for the snow sports most years. It's cold enough there to remind anyone of Westmoreland in December.'

'There's nowhere quite like the lake, though, is there? You feel that, or you wouldn't be here. Don't tell me Peter's invitation was so warm as to make you come back otherwise. He wants you here over a matter of business, I know, but that wouldn't have brought you on its own, would it now?'

'No,' Hal agreed, very glad of the hot coffee into which, without being asked, Rokeby had added a tot of whisky. 'To keep out the cold, Mr Hal.'

'This freeze is bringing them all back,' Sir Henry went on. 'Alix hasn't been home for three years, well, she and her grandmother don't always see eye to eye, but she couldn't resist the frozen lake. She lives and works in London, you know.'

Hal pulled out his memories of the twins, here at Wyncrag. Alix had been a solemn girl with a sudden smile and eyes too old for her years; Caroline had been very harsh with her, he recalled, strict as though she had been a wilful or wayward child. She hadn't looked anything like Helena in those days; had she grown up to resemble her mother? He found the thought somehow alarming. 'Does she take after Helena?' he found himself asking.

'No, she favours my side of the family, she's very like my sister was at that age. Edwin is the one who takes after his mother.'

'Alix was always so attached to Edwin,' Hal said. 'They were inseparable, I remember that.'

'As twins often are, but they grow up and go their different ways. Edwin's gone in for photography, did you hear that?'

'I did, and also that he's making quite a name for himself. Do you mind that he isn't following in your footsteps, going into engineering?'

'He never had a mathematical mind, he would have been wretched if I'd tried to force him into it. Perdita's the one who can do mathematics, but then her head's full of horses and music, and of course girls can't be engineers.'

'Some are, in America.'

'People do anything in America. No, when I'm gone, the works will have to be sold. I've a few more years yet before I give it all up, and if there's another war, even us old 'uns will be kept in harness.'

'I was thinking about Jack when I came past the war memorial. You lost a son, let's hope you don't have to sacrifice a grandson as well.'

'Ah, Jack,' said Sir Henry, wiping traces of coffee from the tip of his bushy moustache with a large silk handkerchief. 'As I said, when you get to my age, you have a different perspective on such things. Jack might not have settled down so well after the war. He had the ability to make a fine engineer, the brains and the mathematical mind, he always was a clever boy, but his outlook . . .' He broke off with a sigh.

Hal was taken aback. He'd always taken it for granted that the Richardsons had no idea what Jack was like. He'd treated Jack with great care ever since he'd discovered for himself what kind of man he was. Would he have prospered after the war if he'd survived? Not in any civilised community he wouldn't. There had been that girl from Askrigg, that had been an ugly affair, and Neville had told him, after Jack's death, that his youngest brother had treated Jane very badly, emotionally and physically, and that she wasn't the only woman who had cause to regret the day she'd met Jack Richardson.

And it had seemed to him at the time that Sir Henry and Caroline had not grieved so very greatly for their youngest son. The war had exhausted Sir Henry, he had worn out his emotions. But Caroline, Aunt Caroline as he had always called her? He would have said she loved Jack beyond anyone and anything, yet her icy self-command betrayed no desperate sense of bereavement. She had simply become more closed and reserved, more demanding of instant compliance and obedience from her children and grandchildren.

Hal realized that Sir Henry was speaking again, and he caught his final words, 'However, it's the season of peace and goodwill, and you'd be well-advised not to mention the possibility of war while you're at the Hall. Caroline won't hear of it, either, so I keep my own counsel.'

Ostriches, thought Hal. Nothing changes. This was why he'd sailed away; nervous, wet behind the ears, expectant, to the New World, to a country not riven by war and class.

'You'll like Alix,' Sir Henry said unexpectedly. 'She's not had an easy time of it, but she's a modern if any one of us is. Good at her job, too,' he added with pride. 'Earns five pounds a week.'

'Does she need to?' asked Hal, surprised. Surely no Richardson, particularly no Richardson woman, needed to earn a living.

'She chooses to, even though she has money of her own. From my sister, she left a considerable fortune and divided it between Neville's children, Neville was her favourite. And Saul has no children.'

Which must be sad for Jane Richardson, who clearly was a woman who would have liked to have children. How old would she be now? About his age. He would like to see her again.

'Saul and Jane are driving up today, they should be here

117

in time for dinner. Everybody's here, Hal, everyone who's still alive. I'm glad of the frost and this freeze, who knows where we'll all be in a year or so?'

'Do you expect war so soon?'

'I do. We'll have until the end of the decade if we're lucky and a couple of years if we're not.'

'Time to negotiate peace?'

'Time to re-arm,' said Sir Henry, ever the realist.

SIXTEEN

Jane refused to go down to breakfast. Saul fretted. 'You know Mother doesn't approve of us having breakfast in bed.'

'If you don't like to tell Chard to bring me up a tray, then I'll go without.'

Saul was horrified. 'That would make her even angrier.'

Jane pulled her bed jacket around her shoulders and smoothed the covers over her knees. 'It's up to you, disapproval or anger. It's a matter of complete indifference to me. I don't eat much breakfast anyway, and, whatever you say, I'm not going down to that mausoleum of a dining room to face a sideboard laden with silver dishes of indigestible food.'

'If you were going out on the ice, you'd want a proper breakfast.'

'I'm not, so I shan't.'

Ice and snow held no appeal for Jane. There was enough ice inside her for her not to care for it out there on the lake. Besides, brought up in the West Country, she wasn't used to the yearly freeze and skating from childhood that had been part of Saul's life. She had never travelled to Switzerland for the winter sports, never skied nor skated, and distinctly remembered taking a nasty tumble from a sledge when she was a little girl and snow had, for once, lain thick in the deep lanes and over the soft, rolling downs of her native county.

Her best months had always been those of summer: tennis on springy green grass, riding along the bridleways above the cliffs, walking the country lanes to exercise the dogs. Not for her this bleak, winter wasteland, white and sterile, as sterile as she was.

There was a tap on the door and Chard, her maid, came into the room, carrying a tray which she placed on Jane's lap. She whisked away the clothes her mistress had taken off the night before, asked if there was anything else, and vanished.

Jane lay back against the pillows, smiling to herself. Her mother-in-law hated her bringing a maid with her to Wyncrag; Caroline felt that members of the family should make do with the household staff. Jane didn't care to be looked after by a strange girl.

'She won't be strange,' Saul argued, every time. 'Phoebe will look after you, and she isn't a strange girl, you've known her for years.'

'Everyone and everything at Wyncrag is strange.'

Jane drank some coffee. That, at least, was good at Wyncrag. It was one of her father-in-law's few domestic rules: the coffee must be strong and well made. He had the beans sent up from London, and made sure they were properly ground in the special machine he had brought back from a trip to Italy.

She ate a slice of toast, and then slid the tray to one side and got out of bed. The room was unnaturally bright; that meant another icy, cloudless day, with reflections from the snow and ice slanting into every room in the house. She picked up her cigarette case from the dressing table and took out a cigarette. She put it in her holder, lit it, and inhaled deeply, tilting her head back and blowing the smoke out through her nostrils.

She was tired, languid; those sleeping pills Dr Barber had given her were too strong. She'd only take half a tablet tonight. Roll on the Brave New World, she could do with a dose of Huxley's happiness drug. What did he call it? Soma, that was it. Pills to make you sleep at night, pills to take away the sting of the day. She half-closed her eyes, unwilling to look into another day of empty existence. She knew exactly how the minutes would tick away.

Saul would go to his mother after breakfast, the invariable ritual of his visits to Wyncrag. Caroline would interrogate him, wanting to know about his career, his colleagues, the government's plans and attitude on this and that subject. Saul, like an eager schoolboy reciting a well-learned lesson, anxious to please an exacting master, would spill it all out, longing for his mother's approval.

'Never marry a younger son,' had been one of her own mother's maxims. 'If you fancy a younger son, ask to meet his older brother.'

'What if the eldest son is married, Mummy?'

'Look elsewhere. One man is much like another when it comes to marriage. As long as he's kind and has money, you'll be happy. A woman's happiness is bound up in her home and family and social life, her husband is not nearly as important to her as you young girls seem to think.'

Her mother would have done better to warn her against middle sons, a son like Saul with an admired older brother, a dashing, attractive younger brother, and a lifelong sense of inferiority as a result.

It was ironic that Saul was now the only brother left. He had taken the place of both the oldest and the youngest, was the one on whom his mother's hopes rested, the son his father greeted as an only son. They went through the motions, but they knew, as he did, that he could never be more than the shadow of his lost brothers.

Saul, to give him his due, had sincerely mourned his older

brother when he died in the mountains of South America; he had loved and looked up to Neville since babyhood. Jane didn't know how he had reacted to Jack's death in 1917. So many deaths, at that most awful of times, and Saul had been facing his own as he went back yet again to the horrors of France. Just luck, she supposed, that he had survived and Jack hadn't.

It was strange how now, all these years later, she couldn't recreate in herself the terrible pain and sense of loss that had overwhelmed her when she heard that Jack was dead. Her life might have been so different if Jack had been the one to come back from the trenches. They could have married, had children, been happy.

Jane stubbed out her cigarette, grinding it into a porcelain dish on the dressing table. Caroline's servants put no ashtrays in the bedrooms; her mother-in-law disapproved of people smoking upstairs in her house. Her hand shook.

Marry her? Jack? No. He wouldn't have wanted to marry her. If she'd told him about the child she was carrying, his child, he would have struck her, denied paternity, told her to go to a woman who knew her way about and ask how to get rid of it. He might even have tried to kick it out of life himself.

She had been sixteen when he had seduced her at her parents' house. In the rose garden, the first time. With that swift and brutal act, he had jolted her out of a girl's romance into the harsh reality of a liaison with a violent man. He enjoyed the experience, aroused by the mixture of excitement, fear and submission, and repeated it wherever and whenever he could get hold of her. She lied to her parents, to her sisters, to her friends, to everyone, to snatch an hour at his rooms. Every time, she swore it would be the last, and every time he drew her back, his violence melting into husky, lecherous words that she couldn't resist.

Years later, she had read what Byron's wife had written

about the noble poet, how he had deliberately corrupted a young and inexperienced woman. His lordship had delighted in her degradation and humiliation, making her accept as normal things that no woman should have to endure against her nature.

Jane never had cared for Byron's poetry.

Yet, when Jack had died, she had lost herself in grief. For what had she grieved? she asked herself now, still amazed at the strength of those vicious chains with which Jack had bound her.

She had miscarried, and had then, a year later, married Saul. It was Caroline's doing, naturally. Caroline had known about her and Jack, or guessed, and Jane suspected to this day that the marriage had been her mother-in-law's way of buying her silence and of keeping it all in the family.

It was the only hold she had over Caroline, and it was the reason why she asserted herself in various pointless ways, such as in the matter of the breakfast tray and her maid. Even now, her liaison with Jack would be considered shocking if it should ever become known. Only think how such a revelation would damage Saul's career; how could he live down a scandal that involved both his brother and his wife? How damaging for the Richardson family!

Jane sighed, and reached out for another cigarette. These ghosts always came out to torment her when she was at Wyncrag. Why hadn't she divorced Saul years ago? Why didn't she divorce him now?

The same old question, and the same old answer. She'd suggested a divorce, pleaded with him, begged him to agree to one. He was adamant. If he were divorced, he would have to resign from the government. So, as far as he was concerned, that was the end of the matter. Jane suspected a mistress, but had no proof of it, and certainly no idea who she might be.

She had thought of setting up a wild affair of her own, impossible for him to ignore. Only, who with? How, when

Jack's treatment of her had destroyed her own capacity for love?

Round and round the thoughts went like a gramophone record, the needle digging sharply in the well-worn grooves and producing the same old tune. She had no money, and no means of earning money.

How she envied Alix her education, the freedom she had to find work and be paid for it. Her niece's generation were fortunate in comparison to her own; did they realize just how lucky they were? Their mothers might long for them to marry, but many of the daughters had their own views on the matter, and chose a different kind of life.

Only she didn't want to be a career woman, wouldn't want it if she were Alix's age now. She wanted a family of her own, as she always had done. It had never occurred to her that her life wouldn't follow a predictable pattern of courtship, marriage, children. She would never have dreamed that she would be denied children by Saul, simply because of his mother's fear of what she called a bad inheritance. Jane sometimes wondered if Caroline's real fear weren't of the deaf mutism that had afflicted one or two of the family in previous generations, but of a double inheritance of Jack's warped nature.

She rang for her maid and told her to draw a bath and put out her clothes. She bathed, dressed, applied cream to her face; one needed protection against the elements at Wyncrag, where it was always excessively wet or windy or cold. And occasionally, in the summer, too-hot, with a burning heat seeming to roll down from the hills.

She whistled to the dogs as she hunted in the downstairs cloakroom for a pair of boots; they were too big, all the Richardsons had big feet. She found some fishing socks and a pair of boots that would just about do, and with Henry's two setters gambolling around her, she clumped out of the house.

The whiteness should have raised her spirits, but it only reminded her of the story of the Snow Queen and the ice splinter, a story she had hated as a child. The sun shone, but it held no warmth in its pale winter aspect. She walked across the terrace and down the steps, taking one of the paths that led to the lake. There, on the frozen shore, she flung sticks for the dogs, watching them slither and slide across the ice, then race back on to the snow to bounce on their paws, flinging white showers into the air, leaving icy yellow puddles by bushes and stones.

There weren't many people on the ice, it was too far away from the delights of hot pie stalls and chestnuts roasting on braziers. Two men were skating a little way out from the shore, strong skaters, jumping and spinning. The taller man's graceful but vigorous movements reminded her of Jack. This would never do. Jack was dead and buried, thank God. It didn't do to brood on old sores the way she had this morning.

A couple skated past. An athletic-looking man, who had to be a foreigner; Englishmen never dressed for the ice like that. The woman skated easily and stylishly, cutting elegant figures on her inside and outside edges. Her hair was hidden under a large woolly hat, her eyes obscured with a pair of sunglasses. The two of them turned in a wide arc to skate steadily back towards the other side of the lake.

Jane walked slowly along the shore, kicking pebbles out of the way with her clumsy boots, throwing stones now for the dogs to retrieve and drop triumphantly at her feet. Then it was time to go back, to shed her boots and wash her hands clean of dog slobber and hair, to present herself exactly on time for her mother-in-law's cold scrutiny and her father-in-law's kindly thanks for taking the dogs for a run. Bloody Wyncrag; bloody, bloody Wyncrag.

The dogs raced ahead of her as she neared Wyncrag, and vanished around the side of the house. She pushed open the back door, hung their leashes on the peg with the other ones and went down the passage that led to the hall. Only to have Lipp jump out on her, her beady eyes bright with disapproval.

'There you are, Mrs Saul. We wondered where you'd gone.'

Jane ignored Lipp, and spared an evil thought for Caroline; she knew exactly what Lipp meant by 'we'.

'Lady Richardson wants to see you,' Lipp said, as though Jane hadn't heard her first request.

Jane made to go past. 'Thank you, Lipp, I'll see her at lunch.'

Lipp stepped into her path, a small, stout, formidable little woman.

'She wants to see you now.'

'Now, I am going to take off my outdoor things. After that I shall go to my room to tidy myself before lunch. When I shall doubtless see my mother-in-law. Please move aside, Lipp, I want to get past.'

Lipp hesitated, glowered, but took a step back. 'Her lady-ship won't be pleased.'

Jane took off her gloves, unwound the scarf from around her neck and handed it to Chard, who had heard her voice and had come hurrying to help. She took Jane's coat and waited for her to take off her hat. Jane patted her hair into place, took off her boots and slipped her feet into the shoes she'd left in the cloakroom.

Lipp was still standing there, her mouth pursed at Jane's smart London maid, who paid no attention to her but swept past, nose in the air, carrying her armful of outdoor clothes.

'That will be all, Lipp,' Jane said, heading for the stairs.

'Her ladyship is anxious about Miss Perdita, and wants to know where she's gone.'

'I haven't seen Perdita this morning, you may tell her that.' She was on the first landing now.

'Not out on your walk?'

'No.' Jane reached her door and the safety of her room.

God, that woman gave her the willies. Creeping about the

place, spying and reporting back to Caroline. Jane sat down at her dressing table, took up a powder puff to take the pink from her cheeks and found her hand was trembling. All because of a servant! Only it wasn't that, it was the servant's mistress who filled her with silent rage. Caroline.

The door opened and Saul came in. 'Lipp's gone fuming off to Mother, you weren't rude to her, were you?'

Jane swivelled around on her stool. 'Rude? To a servant? Why ever should I be? Lipp was impertinent as usual, that's all.'

'She tells me Mama asked to see you, and you wouldn't go.'

'Your mother will be there at lunch, she can see me then. Since she hates unpunctuality, I've come upstairs to wash my hands. The gong will go any minute.'

'Why does Mama want to see you?'

'Only to ask if I know where Perdita is, apparently. I don't, as it happens.'

'Perdita shouldn't go off on her own, she knows how much it upsets Mama. These young people have no consideration for their elders. It isn't good for someone of Mama's age to get upset.'

Jane finished powdering her nose and placed the puff back in the cut-glass powder bowl. She twisted the cap off her lipstick. 'Caroline brings any upset on herself, she treats that girl as though she were a wild animal who has to be kept chained up. Perhaps you know why she's so hard on her. I see no reason for such severity.'

'You can't say that, Jane. It's not easy bringing up a girl who has no parents. Caroline has been more than a mother to Perdita.'

No, much less than a mother. Poor Perdita. 'Perdita's at that awkward age, not a girl, not a woman, not sure how to behave or what to say. It's a difficult time for any girl, and with no mother to guide her, it's not surprising that she's turning out so gauche and strange. She wants affection, a good haircut and pretty clothes. A girl needs all the confidence she can get, not a grandmother who wishes she was still in the nursery, and treats her as though she were. I sometimes think Caroline hates Perdita, and I can't imagine why.'

Saul's face had paled. 'What a ridiculous thing to say. Mama has a lot of experience with young girls, she brought up two of her own, not to mention Alix. She's bound to know more about it than you do.'

'Having no daughters of my own, you mean? Well, we all know who's to blame for that.' The sound of the gong rang out from the hall. Jane sprayed scent behind each ear, then stood up, smoothing down her skirt and flicking a hair off the arm of her blouse. Without looking at Saul, she went to the door, waited for him to open it for her, and went out. He followed her, shaking his head.

SEVENTEEN

Hal was on the ice, glad to have escaped from Grindley Hall for the afternoon, pleased to be away from his brothers and out of reach of Eve's suspicious looks. There, on the smooth, glinting surface of the lake, with the white and mauve mountains towering over him, their shapes etched in his memory from his earliest childhood, he was at peace. For the first time since he'd arrived in England, he thought perhaps it wasn't, after all, a mistake to have come back.

Inside the Hall he felt claustrophobic and found that the memories which clustered about his mind there brought him nothing but unease. It wasn't a question of space, the Hall was large and full of rooms, many of them rarely used – the library, the music room, a print room, offices, bedrooms, dusty attics. It was a matter of what was in his head, and these memories had been forgotten for years, or at least pushed to the very back of his consciousness.

Peter had been the kind of boy and young man who made grown-ups talk approvingly about qualities of leadership. He was blessed with a big, muscular frame and was a first-class rugby player, a bruising rider and a tennis player who liked to win. He was never happier than when engaged in some sporting activity, especially one in which he could beat his opponents. When these opponents changed from men in shorts to men in dark suits, his zeal for winning increased still further. Very few people had ever managed to get the better of him in any commercial or financial contest.

Roger, with a similar build, had won acclaim at school as Captain of Cricket and had run the half-mile in a record time. He had been born, so his mother used to say, with a lawyer's brain; a logical boy and man, with a retentive memory, he possessed much the same competitive spirit as his older brother. In his case, his opponents existed within the enclosed walls of a law court, and there he took the same pleasure in demolishing the opposition that his brother found in his business dealings.

So the famous northern public school that the brothers attended had been delighted to welcome yet another young Grindley to adorn the honours board and bring cups and glory to his house and school.

Only Hal wasn't like his brothers. He was of a different build, destined to grow rather taller than they were, and considerably leaner, the kind of man who wouldn't grow chunky or portly as he aged. He had neither interest nor skill in rugby nor any other team games, and his grace on the ice and brilliance when in control of a yacht brought him no kudos at school. He was, even worse, something of a swot, a boy who always had his nose in a book, who liked poetry and music, and, horror of horrors, the theatre.

Naturally, the bullies moved in for the kill. Not so naturally, they discovered that he was something of a poison pill; not as weedy as he looked, and disinclined to follow any rules of fighting, considering shins and eyes and genitals as perfectly fair targets. Moreover, his viperous tongue made even the densest of the toughs blink. Word went around that old lavatory pan was best left alone. His school felt a startled pride as he took himself off to university covered with scholarships and words of praise from his chosen college, but on the whole were glad to see the back of him, and grateful that there were no more young Grindleys to upset the proper order of school life.

Hal had concluded, in distant America, that after nearly sixteen years his old home and his family could hold no terrors for him. What kind of a daft notion was that? he asked himself as he made some dashing swoops across the ice. Not so much terror, either, as old hostilities and hurts. Gone were the big emotions, enter the trivial, the pinpricks of the first twenty odd years of his life. When he left, he had intended to shake the dust of England, and especially of these northern acres of England, from his feet for ever. America, so far away, so utterly un-Grindley, was the place for him. He had even changed his professional name, wanting to shed the last trace of Grindley-ness. Only, he now realized, Grindley Hall ran in his blood and throbbed in his head; some changes were possible, others weren't.

'You skate awfully well,' said Cecy, gliding up beside him. 'Did you use to skate a lot when you lived at home, before you went away for good?'

'Of course, every year from when I could walk,' he said. 'Just like you. I still go skating every winter when I can get away.'

'Penny for them,' called his niece as she skated away from him, doing some fast backward steps. She was a neat skater, well co-ordinated, moving swiftly and easily and without effort. The same kind of skater that he was, in fact, although he didn't see the likeness, never having considered how he looked on the ice.

'I'm thinking of the States, how New York will be lit up for Christmas.'

'You sound homesick.' Cecy's voice was surprised, why ever should her uncle feel homesick for New York? The other way around was only natural, he would be bound to feel homesick for all this when he was so far away, but now that he was here, home, among his own family and hills, how could he be missing New York?

'I guess I am, a little. They say you have two home towns, where you were born and the place of your heart.'

'And New York's the place of your heart?'

'Maybe. I certainly like it there.'

'More than this?' Cecy asked, the red bobble on her hat flying around after her as she spun through three hundred and sixty degrees, gesturing at the lakes and mountains and sky.

'Maybe.'

'It's only because Eve's getting on your nerves. Eve gets on all our nerves, she makes Mummy growl like anything, and even Daddy, who never criticises anything Uncle Peter does, says that she's bogus.'

'Bogus?' This wasn't the word that would have sprung into Hal's mind.

'She's only been doing the chatelaine bit on you so far. Just wait until she starts on art, then you'll see what I mean by bogus.'

'She's artistic, is she?'

'You could say that.' Cecy skated alongside him as they both gathered speed, then she came to a raking stop in a shower of ice crystals about her ankles. 'I spy Ursula, and that's Perdy with her, must be, good heavens, how she has grown! Have you met her yet? She wasn't born when you went off, isn't that funny, to think of her growing up here just like you did, only you don't know each other at all.' She cupped her hand to her mouth and let out a formidable bellow. 'Ursy! Bring Perdita over to meet Uncle Hal.'

'Do you want to meet my Uncle Hal?' Ursula asked, as she and Perdita made their stately way across the ice with the sledge ropes in their hands.

'I suppose so,' Perdita said.

132

'Good God, you are like your uncle,' Hal exclaimed as Perdita was introduced.

'Don't shake hands, my glove's soaked through, and if I take it off, there's only freezing damp flesh inside. Which uncle do you mean?'

'Your Uncle Jack.'

'Was he gangly, like me?'

'Tall, certainly, very dashing and handsome.'

'Oh, goodie,' she said without enthusiasm. 'Only it's different for a man.' She rubbed the tip of her nose with her icy glove. 'I believe I'm getting frostbite. What do you think, Cecy?'

'Just chilled, I'd say. Go home and have a warm drink, that'll stave it off.'

'That's what we were doing when you called us over,' Ursula pointed out. 'You skate awfully well, Uncle Hal,' she added as she twisted the rope around her wrist to get a better purchase.

'Mind you,' Cecy shouted after them as they skated away, 'if you do get numb toes or fingers or nose, rub some snow on the afflicted part.'

Ursula answered with a lifted hand, and they vanished into the gathering dusk.

'Time for us to be getting back,' Cecy said. 'It does get dark so very early.'

Hal wasn't listening. 'Who's that?' he asked, looking at a solitary figure who was skating close to the shore, taking long, leisurely glides along the ice.

Cecy lifted her hand and looked into the last rays of the setting sun. 'It's Alix. Let's skate over and cut her off.'

'She looks deep in thought,' began Hal, but Cecy was off, flying across the ice, waving as she went.

Hal started after her, arriving just as Alix raised a startled head, and said 'Oh, it's you, Cecy, how you made me jump, whooshing down on me like that.'

It was Helena's voice, the very timbre and pitch of it. No trace of the American accent which she'd always retained, but the rest of it. For a moment Hal felt an ache in his heart, a feeling of such unexpected anguish that he shut his eyes for a moment, catching his breath.

The ice was full of ghosts. Full of people who resembled other people, people from his past, or who reminded him of someone, but he couldn't say who.

Before he had met Perdita, he had seen two distant figures skating out in the middle of the lake. For a moment, the years dropped away, and he was standing on the shore, watching the Richardson brothers skimming over the ice. Neville, fast and determined; Jack hurtling himself forward, unsmiling, but with a look of wild delight on his face. An unusual insight into his emotions; Jack had been born with the ability to mask his feelings.

Of course, when he came out of his reverie, he could see that the men weren't at all like Neville and Jack, it had been a mere trick of sunlight and shadows that had roused the ghosts in his mind.

Then there had been the woman he and Cecy had seen when they skated away from the Grindley shore. A woman in yellow breeches and a matching yellow hat, another good skater, turning and twisting and jumping on the ice.

'That's the mystery tenant of Grindley Cottage,' Cecy told him. 'Ursula says the locals all think she must be a film star. In disguise. She's American, you see. Perhaps you know her.'

Hal had laughed at her. 'There are some hundred and fifty million people in America, and quite a few of them are young women.'

Cecy had laughed, too. 'One thinks of America as being like London, where one is always running unexpectedly into people one knows.'

'Do they think she's any particular film star?'

'No, they haven't recognised her, but she does wear dark glasses, you see.'

'Very sensible, on the ice. I might get out a pair myself.' He narrowed his eyes at the fast-moving woman, now executing a series of figure eights. 'Mind you, she does look in some way familiar.'

What was it, the way she held her head, the smile? There was something about her that stirred a memory, but it was gone as quickly as it had come, no more than an elusive flash.

'Do you go to the pictures a lot? Or would that be busman's holiday, you being an actor?'

'I love the movies,' he said.

'Have you ever gone on the pictures?'

'No, I have to confess I haven't.'

'I thought all actors in America ended up in Hollywood.' Cecy sounded disappointed. 'Haven't you even been there?'

Oh, yes, he'd been there. He'd stayed with the aristocrats of Hollywood, house guest of the Fairbanks, had dined with the Chaplins, danced with Adele Astaire. 'I'm more of a stage man,' he said.

He hadn't intentionally kept the details of his career from his family in England. If any of them had shown the slightest concern for him after his mother had died, he would have sent them cuttings, let them know that he had become a successful and well-known theatrical director, working under the name of Henry Ivison, his first and middle names. If any of them had had any interest in theatre and come across his name they might have put two and two together. Probably not; what happened across the Atlantic didn't seem to be of any importance to any of them. He was unlikely to bring Peter any useful information about rival American firms or Roger any legal anecdotes or gossip, and they certainly didn't care to hear about a third-rate acting career.

Alix was a disappointment, apart from the voice, he thought. Pity that the lively ten-year-old should have turned

135

into this cross-looking young woman with a discontented mouth.

'Where's Edwin?' Cecy asked, taking off her gloves and blowing on her fingers.

'Gone to meet a friend at the station,' Alix said shortly.

'Is he coming to stay at Wyncrag?'

'Who?'

'The friend he's gone to meet.'

Alix was silent for a few moments, then she said, 'It's a woman friend. She's staying at his house in Lowfell. He won't be there, he's staying at Wyncrag over Christmas and New Year.'

'A girlfriend?' Cecy asked.

'She's some kind of refugee,' Alix said. 'She's homeless. You know what a soft heart Edwin has.'

'That's kind of him,' Cecy said. Then she looked more closely at Alix. 'You don't think so.'

'It is kind. I just hope she doesn't impose on him.'

'Is she a photographer?'

'A musician. From Vienna. Jewish.'

'Goodness,' Cecy said. 'Does Lady Richardson know?'

'He hasn't told her.'

'Better not tell Eve, or she'll be down there offering her a job in the kitchen at wages of about ten pounds a year.'

That raised a smile from Alix.

She should smile more, Hal thought, struck by how her face was transformed by the smile. No, she wasn't at all like her mother to look at, but she had good bones, and an interesting face. Her looks were more arresting than beautiful, but what was she so fed up about? Maybe she was the organising kind, like her grandmother, and didn't care for Edwin making quixotic gestures without his discussing it with her. Although twins or no twins, she and Edwin must be twenty-four or -five now, at that age Hal wouldn't have taken any notice of what a sister – or brother – thought about his actions.

136

Not that he had ever been close the way those two were, so it was unreasonable to pass judgement on her reaction to Edwin's behaviour.

'I must be getting back,' Alix said. 'It was nice to see you again, Mr Grindley.'

'Hal, don't you think? I'm the one who used to pull your plaits, remember?'

Now she really laughed. 'No, I don't remember, and I'm sure you were far too grown-up to do any such thing.'

'Don't you think she's grown into a beauty?' Cecy said, as she skated on.

'She's attractive enough, under the scowl,' Hal said, almost to himself. 'I wonder what's eating her?'

Cecy was quick to defend her friend. 'It isn't easy for her, coming back, she hasn't been here for three years. She had the most terrible row with her grandmother before she went, and they didn't give her a penny to live on. She had a tough time of it in London, having to exist on a tiny wage, and living in horrible digs.'

He was surprised to hear it. 'A Richardson, short of money? Surely she has money of her own. Sir Henry said she had, I'm sure he did.'

'She does now, but she didn't then. Sir Henry's one of her trustees, and Lady Richardson wouldn't let him give her an income from her parents' money. Sir Henry always does what Lady Richardson wants, anything for a quiet life. Alix could have taken it up with the other trustees, only they're people like my father, who would say she should live at home and then she wouldn't need any money. Then, luckily, a great-aunt died and left her and Edwin some money, so that made things easier for her.'

Cecy linked arms with her uncle and they skated together towards the Grindley shore. 'Edwin must have upset her. They're terribly close, and I'm sure that's the main reason she's come back, to spend time with him. So if he's got some

137

good cause going that's occupying his mind, she'd be bound to be upset.'

It was more than a brother with a good cause that was bothering Alix, Hal thought, but he didn't say so. He doubted if Cecy would want to hear his opinion, which was that her friend was suffering from a bout of good, old-fashioned jealousy. Cecy seemed to think that Edwin's good deed was a woman of a certain age; he, Hal, would be prepared to bet that she was a lot younger.

Alix struck out across the lake, making for Wyncrag. Her sense of neglect fell away in a sudden rush of joy; she had always loved the lake at the end of the winter's day, watching the shadows of the fells sweeping across the ice, subduing the brilliance to patches of blue shadows as daylight paled into dusk.

So that was Hal Grindley, she said to herself, as she reached the Wyncrag landing stage, its wooden supports rising eerily from the ice. She grasped one to help pull herself on to the small strip of shingle alongside the landing stage, her hand sliding down its skin of ice.

She sat down to unfasten her skates. She didn't remember him very well, he had always been overshadowed by his booming eldest brother. And fourteen years was a huge gap at that age; she'd been a child, he'd been a young man. Now she knew that her adult self was going to dislike him.

Why? she asked herself as she trudged up the slippery bank, her skates dangling from cold fingers. Because he bore all the familiar marks of the sophistication she had walked away from. He was one of them, one of the kind of crowd she had run with, those people who made her feel so sick of herself and of them.

One thing, he wouldn't stay long in Westmoreland. If ever there was a fish out of water, it was Hal Grindley.

He hadn't looked like a gasping fish. Never mind, a few

evenings at Grindley Hall would send him hurrying back to London or New York or wherever he belonged. Unless Peter Grindley's wife was a real charmer, and according to Edwin, she wasn't. 'Social climber,' had been his verdict. 'And full of arty pretentiousness. Talks about Vorticism.'

'Cripes.'

No, this man didn't look the type to put up with that. He'd be off in no time. She dismissed him from her mind, preferring to get back to the thoughts that dominated her mind: Edwin and this Lidia person.

EIGHTEEN

He was cold and frightened.

He wasn't alone among the trees. He could hear someone – or something – else in the forest, out there in the dark, trampling on the icy ground. Awake, his reason would have told him, deer, or maybe a badger. His dream told him, danger. Whatever it was, this growling, whimpering creature was more terrifying than any forest animal.

Michael was dreaming in colour that night. Most of his remembered dreams were in colour. Vaguer, less memorable dreams, forgotten as soon as the morning came, were dreams drained of colour, the sepia of old photographs.

This dream wasn't vague, wasn't sepia, and was full of menace. Twigs, brittle from frost, snapped under his feet. Swaying branches far above him sent snow rustling to the ground; the soft sound was sinister and strange.

It was so dark, that was the worst of it. Even if the moon came out from behind the clouds that had drifted over it, the light wouldn't penetrate this frozen wood. The trees were too dense, too thick, too close together; he was walled in by trees, trapped in a frozen cavern of tree trunks and branches.

He shivered, but knew that he was sweating. Unaware, he pushed the blankets off him as he struck out at the trees

140

and bushes. How could you be cold and sweat at the same time?

More sounds, more rustling; a kind of squeal, cut off; heavy breathing. Oh, Christ, whatever it was, it was coming nearer. It knew his fear, could smell it, must be drawn to him by the scent of fear. Animals could smell fear. His father had told him that when a dog snarled at him.

Boar. It was a wild boar, he was sure it was, with angry red eyes, foaming mouth, vicious tusks. He had seen wild boar, in Hungary.

He stirred in his sleep, confused even as he dreamed. In the dream he was a boy, but the wild boar in Hungary was part of his adult life. And boar had long gone from the forests of England. Except, he thought, as his dream drew him back into its darkness, anything might live in such a wild and cold and desolate place as this.

The creature was quiet now. It was waiting for him to make a move. As soon as he did, it would come crashing through the undergrowth to pounce, rend, tear.

Yet he must move. He had to find a way out. Yes, that was it. Move forward, sliding first one foot then the other so as not to make a sound. Don't tread on twigs, or stumble over a rock. Concentrate.

Then a scream rang through the wood.

He fled; he was running heedlessly through the scratching, grasping undergrowth. Tendrils, sharp and cold, reached out for him, gnarled black roots snatched at his stumbling feet. Whispery things brushed against his face. He ran with his hands crossed before his face, then he could run no more. He stopped, unable to breathe, his back pressed against a tree.

The scream, again. A scream of pain. Of fear. Of protest, even? Cut off as though silenced with a guillotine.

The creature had found its prey. It had killed, so perhaps, oh just perhaps it would be sated, wouldn't bother to come after him.

Now there was only the soft sound of whimpering. Was he whimpering? No, it was someone, something else. His mouth was dry, his heart beating.

'Good morning, Mr Wrexham,' came Mrs Dixon's cheery voice. 'Another fine day. I've brought your water for shaving, and a cup of tea.'

There was a rattle of china, cup against saucer, as she set the tea down on the table beside his bed.

Michael fought with the sheet which was wrapped around him, covering his face, pinning his arms to his side.

'Dear me, you've had a restless night, Mr Wrexham, and no mistake! A cold one, too, with your blankets on the floor.'

He felt the covers being dropped on to his feet, and with a heave he managed to break loose from the crumpled linen sheet. 'I was dreaming.'

'I hope it wasn't the shepherd's pie you had to your dinner last night, for I made it myself.'

He was quick to reassure her. 'Oh, no, it wasn't that, Mrs Dixon. It's a dream I have sometimes. Of when I was a boy. I don't have it so often these days, but it was remarkably vivid.'

Mrs Dixon was sympathetic. 'Tiresome things, dreams, that come troubling a body when you need your rest after a hard day's work. What's the point of them, I'd like to know?'

Michael struggled to a sitting position and reached out for the blankets.

'Your fire isn't quite out, I'll just give it a stir and put more coal on, and the room will be warm in a trice.'

Michael drank his tea, watching Mrs Dixon's large and solid rear, apron straps dangling, as she blew life into the dying embers. There was a reality and a normality to her which he welcomed. Daylight was banishing the fear and the boar and the screams as it always did, but the lingering memory disturbed him still. He hadn't had that dream for more than five years, and this time it was different from all

142

the previous nights in the dark wood. Last night he had, for the first time, moved towards the scream. He felt that if he hadn't been woken up by Mrs Dixon, he would at last have seen what it was that whimpered in the forest.

He wasn't sure that he wanted to know.

'That'll do nicely now,' Mrs Dixon said comfortably, hanging the poker on its hook. 'You get dressed and come down to a good breakfast, you'll be hungry after fighting with your bedclothes all night.'

'Bad night?' enquired Freddie as Michael joined him at the round, highly polished table. The landlord's daughter came in with a tray laden with dishes, and set platefuls of eggs, bacon, sausages, mushrooms, fried bread and tomatoes before each of them.

'Strange dreams,' Michael said, taking his napkin out of its ring and spreading it on his knees. 'Is that mustard you've got there?'

Freddie passed him the mustard pot. 'If you've been having bad dreams, it's because you've been working too hard. I said you've been overdoing things. Up here, with the fresh air and exercise and good food, you should be sleeping like a top. I do.'

'This is a dream I used to have when I was younger.'

'Weren't you taken ill when you were last here? You said you'd had feverish hallucinations. Ones that came back in your dreams.'

Other people's dreams were always an utter bore, why ever had he said anything to Freddie?

'I expect it's being back up here after all that time. It's brought back memories, that's what. Why don't we give the ice a miss today and take the car out for a run? Blow the cobwebs away.'

Mr Dixon had come into the room as they were discussing where they might go. He suggested a run up to Fiend's Fell;

143

the road was clear, that was one pass that never got blocked, he told them. There was a wonderful view, more than thirty miles on a clear day, and a goodish pub half-way down the other side where they could stop for a pint and a bite to eat at lunchtime. Freddie went upstairs to get a map, and they retreated to the parlour for a pipe and a thorough investigation of the route.

Mr Dixon didn't need any maps. 'You'll not want to be going that way,' he said, pausing on a trip through the parlour from the dining room to the bar. He ran the point of a knife along their chosen road. 'It's ice and snow and all sorts along there, and Joe was in this morning, told me there's a tree down. You want to drive back along the lake and take this road here, she'll be passable, and join the other road further up.'

'Excellent,' Freddie said, standing up. He knocked the bowl of his pipe against the side of the ashtray. 'Ten minutes, then, Michael?'

Michael's spirits rose as they drove along the winding road that ran by the shore of the lake. Early skaters were already out on the ice, flying and tumbling, cutting edges and twirling over the shining surface.

'There are those damned Blackshirts,' Freddie said. 'It's a pity anyone was prepared to take them in, nobody needs to have their sort around.'

Michael watched the two men as they advanced over the ice. Good skaters, and fast, they made little allowance for anyone who got in their way. A boy, scampering on unsteady skates to avoid them, lost control and ran into the taller of the men, who thrust him abruptly aside, sending him spinning across the ice.

'Swine,' Freddie said indignantly. 'Just let them bump into me on the ice, that's all.'

'If they're the bullying sort, there's no danger of them taking on anyone their own size.'

'They should be run out of town. Let them stay in the cities, where there are plenty of keen types ready to show what they think of them and their tommy-rot fascism.'

'It's the future,' Michael said, turning his head to keep the skating Blackshirts in sight.

'I jolly well hope not.'

'Look at Italy, and Germany. Fascism has its appeal, it offers hope to all the no-hopers.'

'Hitler and his uncouth gang can do what they like over on the continent, just as long as it doesn't get a hold here. It won't. The English have far too much sense to be hoodwinked by a bunch of thugs dressed up in ridiculous uniforms.'

'One would have said the Germans don't lack for sense.'

'They don't, but they allow themselves to be bamboozled by any passing demagogue.'

Michael thought of what Gibson had said about the way the Germans were building aircraft, but he didn't want to argue with Freddie.

Freddie braked, Germany forgotten. 'Damsel in distress, I do declare.'

Michael had seen her, too, sitting on the bank by the side of the road, pulling at the laces of her boot. A pair of skates lay beside her, and her face was flushed and angry. She hailed them as they slowed down.

'Can you give me a lift? Just a mile or so along the road. I can't walk very well.'

As she spoke, she tried to stand up, obviously keeping her weight on her left foot.

'I say, you've twisted your ankle,' Freddie said. He put on the brake, and both men got out of the car.

'Here, lean on me,' Michael said. 'We'll have you aboard in no time.'

'Thank you.' She hopped towards the car. 'I think I can manage to get in myself.'

'You'll only make matters worse if you do,' Freddie said. 'Let Michael help you in.'

Michael picked her up and sat her on the passenger seat. 'Oh, but there's no room for you.'

'I'll walk,' Michael said cheerfully. 'I shall be glad to stretch my legs.'

'It's most awfully kind of you.'

'Where are you heading for?'

'Wyncrag. The gates are set back from the road, but you can't miss it. Or, I tell you what, there's a short cut across the field. That's how I was going to go, only this blasted ankle wasn't too happy about it. You'd be all right in those boots. You can't miss the house, it looks like it was built by the brothers Grimm.'

'In which case, I know exactly the house you mean. I shall take the short cut and see you there.'

Michael climbed over the stile and set off over the field in the direction she had indicated. That amazing house. He wouldn't mind having a closer look; he had seen it from the lake and from the opposite shore where the road ran through the trees and climbed almost to the top of the fell. He had wondered who lived there.

Others had been this way before him, and the packed snow was icy and treacherous; he found it easier to tramp through the virgin snow to the side of the path. It was slow walking, but he reached a stone wall, climbed over another stile, and after following a narrow track alongside a copse, came out beside what was clearly a drive. It had been cleared of snow and gritted, it would be easier going on this last stretch. Nice girl, he thought, distinctive looking, even when in a temper.

They wouldn't make it to Fiend's Fell today, he'd be prepared to bet on it. A pity, he didn't feel like polite company. The girl would undoubtedly have a mother, who would flutter and fuss around her injured daughter. She'd be profuse in her thanks to her rescuers, there would be offers of refreshments, luncheon . . . What a bore.

Trudie came into the hall as Alix came haltingly in, leaning on Freddie.

'Alix! My dear! What have you done to yourself? A skating accident, well, someone was bound to come a cropper on the ice. Is anything broken?'

She swept into the drawing room ahead of them and whisked cushions into a comforting heap at one end of an enormous sofa. 'There! Alix, tell me where it hurts. Rokeby, tell Phoebe to come at once, bring ice and cloths. Should we ring for the doctor?'

'Don't fuss, Aunt Trudie,' Alix said wearily. Her ankle was hurting a good deal. 'My skate came loose, and my ankle flipped over. That's all. I don't need a doctor. But I do need to get my boot off, I think my ankle's swelling up inside it.'

'Leave it to me,' Freddie said. 'I'll have the wretched thing off in a jiffy.' He unlaced the boot, pulled the lace free, and eased her foot out. He reached for a cushion and lowered her foot on to it.

Alix, looking pale, thanked him. Phoebe hurried into the room with a tray on which lay folded white linen cloths. She held an ice bucket in her other hand. 'Cook says, hot and cold compresses if it's a sprain. She'll see to the hot towels directly.'

'I'm sure she's right,' Trudie said, twisting one of her floating scarves, a chiffon affair in dark red, into a knot at her throat. 'I do hope nothing's broken.'

'I've wrenched my ankle, that's all,' Alix said.

Freddie was feeling the ankle. His hands were firm, knowledgeable, gentle. 'That's all it is. If you rest it, it'll be fine in a day or two. Compresses will ease the pain and the swelling.'

Alix had noticed Lipp out of the corner of her eye as Freddie helped her to the sofa. She had vanished, scuttling off to find Grandmama no doubt. Who would arrive, and . . . Oh, blast, here she was.

'*What* is going on?' Grandmama stood in the doorway, looking at Freddie with cold, unwelcoming eyes. Lipp hovered behind her.

'There's someone at the front door,' Phoebe hissed at Rokeby, who manoeuvred himself past his mistress and crossed the hall to the door.

Alix, feeling slightly sick with the pain of her ankle, heard Michael announce himself to Rokeby, then saw him outside in the hall, watching the scene in the drawing room. Grandmama was beside the sofa now, brushing aside Freddie, her mouth a severe line of dislike; how she hated drama of any kind.

'If Alix has had a fall, she needs peace and quiet. Not all this coming and going. Who are you?' she demanded of Freddie.

'This is Freddie, Grandmama. He brought me back here in his motor. I can't walk properly; I twisted my ankle on the ice. That's all.'

'How do you know that's all?'

'Oh, it is,' Freddie said. 'I've had a feel of it. No bones broken.'

Bother Grandmama, freezing him with that *grande dame* stare. 'Grandmama, he helped me. I'm sure he knows what he's talking about.'

'Why are you so sure?'

One could tell by the way he had felt her ankle, he knew just what he was doing, but of course there was no point in saying that to Grandmama. Freddie was backing away now; hardly surprising. A fine reward for being a Good Samaritan. Oh, Lord, the other man was coming into the room; two strange young men, Grandmama would have a fit.

'Allow me to introduce my friend, Frederick Kerr,' the newcomer was saying, cool and distant and looking as though

148

he wasn't about to make a friend of Grandmama. With that flaming red hair, he'd have a temper, and, judging by the firm line of his jaw, he'd learned to control it. 'My name is Michael Wrexham. We're staying at the Pheasant. We were driving by when we saw this young lady sitting by the road, obviously in pain.'

Grandmama was at her most forbidding, her voice chilly as she addressed Michael. Why did she have to behave like this? 'Are you a judge of pain? Are you qualified in some way?'

Alix flushed, knowing that Grandmama was quite capable of deciding that she had pretended to have hurt her ankle, just to attract the attention of two young men.

Michael ignored the acid tone. 'No, but my friend here is a doctor.'

'Indeed?' Her expression dated back to the day when doctors used the back entrance. 'Of no very great experience, however.'

'Not a lot,' Freddie said with a grin. 'Only I'm quite sound on bones and fractures and so on, because that's my field. I'm training to become an orthopaedic surgeon.'

Alix was defiant. 'And I'm grateful for the lift, for otherwise I should have had to hop and hobble back, which wouldn't have been the least bit fun.'

Then Grandpapa was there, looking the young men up and down in his turn, but in a perfectly civil way. Did the Bentley belong to one of them? A magnificent car. Alix was hurt? Not seriously, though; good, good, let her rest her foot and apply compresses, he was sure that would do the trick. Have a look under the bonnet? He'd be delighted. They must both stay for lunch, no, no, he wouldn't hear of them leaving. 'Rokeby, tell Cook two extra for lunch.'

He and Freddie disappeared, and Grandmama only had the red-haired one, what was his name? Michael, that was it, to vent her spleen on. Alix saw sympathy in his eyes. For her, or for Grandmama? It was impossible to tell. What did Grandmama take her for, a nymphomaniac, unable not to cast out lures to any man who went past? She closed her eyes, feeling slightly sick. She wished they'd all go away.

'I think perhaps she'd rather be alone,' Michael said.

'Yes,' said Trudie, who was wrapping a cold cloth around Alix's ankle. 'I'll stay here with her, I'm sure she'll be all right by lunchtime.'

'Of course she will be. I see no point in making a fuss about a mere twisted ankle. Phoebe, fetch Miss Alix a pair of slippers. Rokeby, bring a tray into the library for Miss Alix, she can hardly sit up at the table if she needs to keep her foot up.'

She swept out, giving Michael a last cold glance.

'I'm sorry,' Alix said from her sofa. 'It's just her way.'

'This young man looks far too sensible to take any notice,' Trudie said, giving him one of her fey smiles. 'Go and join your friend, why don't you; better outside than in here, don't you think?'

'He must think we're such an odd family,' Alix said, fretfully, as Michael went out.

'Well, so we are. Why should he mind, or we mind what he thinks? He and his friend will have lunch, and then be on their way. We shan't see them again.'

'Of course we will. You know Grandpapa. He'll probably invite them to Christmas dinner, oh, the embarrassment of it all.'

'You are ungrateful. For myself, I should be glad of some cheerful extra faces at the dining table. If their owners are young and personable, so much the better, and I have to say that Dr Kerr is a remarkably handsome young man.'

Perdita and Ursula's loud young voices could be heard in the hall, followed by a crash; Perdita walking into the hall table, at a guess. Her sister came in, rubbing her hip.

'Alix! What's up?'

'I fell on the ice and hurt my ankle. I'm going to make my way upstairs, and lunch off a tray.'

'Rokeby's bringing the tray into the library,' Trudie said.

Alix heard the doubt in her voice, and knew that her aunt was thinking that Grandmama might be annoyed at any contravention of her orders. Too bad. 'Tell Phoebe to bring it upstairs. I'd rather be in my room.'

'I say,' Ursula said, 'were you rescued by a knight errant in a Bentley? Two knight errants, actually, counting the heads peering into the engine.'

'It must be knights errant,' Perdita said. 'Were you, Alix? Does Grandmama know? She'll be livid.'

'Strange men in the house,' Ursula said, tut-tutting. 'Does she think they're riff-raff, or fortune hunters?'

'Not in that Bentley,' Perdita said definitely. 'Super car.'

'Which one are you going to fall in love with?' Ursula asked Alix.

'My dear,' Trudie said, looking with alarm towards the door, in case her mother should be listening.

Alix couldn't help laughing, despite her throbbing ankle. 'Is it obligatory?'

'Oh, I think so. Don't you? Only you haven't been properly introduced, so of course your family will disapprove of the match. It will end in an elopement, you know.'

'Whatever next?' Trudie cried. 'Really, Ursula, what an imagination you have.'

'Or maybe it will be a tragic love affair. A Doomed Romance. You'll see him off to the war, your heart breaking because your parents have forbidden the banns, and you know you will never see him again.'

'War?' Trudie said. 'What war?'

'You watch too many soppy films,' Perdita said scornfully. 'If you're going to write books like that, no one will read them.'

'Of course they will. Millions of women will sob over every page, and I'll be incredibly rich and famous.'

'Thank you all the same,' Alix said, 'but count me out. All I ask is that you don't pay any attention at all to either Freddie or Michael, yes, Ursula, that's what they're called, not romantic names at all, I do agree. Don't even look at them, for heaven's sake, Perdy, or Grandmama will hit the roof. She's already made a stink because Freddie drove me back in his car.'

'Is there something wrong with them, apart from the unusual way you made their acquaintance?' asked Ursula, going over to look at herself in the big mirror over the fireplace. She tried to smooth her tousled hair, then gave it up as a bad job. 'They look OK to me.'

'They're strangers, that's all.' Alix had reached the door, and she leaned on the handle before tackling the hall and the stairs.

'Men!' Perdita said. 'The forbidden! Tall, dark and handsome, one of them was, too, just the sort to send Grandmama into a spasm. Lean on me, Alix, and do buck up, old thing. You'll have to get back on your feet pretty quickly, because of the Grindleys' dance.'

'Lord, I'd forgotten all about it,' Alix said. 'I expect it'll be all right by then, I do hope so, otherwise no dancing for me, what a bore, I'll have to sit out with all the dreadful dowagers.'

'And Grandmama,' said Perdita wickedly. 'What a treat. Here's one of them back again, we can ask him.'

'How long will it take to heal?' Freddie looked at the way Alix was taking the weight off her foot, her hand resting on Perdita's shoulder. 'It'll be at least a week before the bruising goes down, and I wouldn't recommend you go back on the ice this season.'

Tears started into her eyes. After all her joy in the frozen lake, she had to do a stupid thing like twist her ankle, and there she was, off the ice for the duration.

'Hurting?' asked Freddie. 'I'd get your doctor to prescribe

152

for you, or at least take some aspirin. Pain does no one any good.'

She could take aspirin for her ankle, but not for what brought the tears to her eyes, not for the wave of disappointment that swept sickeningly over her: no more skating, and Edwin interested in nothing but that Lidia creature, was this why she had come north? Almost, she determined to get Phoebe to pack her suitcase, to summon Eckersley to take her to the station to catch the night sleeper to London. Then she saw the concern in Grandpapa's face, and managed a smile. She despised self-pity, in herself as much as in others, and she struggled to pull herself together. She had run away once, and had come back, and she was damn well going to stick it out, skating or no skating.

'My ankle just jabbed for a moment,' she said lightly. 'I'll do as Freddie says, and take an aspirin. There's the gong for lunch, come on, Perdy, or you'll be late.'

NINETEEN

'In the library, after breakfast, if you have a few minutes to spare,' Peter said to Hal. 'Some business matters to discuss.'

Eve smiled knowingly at her husband over the big silver coffee pot, a Georgian monstrosity that she had unearthed from the silver safe and put out for use when guests were in the house.

It still made Ursula giggle whenever she saw it. 'I wouldn't be surprised if it picked itself up on those ridiculous feet and stalked off the table,' she confided to Cecy, who was picking over the bones of a kipper.

'It must weigh a ton,' Cecy whispered back. 'I dare say it's solid silver. Eve is stronger than she looks.'

'You bet she is,' Ursula said, pinning a polite, neutral expression on her face as her stepmother gave her a disapproving look.

'It's very bad manners to whisper at table,' Eve said.

Cecy and Ursula attended to their plates.

Whether it was the coffee pot or the making, the coffee was vile, and Hal thought longingly of the excellent coffee his godfather had given him. Another visit to Wyncrag might be in order; he missed good coffee to a surprising degree. Surely even undomestic Delia hadn't served anything so watery, he couldn't remember finding the coffee undrinkable in those days. Maybe America was to blame for accustoming his palate to a stronger brew.

He supposed the summons to a business talk was inevitable, he had guessed it was coming when he saw Peter at the breakfast table. Peter usually rose early, breakfasted alone and was in his office at the factory before the rest of his household assembled at the table.

'I'm on holiday until after Christmas,' he said to Hal over his shoulder as he led his brothers out of the dining room.

'Does that go for the workers, too?' Hal enquired, sitting down in what he judged to be the most comfortable of the chairs in that little-used room. He stretched his legs out in front of him, feet crossed at the ankles.

'Don't be foolish,' Peter said irritably. 'They get an extra hour off at Christmas Eve and should be grateful for it, they have no idea what it costs me to pay men when they aren't working.'

'A whole hour, as well as Christmas Day and Boxing Day?' said Hal to no one in particular. 'My, aren't they the lucky ones.' Thoughts of *A Christmas Carol* drifted into his head before he was brought sharply to attention by edgy words from Roger.

'You may scoff, but I notice that you live well on the profits they bring you. For instance that suit you've got on, that sort of tailoring doesn't come cheap. Where did you get it? Not, surely, in America.' Roger was something of a dandy, and had been admiring Hal's tweeds ever since he'd come in to breakfast.

'Savile Row. I go to Urquhart,' Hal said.

'There you are, then,' Peter said. 'Perfectly happy to take the money and yet ready to snipe at me about how the money's made. You ought to be damn grateful to me for taking care of your inheritance so well, I work extremely long hours myself. I shan't be taking much time off over Christmas, I've brought plenty of work home with me.'

155

'I don't doubt it,' murmured Hal.

He had spent a lot of time in the library as a boy and a young man. His grandfather had been a literate man, who had added considerably to the eighteenth-century collection that already existed. Hal had appreciated both the books and the solitude.

Neither Peter nor Roger had much time for such books. Roger took an entirely practical view of his reading matter: if a book was useful to him in some way, he read it, otherwise he didn't. Peter had been known to open the odd book on fishing, but mostly his attention to the printed word was restricted to the daily newspaper and trade literature pertaining to the world of sanitary ware.

This accounted for the unused atmosphere of the library. A shame, thought Hal, for it was a beautiful room, designed after Adam and with a lightness lacking in most of Grindley Hall.

As though he were reading his mind, Peter informed Hal that Eve had great plans for the library. 'She's going to do it over, tremendous taste, Eve has.'

Admiration and adoration glowed in his eyes for a moment, before he turned to more vital and immediate matters.

'How's business in America these days?' he ventured by way of a preamble.

Hal raised his eyebrows. 'My business in particular, or business in general?'

'Your business? What business? You aren't in business over there, are you?'

'I meant the theatrical business.'

'Oh, that. No, Henry Ford, oil, factories, that sort of business.'

'Depressed, one gathers.'

'Depressed! Is that all you can say?'

'The New Deal seems to be paying off.'

'The New Deal is nothing but communism under another

name. That fellow Roosevelt is a blackguard, not fit to be president, I don't know how he came to be voted in, and the sooner the electorate comes to its senses and votes him out, the better.'

'He carries the women voters,' Roger said.

'Women voters!'

Hal sighed. This was going to be even more tedious than he feared. 'Unemployment is intolerably high, since you ask, and coloured people in particular have been very hard hit by the depression.'

'Coloured people? Negroes, do you mean? Wish we had some of those over here, they're prepared to do a good day's work for next to nothing, I dare say.'

'Slavery has been abolished in the United States, I believe.'

Peter glared at him. 'Is that some kind of a joke?'

Roger intervened. 'I think it would be best if we returned to our own business, Peter. You can't expect Hal to be *au fait* with the American economy, he simply doesn't understand that kind of thing.'

Hal felt it was time to get off this dangerous ground. His dislike of Peter and all he stood for was at this moment so intense that he was afraid of losing his temper, and with it any advantage he might have. 'Did you ask me to come in here to discuss America?'

'Of course I didn't, whatever gave you that idea?' Peter said. 'We want to talk about your shares in Jowetts. You still have them?'

'Yes. Why shouldn't I?'

Peter's face was reddening.

'Don't pretend to be a simpleton,' Roger said. 'Naturally we were concerned lest you sell your stake in the company to some stranger, or even a rival firm.'

'I see. But would it make any difference to you who owned my shares? My holdings amount to no more than twenty per cent, I think.'

'Which gives you a controlling interest,' snapped Peter. He had at first sat down at the big round table in the centre of the room, but had now risen and was pacing up and down on the parquet floor in the most irritating way.

How he hates being at any kind of a disadvantage, Hal thought. And just what was he up to? Peter must have more of a reason than this to be so keen to get his hands on those shares. The three brothers held equal shares, and the remaining forty per cent was in the name of their father's sister, who had inherited them when her own father had died, but who never took the slightest interest in anything to do with the firm. Peter was her proxy, so he could always do just as he wanted.

'My twenty per cent would only matter if Aunt Daphne wanted to become involved, and she never has, has she?' Hal asked.

'It's a matter of presenting a united front,' Peter said.

He's lying, thought Hal. Why?

The door opened, and a maid came in with coffee.

'Who asked you to bring that?' Peter said.

The maid's face didn't change an iota at his aggressive manner. 'Mrs Grindley told me to bring the coffee in, sir. Shall I pour for you?'

'No, leave it, leave it. We'll see to it.' Peter waited until the door shut behind the maid with a defiant clunk. 'Where were we?'

Roger took a cup of coffee, added several brown crystal sugar lumps and stirred the brew with neat, precise movements. 'If you'll let me, Peter,' he said, sitting down again. He munched noisily on a biscuit. 'Aren't you having coffee, Hal?'

'No, I had enough at breakfast, thank you.'

'It's like this. Peter and I are concerned about you.' He raised a hand as Hal was about to speak. 'No, let me go on. You are in an uncertain profession, and although one is pleased to see you keeping up appearances, one is aware that your acting career has not been crowned with the kind of success that brings any appreciable financial rewards. Indeed, I think it is true to say that you haven't worked in several years.'

'Now, how the devil do you know that?' said Hal. Really, he had underestimated his brothers' cunning. What were they up to?

'We made enquiries,' Roger said.

Which meant that they must have expended money, quite a lot of money, probably. For whatever reason they wanted his shares, they wanted them badly. Fine, he liked bargaining from a position of strength. No doubt it hadn't occurred to them simply to ask him to sell them, in which case he'd have agreed. He could invest the money elsewhere, the family shares held no sentimental value for him, and if his brothers needed them for some scheme or other, he would be perfectly happy to oblige. However, they had chosen to take the scenic route, so he would watch them sweat a while.

The immediate fulfilment of this pleasure was to be denied him. Even as Peter drew breath to launch into his case, voices could be heard outside the library door. Peter stopped abruptly, a keen and happy look spreading over his face, and, ignoring Roger and Hal, he bounded to the door.

It opened, to reveal an exquisitely fair young woman, wearing what Hal saw at a glance was a Paris model, with a fur tumbling from her shoulders. She had huge blue eyes, a sulky mouth and an affected air.

'Rosalind, dear child,' cried Peter. 'How are you, my petal?'

Petal? What was this? Had Peter succumbed to that most dangerous of yearnings, late middle-age dazzled by an under-twenty? No, Hal decided, watching the pair of them. Peter's affection was definitely paternal, there was a light of pride in his eyes that Hal hadn't noticed when he was with either of his sons or with Ursula.

Clearly Eve, who tripped into the library on her daughter's

heels, had no worries of a more intimate and unseemly liking on her husband's part. And Hal reckoned she was shrewd enough to have instantly noticed any such tendency, Eve was not a woman likely to have any wool pulled over her sharp eyes.

Rosalind's mouth, now more rosebud than sulky, took on a smile as she stood on tiptoe to kiss Peter's cheek. 'Hello, Peterdaddy, have you missed me?'

Peterdaddy! Hal exchanged looks with Roger, who was wearing his court face of profound disapproval and exaggerated disappointment.

'Rosalind, my dear, come and meet your new uncle. This is Hal.'

Hal looked down at his newly acquired niece with appreciation. She certainly was something, even if not remotely the kind of woman he would ever choose to spend time with – not only because she was so young and would therefore bore him, but because she was simply not his type.

She was vamping him shamelessly, after an initial look of surprise.

'You aren't in the least bit like Peterdaddy, nor like Uncle Roger,' she said.

She couldn't, Hal noticed with amusement, quite pronounce her Rs. It wasn't exactly Uncle Woger, but pretty nearly. Uncle Woger, after a brief salutation, was making his getaway. Good, that meant that business was over for the day, and he, too, might escape.

Eve put a hand on his shoulder. It looked light, but her grip was firm. 'You mustn't run away, Hal, just when you've met your new niece.'

Hal was about to say that a step-niece, if that was what she was, was definitely a no-niece as far as he was concerned, but he caught the glint in Eve's eye. Anything for a quiet life. Dammit, though, why did the wretched woman make him feel like a guest in the house he had grown up in? Why did he go along with it, why not say, Sorry, Eve, I have other fish to fry?

Because he hadn't and because to do so would be to annoy Peter, and Hal wasn't in a teasing mood. Besides, he wanted another look at Rosalind; he'd once again felt a tug of familiarity when she came into the library. Was he suffering from some kind of mental kink, brought on by the blinding whiteness of the snow or by the shock of coming home, with this propensity to invest every stranger with the identity of someone he knew or had known?

He laughed at himself, said he'd stay and lunch at the Hall, and headed for the morning room, where he rang for the maid to ask for a cup of coffee, made with double the usual amount of coffee, please, he liked his coffee rich and strong.

The maid looked doubtful. Mrs Grindley was most particular about how coffee should be made, she'd told the kitchen to use a special measure for the grounds, not to be exceeded.

'Then use her measure for the coffee, but make it with only a half, no, a third, of the amount of water. I'm sure that won't cause any problems in the kitchen.'

It was his smile rather than his reasoning that won a stifled giggle and, a little later, a pot of something approximating to coffee.

Not that he was allowed to enjoy it in peace. Roger came prowling into the morning room where Hal had hidden himself with the paper, and sniffed the air.

'That smells good. Mind if I ring for another cup? The stuff they gave us just now was miserable.'

At least Roger wasn't inclined to talk, and the brothers sat wrapped in the taciturn companionship of English families until the luncheon bell went.

Angela gestured to Hal to come and sit beside her. 'What do you think of the young lady?' she asked in an undertone as she took out her napkin.

161

'I reserve judgement,' he replied.

She gave him an amused look. 'You hardly need to say any more. I feel so sorry for Ursula.'

Ursula had a resigned look on her face as Eve encouraged Rosalind to tell the company all about her successes in Munich.

'Bet she had a fling with the fencing master,' Cecy muttered into her napkin. Ursula grinned, and gave her cousin an appreciative kick under the table.

Peter was in an extremely good mood, Eve was triumphant, Rosalind talkative, and the rest of the company glum.

Hal ate his stew without attending to its meagre nature, for he had remembered where he had seen Rosalind. It had been at Euston, when he was boarding the train to come north. She had caught his eye because she looked so young, as though she should have a mother or nurse or governess in charge of her – did English girls still have governesses, he wondered fleetingly, or did they all go to school like Ursula? – yet she was too elegantly dressed for a schoolgirl. Especially with that little hat. The hat served a purpose, though, he noticed, as she had tweaked down its little veil and became an anonymous woman, a creature of mystery.

This creature of mystery had got off the train before him, he'd seen her disembark at Preston, Preston of all unlikely places for a veiled stranger, and hurry, little suitcase in hand, towards the exit.

Yet here she was, talking as though she'd travelled north overnight on the sleeper. He was intrigued. She had, everyone assumed, been staying with friends in London since her arrival from Germany. Important friends, judging by the way Eve repeated their name with intense satisfaction; Hal had never heard of them.

He had his own very good idea of what a seventeen-year-old girl might be up to, pretending to be in one place while travelling alone to other places, and it wasn't something that Eve, still less Peter, would approve of. In fact, they would be appalled. However, he wasn't one to moralize about such matters, and what this piece of perfection got up to meant nothing to him personally, although he might use his knowledge to quell her if she went on patronizing Ursula.

'Don't you know that, Ursula darling?' Rosalind was saying now.

'No, I don't. I've never been abroad, so you can swank away about how foreigners are like this and like that all you want. I can't say it interests me much.'

Attagirl, Hal said to himself, as Ursula dug into her indifferent pudding with an aggressive spoon.

TWENTY

Ursula went off after lunch to write a savage entry in her journal.

'I wouldn't mind half so much if Daddy weren't so stupid about Rosalind. Can't he see what she's like? No, he can't. She's the kind of daughter he'd love to have had, all feminine and pretty and sweet. He can't smell the vinegar on her breath, that's all. And it's no good telling him how mean Eve is when it comes to spending any money on me, since he won't listen to a word I say on the subject. Eve wants to be a mother to me, he tells me, she has my best interests at heart, she knows what's suitable for a girl of my age.

'One of these days, I'm going to lose my temper and shout at him, "I've got a mother and she's worth a hundred Eves." It's grim not being able to see Mummy, I keep thinking that I won't mind so much as time goes on, but I do. Still, I got a letter yesterday. I think Eve's suspicious of Nanny's correspondence, I hope she doesn't start snooping. I'll have to warn Nanny to be on her guard.

'Anyhow, that's enough of me, this journal is for training to be a writer, not for going on about my life. So I'll make a few observations. One, I think Uncle Hal is a dark horse.

Daddy and Uncle Roger had counted on his being a pushover, a down-at-heel actor, grateful for handouts. In which case, of course he'd have sold those shares they go on about ages ago. He must be making a living somehow, he looks awfully prosperous. Perhaps he's a kept man, it's odd that he hasn't married, he's quite old.

'Second, my brothers. Something's up with Nicky, and I don't know what it is, I dare say it's to do with school, but he just clams up when I try to find out. I shall watch him and see what I can glean. Third, Simon is gone on Rosalind, I thought he rather liked her last time he was here, and he has a really jammy expression when he looks at her. He'd better buck up if he's going to take Daddy on about going into the army after Cambridge, rather than joining up for the lav pans; if he spends his time mooning around after Rosalind, no one will take him seriously.

'Shall stop now, as Cecy has shouted up that she and Uncle Hal are going to Wyncrag. Me, too, to see Perdy, and for tea. The food is getting worse and worse here, but it's always heavenly at Wyncrag.'

TWENTY-ONE

'Hal,' said a familiar, well-bred voice.

Hal started, turned, saw Lady Richardson standing beside the drawing-room door.

'Cecy, Alix is in the sitting room,' she said. 'Ursula, I expect you'll find Perdita in the old nursery.'

Hal was amused to see how rapidly Cecy and Ursula vanished in search of their respective friends. Hal had meant to ask for Sir Henry, but before he could say so, Lady Richardson was leading the way across the hall and through a door held open by Rokeby. He followed her obediently into the drawing room.

How big Wyncrag was. Places remembered from childhood were so often disappointingly small when one returned to them years later, but with Wyncrag, the opposite was the case, everything seemed larger, like this vast drawing room, set under an astonishing dome. It belonged to another age, an age of huge families and house parties. He sat down amid a bunch of tall ferns clustered around a palm, his feet sinking into the thick red patterned carpet.

'Tea will be in twenty minutes,' Lady Richardson said. 'I heard that you called on Henry.'

Lipp, that was the name of Lady Richardson's maid, that

appalling Frenchwoman who pried into everything and always wore black. She must have seen him when he was with Sir Henry.

'They tell me you are an actor now.' Lady Richardson's voice held all the scorn of her class and generation for such a reckless and déclassé calling. 'You do not look to me like an actor.'

Lady Richardson had always awed Hal, and he felt the old panic rising in him now. He quelled it. He wasn't a boy, nor a neighbour, politeness was all that could be asked of him.

'I chose a life in the theatrical profession many years ago, when I left home.'

'There are many branches of that profession. One might say that Shakespeare was a member of the theatrical profession.'

How much did she know or guess about his brief career as an actor? He looked at her sitting there, with her inscrutable face and the upright figure of her generation. She carried her years lightly, she didn't look that much older than when last he'd seen her. Her eyes were more hooded, but their penetrating gaze hadn't changed at all, and they still had the power to mesmerize and terrorize.

'I'm no Shakespeare, I've never even contemplated writing a play. My talents do not lie in that direction.'

'No?' There was a world of meaning in her intonation of the simple world.

'A playwright's lot is not an easy one.'

'I would have said, from my knowledge of you as a boy, that even if drawn to a dramatic milieu, you would choose a more authoritative role than that of a mere player.'

Hal looked up into the greenery above his head. 'Really? People so rarely turn out as one expects.'

'Do you speak from your own experience? For my part, I find I am usually right about the kind of adults children become.'

'I haven't caught up with Edwin yet,' Hal said, keen to

change the subject. Lady Richardson was coming a good deal too close to the truth for his liking; not that there was any particular point to secrecy on the subject of his career, but it would be awkward to have to explain himself to his family just now. 'Although I did meet Alix out skating. I hear she's hurt her ankle, not a serious injury, I trust?'

'A twisted ankle is hardly anything to be concerned about.'

Lady Richardson's tone was acidic, better to get away from Alix and her ankle.

She spoke again, before he could gather his wits and light on a safer topic. 'You will find it strange to visit Wyncrag and not find Helena here.'

Hal winced inwardly, but kept a cool expression, or so he hoped. 'That was the saddest thing. And Isabel as well.'

'It was not the greatest of my losses.'

Damned woman. She was implying that Jack was more of a loss than Helena and her granddaughter. Not in his book, he wasn't.

'You were greatly attached to Helena,' she said matter-of-factly. 'Calf love is always so painful.'

Hal simply stared at her. Here he was, a visitor, a stranger almost, paying a call after an absence of sixteen years, how could she make a remark like that to him? About him?

Easily, he told himself. Lady Richardson had always gone for the jugular.

'I don't suppose you heard the details of the accident. It was a very unfortunate affair.'

Unfortunate?

'She was intoxicated, and made the dangerous decision to drive a motor car while under the influence of alcohol. She paid the price, as did her child.'

'I don't remember Helena ever being a heavy drinker.'

'She went to pieces after Neville died.'

Now that Hal didn't believe. And he had Nanny's letters to prove it. Helena had been distraught, but bore up very well, Nanny had said, in trying circumstances. She had been much occupied with Isabel, who had been ill, and that helped to take her mind off the tragic loss of her husband.

Why was Lady Richardson telling him all this? What possible response could she expect from him?

'She had everyone's sympathy. People are such fools, they imagine the loss of a husband is a greater grief than the loss of a son. They are wrong.'

It flashed into his mind that Helena had loved Neville deeply; had Lady Richardson ever had such intense feelings for her husband?

'Are you a single man? Or perhaps married and divorced, I understand that in America, people go in for divorce.'

'I haven't gone in for either marriage or divorce,' he said uncomfortably.

'Surely not wearing the willow for Helena after all these years?'

'I don't know what you imagine I . . .' he began, then stopped. She was goading him, needling him to say more than he wanted to. 'I never met the right woman, and mine is a roving life, we of the stage go hither and thither, hardly conducive to a settled home life, you will agree.' Why was he talking in this stilted way, why did he think that would deflect her?

It probably wouldn't have, but, to his enormous relief, Rokeby came in, leading a stately procession of tea bearers: a tall footman pushing a gently rattling trolley, a parlour maid carrying a silver tray, another maid holding a cake stand aloft. In the lighting of the little spirit stove to boil the kettle, the nice arrangement of the Dresden china, the silver tea caddy, teapot, water jug, strainer on its dish, sugar basin with lumps, sugar bowl with caster sugar, tongs, spoons, muffin dish and various other gleaming items that Hal couldn't guess the purpose of, the subject of Helena and marriage was dropped.

Only temporarily. Alix limped in, leaning on a stick. Cecy hovered beside her, on hand to help her sit down.

'Leave her alone, Cecy,' said Lady Richardson, 'or we shall have to ask Hal, our dramatic expert, to give her some advice. Where are the others?'

'Miss Perdita and Miss Ursula are washing their hands,' Rokeby said, twirling the three-storey cake stand on its base as he took it from the maid and set it on the table. 'Mr Edwin has just come in and is taking off his outdoor clothes. Sir Henry is in his workshop, but will be here directly.'

'Sit there, Alix, and don't fuss,' her grandmother ordered.

That was quite unfair, Hal thought, since Alix wasn't making the least fuss.

'We were just speaking of your late mother,' Lady Richardson went on.

Hal blinked. What was she up to? He noticed, with a practised eye, the slight stiffening of tension in Alix's body, the wary look that came into her eyes.

'Were you?' she said with studied indifference. 'Did you know her well, Mr Grindley?'

'The Grindleys and the Richardsons have always been close neighbours,' he said, at his most noncommittal.

There was a hubbub in the hall, and Perdita came in with Ursula. Lady Richardson pounced.

'This is Mr Grindley, Perdita. He left the lake before you were born, but was a close friend of your mother's.'

'And of your father's,' Hal added.

Perdita didn't seem interested in Hal or her parents; she was eyeing the cakes. 'I met him, on the ice. He was with Cecy,' she said. 'Rokeby, is that coffee cake?'

'What have you been doing this afternoon?' her grandmother asked in a cold, hard voice that shocked Hal. What had Perdita done to deserve that? He wouldn't speak to a dog in that tone, and this child was Lady Richardson's granddaughter, for God's sake.

'Listening to the gramophone in the old nursery,' Perdita lied.

'Dancing,' Ursula said, equally untruthfully. 'Practising our steps.'

Hal could tell they were covering up; he wondered what youthful secrets were being concealed.

Rokeby sprang into action, whipping the silver kettle off the stove, desiring the attendant maids to hand toast, crumpets, muffins, raspberry and strawberry jam, honey, lemon curd, quince jelly.

Hal had forgotten the ritual of northern English afternoon tea. Eve, perhaps for reasons of economy, had dispensed with the full glory of the meal. 'No one wants more than a cup of plain tea and perhaps a biscuit, not after lunch and with dinner to come.'

She should see this, Hal thought, admiring his niece's attack on the food, ably aided by Perdita. Nice kid, though he didn't care to see a child of that age with such a shuttered look to her when she was talking to her grandmother. The same closed, give-nothing-away face that Alix had.

A face that changed totally, in Alix's case, as the door opened and Edwin came in, his cheeks glowing with fresh air. 'Tea,' he cried. 'I'm ravenous.'

'And where have you been?' Lady Richardson's voice had lost some of its sharpness. Edwin, one gathered, enjoyed a different status to that of her granddaughters.

'Oh, in my studio,' Edwin said. 'Developing some pictures I took of the lake.' He advanced on Hal, hand extended. 'You must be Hal. Welcome home! It's a long time since we met.'

Developing pictures indeed; here was another liar, reflected Hal as he shook hands with Edwin. And this twin did bring back Helena: the hair, the eyes, the way he stood, the set of his jaw. It was uncanny, and slightly disturbing. Hal took a deep breath and launched into a series of anodyne remarks about the weather, the ice, the frost, the skaters, was Edwin

171

planning to do any racing, had he got the ice yacht out? Anything not to look at Lady Richardson, who was watching with malice gleaming from her eyes as they darted to and fro to see how Hal reacted to Edwin, who was so like his mother.

He'd confounded her on that one, Hal felt, as he bit into a crumpet, and memories of all the glorious teas of his youth came back to him. There was a timeless quality to this hour towards the end of the afternoon, with the fire in the enormous marble fireplace glowing and crackling. It needed a bigger cast, however, there should be at least a dozen people sitting down with cups and saucers and plates of buttery food to talk over the day's activities.

He noted the colours in the room, the darkness of the glass panes in the dome, the soft lights over each picture – and what pictures they were. Why had he never noticed what a fine collection hung here? A Sargent of Sir Henry's father surveyed the room from above the fireplace, three first-class paintings of the German school on the far wall, that brilliant racing scene must be a Sisley, and several French paintings from the end of the nineteenth century, Impressionists, glowed with light and colour.

Absorbed in the pictures, he didn't notice the other arrivals, and was jolted out of his artistic contemplation to apologize, rise to his feet, be kissed by Jane – good God, what was eating her soul? – and have his hand shaken by Saul, sleek and with that English air of plummy prosperity. A southern look, he felt; northerners had their own aura of wealth and success, but it was less smooth, lacked the polish of a Saul.

'Hal, my dear.'

Trudie, with her floating scarves and vague expression and ways, whom he had always suspected of being a good deal more sharp-minded than she appeared. He gave her a warm embrace.

'How handsome you've become, and so urbane. I can see that America suits you. Rokeby, more tea for Mr Hal. Come

172

and sit beside me here, on this sofa. Then you can tell me about yourself, and you can see everyone, so many old friends, such a shock I dare say, diving back into the past. Not a good idea, in so many cases, and of course last time you were here, it was nineteen twenty, wasn't it? The Christmas of nineteen twenty, you went off to London in the new year, and the next we heard, you were in America. It wasn't a good year, nineteen twenty-one, not in this house, but you know all about that, and one mustn't dwell on the past. In America everyone is so modern, having so little history they don't live in the past so much, I always think.'

Hal listened to Trudie's disjointed but peaceful conversation with only half his attention. Snatches of conversation from the others came to his ears.

Perdita was talking about the past, too. Ghosts, Jemima at school lived in a wing of a castle, her father looked after it, a ruin mostly, but full of ghosts, wandering about the place as though they owned it. 'Which I suppose they do, in a way,' she finished.

Lady Richardson shot her a look of rigid disapproval.

'Grandmama won't have anything to do with the supernatural,' Perdita whispered to Ursula. 'It always annoys her, any mention of ghosts.'

'She isn't listening to you, she's telling your Uncle Saul what to think about Churchill and all his war talk,' Ursula replied. .

'She thinks everything I say is nonsense, anyhow, so it doesn't matter if I talk about ghosts. So you see, I wonder what it's like being somewhere that everything in English history has happened in or to, wars and feuds and Catholics and Protestants and sons going off to war and all that.'

'I wish I had a friend who had a ghost,' Ursula said enviously.

Sir Henry had joined the party, and he chewed a sandwich vigorously as he listened to the girls' chatter. 'They did say there was a ghost over at the Hall, Ursula. You want to ask your father about it. Figures flitting to and fro where the old dairy used to be. All pulled down now, of course.'

Ursula pulled a face. 'No point asking Daddy, he wouldn't take any notice if Charles the First, with his head under his arm, came into the room, he doesn't believe in ghosts. I'd like to dress up as a ghost and give Rosalind a good fright,' she added in an undertone to Perdita. She looked up, and saw Hal's eyes on her. 'You've got long ears, Uncle Hal; don't go telling Eve what I say, will you?'

Hal raised an eyebrow. 'Do you take me for a sneak?'

'Not really.'

'We don't have any ghosts at Wyncrag, do we, Grandpapa? It isn't old enough for ghosts.'

'No, Wyncrag isn't haunted. Just as well, it's the last thing I want, to turn a corner and come face to face with my old guv'nor, he'd be bound to want to tell me I was going about something in quite the wrong way.'

Hal's attention returned to what Trudie was saying. 'Of course, one always imagines actual spectres, only ghosts come in so many forms and far more frightening than a figure in white flitting about the corridors. Recent ghosts are so much more threatening than headless kings, don't you agree? I don't suppose they ever go away. Some people are haunted in their dreams, and that's so tricky, since you think it's only a dream yet it may be so much more. Perhaps some clever man in America will tell us how to control our dreams and banish the nightmares and the hauntings, do you think that may be so, Hal?'

Hal had been looking at Alix, and had to pull himself together to deal with this unexpectedly firm ending to Trudie's sentence. 'Dreams? Oh, American dreams are all good ones, they don't allow any others.'

'But Uncle Hal,' protested Ursula. 'Americans must have . . .'

Perdita dug her in the ribs. 'He's joking.'

Alix's face, when not shadowed and shuttered, but as it was now, laughing at the girls, was captivating. There was something about her, quite unlike Helena's charm and allure, a kind of toughness and character that made Hal want to know her better. The word interesting came to mind again. What did he mean by interesting? Unusual, different? Intelligent, mysterious, intriguing? He came to the conclusion that although Alix might or might not possess any of those qualities, what he meant was that she interested him. He found her attractive, he wanted to know her better, he would like to know what went on inside her head and whether she had a heart.

She might, on closer acquaintance, prove to be a chip off the old block of another kind, the hostility between her and her grandmother could mask an essential similarity. In which case, heaven help anyone who had much to do with her. No one in their right mind would want a Caroline Richardson in their lives.

TWENTY-TWO

Alix's ankle was bothering her. Not because it was excep-
tionally painful; it only hurt if she put her weight on it, but
because she hated having to haul herself about on a stick and
hated even more being an object of anyone's sympathy. Hal
had that look on his face just now, he was feeling sorry for
her, she was sure of it. She frowned at him and smiled encour-
agingly at Jane, who was talking to Cecy about the Simpson
divorce.

'If he marries her, people's attitude to divorce is bound to
change,' Jane was saying.

'Do you think so? I wish that were true,' Cecy said. 'I
know lots of people who are trapped in wretched marriages,
and the reason they stay together is simply fear of social
stigma.'

'Does your generation care about divorce?' Aunt Jane asked,
taking out a slim gold cigarette case and offering it to Cecy.

'Not for me, thanks,' Cecy said. 'I'm trying to break the
habit, patients don't like lady doctors with the smell of cigarette smoke on their breath.'

'Doctors always seem to be smoking,' Jane said, leaning
forward to light her cigarette from Hal's lighter. 'Country
doctors go about with pipes in their mouths, and my Harley

Street man smokes cigars. I suppose it's different for a woman. I have to say, I find the whole idea of women doctors faintly repulsive. Forgive me for saying so.'

'It's an opinion you share with most of the population,' Cecy replied equably. 'Including my father and Uncle Peter.'

'Have they been going on at you again?' Alix asked.

'It's more a matter of never leaving off. They only have to catch sight of me and they start to harangue.' She gave a sudden smile. 'Just you wait, that's nothing to the furore there'll be when Daddy finds out that Mummy's secretly boning up on her medicine. She says that when the war comes, they'll need any doctor who can stand up straight and remember his name. Or her name; old men, drunks, women, they'll have to take anyone they can find.'

Jane gave a little shiver. 'Don't mention the word war, please, Cecy.'

Cecy shot her a quick glance, and went on. 'Mummy flew at Uncle Peter last night for being rather beastly about my training, but it's all water off a duck's back with him. And Eve doesn't help, with her little coos of dismay at how unfeminine I'm becoming and how glad she is that Rosalind doesn't want to do a man's job. Which is as well, since she's got the brains of a peahen and is virtually illiterate.'

Jane fingered her pearls. 'I rather wish I'd never introduced Peter and Eve. You know how it is, two tiresome people, you're quite glad to push them together and escape.'

'Goodness, was it you who did that?' said Cecy. 'Was Uncle Peter in London?'

'Yes, and I knew Eve slightly, from a committee we were both on, although a close friend she was not. Rather a hanger-on if truth be told, she's a terrific snob in that depressing middle-class way. Sucked up to me because of Saul's position, what good could knowing Saul do anyone, I ask you? Anyhow, I do blame myself a bit, for I hear from Trudie that she's not very nice to the children.'

As always, her eyes clouded slightly at the very mention of the word. Alix, made unusually perceptive by having to lie down and keep still, was surprised. Perhaps Aunt Jane regretted not having children. Grandmama had always maintained that she didn't want them on account of the genetic risk, so sensible about that kind of thing, Grandmama had commented more than once.

And Aunt Jane was being more outspoken than usual, there was almost a reckless air about her, as though she'd come to some decision about her life. Perhaps she was going to divorce Uncle Saul, Alix thought, and then laughed at such a preposterous notion; Grandmama wouldn't tolerate divorce in the family, not for a moment. Aunt Jane's only chance of a divorce would be if Uncle Saul agreed to it, and he would never, ever go against his mother's wishes.

In the distance, she could just hear the sound of the front door. Rokeby, who had been standing by the teapot only a second before, was nowhere to be seen, but he reappeared to announce two visitors. 'Dr Kerr and Mr Wrexham,' he said, with a flick of his eyelid towards the more junior of the maids, indicating that she should fetch additional cups and saucers and plates.

Grandpapa drew the visitors closer to the fire, hardly allowing them to make their greetings.

'We came over to enquire after Miss Richardson's ankle,' Freddie said, when he could get a word in. 'Still keeping it up, I see, quite right.'

Alix liked him. He wasn't patronizing or pushy, and she liked his friend, too. Michael Wrexham was not the kind of young man she had had much to do with and she was curious about him. An aircraft designer, her grandfather had told her. A clever young man, in his opinion, and he'd heard of his boss, Giles Gibson, who was doing great things with the company he had founded.

'Come and sit here,' she said to him, seeing that Freddie

and Cecy had recognised one another and had fallen into shop talk about St Luke's Hospital, where Cecy was doing her training and where Freddie had been a junior doctor.

'Tell me about the kind of aeroplanes you work with,' she said. 'Are they the ones people buy for fun, or are you much too serious for that?'

He laughed, and accepted a cup of tea from the maid. He dropped two lumps of sugar into it and stirred it awkwardly with the tiny silver teaspoon. 'All aeroplanes are serious as far as I'm concerned. Now, with what's happening in Spain, everyone's wondering if we're going to need fighter planes and bombers, so that's what I'm working on.'

His words coincided with one of those silences that comes over a gathering of such a kind, and Grindleys and Richardsons alike froze at the mention of the forbidden topic.

Alix was amused by people's expressions, which ranged from a look of mild concern on Grandpapa's face through Edwin and Uncle Saul and Aunt Jane's visible alarm, to Freddie's puzzled look. Hal was watching her watching the others; a smile lurked in his eyes and the corners of his mouth twitched. She averted her gaze and caught a look of contempt from Grandmama.

'I am not quite sure whether you are in business or in a profession, Mr Wrexham,' she said.

'Both, in a way, Lady Richardson,' was his quick reply. 'Without customers, there would be no money for design. We aren't a research establishment, we have to sell our aeroplanes in order to move ahead with new ideas and plans. Giles Gibson, whose firm it is, is a qualified designer, but he is more of a salesman these days. Has to be.'

'Indeed. Isn't that rather a waste of a professional training?'

'Not in my field, no. No one would buy our kind of aircraft from a man who didn't know the machines inside out.'

'I see. And where did you get your training?'

'I was at Edinburgh University, and then I spent three years at the Aeronautical Institute.'

Alix could see that Michael, although standing up well to the interrogation, was beginning to feel uncomfortable. She tried to catch Grandpapa's eye, to get him to put a stop to it, but he was watching Michael with approval and didn't look her way.

Someone had to intervene, she thought. Oh well, it might as well be her, at least she was used to incurring Grandmama's displeasure. 'Do you intend to sell any planes to either side in Spain?' she asked Michael.

He turned gratefully towards her. 'The planes they are using in Spain are all on one side, and they're German. Getting in their practice for bigger things, some people in my field think.'

Lady Richardson's voice was glacial. 'I believe this country is selling aircraft engines to Germany. They wish to build up their flying industry, for transport and passenger traffic. The Prime Minister thoroughly approves of such sales.'

Michael let out a kind of rueful sigh. 'Well, Lady Richardson,' he began, 'Mr Baldwin may want —' when there was a crash and a tinkle of broken china.

'What a butterfingers I am,' cried Edwin. 'So sorry, Grandmama.'

Bother Grandmama, thought Alix. She wasn't going to be deflected, except to nod to one of the maids to clear it up, not now the subject of Germany had come up. 'Your step-sister has just returned from Germany, Ursula, has she not?'

Ursula swallowed the last fragment of a scone too quickly and fell into a fit of coughing, turning scarlet with lack of breath and embarrassment. 'Yes, Lady Richardson,' she managed to say, finally. 'Munich. She's come back terrifically pro-Nazi.'

'It will be interesting to hear what she has to say. Although she can hardly be expected to have any grasp of the economic and political realities of German life, she has at least first-hand experience of the modern Germany.'

'Just so, my dear,' said Sir Henry.

'People in this country are all too ready to condemn the Nazis. I wonder how we should feel if countries across the channel took it upon themselves to denigrate a democratic, elected government of ours.'

Nazis again, Alix thought dispiritedly. Even here, where any talk of war was on the banned list, Grandmama was prepared to extol the virtues of the Nazis, just as Cecy would go on and on about how awful they were. It would end up with one of those polite but vicious English arguments, where so much more was implied than said.

Lipp came into the room, looking furtive, Alix thought, but that was probably just her imagination. She went over to Lady Richardson and murmured something in her ear.

'You will excuse me, but there is a telephone call I wish to take. Good afternoon to you, Mr Wrexham and Mr Kerr, no, of course, it's Dr Kerr, isn't it? Please give my regards to your father and mother, Cecy.'

Alix twisted herself around to watch her grandmother's stately progress from the room. Grandmama take a telephone call in the middle of tea? It was unheard of. Whoever could it be to merit such attention? She saw Edwin watching the door shut behind their grandmother and knew that he was wondering exactly the same thing. He turned and smiled at her, giving a quick shrug to indicate that he had no idea who it might be on the telephone.

'More tea,' said Sir Henry, waving at the trolley. 'Rokeby, I'm sure these young men could do with some more tea. Have you been out on the ice much? Have you ever been in these parts before when the lake is frozen?'

'Never, sir,' said Freddie. 'But Michael was here sixteen years ago, when he was a boy, and he says it was frozen then.'

'Were you, now?' said Sir Henry to Michael. 'With your family? Where did you stay?'

'I don't remember very much about it,' Michael said. 'I went down with pneumonia, and so my memory of it is all rather vague.'

'Just so, just so; tricky thing, pneumonia. Now, I hope that you and Freddie will dine with us while you're here. I want to hear more about this aircraft business.'

Michael called across to Freddie, who was once more deep in conversation with Cecy. 'Sir Henry is asking us to dine one day.'

'That's northern hospitality for you,' said Freddie. 'I take that very kindly, sir, we should like to. And here's Miss Grindley inviting us to a dance at Grindley Hall.'

'Your aunt will be pleased to have two extra men, I dare say,' said Jane.

Meaning, Alix knew, was it all right for Cecy to invite people to the dance.

Cecy knew exactly what Jane meant. 'It's quite all right, Eve said I was to ask any friends from up here. She doesn't know so many people of our age, and she wants lots of young men for Rosalind to meet.'

'Don't look keen, Freddie,' Ursula put in. 'She's simply foul.'

'Ursula, you oughtn't to go first-naming people like that,' Cecy said.

'Oh, Freddie doesn't mind, do you, Freddie?'

Perdita had wandered over to the grand piano when Lady Richardson had left the room and had been quietly playing chords to herself. Alix had asked if she used the piano in here, but Perdita had shaken her head, no, she hardly ever did, she preferred to practise up on the old nursery piano where nobody could hear her. 'If I played here, Lipp would tell on me, even if Grandmama weren't about at the time, you know what she's like. I wish I could play it more, it's quite a good piano. Aunt Trudie makes Rokeby keep it tuned, you know, just in case I get the chance to use it. It's very kind of her.'

Trudie had gone to stand beside Perdita and was encouraging her to play. Perdita gave her a swift smile, and bent her head to continue with her chords.

'Play for us, Perdy,' Alix called out. 'Some carols, why not? It is Christmas.'

Perdita's rather intense expression lightened, and she began to play the tune of *The Holly and the Ivy*, picking up the theme and improvising upon it before moving on to the *Wassail Song*.

'Very evocative,' said Hal, materialising at Alix's elbow in time to help her to her feet.

'The spirit of Christmas isn't conspicuous at Wyncrag, was it the same in your day?' That came out sounding rude; she had only wanted to keep him at a distance.

'Oh, I remember one or two jolly times.'

'When my parents were alive?'

'Yes,' Hal said easily. 'Helena knew how to keep Christmas, I'm sure your childhood Christmases were happy ones.'

'They didn't last, however. No, there's no need to apologize, I was just stating a fact, not trawling for sympathy.'

'I wasn't going to offer it. Here's your stick, you'd better not try to stalk away without it, or you might topple over, and then I'd have to help you up and you'd have to feel grateful for my strong arm.'

TWENTY-THREE

Alix awoke with her mind full of a red dress. Perdita's red evening dress, in fact.

Why? It was a dream she'd had, she couldn't remember the details, only a lingering memory of Perdy wearing giant seashells around her neck, and her thinking how inappropriate it was. Seashells strung together from the collection in the long gallery, no doubt, what an odd thing to dream about.

Yet it did raise a question. What jewellery did Perdy have to wear with the red evening frock she'd bought in Manchester? It wasn't cut especially low in the neck, but she'd need to wear something. Such ornaments as she possessed were probably on a par with her clothes; a shell necklace might not be so very far off the mark.

That must be her, thumping past the door on the way back from the bathroom. Alix slid out of bed and opened her door to call after her sister.

A damp Perdita, with dripping hair, clad in a hideous flannel dressing gown and clutching a sponge, stopped and looked enquiringly around. 'Oh, sorry, Alix, did I wake you up?'

'No,' said Alix. 'Come in here for a moment. Where did you get that horrible dressing gown from?'

Perdita looked down at herself. 'It is ghastly, isn't it? It's a cast-off of Grandpapa's, mine doesn't fit me and I haven't got around to getting a new one.'

'For heaven's sake do so, I never saw anything so depressing. Now, listen, what jewellery have you got to wear for the dance?'

'A silver locket,' Perdita said at once. 'And several glass bangles.'

Alix waited. 'Is that all?'

'You gave me the locket, you and Edwin.'

'That was years ago.'

'I always wear it.'

Not for a dance you don't, Alix said to herself. Then, 'You'll need something a bit more showy, to go with your new dress.'

'Well, as to that,' Perdita said, 'I wish now I hadn't bought it, although it seemed a good idea at the time. I know that the minute Grandmama claps eyes on it, she'll make me take it off, and I'll have to go pinned into my old organdie. Or not allowed to go at all,' she added gloomily.

'Don't expect the worst.'

'Why not? It's what usually happens, or it is if it's anything to do with Grandmama.'

Alix was opening her jewel case. She had some nice pieces that she'd bought herself or had been given by various admirers, but her tastes ran to the modern. There was nothing here that would really do for Perdita, she thought. Apart from anything else, Perdy was so tall and wide-shouldered. Nothing delicate would be right, either for her or for that dress.

She shut the box. 'Leave it with me.'

What had happened to their mother's jewels? Her grandfather's words came back to her, about Neville buying jewellery for Helena. And she had probably had some of her own, from before she was married. Grandmama would know about it, but she didn't feel inclined to tackle her on the subject. She'd ask Grandpapa first.

He was in his study after breakfast, dealing with papers and delighted to see her. 'You're getting some colour back in your cheeks, that's thanks to Cook's excellent work, proper meals are doing you good. You girls living in London don't look after yourselves.'

Alix didn't want to waste time hearing yet again how much better it would be if she'd come back to Wyncrag. 'Grandpapa, where are Mummy's jewels?'

A wary look came into his faded eyes, but his voice was calm and matter-of-fact. A lifetime of dealing with awkward questions had made him an expert. He answered after a pause, a pause that told Alix she wasn't going to achieve anything by this conversation.

'As to your mother's things, your grandmother saw to all that. Trudie helped her, I imagine. It's a terrible task, going through someone's possessions once they're gone.'

'Jewels aren't the same as clothes and hairbrushes. Jewels have a value.'

'Ah, well, as to that, it was a matter for the trustees. It is in such cases, that's perfectly normal.'

'Grandpapa, you are one of the trustees.'

'With so much to do, and it was so very complicated, your poor dear mother meeting with an accident within a few months of Neville's fall in the Andes. Tax was a problem, I do remember that it kept the lawyers busy for some considerable time.'

Alix was too like her grandfather to be taken in by all this. 'The jewels, her jewels, what became of them?'

He was frowning. 'She died in America, do you see? She had her jewels with her, or many of them. Her family –'

'Do you mean to tell me her family took her jewels? Why would they do that? The lawyers would never permit it, they must have had records of insurance valuations and even receipts, for the pieces you said my father bought her. He was an orderly man.'

'Not all of them, but those she had with her I believe, yes, I'm quite sure they remained in America.' He spoke in a firm voice that had more than a hint of impatience and annoyance in it. 'I leave all that side of things to your grandmother, my dear. You'll really have to ask her, I can't help you.'

This was getting her nowhere. She slid off the arm of the fat leather chair where she'd been perching, and sat down on the seat. Her grandfather eyed her without enthusiasm and moved some papers from one side of his desk to the other. Then he opened and shut the hinged lid of his heavy silver inkstand, flicking it with his thumb.

'Is there anything else? I'm rather busy this morning. Have a talk with your grandmother, in due course. I wouldn't disturb her now with a lot of questions, though, she's very busy with Christmas and so on. Not a good time. Ask her later, in the new year.'

Alix was thinking what she'd have done if she'd been Helena. Recently widowed, taking a convalescent daughter to America to stay with her family. At least, that had been why she'd gone, hadn't it? Isabel hadn't been well at new year, and she'd been brought home from school before the end of the spring term, under the weather, they'd said. Then the Easter holidays, with Isabel away, recuperating, the Lord knew where. They hadn't been told, that whole dreadful time had been about doors shutting on her and Edwin, endless 'not in front of the children', and then the blinding unhappiness of the news of their father's climbing accident.

If she'd been Helena, she wouldn't have taken her jewels with her to America, she'd have chosen no more than a few pieces to go with whatever dark clothes she'd taken. She'd gone alone, without a maid, Alix remembered one of the servants at Wyncrag making a comment about that.

'There was a painting of her with pearls on.'

187

'They were beautiful pearls,' Grandpapa said, his eyes looking back into that lost time. 'Such a lustre. Her parents gave them to her as a wedding present.'

Those, she might have taken back with her, Alix thought. But not diamonds, surely. There had been a diamond tiara, she had once put it on, when she was little, and twirled about playing Cinders at the ball. Mummy had laughed and laughed. Then, later, she remembered Mummy wearing it to some very grand do. A red dress, she'd worn a dark red dress, with a droopy hem in the fashion of the day.

Alix shook herself back into the present. 'She must have left some of her jewels here at home. At Wyncrag.'

'Your grandmother knew best what to do with them. They were willed to Helena's daughters, in trust. You'll inherit them when you are twenty-five.'

'So Grandmama has them?'

'Oh, I dare say they're in the bank.'

'And Perdita will inherit hers when she's twenty-five, that's not for another ten years. If I get some when I'm twenty-five, I'll share mine with her. She has so little, she has nothing at all except a locket to wear with her new dress.'

Faced with a specific need for jewels, Grandpapa looked as though he were on firmer ground. 'Can't you lend her a necklace, bracelets, a brooch, whatever she needs?' A thought struck him. 'I suppose you have no jewels, either.'

'I do. I inherited several pieces from my great aunt, surely you remember? She shared the money equally between us, but Edwin got the flat in London and I the jewels. Perdita has some extra shares, only nothing she can touch before she's twenty-one. I had most of it reset, and I have some jewellery of my own. None of it is suitable for Perdy.'

'Perhaps Trudie –'

'Don't worry, Grandpapa,' Alix said. She got up and bent over him to drop a kiss on to his head.

'Bear in mind, Alix, that your grandmother doesn't much

care to have Helena mentioned. She felt the loss most keenly.'

Alix smiled and let herself out of her grandfather's study. Grandmama might have keen feelings, but they weren't for her dead mother, that was for sure.

'Aunt Trudie, I've been asking Grandpapa about Mummy's jewels.'

Trudie was in the Herb Room, long ago used for drying herbs from the garden, now the place where she fed the dogs. She looked at Alix, holding a packet of dog biscuits suspended above the chipped enamel bowls.

'Alix, was that wise? It seems to me −'

'I only wanted to know. I mean, she had jewels, and they must come to me and Perdy. Only, where are they? Grandpapa says he handed them over to Grandmama to take care of, well, in that case they're out of reach, all right, and I suppose she won't want me to have them even when I'm twenty-five, she'll say they aren't suitable for an unmarried woman or some such thing. The other trustees aren't going to ask what Grandpapa's done with them, and he's not going to tell Grandmama to give them to me, is he? Why should she want them, anyhow? She has masses of her own.'

'She'll have put them in the bank, where they belong. There's no point in worrying about them until you're twenty-five.'

'I'm twenty-five next birthday.'

'Are you really? Goodness, how time flies. Well, she'll see to it that you have the jewels then.'

Alix felt there was no real conviction in Aunt Trudie's voice.

'It's not just the jewels. We've so little that belonged to Mummy. Only one snapshot, of her and Daddy. Everything else seems to have been bundled away.'

'A lot of her clothes and so on were sent away for charity. It's what she would have wanted. You had no need for her clothes, with you so small at the time.'

'I was talking to Grandpapa about her pearls. There was

a portrait of her, in evening dress, wearing those pearls.'

Or had she dreamed the painting and the pearls, and perhaps even the face?

Trudie made a little sighing sound, and scooped an evil-smelling mess of meat out of a battered saucepan and into the dogs' bowls. 'It was painted by Tanner. It was so like her, it broke my heart to see it when she . . . when we heard the news from America. Your father commissioned it, and he was so delighted with it.'

'What happened to it?'

'I believe the picture is in the bank.'

'The bank?'

'It might have upset you and Edwin, to be reminded of your mother every time you saw the painting.'

Alix could see that she was going to get nothing more out of her aunt about the portrait. 'And the jewels, did Mummy take all those to America, when she went with Isabel?'

'Is that what your grandfather told you?'

'Sort of, then he fobbed me off by telling me to ask Grandmama, it wasn't anything to do with him. Which may be true, or he may be telling whoppers, one can never tell with him. That's why he's made so much money I suppose, like in a poker game.'

'Mother is rather preoccupied at the moment, you can see . . . He won't want her bothered, and she dislikes having those days mentioned at any time. The past is best left alone, Alix, that's one truth that life has taught me.'

Alix's mind was still on Grandmama. 'Why is she pre-occupied? Grandpapa said she was busy with Christmas, but she isn't, you do everything, not her.'

'I'm not in her confidence.' One of Trudie's unexpectedly firm statements, it made Alix look at her aunt as though seeing her for the first time.

'Aunt Trudie, don't you mind? Not being in her confidence and having no real authority here?'

'I run the house.' Trudie had brought a bit into the house from the stables to clean, and she picked it up to give it a final polish. It gleamed in her hands and gave off a clunking sound as she moved it around. 'And I have my horses.' She smiled at Alix, one of her vague smiles. 'I may not have a job in an office and a wage packet at the end of the week, but I do have a busy life. It's a full-time occupation, looking after a big house like Wyncrag.'

'It doesn't belong to you, though, and it never will. Don't you mind?'

'You probably do a lot of minding. I expect I did, too, when I was your age. My sister minded, your Aunt Dorothea, she minded very much, for years and years. Then, in the end, she got away, and left all this. It did irk her so, living here.'

Alix was struck by her words. Got away. Almost, ran away, only women of forty could hardly be said to have run away from home. 'Do you think Grandmama will ever forgive her? For going off and marrying?'

'No.' Trudie didn't elaborate.

'Grandmama isn't a good forgiver.'

'She neither forgets nor forgives, that's part of what . . . It gives her power.' Trudie held the bit up to the light and rubbed an invisible patch of dullness with a precise finger.

Power, thought Alix. 'Doesn't it mean she never moves on?'

'Why should she? What she most loved is in the past, it makes her indifferent. About the present.'

'Indifferent to all of us, as well?'

Trudie wasn't going to answer that.

Not surprisingly. Trudie had a disconcerting habit of only speaking the truth. When she didn't want to, she said nothing, but retreated into her equable vagueness, her eyes focused elsewhere, mind and spirit detached.

It was a technique Alix could have done with, it would have been useful to keep Grandmama's strictures at bay.

Mention of the jewels seemed to worry everyone, including Trudie, so she wouldn't press her. She might, if she could persuade Edwin to take an interest, tackle Grandmama herself on the subject.

Or she might not.

Saul had come into the house only a short while before his mother returned from a luncheon engagement. He wanted to seize the opportunity offered by the absence of both Lady Richardson and her henchwoman; learning from Eckersley that the chauffeur was on his way to pick the pair up, he had hurried back to Wyncrag. There he had run upstairs to his room to take down the gaudily wrapped present from Mavis. He'd brought it with him, tucked in his official dispatch box, and had hidden it at the top of the large wardrobe. He didn't feel comfortable leaving it there, where Chard might find it.

But even as he stood by the door of the bedroom, the package in his hand, he heard the sound of the returning car. He made his way swiftly downstairs, realized that he had no idea of where to hide it, and then, in desperation, went for the hiding place of his childhood: inside the clock case in the hall. He could hear the car drawing up, and he could hear the click-clack of the door separating the servants' quarters as it swung to and fro, followed by Rokeby's quick footsteps.

Saul whisked himself out of the hall and into the cloak-room to his right, there to entangle himself among the mack-intoshes and gumboots.

'Who's in there?' came his mother's imperious voice. 'Rokeby, what's that noise in the cloakroom?'

Red-faced, he emerged. 'Only me, Mother. I left something in my jacket pocket.'

'How often have I told you that jackets are to be taken upstairs to the bedrooms, not left in the cloakroom, it is not the place for them.'

'No, Mama.'

She swept past him and up the stairs, Lipp trotting along behind her like a tantivy pig, drat the woman for giving him such a suspicious look, as though she knew his jacket wasn't in there at all.

He was alone with Rokeby.

'Rokeby.'

'Yes, Mr Saul? Is there something I can do for you?'

His courage failed him. 'No, no, nothing important.'

Rokeby was used to Mr Saul's ways. 'Very good, sir.'

Saul went towards the billiard room, he wanted to have a cigarette to soothe his nerves. He couldn't bring himself to ask the butler the simple question, had he or had he not seen Rokeby's sister, Mavis, that very morning when he had been driving through Askrigg? By the time he'd stopped and found somewhere to leave the car, she had vanished.

He'd thought she was spending Christmas in London, but she had a perfect right to be in Westmoreland, he told himself as he rubbed a thick layer of chalk on to a cue that didn't need it. It was her home county, and she had worked here at Wyncrag until Mama had dismissed most of the indoors staff after Helena died, and Mavis had gone to London.

Disliking himself for feeling guilty, he rang the bell and told Rokeby to bring him a stiff brandy. Damn Mavis. Damn all women.

TWENTY-FOUR

'I write this under the bedclothes, by torchlight,' Ursula wrote in her journal. 'Today I did a spot of useful eavesdropping. I was in the library, where Eve and Rosalind never go, reading, and hidden by the curtain, with just a little gap I could see through, when Daddy came stalking in with Uncle Roger. They had Uncle Hal in tow, who looked as though he didn't in the least want to be there with them.

'It was all about those shares again. "Now, Hal," Daddy said. "We need to settle this matter. You are aware that Jowetts owns a number of subsidiary companies. All connected with our main business, I don't believe in meddling in all kinds of concerns that have nothing to do with what we know about. However, we have one company, with its main factory over near Appleby, which is highly specialised. It turns out small porcelain items for various industries."

'I could see the surprise on Daddy's face when Uncle Hal came straight back, "You're talking about Palfrey's, I suppose. Someone wants to buy it?"

'Daddy said that it was odd Hal should know the name; Uncle Hal said that, no, it wasn't odd, he remembered their father arranging to buy the company from the man who'd started it, just after the war.

'Roger said, in that precise way he talks, that if Hal knew about the business, it made everything easier. Daddy didn't sound too sure about that, and I could see through my peep-hole that he had that morose look he gets when he isn't in total command of a situation.

'Uncle Hal had his legs stretched out, he has awfully long legs, and he had them crossed at the ankles, quite at his ease, and looking inscrutable. Why did they want to sell the company, he asked.

'Daddy at once launched into facts and figures, goodness he is boring when he's talking money. People say that no one is boring when they're talking about what they most love, which in Daddy's case I should say is money, even though he's so soppy about Eve right now. Anyhow, it isn't true, who would want to hear someone drone on about lizards or postage stamps, unless you were keen yourself?

'Uncle Hal listened, he has these sort of lazy-looking eyes, and they drooped while he was listening, like he was half asleep. Then he shot back, not sleepy at all, cutting Daddy off to say, "Right, you say you need the money from the sale to invest in new machinery for Jowetts. Who wants to buy Palfrey's? Why? And what will happen to the factory and its employees?"

'"We are negotiating with a Mr Philip Shackleton, who is a principal of a company in the south," Uncle Roger said. "They wish to expand in this field."

'"The south?" said Uncle Hal. "The factory and its workers are in the north."

'Then there was some humming and hawing from Daddy and Uncle Roger, but it's quite clear that this Mr Shackleton's bosses will close the factory and move the business elsewhere.

'"How many jobs will that cost?"

'Daddy was going red. "Oh, really, Hal, don't come out with all that unemployment nonsense. The men are skilled, they'll find work again in due course."

'"How many? And are women also employed?"

'"We certainly can't offer work to every woman who loses her job. Women should be at home with their families, in any case, I can't do anything about the women. We'd look to take on a few of the men, if we expand the main business. In due course, all in due course."

'Uncle Hal was playing with them, and I don't think they realized it at all. He was getting them all worked up, I don't know why. I don't think he cares tuppence for the business one way or the other. He began to look bored, and uncrossed his legs and stood up. "Find jobs for the people who'd be thrown out of work, men and women, and then I'll consider voting with you."

'"It would be very much more straightforward, Hal," Uncle Roger said, "if we could arrange to buy you out. Altogether. When this kind of situation arises again, you'll no doubt be back in America, and out of reach when it comes to consultation. You must see how difficult it makes things for us, our hands are tied. And it can't matter to you where your money is."

'"Where do you find the money to buy me out?"

'I could see where, and so could he, but Daddy and Uncle Roger looked solemn and began to talk about banks and so on. Of course they want to use the money from selling this Palfrey's Porcelain.

'"I'll think about your offer," Uncle Hal said. "You might let me know what you consider my shares are worth. Then I can talk to my financial man and see what he advises."

'Goodness, Daddy looked cross. "You don't quite understand," he said, very stiff. "This offer won't remain on the table for long, they'll be looking elsewhere if we don't come to an agreement soon. It so happens that Mr Shackleton is up here now, he's come north for the skating. He would like to see the matter brought to a successful conclusion before the new year."

'Uncle Hal's eyebrows shot up, I wonder how he does that, it looks so impressive. "I call that hasty, Peter," was all he said, and then he nipped out of the library before they could say another word.

'I nearly gave myself away, trying not to make a noise, because I couldn't help laughing to see their chagrin at not getting their own way at once. Mind you, I think someone ought to tell Uncle Hal that this Mr Philip Shackleton is one of those two men everyone says are Blackshirts. Is it wrong to sell a factory to a fascist? Mr Baldwin sells everything to everyone, so Miss Hazelton, our Economics mistress, told us. She's very anti-fascist. Her brother is fighting in Spain against Franco, so you can't blame her for minding.'

TWENTY-FIVE

'Could I possibly borrow some money, do you think?'

Perdita was wearing her aunt's breeches again, and presented a very off appearance. The expedition to Manchester had only provided a few of the things Perdita needed, and threadbare garments in half-empty drawers and closets and having to go around looking a perfect fright was soul-destroying for a female of any age.

Alix felt a surge of anger, startling in its intensity, as she looked at Perdita, standing there with the stiff awkwardness of embarrassment, clearly hating having to ask for money. Her anger was not directed at Perdita, but at the author of her sister's difficulties. It had always been one of Grandmama's weapons, keeping them short of money, she had minded terribly when she was Perdita's age that she had so little to spend.

When she had been at school, Grandmama had sent her off with just enough pocket money to pay for essentials: twelve stamps a term for her letters home, a new tube of toothpaste half-way through the term, a pair of laces if she were unlucky enough to break hers, and shoe polish. In the holidays, she had to ask Grandmama for every penny, with a detailed explanation of how she intended to spend it – and how much she had hated both the asking and the accounting.

None of this, she knew now, sprang from meanness or thriftiness, but from Grandmama's desire to control and suppress any trace of self-sufficiency. Dammit, Perdita shouldn't have to scrimp and save. She stood to inherit a good deal of money from her parents, and from the great-aunt whose bequest had changed Alix's status and brought her independence from her grandmother. Were the trustees aware of how short of money Perdita was? She certainly shouldn't need to borrow from her sister, although Alix felt oddly touched that she'd felt she could.

'Edwin promised to give me some,' Perdita said. 'He has the last two years at Christmas, and he said he would this year, too. So I can pay you back as soon as he does. Only he never seems to be here, and he hasn't remembered I have to do my Christmas shopping before Christmas Day. I'd like to do it today, you see. Eckersley has to go into Lowfell this morning, and I can go with him.'

Damn Edwin for being too wrapped up in his wretched Lidia to think about his sister. 'I'll fetch my purse. Has Grandmama given you nothing to buy presents?'

'Half a crown. It doesn't go very far.'

Half a crown, indeed. Alix was about to go into her room, but she stopped at the door. No, she had a better idea. 'You come with me,' she said, heading back down the stairs.

Grandpapa listened as Alix told him with great firmness that Perdita had to have money for her Christmas shopping. 'I'd give her some, but I think it should come from you.'

He looked taken aback. 'Of course Perdita should have money for shopping. Surely Grandmama has given you some, though, Perdy?'

'Two shillings and sixpence doesn't go far,' Alix said. 'Not when you've got about a dozen people to buy presents for, and then there's wrapping paper and Christmas cards. Edwin gave her an extra ten shillings last year.'

'It made all the difference,' Perdita said. 'I even had a little left over to buy some music.'

Sir Henry stroked his silvery moustache. Alix could see him torn between not wanting any part of this and his better nature. He came to a decision, unlocked the top drawer of his desk, and drew out a tight roll of notes. Pulling off the outside one, he spread the white paper on his desk and reached out for his fountain pen. Then he unscrewed the cap and signed the note.

Perdita had been watching him with interest. 'I always wondered how they got signed. You don't have to give me that much, Grandpapa. Besides, none of the shops in Lowfell will be able to change a five pound note.'

'Quite right. You take that to the bank, and they'll change it for you, they'll give you notes and coins, however you want it. Don't spend it all on presents, save some to buy yourself some more music.'

Perdita was delighted. 'Thank you, Grandpapa.' She shot around the side of his desk and planted a kiss on his cheek. 'I won't tell Grandmama if you don't mind, for she wouldn't let me keep it.'

He looked alarmed. 'No, no, this is just between the three of us. Buy all the presents you want.' A thought struck him, and he opened the drawer again to take out a second note. 'Alix, I want you to take this, to buy something pretty for Perdita to wear with her new dress for the dance. You'll know what to get.'

'Imagine, five whole pounds,' Perdita said as Alix closed the study door behind them. 'I never had half so much money. I can buy a headband for Polly, as well as everything else.'

'I shall give you another ten shillings – no, don't argue – and Edwin shall do the same. You can put it away for next term, if you don't want to spend it now.'

Who was Polly? A friend? One of the servants? Why would Perdita buy any of them a headband?

She asked her, and Perdita went off into a peal of laughter. 'Silly, Polly's a horse.'

'Your horse?'

'No, of course not, she belongs to Grandpapa, but I'm the only one who rides her, Aunt Trudie's too heavy for her. Come and see her, oh, do. Eckersley isn't going until half past eleven, we've got heaps of time.'

Alix, who wasn't very keen on horses, didn't much want to go out to the stables, but she could see that Perdita was offering this treat as a thank you.

'You can put on one of the old jackets and gumboots hanging on the hooks at the end of the passage by the back door,' Perdita told her. 'No need to dress up, you only want to keep a bit warm.'

Alix hugged the coat around her as they went out into the icy air and across the straw laid in the stable yard to Polly's stall. The mare had heard them coming, putting an elegant head over the stable door and pricking up her small, neat ears. Even Alix, no judge of horseflesh, had to admit that Polly was special, as the pretty creature turned intelligent, lustrous eyes on her, whickering softly and nuzzling Perdita who was digging in her breeches' pocket for sugar.

'She's an Arab, isn't she?' Alix asked, stroking the silky neck. ·

'Yes. Fifteen hands, and goes like the wind.'

'Where did she come from? When did Grandpapa buy her?'

'She belonged to Delia Grindley; you know, Ursula's mother, who she's never allowed to mention.'

'Of course I know who Delia is. But why has Polly ended up here?'

Perdita lowered her voice. 'Ursula's father was simply awful when her mother went off with that man. He did the most dreadful thing. He had her dog destroyed.'

Alix stared at her, horrified. 'That beautiful spaniel she was so fond of?'

Perdita nodded. 'And he was going to shoot Polly, because he knew that would hurt Delia most terribly, she adored Polly. But after she heard about the dog, she knew what Peter Grindley might do, and she sent her solicitor to warn him not to, because she owned the horse. He was horrible about money, Ursula says, but her mother had a lot of her own that he couldn't take away from her, and that made him even more angry. Ursula knew her father would shoot Polly whatever any solicitor said, so she begged one of the grooms to spirit her away. Only none of them would, because they knew they'd be sacked as soon as it was found out. But the chauffeur, do you remember Wilbur? he said he'd do it. Ursula said he told her it was a crying shame the way her mum had been treated, and he didn't hold with people taking out their spite on dumb animals. So he stole Polly from her stable and brought her over here, and let Mrs Grindley know where she was. When Peter Grindley found out he nearly went mad, and he threatened Wilbur with all kinds of retribution. Wilbur didn't care, he said he'd been planning to join the army anyhow, and wouldn't be needing a reference from Mr Grindley, and he left the next day.'

'Good Lord,' said Alix. 'I'd no idea all that was going on. Edwin never said a word.'

'Oh, Edwin said you were too busy in London to be interested in our local scandals.'

'Did Grandpapa stand up to Peter? What did Grandmama say?'

'Actually, they were pretty marvellous. You know how canny Grandpapa is, and when Delia telephoned him to ask him to keep Polly, and not let Peter Grindley near her, he immediately said the best thing was for him to buy Polly from her, and he wrote her a cheque then and there and sent it off. You see, the mare was hers, and she could sell it if she wanted, and the Grindley could hardly come storming over and steal her from Grandpapa, could he? Although he did do quite a bit of storming, and ranting, too, said he'd sue Grandpapa and all sorts of things like that. So Grandmama told him that he was behaving in an irrational manner, and she had no patience with him. That shut him up all right,' Perdita said with great satisfaction.

TWENTY-SIX

Michael was dreaming again. Vivid and frightening, just as it had been the previous time and, once again, it ended when he was starting to move towards those weird and suffering sounds.

This time he had woken to find himself alone, with no Mrs Dixon bringing a wave of normality back to him with a cup of tea and a well-stoked fire. This time he woke to darkness, and a cold room, and a sense of foreboding.

There was a knock on his door. He tensed, was he still dreaming? It had happened before, that he'd woken from a dream, apparently lying in his own bed, only to have, in fact, merely passed into another dream. He would gradually notice a subtle strangeness to his familiar surroundings and would realize, when he did finally wake up, that he had been dreaming all along.

He sat up and felt for the switch on the small lamp beside his bed, thankful that the inn had, as Mr Dixon boastfully told him, been provided with electricity to all the rooms only the year before. 'We had candles and oil lamps until then, and although some folk find them picturesque, it's a nasty, dirty way of lighting the house, compared to the electricity.'

He was awake, and he had heard a knock on the door. 'Come in.'

A sleepy-looking Freddie put his head in through the door. 'Are you all right, old thing? I don't mean to butt in, but you were making the devil of a row, calling out in your sleep and all that. One of your nightmares, I suppose. It sounded as though you were having a thoroughly bad time of it and might appreciate being shaken awake.'

'Thanks, Freddie.' Michael unwound himself from the crumpled bedclothes. 'Yes, another one of those damn dreams. Do come in, this room is cold enough without you letting in a howling draught.'

Freddie, attired warmly in a Jaeger dressing gown, came in and shut the door behind him. He dug into a pocket and produced a leather flask. 'I brought this. Emergency rations. Care for a tot?'

'There's only the tooth mug.'

'That'll do, and I'll have the cap. No, you stay where you are, and I'll see if I can't kick these dismal embers into doing their duty.' He handed Michael a good tot of brandy, and saw to the fire, tipping on extra coal and poking it vigorously into life.

The flames at once made the room seem warmer and more homely, and the dark night and the forest much further away. Michael began to relax. 'That's better.'

Rather to Michael's surprise, Freddie didn't go, but instead settled himself comfortably in a wooden chair with arms close to the fire. 'I've been thinking about these dreams of yours. Of course we don't do much of that sort of thing in medical training, although there's a general feeling that we ought. I've got a couple of chums in the business though, who are going in for the brain end, psychiatry and all that. I've read Freud, as I expect you have, and a bit of Jung, who has some crazy ideas, but he's interesting all the same.'

'Spare me Freud,' Michael said, laughing. 'I'm damned if I'd read such stuff. My unconscious or subconscious and those what-do-you-call-'ems, my ego and id and all that, can look after themselves, thank you very much.'

'That's just my point; from the sound of it, they can't. If you've started to have nightmares, and they're repeats of ones you had as a boy, then there's something stirring in that thick skull of yours, and I suspect whatever it is, it's better out than in.'

'You mean, tell some chap in half-glasses my dreams, and he'll tell me my mother beat me when I was a boy?'

'If she did, I dare say you deserved it. No, you ass. Dreams mean something, at least big colourful ones that keep on coming back do.'

Michael was astonished. He'd always considered Freddie one of the most rational men he knew. Clever, of course, very clever, but not given to fancies. 'Are you serious?'

'Couldn't be more so. Something like that rattling around in your brain does you no good at all. Makes you sleep badly for one thing, and if you have too many bad dreams, you get to the point where you don't want to go to sleep at all. That's going to do your work a power of good, isn't it?'

'I've been cracking on with the work for the last few months, that's probably what's put my brain into a spin.'

'Could be, but I doubt it. Let me ask you a few questions.'

'Freddie, if you're planning to psychoanalyse me, I tell you here and now, I'm not having it.'

'I'm not qualified, and besides, it takes seven years and costs a packet. Shut up and let's look at the facts. You said you first had this particular nightmare when you were ill. You'd been up in the lakes, in the winter, and you went down with pneumonia.'

'That's right. High temperature, hallucinations. You don't need me to tell you about pneumonia.'

'Why did you get pneumonia?'

'Oh, for heaven's sake, Freddie, why does anyone get pneumonia? I don't know.'

'Had you had a heavy cold, some other illness?'

Michael sighed, shut his eyes, thought. 'No. It was all a bit surprising, really. I was never ill. I got through all the childhood ailments without any trouble, and I wasn't a wheezy or chesty kind of kid. I was fit and well. Very well. Always. I stayed out late, that was all, got a bit cold.'

'Which turned into pneumonia. I'd call that odd, if you were as healthy as you say.'

'I'd call it just one of those things that happens.'

'Leave the pneumonia then. This illness was in the winter, you said. When in the winter?'

'We were up here over Christmas.'

'Afterwards, when you had the dream again, did it happen at any particular time?'

Blast the man. 'Now you come to mention it, I think it did. This time of year. Christmas, New Year. Good Lord, why had that never occurred to me before?'

'Because you were busy with school and then getting your degree and qualifications and coping with a tough job and had better things to think about. It would be easy and perfectly natural to push something like a bad dream to the back of your mind.'

'Yes, but it wasn't every Christmas. And when I grew up, I didn't have the dream at all for years. Until now. I'd more or less forgotten about it. So it can't be anything to do with Christmas. What are you thinking about, too much excitement and plum pudding having a heating effect on the brain?'

'Do be a little more scientific.'

'I don't call taking dreams seriously at all scientific. Dreams are just a lot of garbage floating about in one's mind that comes to life when one's asleep.'

'Does the dream you've just had, that made you scream like a banshee, sound as though it's simply garbage?'

'So what's your conclusion?'

'My conclusion is that something happened to you when you were here that Christmas. Did you have an accident, fall through the ice, anything like that? A dunking in these icy waters could give the toughest child a bout of pneumonia.'

'Not that I remember.'

Freddie got up. 'Get back to sleep, old man. Let your subconscious do the work for you. There's something buried in there, and it wants out. When you remember what it was all about, I bet you a bottle of good claret you won't be troubled by the dream any more.'

Michael looked at his friend. 'I don't want to keep you up, and in a minute you'll start yawning your head off, but I'd like to tell you the dream.'

Freddie promptly sat down again. 'I shan't yawn. I didn't like to suggest it, but I think it's a good idea.'

'Other people's dreams are a bore.'

'It doesn't sound as though this one is.'

Michael began to laugh. 'It is, it's about a boar.'

'What, the nightmare is that you're being talked to death at a dinner or listening to a dull sermon in church?'

'The other kind of boar. Tusks, burning red eyes and so forth.'

'A wild boar? That sounds much more interesting.'

Michael told him his dream, hesitating at first, as he tried to describe how he felt, and how his surroundings looked. He wasn't used to putting these things into words, but as the dream clarified in his mind, he spoke more easily. He finished, and fell silent.

Freddie didn't say anything for a while. He got up and had another go at the fire, and then he poured more brandy for them both before sitting down again.

'Well?' Michael said.

'A corker,' was Freddie's verdict. 'I think if I had a nightmare like that, I'd wake the house, not merely the chap next door.'

'Freddie, do you think dreams are ever about the future?'

'Predictive, you mean?'

208

'Yes. Could one dream something that hasn't yet happened?'

'I would say no. There's a chap called Dunne who'd say yes. Since you ask, I'd say that this isn't a dream that's sprung up out of nowhere. I'd say it's the other way around, that you're recalling something that happened to you. Only it was such a bad experience that you pushed it down into your unconscious, and tried to forget about it.'

'In which case, it's a great pity I didn't.'

'They say it's better to bring terrors from the past into the conscious mind. Like trauma patients from the war. A bad experience may be buried, but if it hasn't been dealt with, it can cause big trouble later. Like a wound that has healed over an infection.'

'Oh, thanks a lot, Freddie, now my unconscious is septic, is it?'

Freddie laughed. 'Only bits of it.'

'So how do I stop having this dream?' There it was, his weakness out in the open, he was actually admitting to Freddie that he was deeply disturbed by the recurring nightmare.

'The best way is to remember what happened.'

'How exactly do I do that after half a lifetime of not remembering?'

'I think the memory is trying to surface for some reason. Give it a chance, and it may come to you. While you're awake, not in a dream, I mean.'

Somewhere in the distance, a cock crowed. 'That bloody bird,' Freddie said, getting up. 'It sounds off hours before it's light. If I owned it, it'd be in the pot come Christmas Day.'

'Good-night, Freddie. What's left of it. And thanks. You're going to be one hell of a doctor, you know. Wasted on bones, I'd say.'

'Bones are easy compared to minds. You know where you are with bones. Good-night.'

TWENTY-SEVEN

As he was going down the main stairs, Hal heard the sound of an approaching car. He looked out of the landing window to see who it was, a window that was one of Grindley Hall's more picturesque ones, reshaped in a Gothic phase. Through the frame of its elegantly pointed arch, he could see a magnificent Rolls Royce. A shiny purple Rolls Royce.

My God, he said to himself. As he watched, a very smart chauffeur in purple livery was opening the passenger door. A supercilious-looking young woman jumped out, and then there was a pause before a confection of purple and lilac feathers emerged. Beneath this staggering hat he saw the lean and familiar face of a woman dressed in a purple costume that screamed Paris. Her neck and shoulders were swathed in opulent furs.

Aunt Daphne, by all that was wonderful. Not looking a day older than when he'd last seen her, and in just as much of a narky mood, by the look of her. Her voice floated up to him. 'Why is there no one here to receive me?'

He shot down the rest of the stairs, and beating a worried-looking parlourmaid to the front door by several paces, flung it open. Aunt Daphne surged in, and the parlourmaid took a step back, overwhelmed by the aura of expensive scent that hung about the visitor's person.

'Hal,' she said, kissing the air beside his cheeks. 'What are you doing here? The last I heard from you, you were in New York. Back for the ice, I assume, I can't tell you how dreadful this cold is. And the Hall underheated by the feel of it. Tell someone to make sure my room is warmed up properly, will you, and make sure the sitting room is above freezing point? My constitution cannot bear a chill.'

The parlourmaid pulled herself together. 'Whom shall I say is calling, madam?'

'I am Mrs Wolf, and I'm not paying a call, I have come to stay. Don't trouble to announce me, Hal will escort me. I hope tea is ready, I'm famished after my journey, quite famished. My maid and chauffeur will also need tea. See to it, if you please.'

Hal's pleasure in the ensuing scene was undiluted.

Eve was at first inclined to doubt the identity of this visitor, and it was only Roger's walking in and uttering a flabbergasted, 'Aunt Daphne!' that convinced her. Peter was summoned, and when he had got over an equal amazement, he fussed and fidgeted around his aunt in the most amusing way.

Eve was formally introduced to Aunt Daphne, and she tried, unsuccessfully, to look pleased. She was quite confounded when, on Rosalind's coming into the sitting room and being introduced in her turn, Mrs Wolf looked her precious daughter up and down from head to toe, and uttered a withering, 'I see'. Then she asked where Angela was, and were none of her great-nephews and great-nieces sufficiently well-mannered to be in attendance when they knew she would be arriving at this time.

Peter sent a maid scurrying off to round up the younger generation, while Eve, a smile pinned to her lips, explained to Aunt Daphne that her arrival at the Hall was wholly unexpected, although they were naturally delighted to see her.

Aunt Daphne paid her little attention as her eyes scanned

the room, finally coming to rest on the frugal tea tray. 'What time is tea taken these days? It's extremely bad for the digestion to have tea too late, and it spoils one's appetite for dinner. Peter, tell that half-wit of a maid that my luggage is to be taken up to the Red Room. Bonnet will unpack for me.'

A look of horror crossed Eve's face. 'Are you wanting to spend the night?'

'My dear woman, as I made perfectly clear when I telephoned, I have come to pay you a visit for the whole of the Christmas season. I shall leave on the second of January, by which time my constitution will be all to pieces, and I shall have to go on a cure. That is, if I haven't expired from hypothermia long before the new year. Peter, tell them to stoke up the furnace, this is a house, not a refrigerator.'

Eve was looking huffy. 'I am sorry to say that we had no foreknowledge of your intention to pay us a visit.'

'Nonsense, I left a perfectly clear message on the telephone. Now, please order tea directly, I've come a long way today, and the least one can expect in the north of England is a proper tea.'

'I'll tell the maid to bring another cup. And some biscuits, perhaps.'

'Biscuits? What's this about biscuits? Grindley Hall used to be famous for the excellence of its tea, all our guests used to remark upon it. Biscuits?'

'It is quite the custom now, in many houses, merely to take a cup of tea, without –'

'Not while I'm here, I can't imagine where you picked up such a strange notion. Whatever is the country coming to?'

Hal could see two bright red patches forming on Eve's cheeks under her expert *maquillage*. 'As to the room, Mrs Wolf, I'm afraid . . .'

'Don't worry about the room,' Hal put in. 'I'll see that everything's in order for Aunt Daphne.'

That irked Eve still more. 'It is hardly your place to make domestic arrangements at the Hall.'

'Oh, but in this case it is my place. Literally. Don't worry, Eve, I'll be perfectly happy to move into my old room. I'll give instructions about a fire, if I may, I think Aunt Daphne might otherwise find the Red Room a little chilly.'

'Thank you, Hal. Now, Eve, is it? Yes. Please ensure that my maid is lodged somewhere within reach, where I may summon her in the night if I need to. I suffer from insomnia, and she reads to me.'

'Maid?'

'Bonnet. I told, you, Bonnet is her name.'

'A French maid?'

'Of course a French maid.'

In the confusion surrounding the arrival of Aunt Daphne, Hal correctly supposed that no one would miss him. So while his aunt took herself off for the steaming bath and preparation of the elaborate toilette she considered necessary for even a family party, he commandeered one of Peter's cars by the simple expedient of slipping the improbably named Parsons a ten shilling note, and drove over to Wyncrag. Sir Henry would, he knew, be enthralled by the news of Aunt Daphne's arrival.

What about the others, he wondered, as he manoeuvred the big car around the treacherous corners. Would Alix remember Daphne?

'Of course I do,' she said.

She and Sir Henry were playing billiards when he arrived, but his dramatic news brought the game to an abrupt end.

'She's my godmother.'

'Is she, indeed?'

'I hardly remember her, though, I was very small when I met her last, I must have been about five.'

'Yes, that's right,' said Sir Henry, putting his cue away on the rack. 'It will be all of twenty years since she was last up here. I'll take my revenge another evening, Alix.' And to Hal, 'Don't you take her on at billiards, she's a demon player.'

'We must have a game some time,' Hal said courteously to Alix. How well she looked this evening, he thought, with colour in her cheeks for once, and eyes bright from beating her grandfather at the billiard table. She was looking less tense, which might be because her grandmother wasn't on the scene.

'Why hasn't Mrs Wolf been back? Was there a quarrel?' Alix asked. 'Grandpapa, shall I ring and ask for a brandy for you?'

'Yes, do, my dear,' he said, subsiding into one of the armchairs and waving to Hal to take another one. 'Hal? A brandy? Or do you want a whisky, you American types always like whisky? Rokeby,' he said, as the butler glided in. 'We don't have any American whisky in the house, do we?'

'Bourbon, sir? I believe we do.'

'There you are, Hal. Have a bourbon. Alix?'

'A cocktail, please, Rokeby.'

'In answer to your question, Alix,' Sir Henry went on, 'Daphne left Grindley Hall when she married Wolf. He was one of the brewing family, you know, and had a remarkable knack of making money. She made a stay of several weeks during the war, only Peter said some very injudicious things about her husband, and she left in a huff. Wolf died some years ago, she's a very wealthy widow, but I don't think she's ever forgiven Peter. I wonder why she's come to stay now.'

'She lives in France,' said Alix. 'She sends me a card every year on my birthday and an extravagant present, perfume and scarves and things like that. I do appreciate them.'

'She has a villa in the south, near Mentone, and an apartment in Paris,' Hal said. 'That's where I last saw her, in Paris. About ten years ago.'

'You were over in Europe ten years ago?' said Alix. 'You didn't come to Westmoreland.'

214

'I did not. I spent a few weeks in London and then took the boat back to New York.' He could see the quizzical look in Alix's eye. 'You're wondering how a strolling player can afford the fares and hotel bills?'

'Hal's a Grindley,' Sir Henry said. 'You did all right by your father's will, and your mother left you a bit, too, didn't she, Hal? No reason why you shouldn't cross the Atlantic now and again.'

The butler reappeared, carrying a silver tray with decanters and glasses and a cocktail shaker. 'Alix, what is that concoction you've got there?'

'Rokeby knows. Rokeby mixes a terrific cocktail. You should try one, Grandpapa.'

'I'll stay with my brandy and soda, thank you.'

'Your aunt hasn't met Eve before, has she?' Alix asked Hal.

'No, and judging from first impressions, I don't think Aunt Daphne's going to take to Eve. I feel we may be in for a merrier Christmas than we had expected.'

'Daphne must dine at Wyncrag,' Sir Henry said. 'I'm asking those young men who are staying at the Pheasant up for a meal. They can come at the same time. To be honest, Daphne and Caroline haven't always seen eye to eye.'

'Safety in numbers, Grandpapa?'

He laughed. 'The two of them go back a long way, and there never was much love lost between them. Chalk and cheese, chalk and cheese. Daphne's a demonstrative woman, wouldn't you agree, Hal? A keen sense of drama, that must be where you got it from, now I come to think of it.'

'I doubt if dramatic tendencies are inherited.'

'Oh, they must be,' said Alix. 'Look at the great theatrical dynasties.'

'That may just be opportunity and nepotism,' said Hal. 'And what about the first member of a family to spring to success and fame on the boards? Where did they get it from? Your sister Isabel, now she had all the makings of an actress, she was wonderful at charades from a tiny girl. Where did that talent come from?'

'Not from her grandmother,' said Sir Henry with a croak and a chuckle. 'No, indeed, not from Caroline. Nor from me. I wonder if she would have grown up to go on the stage, poor child.'

'Not if Grandmama had anything to do with it,' said Alix. 'Can you imagine it?'

Alix drank her cocktail slowly, only half-listening to Hal and Grandpapa talking about New York, a city that Grandpapa had visited several times, and then on to other parts of America: Chicago, Texas, the pleasantness of California, the wicked winter weather in Boston . . .

Alix had never been to America, and felt slightly excluded by their conversation, which meant little to her. However, she wasn't resentful. Her mind was at ease for once, and the warm room with its subdued lighting, the crackle of the fire, the slight odour of cigars that hung in the air, were conducive to relaxation. Her thoughts drifted to and fro, coming to rest on her cocktail, as she lifted her glass and watched the flickering flames through it.

Had her mother really been drunk when her car crashed? How reliable was the memory of a nine-year-old girl? Did the fact of her never having seen her mother in the least the worse for drink mean anything? It was not as though she had no experience of people being drunk, she could clearly remember visitors to the house all too merry after a good dinner and several glasses of port; Uncle Saul, pale and unhappy and speaking in a slurred voice; Peter Grindley at the Hall shouting at Delia, who had simply moved out of earshot, remarking to Helena that her husband had a terrible hangover, had been to an official dinner, his liver was all to pieces.

She knew of plenty of women in London who regularly

drank far too much, contemporaries of hers who glided boozily from party to party, older women clasping glasses of gin, all part and parcel of the social round. Young men got happily plastered and tore off in their noisy cars, a menace to themselves and to anyone else on the road or pavements. It had been worse in the twenties, people said, the roaring twenties, when her mother had died. And alcohol in America, home-made and bootlegged, one gathered, under the oppressive prohibition laws, might be far more powerful and dangerous in its effects than anything people drank in England.

Even so.

She had questioned Edwin, no, he never remembered their mother drinking much, 'Only it was all such a time ago, Lexy, and we were too little to be aware of that kind of thing. And after all, no one would make up a story like that if it weren't true. Do stop dwelling on it. If you want to make yourself miserable, do find some other way of doing it. Or start thinking about all the people in the world who are far more wretched than we are, it does restore a sense of proportion to do that, you know.'

Yes, meaning Lidia, Alix thought bitterly.

She'd asked Aunt Trudie, who hadn't been very helpful, no, of course Helena wasn't an alcoholic, nothing like that, but it had been a very distressing time for her, it wasn't unusual for people to drown their sorrows in such a time-honoured manner. And she, too, advised Alix not to dwell on it. 'Remember your mother as you knew her. That's the kindest way you can honour her memory.'

Alix didn't want kindness, she wanted the truth.

Since coming back to Wyncrag this time, she saw her family in a different light, as one did after such a gap of time, and she asked herself questions that had never previously occurred to her. What had been the matter with Isabel? Why had Daddy gone off climbing in the Andes when his eldest daughter, of whom he was, everyone said, extremely fond, was unwell? Why had America been deemed a suitable place for her to convalesce? Why not the south coast, or Switzerland?

'Penny for them.'

Hal's voice broke into her thoughts. She blinked. 'Where's Grandpapa?'

'He's gone to look for some photographs for me. Pictures he took when he was in the Far East.'

'When was that? I don't recall any trip of his to the East.'

'He went in the early twenties, he was planning the journey about the time I went to America. He visited Singapore and I believe Shanghai and even Japan. Engineers are often great travellers, you know how he likes to go abroad.'

Grandpapa had been away that autumn when her mother had died, she remembered. She hadn't known where he'd gone, although it must have been mentioned. Too much else was happening for an absent grandfather to be much noticed by a nine-year-old. She had a sudden flash of recollection, of Grandmama standing in the hall, talking to a subdued and worried Aunt Trudie, her forehead puckered up in the way it still did when she was distressed, and Grandmama saying what a mercy it was that Henry was away, she could manage so much better by herself without him making difficulties about everything.

'Did he take that big camera of his with him, the one that Edwin likes to borrow? He must have needed a team of coolies to cope with his luggage.'

'That's the English abroad for you.'

'You travel light, of course.'

'My generation has a different attitude to travel. Speed and ease counts for more than creature comforts and taking half your wardrobe with you. You should have seen how many trunks and cases my mother considered necessary to pack for a couple of weeks in London.'

'You know, that's what I most miss, those details about

my mother that you remember so readily about yours. I was just too young for much to have registered with me. Although a lot of trunks rings a faint bell.' She looked across at Hal, who seemed this evening to belong in these surroundings of tranquil English winter darkness and fire and silence. He had a solid, reassuring air of easy competence, a world away from the brittle life she imagined he led. He was, after all, one of them; he might have fled his northern roots, but he had been born and bred among these hills. He was a Grindley, not a stranger.

'Did you like my mother?' she asked abruptly. If she was going to fulfil her desire to find out more about her mother as a person, someone with an existence independent of her role as mother, then she needed to talk to anyone who had known her.

'Like?' said Hal, stretching his hands out in front of him with his fingers linked and turned inwards. He got up. 'Cigarette?'

'Please,' said Alix. He opened his cigarette case, and lit hers and then his. He tossed the spent match into the fire, and watched the momentary glow as it was absorbed by the flames.

'I wasn't a contemporary of Helena's,' he began.

Alix heard the wariness in his voice, and she became more alert.

'She was a good bit older than I was, so I didn't see her in the same way that your uncles and aunts would, or even as my brothers did. If you want me to be honest . . .' his voice trailed away as he gazed into the fire. 'You see, I was infatuated by Helena. It's not uncommon, you'll know of other cases: a very young man and a somewhat older woman.'

'You were in love with her?'

His face was in shadow, she wasn't sure if he were serious. If so, why was he telling her, of all people?

'If you have anything of Helena's make up, you'll share

one of her outstanding characteristics, which was honesty. Helena didn't like unpleasantness of any kind, but she never pretended it couldn't, or didn't, happen. The truth is that I was in love with Helena. Calf love, a boy's passion when he's discovering what love is about.'

'But she didn't . . . I mean, it wasn't that . . .' God, thought Alix, I sound like Aunt Trudie. How did you ask a man outright if he had had an affair with your mother? The idea of it appalled her, even though she didn't stop to ask how much of her distaste was because the woman was her mother, and how much because such an affair would mean Hal was despicable.

'Were we lovers? Of course not. Apart from the fact that your mother was devoted to Neville, and never looked at another man, she was a most moral creature, she regarded adultery with real horror as a breaking of solemn vows.'

Alix felt obscurely corrected, but it had been a reasonable enough question.

'Was it a secret love?' she asked, and then, spitefully, 'Or one of those adorations from afar, the object of affection taking on the persona of some divine being?'

'Claws, I see,' said Hal appreciatively. 'She knew. She treated me with kindness and tact, and yes, I'm afraid I did worship her as someone beyond ordinary womankind.'

Alix made a noise of distaste.

Hal laughed. 'Haven't you ever had a crush on a man? Or a woman, even, given your upbringing? Let me tell you, however, that I wasn't the only one. She was a siren, your mother, only the rarest kind of siren, in that she was quite unaware of the mesmeric power she had over a lot of men. It was why your father fell for her in such a thundering way, and why Sir Henry defended her against your grandmother's hostility; normally he agreed with her on everything.'

'He still does. It makes for an easier life.'

'Exactly.' He paused and blew a few neat smoke rings into

220

the air. 'I can't help you much, you see, since the woman I so adored was as much a creature of my imagination as a real woman. You know all about projection, being a modern young woman. I can tell you that she had a sense of humour and laughed a lot, she had a lovely laugh, deep throated and very infectious. I can't tell if you've inherited that, since you don't seem to do a lot of laughing.'

He was laughing himself, at her. Damn the man.

'Angela's the one you want to talk to. Jane knew her well, but you won't get an honest picture out of her. Your own family, well, you know best about that. But Angela was much the same age as she was, and she's a perceptive woman.'

'Did everyone know you had a pash on Mummy, or did you keep it a secret?'

He winced at 'pash'. 'I fancied no one had a clue. In reality, they all knew quite well, and were amused or sympathetic or annoyed according to temperament. Peter told me to stop mooning around another man's wife and grow up. He was having trouble with Delia at the time. And your grandmother knew all right. She never said a word about it then, but she threw it in my face only the other day. Is she perfectly well, by the way? She appears a little strained.'

'People change after sixteen years.'

TWENTY-EIGHT

Lowfell was bustling with Christmas shoppers and looked very gay with gaudy decorations strung across the main square, a Christmas tree decked with lanterns and the light grey stone of the area glistening and sparkling with frost and sunshine. Shoppers and errand boys had bright pink cheeks, and the draper's on the corner of the square was doing a brisk trade in knitted hats with pompoms.

Alix was wondering whether to buy a hat for Ursula when she spotted Angela and Cecy, baskets laden, going into the town's principal tea shop. She hastened across the square, cursing as her stick caught between the cobbles.

The two Grindleys were already sitting at a small round table, and they moved parcels and bags to make room for her. Cecy attracted a waitress's attention, jumping ahead of several offcomers waiting for service by the simple expedient of calling out, 'Oy, Rose,' to a hurrying young woman in a flowered apron.

'Hello, Rose,' Alix said, recognising an old friend from the village. 'I thought you'd moved to Manchester when you got married.'

'I did, Miss Alix, but we're home for Christmas, we weren't going to miss the ice. So I'm giving my ma a hand in the tea shop, we're that busy with all the visitors. Do you want a pot of coffee for three? And the walnut cake's very good today.'

Alix unwound her scarf, glad of the steamy warmth of the tea shop. She hesitated, then plunged in. 'Angela, may I talk to you about Mummy?'

'About Helena? Of course, if you want to.'

'I've come to the conclusion that I never knew her. Well, that's obvious, I was only nine when she died, a child, with a child's recollections. To me she was just Mummy, not a person in her own right.'

Angela waited while Rose came back with a tray and set cups and plates down in front of them. Then she said, 'Surely your family are the people to ask.'

'You think so? Aunt Trudie just gets twice as vague as usual if I mention her name. Grandpapa says what a good wife she was to Neville, and I get the feeling he liked her very much, only he clams up, rather. Uncle Saul's hopeless, you never get anything except platitudes, it's all *nihil nisi* with a man like him. Jane says she knew her very well and was extremely fond of her, but what use is that?'

'Yes, Jane and Helena were good friends. Much of a muchness in some ways, home and family centred, not that poor Jane had the family she wanted, but they shared the same conventional views on women's place.'

'Conventional?'

'Helena was very conventional. I'm not the best person to ask, Alix, for your mother and I never hit it off. She was well-educated herself, she attended one of those American women's colleges, but she thoroughly disapproved of working women. My being a doctor put her off straight away, she felt I had taken a career away from a man, and had been very wrong to want to enter a masculine profession, where I would never be on equal terms with my male colleagues; no woman could hope to match a man for ability or brains, do you see?'

223

'What's changed?' said Cecy cheerfully. 'This cake is good, try it, Alix.'

Alix looked at the cake on her plate and pulled off a chunk of walnut.

'You may think it's hard now, Cecy,' Angela said, quite sharp. 'It was very much worse when I trained. We were curiosities, back before the war, treated as freaks. There was a great deal of prejudice and hostility from professors and other medical students, and the nurses loathed us.'

'You think that Mummy wouldn't have liked my going to London and getting a job?'

'She would have been bitterly opposed to such a plan. You wouldn't have gone, you know. She had a very strong character, steel when she felt she was in the right.'

'Grandmama didn't like her.'

'Caroline was angry with Neville for choosing a wife for himself, she would have hated whoever he'd married as long as the match wasn't of her making. Then Helena was a religious woman, and you know how Caroline feels about the church.'

'Religious?' said Alix, visions of crucifixes and statues of the Blessed Virgin rising before her eyes.

'Don't sound so amazed, I don't mean she went in for Catholicism or fasting or that kind of thing. No, she came from the part of America where they take their faith very seriously. I don't know what she was brought up to be, but she was perfectly happy to worship at the church here, she once told me that good Christian principles weren't the preserve of one or other branch of the church.'

'Grandmama must have hated that.'

'She did. Words like idolatrous and misguided superstition were some of her milder comments.'

'Helena was a Christian Scientist,' Cecy said.

'A what?' said Alix.

'Surely not,' said Angela.

'I'm not making it up. Lots of Americans are Christian Scientists. We had one at our college at Oxford, Alix, that tall girl who always wore a plait. No birthdays and no doctors is more or less all I know about them.'

'We had birthdays.'

'I expect your father insisted on birthdays. Though I don't remember you having parties.'

Alix thought back. Come to think of it, her and Edwin's birthdays had been quiet affairs. A present each from their parents; she still had the teddy bear bestowed on her for her fourth birthday, an oddly coloured pale green bear, to distinguish it from an identical golden one for Edwin. Nanny had given them useful presents, such things as a hanky or pyjama case, embroidered with their names in cross-stitch. Grandmama gave them books, not very interesting books, either, although the *Boys' Book of Photography* had been a hit with Edwin.

The only extravagant gestures came from Grandpapa, who brought back marvellous toys from Manchester. Meccano, a train set, a rocking horse. And yes, their joy in these delights had been tempered by Mummy's subdued reception of them. 'Christmas is the time for presents, Henry,' she had said to him, thinking the twins out of earshot.

'Wherever did you pick up such an idea?' Angela asked Cecy. 'Really, I don't know how you manage your studies, your head is so full of snippets of information about people, much of it quite wrong, I feel sure.'

'Dr Johnstone told me.'

'What, that old gargoyle? Is he still alive?' asked Alix.

'Very much so, spends all his time fishing, if you mean old Dr Johnstone. It's his son who told me, he took over the practice when his father retired. Pushed the old man out, I expect; anxious about the number of patients popping off under the aged parent's doddery care, if you ask me.'

'Cecy, you really should not say such things. Apart from anything else, it's unprofessional.'

'I'm not qualified yet, so I can say what I like about other doctors. Anyhow, it's true. Young Dr Johnstone, who must be about fifty, told me about your mother, Alix. There was a fearful row when you and Edwin had the measles, and your mother wouldn't call him in. In the end Grandmama did, and it caused all sorts of ructions.'

'Did Daddy go along with these Christian Scientist beliefs?'

'Neville was the healthiest of men,' Angela said. 'I don't suppose he ever went near a doctor. He'd have left any medical attention you and Edwin needed to your mother, would never have given it a thought.'

'Maybe that's why Isabel was ill for so long, that winter before she was killed. Because Mummy wouldn't let her see a doctor. Do you know what was wrong with her, Angela?'

Angela shook her head. Her hands were wrapped around her coffee cup and she was gazing into the swirl of cream on its surface, seeing the past. 'She was taken ill a few days after Christmas. Roger and I and the children left on Boxing Day that year, we went to stay with my parents for the rest of the Christmas holiday. Delia wrote and told me that Isabel was unwell, but she didn't give details, no one seemed to know what was wrong with her.'

'A sudden illness, it must have been,' Alix said. 'It was awfully sudden, one afternoon all this rumpus and we were shooed away to the nursery, and Isabel was shut away in a room on the other side of the house. That means it was infectious, I suppose.'

'I did wonder about TB,' Angela said. 'People can be funny about it, and take a lot of trouble to keep it quiet. Only, Delia said she saw Isabel just before she and Helena went to America, and she thought Isabel looked very stout. Literally stout, I gathered; she was afflicted with puppy fat. You were lucky that way, Alix, you never got podgy.'

'Unlike me,' said Cecy. 'Lord, roly poly wasn't in it. And

then, mercifully most of it vanished one summer holidays. What about appendicitis, something like that?'

'One would have heard if there'd been an operation. And whatever Helena's beliefs, Neville and Caroline would have rushed her into hospital for that, and if they hadn't, she wouldn't have survived.'

'Which she didn't, anyhow,' said Alix. 'If she hadn't got ill, she and Mummy wouldn't have gone to America, and they'd both be alive today.'

'There's nothing to be gained from those kind of thoughts.' Angela was brisk. 'What happened, happened, there's no point in might-have-beens.'

They were silent for a few minutes. Alix crumbled cake between her fingers, trying to come to terms with the idea of a religiously-inclined mother. No one had ever said anything about that. Did Edwin know? Aunt Trudie must have, why hadn't she mentioned it?

'Was she very pi, Alix's mother?' Cecy asked.

'She had a strong moral sense, a clear idea of right and wrong. On sexual morality in particular. That was her one redeeming feature as far as Caroline was concerned, for you know how strait-laced she is about sex, Alix. All that wanting her daughters, and then you and Perdita kept safe from predatory males. However, although the end was the same, she and Helena differed on their grounds. Helena held that men were nearly always to blame for what she called "moral lapses"; Caroline believes that women are the predators and need to be kept safe from their own wicked inclinations, that they seduce and mislead men into bad ways.'

Cecy laughed, sending a few crumbs flying. 'Oh, how very convenient for the men. Mind you, it turns out the same, prim and proper for the girls so they don't get into trouble, and the men can do as they like. How did Lady Richardson square that with her son Jack's goings on? Wasn't he dreadfully wild?'

Angela's face took on a stony look. 'Even now, I don't care to think about Jack. He was savage. He was like an illness that you get over but are never the same again. Look at Jane.'

'Aunt Jane?' cried Alix, causing several heads to turn in their direction. She lowered her voice. 'What did Aunt Jane have to do with Jack?'

'It's nothing,' Angela said. 'I can't think why I mentioned it. It's an old story, and Jane married Saul, so . . .'

'Spit it out, Mummy dear,' Cecy said. 'Whisper it to us.'

'No, indeed I shan't. We're talking about Helena, not about Jane, whose private life is her own affair, not yours. I'm sorry not to be more helpful, Alix, but you see why your mother and I didn't get on very well. We never argued, one didn't argue with Helena, somehow, but we disagreed fundamentally on too many things to be real friends. And I was close to Delia, who was already . . . Well, that marriage was never a happy one, and who can blame Delia for what she did? Helena made no allowances. Marriage was for life, one made one's bed and had to go on sharing it with one's husband come hell or high water. Divorce was unthinkable, infidelity unforgivable, a wife who committed adultery was beyond the pale.'

Alix's head was in a whirl. Whatever she had thought her mother might have been like, it wasn't this. Perhaps Edwin had the right of it; she certainly felt as though she'd been walking along a supposedly secure path only to find the ground vanishing underfoot.

'You may feel you had a restricted upbringing with your grandmother breathing down your neck, Alix, but I can tell you that it would have been just as hard had your mother lived.'

How much did Angela know about her life in London? Had Cecy been carrying tales?

'Don't look at me,' Cecy said. 'I've hardly seen anything of you, as you very well know, and I haven't said a word to Mummy about you.'

'Word does get about,' Angela said. 'Not, I do hope, to your grandmother's ears.'

Alix shrugged. 'What I've done, I've done. I'm of age, independent financially, she has no hold over me any more.'

Angela snorted.

'All right, I'm still frightened of her, and it's difficult to stand up to her when I'm at Wyncrag, but I'm not here for more than a couple of weeks. And somehow, she seems less inclined to sit on me. I suppose she keeps her best efforts for Perdita. Is she quite well, do you think, Angela? She seems to be less on her toes than she used to be.'

'She's nearly seventy, one has to remember that, but from the little I've seen of her these holidays she seems in splendid shape. Quite as vigorous as she always has been.'

'Distracted, that's what she is. As though she's got something on her mind, and for once it isn't us. She lays into Perdy, though, just as much as she ever did to me. Worse, actually.'

'So Ursula tells me.'

'And talking of Ursula, she's been looking a bit blue recently,' Cecy said. 'Oppressed by Eve, I suppose. Lord, what a dark labyrinth family life is. I plan to stay single, either that, or marry someone so ordinary that there's no danger in it.'

Angela laughed. 'The ordinary ones turn out to have the darkest secrets and the most malevolent relatives. And mild men grow into monsters once they're married. No, it's walking on glass whoever you marry.'

'Forewarned is forearmed when you've grown up knowing the Grindleys and the Richardsons,' Cecy said. 'It's single blessedness for me, I can see nothing else for it.'

TWENTY-NINE

'Hell,' Ursula wrote in her journal. 'Ghastly Rosalind has been prying in my room. Looking for a pair of silk stockings to borrow is her pathetic excuse, as if I had any silk stockings to spare. Not that it matters, what is so dreadful is that she found a letter from Mummy and read it. Where was she brought up to go uninvited into someone's room and then to read their correspondence?

'I said that to her, but she laughed and tossed her head about a bit and said wouldn't Peterdaddy be interested to read the letter? I snatched it away, she was a bit surprised at that, but I am bigger than she is. Then she got down to the nitty gritty. If I act as a go-between, which means I take notes from her to some man she's carrying on with, then she says she won't tell on me to Daddy.

'I told her to get lost, that if she split on me over the letter, I'd tell them about this man, obviously someone unsuitable or why notes and not asking him up to the Hall? She says it's not only me, the letter was in an envelope addressed to Nanny and she's sure Nanny will be turned out if they find out what she's been doing.

'It's blackmail. I had no idea she was as foul as that. I don't know what to do. I talked it over with Perdy, and she said, tell her to publish and be damned, like the Duke of Wellington did. Which is all very well, but what about Nanny? However, Perdy then said, take the note and find out who Rosalind's boyfriend is. If it's someone that dear Eve and darling Peterdaddy would throw a wobbly over, then I'll have a hold on her. More of a stand-off, I'd say. But what else can I do?

'She's just been in to give me a sealed envelope. It's only addressed with initials: JR. He's staying at Mrs McKechnie's house, she says. What Rosalind doesn't know is that Mrs McKechnie is an evil woman. I don't suppose she'll let me through the front door to deliver anything. And stupid Rosalind doesn't realize that the McKechnie will have the envelope over a steaming kettle in a trice. She thinks she's awfully clever; actually, she's being incredibly stupid.

'She's spoilt everything. I can't write about her in a calm way or think of her as fodder for my writing, because she makes me want to spit, and everyone knows writing must deal with processed and analysed emotions, and raw emotion is just embarrassing on the page.

'I'd like to see Rosalind on the page all right – squashed, like a fly.'

THIRTY

Hal found Alix sitting on the Wyncrag landing stage, her stick lying beside her and her legs dangling over the side. He skated over to her.

'Is this wise? You may be found frozen in place, a kind of latter-day garden gnome, lacking only a fishing rod.'

'Did you know Mummy was a religious maniac?'

He slid away from her and clumped on to the patch of shingle beside the landing stage. He unfastened his skates, hung them over the post at the end and walked along the wooden planks to sit beside her.

'Dangerous, these wooden slats, even if they weren't covered with ice and you didn't have to walk with a stick. Are you planning on breaking a leg or two to pass the time?'

'If you want to know, I sat down over there and edged along on my behind. If I can't be on the lake, I can at least be over it. You haven't answered my question.'

'It's an absurd question. Of course Helena wasn't a religious maniac. She was a devout woman in that she went to church and I believe held strongish views on God healing rather than doctors, but who's to say she was wrong? Did you know that there's a tomb on the Appian Way in Rome with an inscription that reads, *Beware of doctors, they were the ones who killed me.*'

'Really?' Alix laughed, despite herself. 'I've never been to Rome.'

'It's an interesting place, although marred at present by the Generalissimo's Blackshirts.'

'Angela says Mummy was a firm Christian who disapproved of adultery and divorce and lax behaviour.'

'Oh, so do I. Don't you?' He could hear the desperation in her questions and wanted to turn her off the subject, since it evidently distressed her. 'I'm not suggesting that you would ever be guilty of lax behaviour, but are you by any chance wondering how your mother might have judged you? If so, don't. It's inevitable that one generation finds fault with the morals of the next. Religious mania really doesn't come into it. Whatever you did, I dare say your parents would have disapproved. Unless you'd got engaged to a dull young man at eighteen and settled down in a nice house to have a brood of nice children. That's safety for a woman, or apparently so, and parents do seem to want their offspring to be safe and happy.'

'Whereas the offspring want to be adventurous and go out in the world. Like you.'

'And you. Or go to train to be a doctor like Cecy. What do you think young Perdita will do to shock her elders?'

Alix sighed. 'She's musical. She wants to go to a music conservatory.'

'Ah. Not the dull husband route, in that case. Just one thing: I can't quite see Lady Richardson giving a musical career her blessing. What does Perdita play – or, heavens, don't tell me she's a song and dance girl. Not with her height and build, surely.'

'Piano. Beethoven and so on. She plays very well, but she's had to be duplicitous in the extreme to get herself the lessons she needs.'

'Duplicitous. I love the way that rolls off your tongue, it isn't a word you hear every day.'

'You might if you came from Wyncrag. It's how we all live.'

Another silence.

'You could say the same about Grindley Hall.'

'When did you ever have to resort to trickery to get what you wanted?'

'My dear girl, ever since I was old enough to walk and talk. With my brothers, what do you think?'

'You know them better than I do.'

'The great thing about families is that one can get away from them.'

Was that true? he asked himself. No. You left physically, yet with a psychic web of childhood and adolescence so entwined in your system that it was part of you. Inalienable, untouchable, as integral as teeth and bones and sinews. The people you grew up with were the people who taught you what human beings were like. You never knew anyone better than you knew your family. Everyone else you lived with, you came to with an adult's sensibilities and mind and emotions. And defences. Which wasn't the same.

He kicked at the strut beneath him. He found it a depressing thought, and hoped that he was wrong.

'You can't undo your childhood, that's the thing,' said Alix. 'They say you can have it all psychoanalysed away, but it would only scratch the surface, heave away at the big things like your father beating you or your mother loving you too much or too little. It couldn't wipe out the minutes and hours and days and weeks that you spent growing up with your family around you. I don't suppose old Sigmund himself could get Grandmama out of my unconscious.'

'I'm quite sure that Lady Richardson would be more than a match for Freud, Adler, Jung or any other master of our hidden selves.'

'I have a friend who's being analysed. It seems frightfully

dreary, just talking about yourself and your dreams and your repressions week after week. Seven years, she says it takes. And she's not supposed to make any major changes to her life during analysis. I ask you. Still, even a psychoanalyst couldn't get to the bottom of Grandmama, only think of the complexes he'd come across along the way.'

'Oedipus springs to mind,' said Hal, without thinking.

'Oedipus? What do you mean? How can she have an Oedipus complex, that's what men have, isn't it?'

'Of course, I wasn't expressing myself very clearly.'

'You meant something. Out with it. Do you mean Grandmama was in love with her sons?'

'Your grandmother, as you must be well aware, was deeply attached to your Uncle Jack.'

'Oh, him. He sounds a complete cad. Did she spoil him dreadfully? I can't imagine her showing any of her children any real affection. You knew Jack, wasn't he the same age as you? Childhood friends and all that.'

'Jack didn't have friends. He was slightly older than me, and I took good care to keep out of his way. Mind you, he died young, who can say how he would have grown up? The war changed a lot of people, and Jack had great abilities, he was clever and perceptive and a fine athlete and sportsman. Away from his mother, out in the world, with a profession and a purpose in life, he might have grown into a useful member of society.'

Alix took off her gloves and blew on numb fingers. 'You don't believe a word of that. You think he was wicked and vicious and would have stayed that way. I can see that's what everyone thinks, except for Grandmama and perhaps Grandpapa, for I get the impression that she managed to hide a lot of things about Jack from him.'

'That's probably true,' said Hal. 'Although Sir Henry is an astute old bird. I dare say he saw more than your grandmother wanted him to.'

Alix turned to look at him. Her face was chilled, her nose and cheeks pinched with cold, her eyes troubled.

'You see, that's just why I want to know more about my mother. I know what my inheritance from the Richardson side of the family might be, but not the other half of what I am.'

'And you hoped for a fairy princess of a mother, loving and kind, which she was, and all-forgiving and tolerant and wise and broad-minded, which she wasn't. And someone secure and stable and without a hint of neurosis. As it was, she was a clever, complicated woman with a sense of humour and a lot of beliefs and ideas you have little sympathy with. What does it matter? Do you climb?' he ended abruptly.

'Climb? With this leg?'

'No, when you're hale and hearty. Do you like climbing?'

'I get vertigo if I go three rungs up a ladder.'

'So, your father was a mountaineer, you aren't. Your mother had a religious nature, you don't. You probably take after distant ancestors who were quite unlike anyone else in your family now. Look at Trudie, is she like either of her parents?'

Alix laughed. 'Aunt Trudie's a one-off.'

'There you are, then.' He shaded his eyes, looking into the slanting sunlight. 'Isn't that Cecy?' He waved vigorously.

'All this stuff is beside the point,' Alix said unexpectedly. 'It's actually about wanting to know why my mother was drunk and why she crashed that car and what she was doing in America in the first place. It's wanting to know what happened fifteen years ago, and nobody is prepared to tell me.'

Hal made a whistling sound. 'A matter of those who know won't tell and those who will talk have nothing to tell. I can see the frustration. But honestly, Alix, aren't you creating a mystery where there is none? Illness, accidents, does there have to be more to it than that?'

'There doesn't have to be, but I'm sure there is.'

Cecy reached the landing and made a dramatic halt, sending up a shower of icy crystals from her blades. 'Hello, Uncle Hal. You can be a husky and help me pull Alix. The sledge is on the other side of the landing stage.'

He let himself down on to the ice and peered under the wooden structure. 'That's how you got here,' he said to Alix. He held out his arms. 'Slide down and I'll catch you before you hit the ice.'

'And send both of us flying and add a few broken bones to the casualty list? No, thank you, I'll be safer wriggling back to the end of the stage.'

'You don't trust me,' he complained.

'I don't trust anyone,' was her rejoinder. 'Lessons we learn in childhood, remember what we were talking about?'

'You are nonsensical,' Cecy said, emerging from beneath the landing stage and standing upright as she swung the sledge around. 'You trust Edwin.'

'Not any more,' said Alix.

THIRTY-ONE

Ursula and Perdita skated slowly, since Ursula was reluctant to reach her destination.

'She said, just the one note, and then she'd promise not to say anything to Eve. Do you think I can believe her?'

Perdita slid to a halt and gave her oversized breeches a hitch up before kicking off and catching up with her friend. 'No. Blackmailers are never satisfied.'

'You're right, they never are in books. Blackmailers are always completely bad and villainous. No author ever has a good word to say for them.'

Perdita considered the point. 'You can't take everything you read in books as the truth, though. Books aren't life.'

'Where else can I find out about what blackmailers are like? The newspapers, I suppose, the ones I'm not supposed to read, but although they're full of screaming headlines and shock, horror, misery, they don't actually tell you anything. No details that might help one to deal with a Rosalind.'

'I think the point about blackmailers is that they like doing it. So they go on, whether you give them what they want or not.'

'Rosalind enjoys making people squirm, but this blackmail is a means to an end, she's making use of me.'

'Yes, and even if you do what she wants, she might split on you and Nanny just for the fun of it.'

Ursula gave a wail of dismay. 'It's hopeless.'

'Do your best, that's all you can do. Buck up, we're almost there, that's Mrs McKechnie's boathouse, near where the beck comes out.'

'Used to come out,' said Ursula as they clumped on to the path beside the lake. 'It's frozen solid.'

They sat down to unfasten their skates. 'If all the water coming into the lake is frozen, and the river running out of it isn't, then the lake must be shrinking,' said Perdita.

Ursula stood up. 'It'll all even out when it thaws, stands to reason. Do get a move on.'

'There's no need for me to get a move on, for I'm not coming with you. I'll stay here and guard the skates.'

Ursula bit her lip and dug her hand into her coat pocket to check that she had the scented note which Rosalind had given her. 'I wish you would come.'

'That's stupid. You don't want to play into Rosalind's hands. She said you had to do it by yourself. She'll hear about it if you don't and then she'll think up some new piece of nastiness. Go on, get it over with.'

Perdita watched her friend trudge up to the square grey stone house. She did look dismal, not surprising, really. Nanny was the only person at Grindley Hall who cared about Ursula, and if Eve managed to get her sent away it wouldn't just break Nanny's heart, it would leave Ursula completely at her stepmother's mercy.

Perdita knew all about being at someone's mercy.

The black front door was opened by Mrs McKechnie, who was as square and grey as her house. She glowered at Ursula. 'What would you be wanting?'

'I've brought a note. For one of your guests.'

'Give it to me, and I'll put it on the hall table.' She held out a claw-like hand, but Ursula clamped the envelope to her breast. 'No, I'm to give it to him myself.'

'Come in, then. Wipe your boots, I don't want that muck spread over my clean floors.'

'It's a horrible house inside,' Ursula told Perdita, panting, as they flew back across the ice, filled with relief that the mission had been accomplished. 'Dark and pongy.'

'Dogs?'

'Nothing so nice. Jeyes fluid and cheap polish and cabbage. Mrs McKechnie took me to the back of the house, and opened the door to this big, dingy room. There was a fire going, a proper fire, which cheered things up a bit.'

'Her lodgers must have gone and got the coal themselves, you know how mean she is.'

'I think she's frightened of them. I didn't think she'd let me in, but when I said the person who the note was for would be angry if I didn't deliver it to him personally, she didn't argue at all.'

'What's this man like?'

'Creepy. He's got a great scar down one cheek and he's quite old. He's tall, and has his hair cut very short. He has the kind of face that doesn't move, expressionless is the word. He looked at me as though I were a spider that had just walked across the floor. I held out the letter and he took it without so much as a thank you. He asked who I was, and I said I didn't think he needed to know. Then he began to read the letter, and I was about to go when he looked up and said, "So you're Ursula, Peter's youngest. Well, well, well." He said it in such a horrible way, it made me go all cold.'

'You *were* cold, just off the ice,' said Perdita practically.

'No, shivers down the spine, that sort of cold. I suppose Rosalind's told him all about the family.'

'If he's quite old, I bet he's even more unsuitable for Rosalind than you thought. Was he wearing a black shirt?'

240

Ursula slowed down and put out a hand to stop Perdita. 'How did you know that?'

Perdita launched herself into a sinuous figure eight before coming back to Ursula. 'That's what everyone says those men are. Blackshirts, Fascists. Mosleyites. You know.'

'I wonder if she met him when she was in Munich.'

'He wasn't a German, was he?'

'He didn't sound German. He sounded perfectly normal, just the same as us.'

'Still, I expect all these fascists like to visit fascist countries like Germany and Italy, so she might have met him there.'

'She must have known him before she came to the Hall, in any case. She just hasn't had the chance to meet any strangers since she's been here, what with Eve and Daddy cooing over her all the time.'

'I expect the note's to fix an assignation. You keep an eye on her, see if you can catch her creeping out of the house. Then you can nip into her room and reclaim your property, before spilling the beans on what she's up to.'

'More likely that she'd be creeping out with my letter in her pocket. And, even if they believed me, which they wouldn't, it doesn't matter what frightful things she gets up to. If they were cross with her, they'd be twice as cross with me, you know how Daddy is about Mummy. And Nanny will be turned out into the snow.'

'Don't think about it,' Perdita advised. 'Listen, do you think they'd let you come to Wyncrag for Christmas Eve? And stay on a bit afterwards? Aunt Trudie said I should ask you.'

'What about Lady Richardson?'

'Aunt Trudie said she'd square it with her.' Aunt Trudie would manage it, she always kept her word, and it would be awfully nice to have Ursula there. What with Edwin spending all his time at Lowfell with that so-called friend he had visiting, and Alix moody and uncommunicative most of the time, she didn't find having her brother and sister both at home for Christmas made much difference to her rather lonely life there. And not being able to take Polly out made it all worse.

'I'll ask. Don't count on it, though, the place is all at sixes and sevens with Great Aunt Daphne throwing her weight around.'

'Does she want you to be there?'

'I shouldn't think so. I never saw an aunt with less family feeling. She looked me up and down and just said, "Oh, dear," and then, "Well, she's still young, there's time for her to improve."'

'How perfectly foul. Why did she come?'

'Don't know. Come on, I'll race you around the island.'

THIRTY-TWO

Daphne had taken it into her head to beat the bounds of Grindley Hall, inside and out. She had bidden Hal to accompany her, saying that she wanted to hear all about his life in New York; this he found slightly worrying, as Eve rose from the breakfast table with the evident intention of coming along too.

'What do you want to see, Aunt Daphne?' she said.

'Just Daphne will do, or Mrs Wolf if you prefer, thank you, Eve. Aunts are all very well when your nephews and nieces are in the nursery, but ridiculous when they're grown up. Besides, I'm not your aunt. Hal, you go first, I want to visit the kitchens, and if I fall down that tiresome flight of stairs at the back, then at least I'll land on you.'

'The kitchens?' said Eve. Humour her, be nice to her, charm her, had been Peter's instructions. He needed her support over that matter of the shares, Eve knew this, so she pinned a smile on her mouth and told Daphne that the door on the left in the hall would take them down to the kitchens.

'You don't have to do a guided tour,' Daphne said. 'I grew up in this house, I know it far better than you do, how long have you been here? A year? Well, then.' And, as they went down the short flight of stairs which led down to the kitchen

243

realms, 'I always told Delia she should have these stairs carpeted. Something plain and hard-wearing; the maids were always tripping up and breaking limbs and china in my day.'

Daphne had a very precise memory of how things had been in her day, Hal noticed. He did some swift arithmetic: her day would have been the eighteen-nineties.

'Of course, we have far too many rooms and offices down here for our present-day needs,' said Eve, unwisely adding that she was planning to shut off the Still Room, Bottle Room and Boot Room as being unnecessary in the modern world.

'So where does the boot-boy clean the shoes?'

'We no longer have a boot-boy. The maids clean the shoes.'

'I noticed one of them had black marks on her hands. It's false economy to dispense with staff, it makes too much work for the ones who are left, and then they get resentful and leave.'

'Most of our staff are so grateful for the work that they wouldn't dream of leaving,' said Eve.

'From the few I've spoken to, most of them only stay because they don't speak enough English to look for other jobs,' said Daphne. 'The house is full of foreigners, Bonnet was telling me. She doesn't care for foreigners.'

'I thought Bonnet was French,' Hal said.

'She is. French isn't foreign, you know better than that, Hal. Good heavens, what have you done to the kitchen, Eve? Where's the old range?'

Eve looked wildly at Hal, who took pity on her. 'You can't blame Eve for that, Delia had it taken out years ago, and a modern stove installed.'

'I can't be doing with these newfangled stoves,' said Daphne.

Hal thought of the modern, labour-saving kitchen in his aunt's Paris apartment, but he said nothing.

'And an enormous refrigerator, of course we had the ice house in my day, all the ice you could want, all year round.'

'Peter's converted the old ice house into a summer house,' Hal said.

'Just the kind of stupid thing he would do, what's the use of a summer house built in a place which is intended to remain in shadow for as much of the year as possible?'

'It catches the evening sun,' said Eve. 'It is really most pleasant out there on summer evenings.'

'No, it isn't, not unless the climate here has changed a good deal. Of course, in the south of France one may sit out as often and as long as one wants, the weather is another of those things the French do so much better than the English. Is this your cook?'

The little nut of a man in a chef's hat looked at Daphne with deep suspicion.

'He isn't English, I can see that.' She addressed him in French, and he looked startled, and then replied in the same language, spoken with a thick accent.

'Russian. I thought so.'

'He trained in Paris,' Eve said.

'Trained as what?' Daphne asked as she opened the door into the scullery, sniffed and announced that the drains still hadn't been put right, it was extraordinary how that scullery drain defied all efforts to cure its problems.

'She wasn't ever in charge of the house, only a daughter, why are we hearing about drains and kitchen stairs?' Eve said crossly to Hal.

'Ah, you're out there. When my grandmother died, Daphne became mistress of the house, and she ran it for several years before she married and went away.'

'Do you suppose she'll want to inspect the attics?'

'I shouldn't be surprised.'

However, Daphne was content to make a sweep through the bedrooms, criticising furniture, curtains, carpets, commenting on the softness of the mattresses, 'One always sleeps better on a hard mattress,' and sniffing at the extravagance of the extra bathrooms that had been installed.

'Advertising the family wares, rather vulgar, all this marble.'

Her house in the south of France had several huge bathrooms, predominantly of marble, Hal knew.

'It's English marble,' Eve said.

Hal wondered if Eve hoped that native marble might make up for the foreign element among her staff.

'A mistake. Italian marble is better in every way.'

Flushed with chagrin and temper, Eve watched Daphne sail into Rosalind's bedroom without knocking on the door.

It was rather squalid, Hal had to admit, but was it necessary for her to tell Eve that her daughter had sluttish tendencies which should be seen to? 'If a girl doesn't keep her room neat, what hope is there for her manners or morals?'

Eve said crossly that the maid hadn't been in yet.

'Maid! It needs more than a maid to clear up that kind of mess. And I noticed the girl wasn't down to breakfast, and I see why, sitting there in a *peignoir* looking like something out of a servants' magazine. At this time in the morning! I'm glad she's no relation of mine.'

'Peter thinks of her as a daughter.'

'More fool he.'

Eve could stand it no longer. She said coffee would be served in the morning room in a few minutes, she had one or two things to attend to, and Mrs Wolf must excuse her. She fled, hearing Daphne's ringing voice pointing out to Hal that the picture rail on the landing clearly hadn't been dusted for weeks.

'You are a card,' Hal told her. 'When was that picture rail ever dusted? What do you care about dust, anyhow?'

'Keeping up standards is important. Peter's married this nobody who has an essentially suburban nature, one can see that right away, and she has to learn what running a house like this is all about. And that daughter of hers is a disgrace. How old is she? Seventeen? If her mother has any sense she'll marry her off straight away. If she doesn't, she'll have trouble with her, mark my words.'

'Have a heart. She's only just got back from finishing school.'

'Finishing school! What good does that do a girl like her? Provides her with opportunities to get up to mischief, that's all. Where's she been, Switzerland?'

'Germany.'

'Unfortunate. I have to tell you, Hal, Germany's in a bad way. Myself, I wouldn't set foot in Germany these days. Let's have that coffee, and I hope they remember to put some coffee grounds in the pot this time.'

'I'll see to it,' Hal said. He pondered on his aunt's remarks as they went along the landing. Daphne had always been able to spot an intrigue a mile off, she wouldn't need to see Rosalind disembarking from trains at Preston to know she was up to something.

'At least the banister rail is properly looked after,' said Daphne, running her hand over the silken mahogany. 'And the wrought iron supports don't look dusty, either.'

Below them in the hall, Peter was talking to a big man in a dark suit. The maid was standing by with an overcoat over her arm and a black felt hat in her hand. The two men shook hands, the visitor shrugged himself into his coat, and the door opened to let in a gust of icy air. The maid shut it quickly behind him.

'Who was that?' asked Daphne, sailing down the beautiful curved staircase.

'A business acquaintance,' Peter said.

'Mr Shackleton?' Hal asked in a moment of inspiration.

Peter gave him a sharp look. 'Yes, as it happens. He is anxious to press on, I told you he was staying up here for a few days.'

'I don't like his haircut,' Daphne said. 'Too short. Are businessmen wearing their hair so short in England these days? Almost a military cut, one would say.'

'I'm glad to catch you,' Peter said. 'I've been wanting to have a chat.'

'Plenty of opportunity for talking, I'm here for several days yet. I'm about to have my coffee.'

Peter turned to the maid who was about to make her getaway. 'Bring coffee into the library. Hal, we need you too.'

Daphne gave Hal a wink. 'Shareholders' meeting, I think,' she said to him in a penetrating whisper. 'You can have half an hour of my time, Peter, no more. Then I'm going out for a walk, I want to see if you've cut the hedges into the shapes of cockerels and squirrels.'

'What? What are you talking about?'

'So many changes at the Hall. It seems to be quite a different sort of house.'

'That's Eve, she's full of wonderful plans,' Peter's face softened, and took on a look of pride. 'The conservatory, for instance, it's small and inconvenient, she's going to have it down and a much better one put in its place. Time the Hall was given a new look, you must agree.'

'That depends on who's doing the giving and who's doing the looking,' Daphne said. 'Surrey is all very well in its place, but that's hardly here.'

'What has Surrey got to do with anything?'

'My dear man, if you don't know, I shan't take the trouble to tell you. Ah, coffee. Strong, I do so hope. The coffee at breakfast was undrinkable, Peter, it tasted as though it had been decanted from the rain butt.'

The chairs in the library had been arranged in a semicircle around the fireplace, in which a meagre fire was burning. Daphne sat herself in the central chair, which Hal could see was where Peter had been intending to sit.

'You'll be more comfortable here, closer to the fire,' his brother said.

'No, I won't, although you can put some more coal on the fire, it's quite inadequate for a room of this size.'

Hal took pity on his brother, whose neck was becoming dangerously red, always a warning sign with Peter, and heaped several shovels of coal on to the fire.

'That's better,' said Daphne.

'Roger will be here in a moment,' Peter said. 'Ah, this is him. Now we're all here.'

'Let me tell you right away, Peter, and you, Roger, that if this is about the sale of Palfrey's Porcelain to Hardy's, I will have nothing to do with it,' Daphne said. 'And if Hal will be advised by me, he won't let the plan go ahead either. Now don't start to address me as though I were a public meeting, Peter, for I won't put up with it. And don't think you can hector me, either, Roger, save your forensic skills for the courtroom.'

That was laying it on the line, Hal thought appreciatively. Steamroller tactics were undoubtedly the best way to deal with his brothers, although he could see that they felt battle had only just begun.

'Well, Aunt Daphne . . .'

'Daphne will do.'

'I'm not sure I understand why you are taking this stand on what is a very routine matter of company business. After all, we have acted for years on your behalf, using your proxy, and you've never interfered nor complained.'

'I haven't seen any need to. Now I do. This deal sounds fishy to me. It won't come as a surprise to you that Hardy's is now owned by Morton and Sons, who are in turn a subsidiary of a German company.'

Hal was amused to see Peter and Roger trying to put expressions of surprise on their faces, it was clear that they knew this perfectly well. Peter, however, was inclined to brazen it out.

'Nonsense, Hardy's is as English as they come. A highly respected firm, been going for donkey's years.'

'Indeed they have, and they were English until they were bought two years ago by Morton. The major shareholder of that concern is now Heinrich Scholler Industrie, which is part of the Fürst & Söhne empire.'

'Really, Daphne,' Peter protested. 'I hardly think we need

you to ferret around looking for conspiracies which don't exist.'

'Who said anything about conspiracies? There's no conspiracy about this, it's all there on the record for anyone who cares to take a look.'

'I can't believe you've gone to so much trouble to delve into such a very minor matter.'

Daphne gave Roger a withering look. 'I am a rich woman, Roger, and I intend to remain so. I have several very efficient people who handle my affairs, and are paid to look into this kind of thing. My stake in the family business is not one of my major interests, and I have been happy to leave the running of the company to Peter and you. Until now. I gather Hal has done the same.'

'Hal simply took himself and his shares off to another continent, not even leaving us a proxy,' said Peter crossly.

Of course, that was his brothers' problem, as he knew, and, it seemed, as Daphne knew, too. With their aunt's shares in their pockets, Peter and Roger had no need to bother about Hal. With Daphne kicking up a stink, they needed his vote. It seemed irrational of Daphne to object to selling a porcelain business to a company who happened to be owned by another company with German connections, and Hal said so.

'There's more to this than meets the eye,' said Daphne. 'I'm deeply suspicious about why, at this time, Hardy's should be so keen to buy this particular company. What's special about it?'

'Really, Daphne, nothing at all.'

'No, that's my point. Old-fashioned plant, old-fashioned products, why should anyone want to buy it? Were you trying to sell it?'

'Not exactly,' said Peter uncomfortably.

'We were approached by Hardy's,' said Roger. 'Perfectly normal, an everyday matter in the business world, nothing sinister about it.'

Daphne hadn't been married all those years to the spectacularly successful Daniel Wolf without learning a thing or two about business. Hal could see from the sceptical glint in her eye that this explanation wouldn't wash with her.

'Mr Shackleton is up here to conclude the sale,' Peter said. 'They will go elsewhere if we start shillyshallying. It's nearly Christmas, there isn't time to go delving into why they want to buy.'

'Then let us consider why you're so keen to sell.'

Silence.

'So, I shall have to find out that as well.'

Roger cleared his throat. 'Aunt, I mean, Daphne, we are prepared to make a very generous offer for your shares. You said yourself that they are of no real importance in your portfolio, and –'

Daphne interrupted him. 'I said of no key financial importance. From a family point of view, they are very important to me. Go on. Who's offering for my shares?'

'Why, Peter and myself.'

'Not Hal?'

'They've offered to buy mine,' Hal said. 'I said I'd think about it.'

'By the time you two have dug around and thought, all to absolutely no purpose,' said Peter irritably, 'the deal will have fallen through.'

'In which case, there'll be someone else willing to buy the company. If Hardy's see a future for it, why not another purchaser?'

'No one else would pay that much,' said Roger, forgetting himself and earning a furious look from Peter.

Hal felt like giving the pot another stir. 'Of course, if the company is worth so much, perhaps you should be looking into why its returns are presently so low? It's strange that Hardy's are prepared to pay so much for an ailing concern, is it not?'

Daphne nodded her head in emphatic approval. 'You put the matter in a nutshell, Hal. Peter, don't say any more. I said you could have half an hour of my time, and you've had thirty-three minutes. Quite enough. I shan't be bullied or threatened or charmed into doing what I don't want. If you can show me why a German company wants this unsuccessful part of the family business, and the reason is an innocent one, then I may change my mind. However, I may not. I don't feel like doing any favours for the Germans just at present.'

She rose from her chair, picking up her purple crocodile handbag from the floor and taking herself nimbly out of the room, almost before the men had stood up.

'Bloody woman,' said Peter, taking care not to speak until the door had closed behind her. 'Who does she think she is? Hal, you don't give a damn about German holding companies and all that rubbish. Stop sitting on the fence and say you'll vote with us, or if you want to keep your hands clean, make over your shares to us, we've said we'll give you a good price. Whatever it is that's making Daphne so fussy, it needn't bother you. Frankly, I think her age is getting to her, she's gone a bit potty, if you ask me.'

'She isn't potty. You forget that Wolf was a Jew. I think you'll find that's what's behind this,' Hal said, making for the door himself.

'Wolf? What's he got to do with it?'

'Well, Peter, if you can't work that one out, I think it's you who's going potty.'

THIRTY-THREE

'Jew!'

Lidia froze. She gripped the handle of her shopping basket so hard, it began to shake. An apple tipped out, rolled along the pavement and fell into the gutter.

'Get down there with it, into the gutter where you belong.' The voice rang out on the cold air.

She was no longer in a small northern town in England. She was back in Vienna, being shouldered aside by a group of *Heimwehr* officers, one of them reaching for her basket, turning it upside down, laughing at the joke. She had bought eggs; they smashed on the pavement, broken yellow yolks and slime trickling into the wet gutter.

They had laughed even more. 'You're next, Jew girl. You and all your kind.'

She forced herself back into the present, a present which until that moment had been a world away from the dangerous streets of Europe and the daily humiliations dealt out to those of her race. She was in Lowfell, where the locals were polite to her and where the English police constable put up a hand to stop the traffic when she needed to cross the road. But even here, here in this remote and peaceful place, someone was saying these dreadful words.

She wanted to drop her basket, and run, get away from the taunting voice. Only where was there to run to, if she weren't safe here? From deep inside her, anger welled up, swamping her fear.

She rounded on her persecutor, her eyes ablaze with fury. 'Are you speaking to me?' she said, in English.

It was one of the men people said were Blackshirts. She had heard people talking about them, there were two of them, staying at the home of Mrs McKechnie, a Scottish woman who let out rooms. English Blackshirts, not at all like the ones in Germany, she'd told herself. The English wouldn't put up with that sort. These would be overgrown boy scouts, nothing more.

The second she laid eyes on this man, she knew she had been wrong. This wasn't some provincial dressed up to disguise a timid and unsuccessful nature. This man wasn't a braggart or a fool. This was one of them, one of the terrible men who set the gangs of uniformed, officially-sanctioned thugs and criminals on to those enemies of the state: Jews, gypsies, homosexuals.

'Yes, I'm speaking to you, Jew.'

His eyes held nothing but menace, his stance was threatening, his face, marked with a livid scar from eye to mouth, was hard and lean in that Aryan way the German Nazis loved. He wasn't a fool, nor did he look a man to be threatened by the accomplishments of those unlike himself; his eyes weren't those of the fanatic. This was a man chock full of violent energy, who liked to inflict hurt and pain, untouchable himself in all his English maleness and strength. His voice was the voice of the upper classes, he had the certainty of a man who knows he was born to rule. A man who had been brought up to chase and shoot and hunt and prey on creatures smaller and weaker than himself.

Now she was the prey.

He was standing just across on the other side of the narrow

street. There weren't many people about, it was lunchtime, the shops were shut, she'd hurried out to buy fruit for her lunch before the greengrocer's closed. The butcher's boy came past on his bike, cast a curious glance at the man and at her, rode on, whistling and heedless. The girl from the draper's, on her way home for the midday meal, crossed to her side of the road rather than push past the man.

Panic rose in Lidia. There were two of these men, she had heard. Such men didn't hunt alone, they went about in groups, packs, they liked numbers, having others to urge them on, to behave in a way all their upbringing and social code told them was wrong. Or, in the case of a man like this one, they liked having others to give orders to. There was a pleasure and satisfaction in watching men go open-eyed into beastliness at your command.

'Jew!' he called again. 'Jew girl scum. Get back to your rat hole where you belong, among the greasy locks and hook noses of your race. We know how to deal with you as you deserve, like rats.'

'Shut up!' she shouted back, her voice high and uncontrolled. She mustn't let herself sound like a victim, she mustn't lose her sense of who she was. 'This is England, do you think people here let you behave in such a way?'

He cast a contemptuous glance up and down the street. 'I see no people. No citizens rushing to defend you. Nobody cares about you, Jew bitch. No more than they do for vermin in the fields.'

Lidia backed away. Why did nobody come? Couldn't they hear what he was saying, didn't they know that he would like to kill her, just for being what she was? No, he couldn't kill her, even if he wanted to. She was in a country where you couldn't kill a woman and get away with it because you were from the ruling classes and your victim was a refugee, a Jew. However much they disliked foreigners, that was not the way English people behaved.

Was it?

'Is this man bothering you, miss?'

Lidia couldn't believe it: before her swimming eyes stood the stolid, six-foot, blue-uniformed figure of PC Ogilvy.

'Only I heard a disturbance out here as I was eating my dinner and I thought I'd just step out and see what was going on. Do you know this gentleman, miss? I mean, he isn't your husband or brother or young man, like?'

She shook her head, trembling now from relief as well as from the shock of it all. 'No, oh no, I don't know him at all.'

'I'd just like a word with you, sir,' he said. He pulled out a notebook from the breast pocket of his tunic and began to cross the road.

'You all right, honey?'

Lidia had turned away as the policeman had accosted the man, and started to run, heart pounding in her chest. Along the street, around the corner and up the slight slope to Edwin's house. She whirled around as she heard the voice behind her. 'Who are you?'

She knew who it was, it was the American woman with the headscarves and dark glasses, the one who wore trousers that caused locals to shake their heads and predict all kinds of disaster if their young women ever took to dressing like that. The one they reckoned was a film star, American and dark glasses and all.

She was young, behind the dark glasses her eyes were unlined. She smiled, showing white, even teeth. Americans always had such lovely teeth.

'Call me Tina, OK? Did something happen back there? I saw the policeman, and then you running away. Are you in trouble?'

'Oh, thank you, I did not mean to be rude. No, I'm not in trouble, it was just that the man, who is a Blackshirt . . .

256

I'm Jewish, you see, and foreign, and it is only that I didn't expect . . . here.'

Her hand was shaking as she tried to push the key into the lock.

'Let me.' The woman took the key from her. She turned the key in the lock, the door opened, and Lidia almost fell into the house. Followed by the American.

'You need a cup of something hot,' Tina said, 'and sweet. This appears to be some kind of a photographic studio, are you a photographer?'

'No, no. I'm staying upstairs.'

'How do you get to your apartment?'

Lidia didn't want this strange woman in her rooms. On the other hand, her legs felt so weak that she wasn't sure if she would manage the stairs without help. She was furious with herself, no one had touched her, she hadn't been in an accident, and what the man had said and what he was were no novelty to her. Yet here she was, trembling and useless. 'It's that door, over there.'

'Let's go.'

Upstairs, Lidia sank down on the sofa, still in her coat and boots.

'If you feel like you're going to pass out, dip your head down between your knees, honey.'

The faintness passed, her eyes stopped watering, her hands no longer shook. She had control of herself once more. She stood up and took off her coat and stooped to remove her boots.

'I felt so safe here. Not that I was in danger in London, it isn't that I have done anything or am anyone special.'

'You just happen to be Jewish, and foreign, and that's enough for these grotesque people who've got their heads where the sun never shines.' Tina handed her a cup of coffee. 'I don't know how you usually take it, but sweet and milky is how you need it right now.'

She sat down opposite Lidia. 'I've read about these Blackshirts. We don't get them back in the States, at least not where I come from. However, we have our problems, especially in the south, where there's a good deal of racial intolerance.'

Lidia gulped the sweet coffee, grateful for its warmth and strength. She must make an effort. 'Where in America is that? Where you come from?'

'California.'

'Oranges,' Lidia said. 'Oranges and sunshine, is that right?'

'Lots of oranges, and sunshine too.'

'You must find it cold here. After the sunshine.'

'I grew up in the north of England. Before I went to America. I'm kind of getting used to it again, although I sure need to wrap up warm. The English aren't good at central heating.'

'It is warm in here.'

'This is some guy's place, isn't it?'

'I'm sorry?'

'A man lives here. He your lover?'

Lidia stared at her. 'What?'

Tina laughed. 'Don't mind me. I'm just naturally curious about people, and I shed my English reticence a long time ago. I can tell a man lives here from the way it looks.'

'He isn't living here now. Not when I am here. It wouldn't be suitable, he has family and friends here, they would be shocked and would call me a whore.'

'I doubt it, honey, it's not a word these people would use. Where does he live, while you're in his apartment?'

'At his home. On the other side of the lake. This is his workplace, his studio, and also sometimes he stays here. But not while I am here, I am strict about this.'

'What do you do with yourself all day? Do you go skating?'

Lidia's face lit up. 'I love to skate, and I have skates, so I go on the ice nearly every morning, almost before it is light.'

'You're an early riser, then. Me, I cling to my bed when I can. What do you do for the rest of the day?'

'I practise, for some hours every day.'

'You a musician? Is that some kind of a piano?'

'It's a harpsichord.'

Tina got up and went to examine the instrument. 'It's kind of pretty, isn't it? Is this the one that makes the tinkly sound?'

'I show you.' Lidia finished her coffee and went to the harpsichord.

'Play something light,' Tina said, as Lidia hesitated, her hands hovering over the black keys. 'I'm not a big fan of classical music.'

Lidia made a little gesture with her head, and played.

'I like that,' Tina said, when Lidia had finished and lowered her hands into her lap. 'What's it called?'

'It is by Handel, a German composer who lived and worked in this country. It's called *Air and Variations*.'

'I know Handel. He wrote the *Messiah*. They sing it every Christmas in halls all over the country. My father used to sing in it.'

'Your family are musical?'

'Lord, no. My father just sang in some choir. He enjoyed it. Strictly amateur. You aren't an amateur, are you?'

'No, I have trained. I played professionally. In Europe.'

'And now?'

'Now, I'm a refugee, and it is only thanks to my friend that I have a harpsichord at all.'

'Who is this friend of yours?'

Lidia hesitated.

'If he's the owner here, there'll be no secret about it. I only have to ask around.'

'His name is Edwin.'

'Edwin!'

'You sound surprised. Is this an unusual name?'

'What's his surname?'

'Richardson. They are a rich and important family here, I believe. They have a big, big house. Wyncrag.'

She pronounced the W as a V. Tina corrected her, but absently. 'Wyncrag, you mean. Is he a nice guy, this Edwin Richardson? Tell me about him.'

THIRTY-FOUR

Perdita ate a substantial tea: crumpets, several sandwiches, a large slice of chocolate cake. They were dining at Grindley Hall before the dance, and Ursula had warned her to have a good tea at Wyncrag. 'You've no idea how sparse the meals have become, although I think Eve might have to do something about it, Great Aunt Daphne doesn't seem too happy with the menus.'

'She lives in France, she probably likes frogs' legs and things like that.'

'Goodness, only imagine the horror if they served them at Grindley Hall.'

'Just as well if they don't, I won't eat them if they appear on my plate tonight.'

Perdita paused in the door on her way out to go upstairs and dress. 'Aren't you going up to get changed, Alix?'

'I'm not sure that I'm going to the dance. My ankle's swollen up again, so much so that I can't get a shoe on. I simply refuse to go to a dance wearing a sock on one foot.'

'Whatever will Grandmama say if you don't go? You know what her rule is: once you've accepted an invitation, you have to go.'

'Where's the fun of going to a dance if you can't actually

261

dance? I know, Grandmama will insist that I go and say I must sit and make conversation with the mothers and dowagers. I don't want to talk to them, and they jolly well don't want to talk to me. I can't talk about nannies or governesses or servants or operations or who's having an affair with whom; I'm not married. So I cramp their style. Frankly, Perdy, I don't much care what Grandmama says.'

'But do come, Alix. Michael and Freddie are going to be there, you know you like them.'

'I'll remind Grandmama of that. She'll be glad that I'm not hobnobbing with such a dangerous pair.'

'What's dangerous about them?'

'They're young men. Therefore, dangerous to young women. Oh, you know how she is. Off you go now, or you'll be late, and then you'll be in real trouble.'

It seemed that Alix was resolute in her intention not to go, for when Perdita came down an hour later, her sister was still in the sitting room, her foot propped up on a footstool. She had been gazing into the flames, brooding and thinking, and quite unaware of the passing time, until she looked up and saw Perdita standing there.

Perdita was wearing the red dress they had bought in Manchester. The silk velvet was sumptuous in the soft lighting, and it turned the gold and garnet ornament she had around her neck into something more than a trinket. She looked magnificent.

'Perdy!' Alix exclaimed. The dress was entirely unsuitable for a fifteen-year-old, she realized that now; it was designed for an older and much more sophisticated woman. Perdita's long legs and wide, bony frame showed it off to perfection. Why hadn't she noticed how inappropriate it was when they were in the shop? Because it was the only dress that fitted Perdita, and in the fitting room, with the not very good lighting, and Perdy's hair hanging about her face, it hadn't seemed so striking. 'You look about twenty-five,' she said.

'Oh dear, don't say that, how awful, Grandmama will tell me to take it off at once.'

'You're right. It's perfectly lovely, and you do look nice, but Grandmama isn't going to like it.'

'Oh well, I'll just sit here and wait for the onslaught,' Perdita said philosophically. 'At least I'll have worn it for a bit. I don't suppose they'll take it back now, will they? Grandmama will lock it away or send it to the jumble sale, I suppose. I'll spend the evening here with you, although that won't seem very good manners, if neither of us goes. Are you sure you won't come? Why, you might meet the man of your life there.'

Alix laughed. 'I know everyone who'll be there, I've known most of them for most of my life. I'm quite sure none of them is my soulmate.'

'It's a shame.'

'What's a shame?' asked Edwin, joining them by the fire. He was wearing tails, and he propped a gleaming patent-clad foot on the fender. He took in Alix's clothes. 'Aren't you coming, Lexy? Is your ankle still hurting?'

'It is, rather. So I'm staying behind, Cinders in the fireplace.'

'Have you broken the news to Grandmama?'

'No, Perdy and I are sitting here in a state of trepidation, waiting for her to descend.'

'You're in luck. So are you, Perdy, I must say you look a treat in that dress, but I can't see Grandmama taking to it. Let me be the one to tell you the glad tidings. Lipp met me in the hall just now and announced in her irritating way that Madame has the headache, has taken a powder, and is spending the evening in a darkened room. We are to make not a sound in our going or coming.'

Alix felt an overwhelming sense of relief. 'Thank goodness. It isn't a migraine, by any wonderful chance, is it?'

'Lipp is very much afraid it is.'

'Oh, goodie,' said Perdita, forgetting to be grown-up. 'It was three days last time, that would just take us through to Christmas Eve.'

'Vile child,' said Edwin. 'Have you no pity? Migraines are very painful, so I've been told.'

'I expect it's bad temper that's brought it on,' Alix said. 'Michael and Freddie called this morning, and I won't tell you how rude she was.'

'I can't help being pleased, for now she can't stop me going,' said Perdita, pink with pleasure. 'And fancy her pulling out of an engagement, and at the last minute, too. Her head must be very bad. Alix, you must come now. Don't you see, it will be much more fun if Grandmama isn't there disapproving of us? Lots of people will sit out with you and chat, you know they will.'

'Yes, do come,' Edwin said. 'I shan't dance more than politeness dictates, we can sit together and pass judgements on the dancing couples.'

Alix knew that Edwin wasn't planning to dance much because the woman he'd really like to dance with wouldn't be there. On the other hand, the prospect of several hours of his company was more than she could lightly forgo. Even if he ended up talking about Lidia, he would be with her at Grindley Hall, not in Lowfell with Lidia.

'You've got some gold slippers with no backs,' Perdita said; she had spent several happy hours inspecting all Alix's clothes. 'Wear those, they'll hide the bandage.'

'All right,' Alix said, getting awkwardly to her feet. 'I'll be as quick as I can.'

Trudie came tsk-tsking into the room, a stream of dark blue chiffon. 'Alix, my dear, not changed yet, we shall be late, whatever are you thinking of? And Mama isn't coming, as I expect you know. Good heavens, Perdita, is that the dress you bought in Manchester? Perhaps it's as well that Mama is indisposed. I'll come and help you dress, if you like, Alix. Edwin, tell Pa that we will be down directly, and that Saul is just waiting for Jane to finish dressing.'

'Well, well,' said Sir Henry, looking his youngest grand-daughter over with an approving eye. 'You do look hand-some this evening, Perdita. Is that the frock you bought in Manchester?'

'Do you like it?'

'I do, although I'm not sure that your grandmother would consider it suitable.'

'You won't tell her about it?'

'Never a word.'

Alix looked down at her family from where she had paused on her way down the stairs. Grandpapa was smoking a cigar, something Grandmama wouldn't have countenanced, his gleaming starched shirt brilliant against the black broadcloth. Perdy, a stranger in the red velvet dress. Aunt Trudie standing slightly back from the others, as she so often did, a fur stole around her shoulders. Uncle Saul stood beside his sister, sleek, assured and worried, the frown lines at the ridge of his nose more pronounced in a hall lit by wall sconces with fat flame globes, none of which shed much light. Aunt Jane stood apart from him, exquisitely elegant in palest green. Too thin, thought Alix, looking at her aunt's huge, hungry eyes. She shivered, God save her from ever looking like that.

And Edwin, at ease, his hair for once not falling over his forehead, but slicked back into conformity.

She went down the remaining stairs to join them.

Perdita heaved herself into her old tweed coat, and the others all looked startled at the strangely tramp-like figure that emerged.

'Good heavens, haven't you got a cloak or a wrap?' said Grandpapa.

Trudie, who had disappeared as Perdita was thrusting her

arm into a sleeve, came back into the hall. 'I have just the thing,' she said. 'Take off that coat, Perdita.' She had in her hand a black velvet half-cape, which she draped over Perdita's shoulders. 'It won't keep you warm, but you'll only be outside for a few minutes, and you can wrap up in the car.'

Rokeby helped Alix into her evening cloak, handed Sir Henry his top hat and gloves and then his silver-headed cane.

'Are you driving yourself, Saul?'

'Yes.'

'We'll see you there, in that case.'

Rokeby opened the front door.

THIRTY-FIVE

'I'm snatching time to write my journal, in my room, at my table, with no fear of prying eyes. I'm sitting in my underwear, my disgraceful underwear, judging by Bonnet's drawn breath and clicking tongue. I never thought very much about underwear, but I agree that my slip has seen better days and in fact looks a bit dismal. Never mind, no one will see it.

'Except Bonnet, which is why I'm here, half an hour before the dinner guests will start arriving, while the others are downstairs in the drawing room, listening to Great Aunt Daphne tell them a thing or two about what it was like at Grindley Hall in the Good Old Days when dances were dances, and none of this penny-pinching nonsense.

'I came upstairs to dress when everyone else did, and it took me about five minutes to put on my old green dress and go back down. I was there before the others, of course, since they primp and preen so, especially horrible Eve and dear Rosalind, or, if male, bath and shave and potter.

'That was all right, because it allowed me to make a killing with the little biccies and small eats thoughtfully left out by a footman, one of the staff hired for the evening, I may say, and doubtless horrified by the babble of tongues below stairs.

'Daddy and Roger appeared, very starched and black-and-white and shining, then Angela, who always looks nice, but seemed to be in a bit of a temper, and Cecy, who looked as though she'd been crying. Then Uncle Hal made his appearance, and I have to say he does look frightfully dashing, I suppose it's being younger and leaner than Daddy and Uncle Roger, although Uncle Roger did make a sharp remark about Savile Row tailoring and supposing that actors needed well-cut evening dress to wear on stage.

'Simon and Nicky sloped in, Nicky wearing Simon's old tail suit, which doesn't really fit him, and then horrible Eve looking very glam and slinky, and after a while Rosalind made her entrance. Well! Simon just goggled at her, and she did look fairy princess-like, all in white flecked with silver. I heard Uncle Hal mutter something about meringues, which made me giggle, and that made Eve cross. Only she was crosser still shortly afterwards, because Rosalind was upstaged by Great Aunt Daphne coming in only seconds behind her, dressed in purple, as always, and looking like something on the pictures. You can see she has tremendous style and spends a fortune on her clothes.

'She told the footman to bring her a glass of champagne, and Eve was stupid enough to say that she was serving sherry. Daphne told her that she, Eve, knew perfectly well that she never touched sherry, which she doesn't, she downs cocktails like anything most evenings, and that the proper drink before dinner and a dance was champagne. Daddy put a stop to a promising argument by telling the footman to open a bottle of champagne, you can tell he's trying to keep her sweet on account of those shares of hers. Goodness, how Eve did glare! Then Great Aunt Daphne told Rosalind that she looked like a Christmas decoration, far too fussy for the current mode and how it was thoroughly provincial to wear a dress like that to a winter dance at home.

'Rosalind's mouth drooped, and you could see hatred and sulk written all over her face, but before she or Eve could say anything else, Great Aunt Daphne turned her attention on me. "Good God, girl," she cried. "You can't appear in public looking like that. Go upstairs and change at once, you're a disgrace to the family, how could Delia's daughter have such dreadful taste?"

'So there was Daddy apoplectic what with Rosalind being criticised and the Great Aunt daring to speak Mummy's name; I notice he didn't seem to mind my being criticised. Simon was gaping like a fish at his adored one being upset, Eve was white with temper, Angela was laughing, and even Cecy looked a good deal more cheerful. Uncle Hal was watching it all with what I can only describe as a supercilious air, and a wicked smile on his face. Nicky was the only one who came to my defence, bless him, he went quite red and turned on Great Aunt Daphne, saying it wasn't my fault, that it was the only dress I possessed, and that there was plenty of money to spend on Rosalind's clothes and nobody cared tuppence about how I looked.

'Uncle Hal said, under his breath, but I heard him, "Good for you, Nicky." Eve leapt into battle and said that I was only a schoolgirl, that my turn would come, that I was still growing and it wasn't worth spending money on good clothes that I'd grow out of.

'Great Aunt Daphne then advanced on me, and demanded to be taken up to my room to inspect my wardrobe. Eve wasn't at all keen on that, but the Great Aunt just swept over her. In about two seconds she was in here, demanding that Bonnet be summoned, that instant, and making all kinds of appalled remarks at the meagre contents of my cupboards.

'"I cannot believe my eyes, but I see that you are telling the truth, Ursula, when you say that's your only party dress. Bonnet, where is that dratted woman? Bonnet, you see how Miss Ursula looks."

'Bonnet's face was a picture.

'"Take it off, Ursula, and Bonnet can at least put in a few

269

stitches so that it fits you properly. And when you've done that, Bonnet, you can dress Miss Ursula's hair and make her powder her nose. And fetch that diamond filigree necklace I never wear – I keep it for sentimental reasons," she said to me, "since my dear Wolf gave it to me in a cracker – and the thin gold and diamond bracelet and earrings."

'Then she noticed my shoes, which have seen better days. More cries of dismay. She took a good look at my feet, which unlike the rest of me are quite OK, slim and a perfectly reasonable size. Not like Perdy's, she has feet to go with her height and she has an awful time finding shoes to fit her. Alix says she's going to have to have them made, and apparently her grandmother agrees, shoes not being something she can really object to, although you may be sure Perdy will be allowed nothing but sensible lace-ups. Anyway, Great Aunt Daphne and Bonnet concluded that my feet were the same size as the Great Aunt's, and Bonnet was instructed to bring some gold shoes as well as the jewellery. I don't think even a French maid can make my dress look like anything much, but I shall feel frightfully grand in diamonds, however small. I hope the shoes don't pinch, for even if no one else dances with me, I know Nicky will.

'Great Aunt Daphne then said some very rude things about horrible Eve, which I enjoyed, and how distressed Mummy would be if she knew how I was being treated, which rather upset me.'

THIRTY-SIX

Torches flared on either side of the drive up to the Hall, their flames and faint trails of smoke clear against the black sky.

Grandpapa grunted. 'Doing it in style, I see.'

Alix, wrapped in a fur rug in the back of the car, looked out of the window at the flares and at the little electric lights which had been run along the front of the house. She felt a sudden aching sense of memory, of the last dance she had come to here at Grindley Hall, when she was twenty-one, on vacation from Oxford, dressed in a dowdy frock and pining for the absent John.

They joined a line of cars. 'Giving a big dinner party, I see,' remarked Grandpapa.

'I think thirty, apart from family,' Trudie said out of the darkness.

In her mind's eye, Alix could see just what lay ahead of them. Dinner, five courses at least, in the dining room. This was one of her favourite rooms at the Hall: a beautiful oval room built in the time of an Adam-loving Grindley ancestor, it had a fine plasterwork ceiling with an oval painting of the muses above the oval table, the ceiling painting matched by an oval Aubusson carpet in shades of pink and grey.

Alix always felt that the muses were hardly appropriate

for the family business, and she and the younger Grindleys had often speculated on which of the Greek pantheon might be more suitable, with Simon's vote for the Titans being regarded as the best suggestion.

The food would be plentiful, the wines good, the conversation that of friends and neighbours, most of whom met each other several times a week, had known one another for much of their lives and therefore had plenty to talk about. Normally, talk of the favoured pursuit of killing things of the furry, feathery or finny variety would have figured largely, but now all they could do was bemoan how the ice had put a stop to all their favourite sports.

There would be a leavening of less familiar faces this year, with the ice drawing so many exiles home to the lake. Hal, for instance. His last dance at the Hall would have been when he, too, was a young man home from university. She might have changed over the last three years; how much more Hal had changed in the intervening years since he had been back to Westmoreland. He wasn't really a Grindley, she decided; he was much too cultured. He must take after his mother's side of the family, or maybe he was a throwback to the Grindley who had built the dining room.

After dinner, more guests would arrive. The band, possibly a Manchester one if Peter was pushing out the boat, would tune up for the first dance, and they would assemble in the ballroom, a less fortunate addition to the house as far as aesthetics went, being mid-Victorian and rather overpowering as to woodwork and pillars. The joy of it was the Orangery leading off the ballroom, which ran along the length of the house; here the band would sit and play amid palms and exotic plants. The huge pots with their orange and lemon trees would be pushed to the sides to make extra room for dancing, and the glass roof would be strung with hundreds of little lights.

For a summer dance, all the doors of the Orangery would

be left open on to the terrace; tonight, for a Christmas dance, great swagged curtains would be hung to shut out the chill night and the clear, moonlit sky.

The headlamps of the slowly moving cars sent patterns of light dancing over the frosty lawns. Eckersley drew up by the front door and climbed out to open doors, fold rugs away and hold Alix's stick while her grandfather and brother heaved her unceremoniously out and on to her sound foot. The cold made her eyes tingle, and Trudie shooed Perdita through the door and into the house rather as though she had been one of the dogs, murmuring disjointedly about cold, chests, bronchitis when younger, proper cloaks and the folly of midwinter outings in sleeveless, low-cut, backless dresses.

Alix made her way with care up the pair of shallow steps, and into the warmth and light of the hall. A maid took her cloak, and attempted to relieve her of her stick, which Grandpapa rescued with a snort of annoyance at the maid's temerity.

She was glad to find herself sitting next to Hal at dinner, although rather thrown when he told her he had switched the place cards in order to enjoy her company. 'Eve had put me next to Sybil Braithwaite. I may not have been back for nearly sixteen years, but a lifetime is not enough to forget that particular woman.'

Alix laughed, but was pleased by the compliment. 'Who was to have sat where you are?'

'One Gerald Carson. Do you know him?'

'A frightful bore. Well, I am glad to have been spared an hour or so of his company, but you've done better than you realized, for the Carsons and the Braithwaites have been sworn enemies for years, something to do with a boundary.'

'Excellent. That's the delight of these kind of gatherings, nothing but friends and enemies, and all so happy to see one another. Now, a lot of these people I know from days of yore, some sadly aged, I notice, others who don't seem to have changed a jot. Some are total strangers; who, for example, is the young man with red hair who so closely resembles a salmon?'

Alix had never been so well entertained in that room. On Hal's other side was a lively woman of about Hal's age, who talked to him about life in New York. On Alix's other side was a very deaf Grindley cousin, who never made any kind of conversation, concentrating entirely on his food and wine. So Alix was free to devote her attention to Hal; she was amused to find herself slightly resentful of the assured way Pansy, as Hal's neighbour was unfortunately called, talked to Hal, but there was nothing flirtatious in his response, and he swiftly drew Alix into their talk when it became obvious that Joseph Grindley wasn't going to say a word to her.

Afterwards, when they went upstairs to powder their noses, Pansy commiserated with Alix for having been sat next to such a dull man.

'He's a famously dreadful guest,' Alix told her with a grin, 'but since he's both childless and rich, Peter Grindley wouldn't dream of not inviting him to dine before a dance.'

Pansy, it turned out, was married to one of the exiles, and this was her first visit to Westmoreland in the winter. 'And my last, if I have anything to do with it,' she confided. 'I know the ice is pretty and all that, but so is Switzerland, and that has the great benefit of being a civilised country. Do you know, my mother-in-law allows no heating in the bedrooms? I can't tell you how cold it gets. I go to bed in woollen jumpers and socks, and put my fur coat on top of the bedclothes, and I'm still frozen in the morning. We have a two-bar electric fire in our room, and when I left it on one night, fearing hypothermia, you understand, my mother-in-law crept in at three in the morning and turned it off. She must have been watching the little wheel on the meter going around, and snooped around until she found out what was on.'

Alix laughed, and thought that she rather liked Pansy, despite her loudly expressed liking for Hal's company.

'My dear, what a find, what a delight in this wilderness of dull men! A man who can talk and not bore on about shooting and fishing, not that they can do any of that now, and you'd think that would shut them up, but no, they go on and on. My Reggie is quite normal in London, but once in the north he turns thoroughly peculiar; I wonder why I ever married him. Imagine Hal being a Grindley, so unlike the rest of the family. Have you met him before? You aren't local, are you, not in that dress?'

Alix had chosen a pewter dress in heavy silk, cut on the bias so that it clung to her figure and would have swayed as she walked had not the stick taken away any grace of movement. Her hair was sleeked back and held in a clasp of grey silk and feathers.

'You look very modern,' Hal said, as he asked her for a dance.

'Pansy said the same about you. She is amazed that you're a Grindley. And I can't dance, by the way.'

'I'm well aware of that, so I propose we sit out together.'

'You'd much better do your duty on the floor. Son of the house and all that.'

'There are plenty of other sons of the house, I shall do as I please. Mind you, I must dance with Daphne, isn't she wonderful?'

Daphne was holding court among a bevy of old acquaintances. 'Several old flames of hers here, I should think,' said Hal. 'Have you seen the change she wrought in Ursula?'

Alix looked, and blinked. 'Good heavens, what a difference, and with her hair like that, she looks even more like Delia. Which is unfortunate when you think of the grudges Peter carries. Have you seen my sister?'

'Perdita? What a wow of a dress. I haven't seen Lady Richardson this evening, however. Isn't she here?'

'No, she has a migraine, and that's why Perdy is looking like she does.'

Alix's attention was caught by the entrance of Michael and Freddie, Michael in unexceptionable tails, Freddie looking darkly handsome and very dashing in full Highland dress.

'It's so unfair,' Hal complained. 'How can we Englishmen compete with that?'

Freddie wasn't the only Scot wearing the kilt and velvet jacket at the dance, but he was much the most striking.

'Who is that man?' Alix heard a stout matron ask. 'If he's going to be around at New Year, we must get him to be our first-footer.'

Freddie and Michael came over to say hello to her. 'Freddie, there's a woman who's going to pounce on you to first-foot at New Year, so I shall bag you first, on behalf of Wyncrag.' She called across to Grandpapa, who was surveying the scene with great satisfaction. He joined them, shaking hands with the young men and looking pleased to see them.

'Don't you agree, Grandpapa, that Freddie will make a perfect bearer of the New Year coal?'

'Certainly, certainly, and I hope also that Michael and Freddie will dine with us on Christmas Day. We shall be quite a crowd, it's the custom for the Grindleys to join us, but the more the merrier, you can't have too big a party on Christmas night.'

It was hard on Grandpapa, Alix knew; he loved Christmas, whereas Grandmama would have left the season unmarked by any festivities if she could have managed it. They had never sat down alone as a family at Christmas, not for as long as she could remember. Grandpapa knew very well that hospitality was the only way to keep his wife's dislike of the occasion under control.

Alix had wondered if it had anything to do with her Uncle Jack's having been killed in December, but when she had asked Aunt Trudie, who was at the time happily threading extra swags of foliage through the banisters, her aunt had said not. 'It goes back much earlier, I think it was on account of Mama's being brought up in such an atheistical household.'

'How dull her parents must have been, what did they celebrate?'

'I don't remember them awfully well, they died, you see, when I was quite small. They were very serious people, with a scientific approach to everything, science had all the answers. Not puritanical, exactly; clear-headed realists, they would say. Only realism is so often used to mean negative, I find, and that's so disheartening.'

'You aren't serious or negative, Aunt Trudie,' Alix had said, giving her aunt an impulsive hug. 'I wish I hadn't hurt my ankle, I could help you put up more decorations.'

'Last time you were here for Christmas, you scorned the tree and lights and decorations. I believe you said the money would be better spent on the poor. Not that it is a matter of spending, since the greenery is from outside, and the lights go from year to year.'

'Did I really say that? How dreadfully priggish of me.' That had been a combination of youthful hatred of all things familial, mixed with a good dose of John's austere views on anything that smacked of frivolity. 'Well, Aunt Trudie, I think the house looks quite lovely, decorated for Christmas and with vistas of snow from every window.'

She could see Aunt Trudie now, engaged in what was, for her, animated conversation with the vicar. New since she was here, an agreeable-looking man in his forties, with a humorous face and nothing of the pompous cleric about him. Unlike the previous incumbent, she thought, who had been the most tedious man.

She would so have liked to dance, she fretted at having to sit and envy those out on the floor. Yet there was a novelty and a certain interest in being an observer; not one to have spent any time as a wallflower, she had never before had the opportunity just to sit and watch the constantly moving throng of people.

Michael was dancing with Cecy. She was wearing a rose-pink dress which suited her fairness. She had abandoned her spectacles, which meant, she confessed to Michael, that she could hardly see a thing.

On the other hand, Michael, who had excellent eyesight, could see that she had been crying not so long ago. He held her a little more firmly and asked her what the matter was. Cecy, he felt, was a person who should be happy, and he didn't care for the taut look about her eyes and mouth.

'Matter? Why should anything be the matter? Everything's perfectly fine.'

'No, it isn't. Don't tell me if you don't want to, but is there anything I can do to help? Ask advice from Uncle Michael, all letters replied to and a guinea to any reader whose letter is printed on my page.'

She laughed, despite herself. 'It's a family problem.'

They danced for a while in silence. 'I don't have any family to speak of,' Michael said. 'My parents are both dead, and I was an only child. I have an aunt who lives in the Borders, who saw me through university, but she's a tough old biddy, and so you see, problems don't arise.'

'Are you politely telling me I should be grateful to have a family, with or without problems?'

'Good gracious, no,' Michael said, taken aback. 'That would be unpardonable. What I mean is, you can tell me and get a disinterested and un-familied viewpoint on the problem if you cared to.' He spoke lightly, not wanting to tell Cecy how much he disliked seeing her unhappiness.

'It isn't really a secret, since it'll be obvious enough when I don't go back to London after the Christmas break.'

'Not go back to London? Are you continuing your medical training up north, then?'

'I'm not continuing it anywhere. Daddy says he won't pay for me any more. Not won't, he says, can't; that he has to retrench. I don't know why, he has his share of the family business, beside his legal earnings, and his fees are huge now he's a KC. I thought it was just spite, he's always threatening to stop me becoming a doctor, but that's because he disapproves in principle, it isn't the money. Only now it is. Mummy won't say much, but I think Daddy's been plunging on the stock market, and the way things are I suppose he could have lost a lot of money.'

Michael wasn't a man with a portfolio of stocks and shares, or one who took any particular interest in the City, but he had friends who did, and he knew that one or two of them had been badly burned in recent months.

'Aren't there schemes to help trainee doctors who run out of funds? Or scholarships?'

'There are, but they prefer to hand out any money there is to men. They all say women train and qualify and then get married and it's all wasted. I can swear until I'm blue in the face that I don't ever intend to get married, but they don't believe me.'

'Is it true?' said Michael. 'Are you really set against marriage?'

Close to tears again, she merely nodded.

'You'll change your mind.'

'I won't. I expect you miss your parents, and I dare say they were happily married, but when I see what marriage has done to my mother, I'm sure I don't want to be caught in the same trap.'

These were wild words to Michael. He regarded Cecy with a kind of awed surprise. 'Surely every woman dreams of getting married and having a family?'

'Not this one, and you'd be amazed how many women of my generation are chary about getting married. You lose everything when you marry, I mean you can keep your money now, if you've got any, but you just become part of your husband's life, you can't have a career of your own.'

'Do many women want careers?'

'I don't suppose there are many women in your field, so you wouldn't know, but yes, lots of women would like to have careers.'

'I had no idea.'

Alix found some amusement in the fact that many of her previous friends and acquaintances didn't immediately recognise her.

'Alix? Alix Richardson? Is it really you? My dear, I would never have known you.'

'Goodness, Lexy, I had to look twice to know it was you. I heard you were coming north, and I was longing to see you again. I'm married now and living in Herefordshire, I asked you to the wedding, if you remember, but you were abroad or something. Do tell what you've been up to, I'm sure your life in London is madly exciting.'

'Hello, Alix. You do look different. Edwin told me you'd be here, or I wouldn't have recognised you, so smart as you've become. I noticed you at dinner, sitting next to Hal Grindley, lucky you, he's devastatingly attractive, isn't he?'

Bother Hal, thought Alix. 'Is he?'

'Oh, come on. Even in London, men like him don't grow on trees. Now, tell me what Edwin's up to, who's this woman he's got holed up in Lowfell? Rumour is rife, I can tell you.'

'Marjorie, she's a friend, from abroad, who's looking for a place to live, which you can't do over Christmas. Nothing more.'

Why was she defending Edwin, when she felt Marjorie was more than justified in her gossipy suspicions? Because she was his twin, and while she herself might harbour evil thoughts about Lidia, she was damned if Marjorie Geddison was going to run Edwin down, for whatever reason.

Cries of delight from an old schoolfriend, who had a willowy young man in tow, a young man Alix had known since they were both in the nursery.

'Alix, it is Alix, I knew it was; my dear, what a divine dress! And what have you done to your leg, no dancing, you poor sweet? Tony, look who's here, it's Alix, no less, after all this time. We quite thought you'd never be on speakers with your gran again, and one would only see you if one visited wicked old London, which I must say I'm jolly happy to do.'

Her friends drifted away to the dance floor, and she found herself alone. An older man was looking at her, and as she caught his eye, he came up to her. She was sure that she knew him, but she couldn't put a name to the face. He was a well-built man, with a very tanned face and the look to his eyes of a person who spent most of his time in the open air.

'Alix? You won't remember me, the last time we met you were a child.' He held out a hand. 'I'm Alan Hemmings, and I was a friend of your father's. I see you're laid up,' he pointed to her foot. 'Nothing serious, I trust? May I sit down?'

Alix said that she had merely given her ankle a nasty wrench on the ice. 'You're the mountaineer and explorer, aren't you? I've read about you in the papers.'

'That's it. I used to climb a lot with your father. I can't tell you how grieved I was when Neville was killed. I still miss him. I never had a better climbing partner. What a loss it was to our sport when he died.'

'Was he really such a good mountaineer?'

'Oh, one of the very best. He grew up climbing all these hills, that's the kind of background all our top men have, Scotland or the Lake District or the Welsh hills. He was a meticulous climber, instinctive but always clear-headed. Not one to take risks, and I can tell you, when you're at one end of the rope, you don't want a risk-taker at the other end.'

'Yet he fell.'

'That can happen to anyone. He loved the mountains, and

although it was a tragedy he died so young, I know he would have been glad to end his days up there amid the high peaks.'

Alix thought back to that momentous year. Daddy packing, calling for his equipment, his boots, discussing the fastening on his goggles with someone. Barely talking to Mummy, and she had been white-faced, tight-lipped, anxious, drawn; Alix could see her quite clearly in her mind's eye. How odd, after all these years of not being able to visualise her at all, to suddenly see her so clearly.

'I don't think Mummy wanted him to go.'

'No, she didn't. She told me that it was a bad time for him to go, some trouble in the family, I believe.'

'My sister was ill.'

'That would be it. And she told me just before he went that she felt he wasn't in the right frame of mind for the kind of mountain he would be tackling. She wouldn't have minded so much if it had been the Alps, which he knew so well and which were close. It was his going off to the Andes, where he'd never climbed before, that alarmed her. That and the distance. I couldn't go with him, and I've always blamed myself for that. Perhaps if I'd gone . . . However, I didn't.'

'Mummy was expecting another baby; it's always seemed odd that Daddy should go so far away, with that and with Isabel being ill.'

'He was worried about you all,' Hemmings said. 'I saw him in London just before he left. He was going up to Liverpool the next day, to catch the boat for Chile. We were at a Royal Society dinner, and walked back to his club afterwards. I didn't know about Helena and the baby. I assume he intended to be back before the child was born. That would be your younger sister?'

Alix nodded. 'Perdita. She's the tall girl there, in the red dress.'

'Is she now? Good heavens, so that's Neville's youngest

daughter. He would have been proud of her. She takes after that younger brother of Neville's, what was his name?'

'Jack.'

'Jack, yes, that's it. I only met him a couple of times, that would have been around nineteen sixteen, when I was home on leave. Of course, he and Neville didn't get on.'

'Didn't they? Uncle Jack died when I was very small, so I never knew him.'

'Neville was a very even-tempered man. Most of us climbers are, you know, you need an equable temperament to make a good mountaineer. But whenever Jack's name was mentioned, even after he was dead, Neville would get quite heated, and say some very bitter things about him. But all this is old history, my dear, it doesn't do to rake up the past, I find. I am glad to see you again, and looking so lovely if I may say so. And young Perdita – how old is she? Fifteen, my word how the years do fly past, it seems only yesterday I was seeing Neville on to the boat train. Is your brother here?'

'Edwin, yes.'

'I shall say hello.'

'Mr Hemmings,' Alix said, as her companion got up. 'You say Daddy was worried about us, when you saw him in London. Was that all? I mean, was he angry or depressed . . . Anything that might have meant he wasn't as careful climbing as he should have been?'

'Depressed? His spirits were down, I can't say he was in a very lively frame of mind, but that's only natural when you're starting a long trip which is taking you away from your family for several months.'

'Do you think that's why he fell?'

'Oh, no, not a bit of it. Trust me, once Neville was there, he would have been completely focused on the mountains, and the task in hand. That was the kind of man he was.'

'Yet he made a mistake, he slipped and fell.' She closed her eyes to shut out the image of a figure falling from unimaginable heights, plunging to the rocks and ice and snow thousands of feet beneath him.

'My dear, that can happen to any one of us.'

He smiled and moved away, leaving Alix lost in thought. Now, from the vantage point of her twenty-four years, her father's behaviour in nineteen twenty-one seemed quite extraordinary. What kind of a man would leave – abandon, almost – his pregnant wife and an ill daughter to travel to the other side of the world to climb mountains?

Hal had gone in search of refreshments, thirsty after a very lively foxtrot with Pansy. He took a glass of punch from a passing waiter, and moved to one side to drink it.

'Ghastly stuff, that punch,' said a voice from the other side of the pillar, and Simon, looking rather flushed, came around to stand beside Hal. 'Stick to whisky if I were you.'

And you've already had more whisky than is good for you, Hal said to himself. If he knew the signs, Simon would shortly be retreating to the bathroom for a nasty session. What possessed the young man to get drunk at a dance in his own home, and so early in the evening? Or was he one of those unfortunates who simply couldn't hold his liquor?

'I decided to get drunk,' Simon informed him. 'Best to live in a blur, stops one thinking and worrying about things.'

Hal sighed. He was used to dealing with young men in his work, and he could see the signs of imminent confession and confusion. Simon wasn't a young actor nor a writer, but Hal didn't suppose his problems were much different at root. 'Worrying about what things?' he said obligingly.

'The Guv'nor, and going into the business, and how do I tell him I don't want to spend the rest of my life making lavatories.'

'When you put it like that, it does seem a dull existence, but it isn't quite fair, is it, in reality? Many young men would think a thriving family business a tremendous inheritance.'

'It won't thrive long if I'm in charge of any of it,' said Simon glumly. 'I'm hopeless at figures, and the last thing I want to do is sit in an office all day.'

'I hardly think Peter does that.'

'No, but he'll expect me to. Learning the ropes, he calls it, and then I'm to spend six months on the factory floor, making the damn lavs.'

'They do provide the family fortune, and someone has to make them.'

'Let someone who needs the work do it, I'll just be taking the bread out of some poor chap's mouth, if you think about it. And you know what? If there's a war, which there's bound to be, everyone says so, all the chaps at Cambridge, the ones who are much brainier than I am, they all say it's coming, if, as I say, there's a war and I'm in the business, the Guv'nor will move heaven and earth to keep me there for the duration.'

Hal thought this was all too likely. 'Would you rather be in uniform if the balloon goes up?' Good God, he was beginning to talk the way they had all done back in nineteen eighteen.

'Would I?' Simon's face took on an even deeper shade of red. 'Oh, wouldn't I just! You know how it is, Uncle Hal, you were in the last war.'

'Yes.' Should he mention how truly appalling the whole experience had been?

'It isn't only knowing there's going to be a war and wanting to get in quickly. I hope to be a soldier, a professional soldier. It's all I've ever wanted to be. Only if there's a war, and I've wasted all that time, hanging about up north, well, even if I can get out of the factory, I'd have a job getting into a decent regiment, because, don't you see, all the other chaps will be there before me.'

'Simon, why on earth do you want to be a soldier?' This was an ambition that really was beyond Hal's understanding.

'It's a grim life. Do you have any idea what you'd be letting yourself in for?'

Simon's face glowed with enthusiasm. 'It's the best life one could have. I could go to Sandhurst in the autumn if I crammed a bit on the old maths, and then I'd get a commission in bags of time before they all start shooting at each other.'

'Being a soldier means you train to kill other men.'

'Doesn't it just, and get them before they get you. That's what war means, Uncle Hal, they want to kill or imprison you and me and all the women and children. Someone's got to fight for them. Why shouldn't it be me?'

'Why not, indeed?' Hal murmured.

Simon took hold of his uncle's sleeve. 'The thing is, Uncle Hal, could you have a word with the old man? You're his brother and all that, he'd listen to you.'

'The only result of Peter's listening to me, I'm afraid, would be that he'd do the exact opposite of whatever I asked.'

'You could bargain with him. Over those shares. If you don't mind much either way. He minds a lot, you see, he's simply gone on selling that porcelain company. He'd say yes to my going into the army if it meant his getting his hands on your share of the business. I'm desperate, Uncle Hal. I'd hoped that Rosalind might put in a word for me, the Guv'nor's potty about her, she can twist him around her little finger, and I'm not surprised. I want to ask her to marry me, you see, once I've got a commission and all that. Only she won't do it, she just laughs at me and tells me to fight my own battles, and that there won't be a silly war anyhow and then I'd be a soldier with no one to fight and she couldn't imagine anything more pointless.'

Simon was beginning to slide floorwards. Hal caught a footman's eye and gestured to his nephew. 'Escort Mr Simon to the nearest bathroom,' he said. Then he looked more closely at the footman. 'Hello, aren't you Parsons, the chauffeur?'

'Tonight, I am footman. Is fun. I take the young gentleman to be sick, and then I mix him something to make him better.'

'No more alcohol.'

Parsons was hurt. 'I know this. My brother, when he isn't fighting Franco, he is getting drunk. I deal with it.'

Two women went by, giving the trio sidelong glances. Hal overheard their whispered talk.

'My dear, that's Hal, the black sheep, back from America or wherever he went. And Simon, pie-eyed.'

'Isn't that footman one of Eve's foreigners?'

'Yes, she has a household of them. Imagine, up here! She says they're cheap.'

'She's only got two or three, this man and a maid who's from Portugal, so she can't be saving herself so much on the bills. Besides, it's folly, the locals don't care for it at all, they aren't deceived by her giving them English names. It isn't like in London where we're all getting used to Spaniards and Austrians and the Lord knows who arriving by every train. It doesn't do to put people's backs up, not when you're an offcomer to start with, like Eve is. Poor Simon, I don't wonder he's tipsy, it must be hell for those children with a stepmother like that.'

'Delia should have thought of that before she chucked Peter.'

'The chucking was done by Peter.'

'Oh, yes, but only after . . .'

'Simon drunk again?' asked Nicky, materialising at his side. 'I wish he wouldn't, it isn't good for him and it makes him look such an ass.'

'Is it a habit with him?'

'It is rather. Only recently though, what with his doomed love for Rosalind and being at his wit's end about what he'll do when he finishes at Cambridge in the summer.'

'He tells me he wants to be a soldier.'

'He's mad, completely mad. I suppose he'd be rather good

at it, though, to be honest. I can see him in a uniform leading the troops into battle. Do you think there'll be a war, Uncle Hal?'

Hal looked at his younger nephew with mild irritation. These boys were making him feel old, which he wasn't, and useless, which in their terms, he was.

'I'm not the person to ask,' he said as lightly as he could. 'On my side of the Atlantic, we see things differently.'

'I suppose you do. Are you doing any directing while you're over here, or is it just a holiday for you?'

Hal jumped. 'What did you say?'

'I know you aren't the unsuccessful actor they all think you are. Don't worry, I shan't say anything, I'm not stupid, I can see you prefer to keep it quiet. Is that why you changed your name?'

'I didn't. Henry is my name, of course, and Ivison is my middle name.'

'I thought the "I" stood for Ian.'

'No, Ivison, which was my grandmother's maiden name.'

'Does Great Aunt Daphne know? I shouldn't think one could keep many secrets from her.'

'Very true, and yes, she does. Be a good chap and continue to keep it under your hat, would you?'

'Nobody ever listens to anything I say anyhow,' said Nicky cheerfully. 'I could shout it from the chimney pots and they wouldn't pay any attention, they'd just say, what's Nicky making a to do about, and go on with what they were doing. I wish Simon could be a soldier, and then maybe my father would let me go into the firm instead of him.'

There was no end to the surprises Hal's family were handing out this evening. 'Is that what you want?'

'I'd like it very much. Everything we make is fearfully old-fashioned, you know. One has to keep up with the times, you'd appreciate that, living in America.'

Hal was about to demur on that one, but perhaps Nicky

had the truth of it. 'If there's war, which, as I say, I can't predict, then I dare say what Jowetts will be turning out is thousands of plain lavatories and urinals for the troops.'

'I know that. You can make terrific amounts of money in wartime, if you supply the forces or make weapons. Then, after it's over, there'll be money to invest in new plant and new ideas.'

'Always supposing the country isn't being run as part of the Reich.'

'Do you think we might lose?' Nicky was taken aback. 'Well, even then, they'll still need lavs and baths and basins, won't they?'

Hal decided that he simply didn't understand the younger generation. 'Don't you want to go to the university?'

'No. I've discussed it very carefully with Berris, he's my best friend at school, and both of us think it's a frightful waste of time, unless you want to go in for school mastering or something like that. Berris is going to be a painter. I wish you could meet him, I know you'd like him.'

'I see.'

Nicky's eyes were following Freddie, who was dancing on the other side of the room. 'That's Dr Kerr. Don't you think he's awfully good looking?'

Well, Hal thought, as the dance ended and he went to look for his partner for the next one, Nicky might do brilliantly in the family business. He had brains and flair, and anything that kept him out of uniform would be a blessing. Did Peter have the slightest idea of how his younger son was shaping up, or what his inclinations seemed likely to be? Hal thought not. Nicky might have a tougher path to travel than any Simon was dreaming of, battlefields or no battlefields.

THIRTY-SEVEN

Daphne bore down on Alix in a blaze of purple. Alix, startled, seized her stick, ready to haul herself upright, but Daphne forestalled her. 'No, no, don't get up. Do you know who I am?'

'Mrs Wolf? My godmother?'

'How clever of you to know.'

Not so clever, when the purple Rolls and livery and clothes – even some of her furs were purple, only imagine! – had been the talk of the lake, and Alix had had a blow-by-blow description of Great Aunt Daphne's descent on Grindley Hall from Cecy.

'So sad, not to be dancing, a young thing like you. Now, let me compliment you on your dress. How wise you are to dress up even when you aren't dancing. Céline, is it? Yes, one can always tell, there's no one in London to touch her for cut when it comes to evening gowns. Plenty in Paris, of course, but it's different there. How do you come to afford such clothes, are you a kept woman?'

Alix felt she should protest, but instead she laughed. 'No, sadly not.'

'I can't see Caroline letting Henry give you a sufficiently large allowance to buy clothes like that.'

'I came into some money from one of Grandpapa's sisters.'

'Ah, that would be Gertrude, I dare say she left a tidy sum, she was always a mean creature. The psychoanalysts say it's all down to potty training, don't they, or being smacked or not smacked enough in the nursery. I don't believe a word of it, Gertrude was born mean. Still, I'm glad she left you some money, a girl can't have too much money. What about your parents, they must have left you well provided for? That was a shocking loss for you, both parents and a sister. Neville inherited a lot from his grandfather, I don't know about your mother, she was an American.'

'What they left us is in trust until we're twenty-five.'

'We? Oh, you and Edwin, twins, of course. Well, that will come in handy. Does that tall child have to wait until she's twenty-five, what's her name?'

'Perdita. She'll come into Great Aunt Gertrude's inheritance at twenty-one. She'll be very glad of it, too.'

Daphne's eyebrows shot up. 'Caroline up to her old tricks is she, keeping the girl under iron control and short of spending money? It doesn't seem to have worked in your case. Do you still live at Wyncrag?'

'No, I have a job in London.'

'A job?' Daphne's voice was incredulous, and Alix flushed.

'I work in an advertising agency.'

'Whatever for, if you've got plenty of money?'

'I want to.'

'I simply don't understand you young things. Either you're intoxicated all the time, full of cocktails and cocaine, or you're going off to dull offices or running dull charities. Where's the fun in that?'

Alix thought it prudent not to answer.

'And advertising, why advertising?'

'I happen to be rather good at writing copy.'

'You'll never get a husband if you carry on with that sort of thing. How old are you now?'

'Twenty-four.'

'Good gracious, it's high time you were married. Engaged?'

Alix shook her head.

'My nephew Hal, do you like him?'

'Hal?' What had Hal got to do with this?

'Yes, Hal. He's an interesting man. Attractive.'

'I'm sure he is.'

'He likes you.'

Alix gave Daphne what she hoped was a repressive look, but Daphne had hopped off on to another topic. 'Now, that sister of yours may look like her uncle, but the one you take after is Caroline.'

That was all she needed. 'I don't think so, not judging by the picture of her at Wyncrag when she was about my age.'

'It's not a matter of features, more a direct look you both have. I knew her when she was a girl. I introduced her to Henry as a matter of fact. Worst day's work I ever did, although I suppose he's been happy after a fashion with her. He was my beau in those days, and he came with me to a dance in Cambridge. He met Caroline, and that was that.'

'Did you mind?' Meaning, had Daphne been in love with Grandpapa; it seemed incredible, absurd, to think of that generation being torn apart by the kind of emotions that ruled her contemporaries.

'My pride was piqued, that's all, for that very week I'd met Wolf, and really, there was no one else for me after that. Lord, what a fuss there was. My father, and my brother – he was Peter and Hal's father – had made up their minds I was to marry Henry and live at Wyncrag, unite the two houses, a perfect match. Instead of which, Henry brought home the daughter of a Cambridge professor, of all things, and I married a Jew. I know who got the better deal, but that's life.'

Alix was intrigued by these family ructions of long ago. 'What about Grandpapa's family? Didn't they like Caroline?'

'They mistrusted her, with her atheism and enthusiasm for

science and her rigid code. Mind you, she was very beautiful and had tremendous charm.'

'You wouldn't know it these days,' Alix muttered.

'What was that?'

Nothing wrong with her godmother's ears, even if she was the same age as Grandmama and Grandpapa.

'Nothing.'

'It was a shame that the only one of her children to inherit her charm was Jack. Heredity is a funny thing.'

'Uncle Jack? Everyone just goes on about how awful he was, a bully and all that, no one ever mentions charm.'

Daphne made a rather inelegant snorting sound. 'Bully? That's as may be, but what he was was a seducer, that was the really tiresome thing about Jack. And that's where the charm came in, they couldn't resist him.'

'Married women?' asked Alix.

'That wouldn't have been half so bad. No, Jack liked them young, the younger the better.' Her face took on a foxy expression. 'Ask your Aunt Jane about that.'

There it was again, Aunt Jane's name linked with Jack.

'Violence, he had a reputation for liking violence. With women. And given that the women in question were mostly so very young, and therefore ignorant and innocent, it was a distinctly unpleasant habit.' Daphne gave Alix a sharp look. 'I dare say you know what I mean, from hearsay if not from your own experience. No, don't attempt to put on a shocked expression, no girl of twenty-four who looks the way you do in that dress is going to persuade me that she's an innocent miss. Have a cigarette.'

Why was her godmother telling her all this? Alix stared at the cigarette between her fingers. Purple? A purple cigarette?

'I have them specially made for me,' Daphne said, tucking her cigarette into the end of a long holder decorated with amethysts. 'Anyway, good riddance to your Uncle Jack,' she went on. 'Getting himself killed in the war was the best thing he could have done. Caroline doesn't think so, but everyone else heaved a sigh of relief. Including his brothers and sisters, I may add, so don't be taken in by any Jack the hero nonsense, MC or no MC.'

Alix hadn't finished with the subject. 'So Aunt Jane married Uncle Saul on the rebound.'

Another snort of laughter. 'Rebound! That's one word for it. It was your grandmother fixed that match up, what an interfering woman she turned out to be. Quite ruthless in arranging other people's lives to fit in with her convenience and wishes.'

'Aunt Jane and Uncle Saul can't have children. Because of being cousins, Grandmama says.'

'Ah, afraid of the close connection throwing up freaks?'

'It has to do with Aunt Trudie being born with a sixth finger and there being deaf-mutism in the family, way back. Grandmama says that by the laws of inheritance, cousins are much more likely to produce abnormal children.'

'Yes, I remember Trudie's extra finger. Jane is a cousin on the male side.'

Alix looked puzzled.

'If you can't work it out, you can't. Is Caroline into eugenics? That's the kind of dangerous nonsense she would go for.'

'She has mentioned it.'

'I sometimes think Caroline should have been locked away.'

Was Mrs Wolf drunk? Alix couldn't think why she was saying these things, none of which seemed to make much sense. Of course, she was getting on, she might be a bit gaga.

Jane was dancing with Freddie and enjoying the music, her partner's company and the feeling of freedom that dancing always gave her. Saul rarely danced these days. 'My dancing days are behind me,' he was inclined to say. As though it were something to be proud of.

Jane did not ever intend to put her dancing days behind her. Look at Daphne Wolf, seventy if she was a day, and lighter on her feet than many of the younger women. How did she do it? Jane had asked her, over supper.

'Live abroad, my dear. There's nothing like warmth and sunshine in the air to keep one supple. Plus the light. The light is the great gift of the south, especially to the English, born and bred in greyness. It's no wonder our bones turn brittle and our sinews shrink. Yes, sunshine is the key. Plus young men about you, to remind you what life is for.'

Jane had looked prim. Mrs Wolf was jesting.

Mrs Wolf wasn't. 'If one has plenty of money, which is another great secret of eternal youth, one finds young men are very happy to spend time in one's company.'

Jane thought this was no way for a widow of advancing years, however lightly she might trip on the dance floor, to talk. 'Your husband's memory,' she began.

'I loved Wolf very dearly, until the day he died, and mourned him very sincerely. But it is precisely because he was such an excellent husband in every way that I grew accustomed to male company, and so I make a point of not depriving myself of it.'

Jane had thought of Saul, whom she would not describe as an excellent husband on any grounds, and said that the south of England was as far as her ambition reached.

'Take my word for it,' Daphne said. 'It's not the same as Mentone.'

Freddie was a medical man, Freddie might know what gave a woman like Daphne Wolf her amazing pep.

'Her constitution, I dare say. Some people are built to last, and she's obviously one of them.'

'It's all down to heredity, I suppose,' said Jane.

'The laws of inheritance are too complicated for us to understand completely, but yes, a vigorous parent may well pass that vigour on to the next generation. Or not, there's many a sickly offspring of hale and hearty parents.'

'The Germans don't think so, do they? Aren't they very keen on breeding superheroes?'

'Such as Hitler, and that fine specimen of Aryan manhood, Dr Goebbels. I doubt if they'll get very far. The Americans have some men who are keen on the field, but there'd be a public outcry if they ever try to put their theories into practice. Would you care to be told that you could or couldn't have children because of some supposed fault in your heredity, in your genes?'

Jane froze, halted, stared at Freddie, tears starting into her eyes. 'How could you?'

Freddie stared at her. 'Why, whatever have I said?'

Jane broke away from him and walked off the dance floor, her head held high. 'I turned my ankle,' she said in reply to a polite enquiry from Cecy, who had been dancing with Michael and had paused on seeing Jane's stricken face.

'Ankle?' asked Freddie, catching up with her and guiding her to a chair. 'It seems to be a habit in your family.'

She wished he would go away, and leave her alone. Who had been talking about her to him? Who would be callous or tactless enough to talk about why she and Saul had no children to anyone outside the immediate family? And to a man who was almost a total stranger.

'Now, listen to me,' said Freddie. 'I don't think you hurt your foot, I think I hurt you very much by something I said. I had no intention of hurting you, I had no idea I was talking about a sensitive subject. I assure you, there was nothing personal in any remarks I made. If I touched a nerve, I can only apologize.'

Jane considered what he was saying. He sounded sincere, and she wanted to believe him so. 'I have no children.'

'I know that.'

'Has anyone from Wyncrag ever said why my husband and I are childless? Or have any of the Grindleys mentioned it to you?'

'They have not.'

She searched his face with her big, troubled eyes, and read nothing but concern and some alarm there. 'I'm sorry,' she said, getting up from her seat. 'I made too much of what was clearly a casual remark. Shall we go back to the dance?'

He hooked his arm and they took their places on the floor again.

After a while, Jane said, 'If you wouldn't mind, I'd like to tell you why I flared up at what you said. I think I owe you an explanation.'

'You don't, but if you want to talk, go ahead. I'm listening.'

'Glandular fever. Or some disorder of that kind.'

Alix had found herself standing next to the elder Dr Johnstone at supper, and had thought it too good an opportunity to miss. She wanted to know what had been wrong with Isabel fifteen years ago.

'Why glandular fever?'

'Girls of that age often succumb to it. I have no idea what ailed your sister, so glandular fever is as good a guess as any. Like any diagnosis, it fits the facts.'

'But you don't know. Why weren't you called in? Or were you?'

Dr Johnstone had brought Alix and Edwin into the world, along with at least half the assembled company, and he wasn't going to mince his words.

'What you are doing, my dear Alix, is disobeying that excellent old maxim about sleeping dogs, and, knowing you, you aren't just disturbing them, but kicking them into howling, barking life. Take an old man's advice. Don't.'

'Don't what, exactly?'

'Don't ask too many questions. Let the dead past bury its dead.'

'Dr Johnstone, I was nine when my parents died, and my sister. Now I'm twenty-four. It was a long time ago, and that means that it no longer hurts the way it did, but it also means that I want to know. I want to sort it all out in my mind. What happened that year has gone on affecting me and Edwin and Perdy, you can understand that, I'm sure.'

Which was a veiled way of reminding him how hard it was to have been brought up by Grandmama rather than her own mother and father.

He said nothing.

'It was the most terrible year of my life, and the first thing that went wrong was Isabel suddenly getting ill. It's a missing piece of the jigsaw puzzle, I'd like to know what her illness was. It might have been life threatening, it might have been that she wouldn't have lived to make old bones in any case. I was thinking about TB.'

'Tuberculosis?' Dr Johnstone was taken aback. 'Oh, I don't think so. Isabel wasn't the consumptive type. Anything is possible, but I would be surprised.'

'You didn't see her? You weren't called in?'

'Your mother, dear Mrs Neville, had strong views on the medical profession. I believe her distrust or dislike of physicians came from her religious principles. No, I wasn't called in to see Isabel. And, you know, if it were glandular fever, which is a most debilitating disease, although not fatal, there would be nothing I could do but prescribe rest and perhaps a tonic. Time is the only healer. And if her mother, your mother, chose to pray for her, who can say that prayers might not help?'

'We woke up one morning to find that Isabel had been closeted in the other wing, we were strictly forbidden to go anywhere near her.'

'That does sound like an infection of some kind. Scarlet fever? No, she had the scarlet fever when she was an infant. Very mildly, fortunately.'

'She went back to school a fortnight later, in the January. If it had been anything really infectious, she couldn't have gone, and nor could Edwin and I have gone back to the village school. We'd have been kept in quarantine.'

'Very true, very true. That didn't strike me. Of course, since I was never consulted, I never gave it any thought.'

'She went away in the Easter holidays. To convalesce, Nanny told us.'

'Your nanny, she would know what was the trouble.'

'Dr Johnstone, you know as well as I do that Nanny left us years ago.'

'Did she? Yes, so she did, so she did. Well, then, it doesn't seem that anyone can help you. Your grandmother, Lady Richardson, will know. You could ask her.'

Was Dr Johnstone being deliberately obtuse or wilful or malicious? Possibly all three.

'I could, but I wouldn't get an answer.'

'Lady Richardson knows everything that has happened at Wyncrag these last fifty years. Everything.'

'If she does, she won't tell.'

'Ah, dear Alix, that's her privilege. We all need our secrets. And there are some secrets much better kept that way. Sleeping dogs, as I said; even the most somnolent of hounds may turn out to have a savage bite if roused.'

Michael was beginning to wish he hadn't come. These weren't his sort of people, and he was hot and uncomfortable and, except when he could dance or talk to Cecy, bored. His white tie was too tight and his collar rubbed.

Freddie was enjoying himself, dancing every dance, flirting with several pretty girls and even with Jane Richardson, who must be quite ten years older than him, apart from being married. Michael didn't spend much time thinking about morals, his head was too full of aeroplanes, but he held the simple and straightforward notion that married people had best stay married and that married women were off limits – even for flirting.

Freddie would stay till the bitter end, there were going to be reels later on, and Freddie loved dancing reels.

Could he open a window? The place seemed hermetically sealed, with velvet and damask curtains, each one enough to curtain all the windows in his landlady's abode, covering every inch of glass.

'Hot?' said Ursula, appearing at his elbow.

'Very,' said Michael.

'You are wilting, rather. I tell you what, come with me. I know a really cool place.'

The cool place was the top of the cellar steps, with the door propped open. Michael had known pleasanter spots, he thought, as the mephitic chill wafting up from the deep began to lower his temperature. 'Good God, what lives down there?'

'Not much. Mushrooms, mostly. This isn't the wine cellar, that's on the other side of the house. This is the smugglers' cellar, where all the contraband wine and brandy used to be hidden from the excise men.'

'Smugglers? But this is nowhere near the sea.'

'Nearer than you think, and it must have been worth the contrabanders' while bringing it here, because they did, for years and years, back in the eighteenth century.'

'Four and twenty ponies, trotting through the dark,' Michael said, the line floating up from some long ago school task.

'Brandy for the parson, baccy for the clerk,' said Ursula. 'Cooler now?'

'I shall get pneumonia if I stay here.'

'Have you ever had pneumonia?'

'When I was a boy.'

'Was it awful? Did you have bubbling breath and terrible visions?'

'I don't remember much about it, thankfully. It was when I was up here for Christmas. I went out at night and caught a nasty chill. As I will now, come on, let's go back to the ballroom.'

'When was that?'

'Nineteen twenty.'

'When the lake last froze over.'

'That's right. I went skating by moonlight.' His voice was quiet, for into his mind now came a clear, sharp memory, of being on the ice, swooping and curving to avoid the strange blue shadows cast by the full moon. He was wearing tweed plus fours and a Norfolk jacket. The jacket was too tight, that was the year he began to shoot up.

'Penny for them,' said Ursula.

'What? Oh, sorry, how rude of me. I suddenly remembered being out on the ice, when I was a boy. Isn't it odd how a memory like that flashes into one's mind? It hasn't, in all these years. Even the clothes I was wearing . . .'

'I expect you're a seething mass of repressions,' Ursula said in a kindly voice. 'Most people are. Perhaps you have a complex about ice, do you feel dizzy or disoriented when you go on the ice?'

'I do not. Which way do we go?'

'I'll show you. Are you sure you want to go back? My stepmother will probably pounce on you and make you dance. There aren't enough young men to go around, she says. She's furious because my great aunt and people like Jane Richardson are dancing. They take up the men, you see, and leave the girls as wallflowers. I don't know why she frets about it, Rosalind has a thousand applicants clamouring for her hand. Have you been clamouring?'

'To dance with your stepsister? I have not.'

'Nor has Edwin, and she's been making up to him shamelessly. It makes poor Simon so cross, but he's a bit the worse for wear anyhow. Edwin looks at her as if she were a worm, and she pouts and throws her head about and questions him about photography with many a meaningful glance from beneath her lustrous lashes.'

'Good Lord,' said Michael, stopping to look at his strange companion. Had she been at the champagne?

'I'm not tipsy. I'm training to be a writer, so I watch and listen.'

'Are we talking about eavesdropping?'

Ursula shrugged. 'In a family like mine, that's often the only way you find out what's going on. Are you shocked?'

'I don't care for eavesdroppers. They hear no good of themselves, you know.'

'That's the kind of rot they tell you at school. It's simply not true. If I didn't keep my ears open, I'd find myself bundled off to finishing school, or sent to stay with Cousin Adelaide in Bognor Regis, they're always discussing that kind of thing behind my back. Forewarned is forearmed, you must agree.'

'So, you are an observer of your fellow men.'

'Yes. I look and overhear what they're saying, and if it's interesting, I find out more. It's great fun.'

And a great way to make enemies, thought Michael, but he didn't say so. 'What kind of a writer? Newspaper reporter? Novelist? Biographer?'

'It would be awfully grand to be a biographer, don't you think? I'd find it tiresome, maybe, to have to restrict myself to one life at a time. And the trouble with being a newspaperman – or woman, in my case – is that you have to stick to the facts.'

'I'm not so sure about that.'

'They're meant to. I plan to write novels. Full of human interest, showing the pale underbelly of the upper classes.'

'Good Lord.'

'My family might not care for it. At first they'll just say it's unsuitable, and have I thought of secretarial work. To fill in. Until I get married, they mean. Later, when I'm a famous writer, they'll worry that I'm putting them in my books.'

'I can see that. Are you gathering material this evening?'

'Meaning you? Don't be so vain. I don't know enough about you to know whether I could base a character on you or not. Have you any secrets?'

302

'What?' He couldn't believe he was having this conversation. How old was Ursula Grindley? Fifteen? God help her family when she grew up, that was all.

'Secrets. Dark deeds in the past. Are you who you seem to be? I know what you do for a living, or what you say you do, you fly aeroplanes.'

'I design aircraft.' That should quell her enthusiasm for grilling him, there was nothing exciting, secretive or upper class about aircraft design. But no, her eyes gleamed.

'War planes?'

'All kinds of aeroplanes.'

'Do you think there's going to be a war? I do. If there is, you'll have to design fighters and bombers like billy-oh, won't you?'

'I suppose I will.'

'I don't think you've got any time for secrets. Not if your head is full of aeroplanes. Are there no terrible secrets from your childhood?'

'No.' And if there were, he wouldn't tell Ursula about them, the girl was clearly going to grow up a menace to all her friends and acquaintances, never mind her family. Almost, he pitied the Grindleys.

'All repressed, I dare say,' she said philosophically. 'Pity, really. Will you get me an ice? Strawberry would be best.'

He made his way along the edge of the dance floor to where the ices were. What a disconcerting girl she was. He must ask Cecy about her. Dark secrets, indeed.

Then he remembered the cold blackness of his nightmares, and, forgetting all about the ices, went in search of another drink.

THIRTY-EIGHT

By eleven o'clock, the Orangery was almost too warm. The aroma of cigar and cigarette smoke mingled with women's scents and the faint, darker smell of sweat. Edwin opened his cigarette case and took out a cigarette. He lit it, blew a trail of smoke into the heavy air, and surveyed the shifting scene.

He had a sense of detachment. This was the world he had grown up in, these people were his family, his kind. The younger people here were almost all long-standing friends and neighbours. He had played cowboys and Indians with them at Wyncrag, made one of Robin Hood's merry band in the trees at Grindley Hall, had been a pirate and explorer on the lake in the summer, polar survivor and mountain rescuer in the winter. He had gone to school with them, to university, and then, more frequently now, had donned his morning suit to be best man or usher at their weddings as they married other people of the same sort.

Only now a wall had gone up between them. Of his own making, the foundations laid when he began to spend more and more time on photography, and an unacceptable hobby became a profession outside those approved of by his set. With the arrival of Lidia in his life, the wall was higher, much higher; he and Lidia on one side, his old life continuing on the other.

So far he had managed to juggle the two. Juggling would not do for ever. He had no doubts about where his choice would lie, but he couldn't yet face the full implications and consequences of his decision to march to a different tune.

He smoked, and listened with half his mind to the conversations flowing around him

One of the younger wives was cursing her silver lamé dress.

'Not at all a bad band, at least, not for these parts,' Pansy said as the music ended and she abandoned her partner to join her friend.

'Hello, Pansy. God, I feel like a tin of salmon in this dress. Heavenly to look at, I admit, but a pig to wear, one gets so hot.'

'Open a window, Vee. You'll be screamed at, but you'll get cool frightfully quickly.'

'Get pneumonia frightfully quickly, too. Any more bright ideas?'

'Dance with some divine man, and then you'll forget about the heat. How about that smooth, delectable Hal Grindley? Where is he? Lord, sitting out with the Richardson girl with the gammy leg, I suppose she fell on the ice. We could cruise over and winkle the man away.'

'They look too deep in conversation for him to be winkled. Lovely dress she's wearing. Now, I know what I wanted to ask you, Pansy. Do you know anything about the woman who's staying at Grindley Cottage?'

'Oh, the mysterious American all the servants are convinced is a film star. They know more about her than I do. It seems that the young man with her isn't her husband, but a secretary.'

'Secretary?' Vee exclaimed.

'He doesn't look the sort of man to have a wife, and he's hardly more than a boy, he must be at least ten years younger than she is. Five, anyhow, she must be nearly thirty.'

Vee was ready to be impressed by the worldly-wise Pansy's knowledge of men. 'You mean he's a Lothario?'

'Women aren't his thing, darling, that's all. Rory says he's a homo.'

'What, the secretary? No!'

'That's what he says. He spotted it at once, and after all, he should know one if anyone up here does.'

'Perhaps she is a film star, and he's her minder. These Hollywood actresses are terribly neurotic, you know, they have the most tremendous trouble getting them to work in the mornings.'

'How do you know that?'

'I read it in some ghastly mag that my maid takes.'

'Of course, they think everyone from America must be a film star.'

Vee was thinking. 'Why should Rory be such an expert?'

'Darling, you are a hoot. Everyone knows about Rory.'

'Knows what? He is my cousin, after all, and I don't know what you mean.'

Bony shoulders shrugged. 'Just that, you know . . .' Pansy slithered off to find new prey. Vee watched her go, envying the elegant line of her body in a very backless dress. 'I don't know what you're talking about,' she called after her.

Edwin felt sorry for the unknown American at Grindley Cottage. That was the trouble with small-town anywhere, gossip ran riot over any stranger who didn't immediately identify herself or himself. No doubt tongues were wagging furiously over Lidia.

He was accosted by one of his oldest friends. 'What's this I hear about you having a popsy installed in your little nest in Lowfell? Naughty, naughty, Sir Henry and Lady Richardson won't care for that, old thing.' He finished by giving Edwin a poke in the ribs.

Edwin considered giving him a much harder jab back, but he kept his temper. 'Don't know what you're talking about.'

Another young man joined them, a red-faced, stocky person who owned an enormous number of rather useless acres on the other side of the lake. Bertie greeted him cheerily. 'Hello, Toby. Have a drink.'

Toby accepted the drink and turned his rather protuberant eyes on Edwin. 'Bertie's talking about that woman of yours, isn't he? She's a bit of all right, I must say.' His hands curved a lascivious figure in the air. 'Foreign, that's the only problem.'

'Doesn't even speak the lingo properly,' Bertie said with a hearty laugh. 'Myself, I find a foreign accent rather charming. In the right place at the right time.'

Another poke in the ribs, curse Bertie for being such an offensive ass.

'Still, I don't suppose that matters to you, old boy, does it? I mean, you Richardsons are practically born speaking German, aren't you?'

God, what morons these people were. Boors. Savages. And bloody vulgar. He told them so.

'I say, steady on, Edwin, old boy.' Toby was aggrieved. 'All chaps together, you know.'

Why was it, Edwin asked inwardly, that among a group of people whose interest in sex was probably the lowest in the world, certainly way down below dogs and hunting and guns, he had to end up alongside these two, who had the morals and predatory instincts of some sheikh on the flicks.

'I don't make unpleasant remarks about your tenants, so why don't you just shut up?'

'Tenant, is she? That's a good word for it.' Toby made the whooping sound that was his laugh.

'She was roughed up today, by one of those chaps who goes around looking tough. Wears a black shirt, they say he's a Mosley supporter. In the street. Did you hear about it?'

'What?' Edwin went cold. Surely Bertie was making this up, it couldn't be true.

'No!' Toby said, impressed. 'I thought those types were all strut and salute and no do.'

Bertie lowered his voice to a hoarse whisper. 'Called her bitch and whore and all sorts. She's Jewish, or he thinks she is, of course, they can't stand Jews.'

'They've got a point there,' said Toby.

'Still, you can't go shouting at women in the street, whoever they are. Frightens the horses and all that, and it's awfully bad form. I say, Edwin, no need to push past me like that.'

'All these Richardsons seem to have left their manners at home this evening,' Toby grumbled. 'I gave Perdita a dance, just to humour her, Christ, she's really only a baby, and she got the wrong idea when I gave her a bit of a squeeze, you know.' His voice rose with indignation. 'She ran her heel into my shin.'

'Wonder where she picked up that trick,' Bertie said. 'Wouldn't have recognised her myself, not in that dress, she usually looks a perfect fright.'

Alix was in the drawing room, watching Perdita. She was sitting at the piano; someone had produced sheet music, dance tunes, and she was playing these to an admiring audience. They were old-fashioned pieces, ragtime and charlestons; the slightly older men and women were tapping feet and singing snatches of the songs with great enthusiasm.

Saul was looking for Jane. 'We really must get back, I don't like Mama to be alone for the whole evening, what if she isn't well?'

'She isn't, Uncle Saul. She has a migraine.'

'It's all very well for you young things to be so casual. Someone has to take care of her.'

'There's Lipp.' Alix could have added that she knew no one more capable of taking care of herself than Grandmama.

She watched as her uncle threaded his way through the knot of people at the piano and reached Jane's side. He spoke to her, she turned to him, and Alix blanched. That Aunt Jane should look like that. That any woman should have such hatred in her eyes when she spoke to her husband. Did Aunt Jane really loathe Uncle Saul? Or had they just had a row?

Perhaps her father and mother used to look at each other in that way. She would never know. What about her grandparents? Grandpapa was always affectionately polite with Grandmama – but that was in public. She'd never heard them quarrel, not in the way of raised voices and hot tempers. There were disagreements, nobody could be in contact with Grandmama and not disagree with her, but somehow Grandpapa smoothed things over, defused, deferred, withdrew from confrontation.

Watching her uncle and aunt, and considering Aunt Trudie's apparent contentment and even enjoyment of life, and thinking about Grandpapa living for fifty years with Grandmama, it occurred to Alix for the first time that marriage might represent danger as much as love, contentment or security.

'You look very severe,' Cecy said. She had come into the drawing room with Michael. 'Michael is bored, he denies it, but I can see it in his eyes. So I brought him in here to listen to Perdy. What were you thinking about to make you so cross?'

'I wasn't cross, just reflective. I was watching Uncle Saul and Aunt Jane, and wondering if I want ever to get married.'

'You, too?' said Michael with a grin. 'Cecy's been lecturing me on the advantages of the single state. Only what about children? Someone has to have children. Are they enough of a nuisance to make you swear off matrimony?'

'Children are no problem at all when they're little. It's when they grow up that the troubles begin.'

Across the room, Jane's voice was raised. 'No, I won't ssh. I don't see why we have to leave early just so that you can see how your mother is. Your mother will be fast asleep with the evil Lipp hovering about her door. I'm enjoying myself for once, there's no one here I have to be polite to because they might or might not vote for you. If you want to go home, do so. I'm staying.'

'Jane, be reasonable,' Saul was saying, his face red with embarrassment. 'You can't stay if I go. It's absurd to carry on like this. You're behaving like a debutante in her first Season, staying up late at dances is for young people.'

'I'm to consider myself old, and sit with the dowagers, am I? They have children and grandchildren to talk about, I don't, please remember. I certainly feel old when I'm with you.'

Then, thank goodness, Grandpapa was at Uncle Saul's elbow. 'Why don't you come home with me, Saul? I shan't be staying much longer. Edwin's left, I believe, so there's room in the Benz for you. Leave Jane to enjoy herself, it's a pleasure to see her looking so happy. She can drive herself home in your car later on.'

'No, she can't. She's had far too much to drink, just look at her. She's tight.'

'If I look tight, it's the effect of music and agreeable company. I've drunk precisely one glass of champagne, and otherwise nothing but fruit punch. I can perfectly well drive myself back.'

Cecy and Michael drew nearer to the piano. Alix felt an urgent tug at her arm and turned around to see who it was. 'Edwin! You look ghastly, what's the matter? I thought you'd gone. Has something happened?'

'I need your help, Lexy. Now. Come outside where Grandpapa won't see or hear us. Ask someone for your cloak, we have to go, right now.'

'Go? Why?' Alix was by now thoroughly alarmed.

'I just heard the most terrible news; I must go to see her, right now, there isn't a moment to lose. Only I can't go alone, not at this time of night.'

'See who? And why ever not alone? Are there thugs and

bandits about all of a sudden? For heaven's sake, Edwin, you're not making any sense.'

'You're not so far off the mark at that, when you talk about thugs, but no, it's not that, it's the proprieties, damn it. If I go to the house at this time of night, someone's bound to see me, all those twitching curtains, you know what the Lowfell tabbies are like. I've made enough trouble for her, it seems, without that.'

'Edwin, calm down, and tell me what you're talking about.' This was a new Edwin; the brother she knew was calm and rational and never put out. He looked perfectly distracted.

They were in the gun room now, alone. Edwin leaned back against a chest, and ran his fingers through his hair. The strands looked almost black against his hand she noticed, with the irrelevant, heightened awareness triggered by her brother's anxiety.

'It's Lidia. Two men here were talking about her, in an offensive way, you know the sort of thing. As if that weren't bad enough, Bertie then said, quite casually, that she'd been attacked by one of those fascists who are staying in Mrs McKechnie's house.'

'Bertie who?'

'Bertie whatsisname, oh, you know, Bertie Longton. What does it matter? The point is that this man, this bastard, had a go at Lidia. What must she have felt? What must she be feeling now? Lexy, for all I know, she may have packed her bags and left.'

Which mightn't be such a bad thing, Alix thought, but she could hardly say that to Edwin.

'I didn't see her this afternoon. I could kick myself for that. I try not to go every day, though God knows I'd happily spend the whole day with her. But I had to take that damned ice yacht across to the blacksmith, one of the blades needs adjusting, so I didn't go skating with her this morning, and then I thought I'd leave it until tomorrow. I wanted to be with her, why wasn't I there?'

'You'd probably have got into a brawl with the Blackshirt and ended up in jug and then there'd have been the devil to pay,' Alix said calmly. 'Did the wretched man actually hurt her?'

'I don't know . . . I'm not sure. That idiot Bertie said that the Blackshirt called her a whore and a bitch. And a Jew, of course.'

'That'll have startled the neighbours.'

'It isn't funny!'

'For God's sake, Edwin, I never said it was. I think it's horrible. All right, I'll come. Get someone to find Eckersley, he can run us home and come back for the others. You go and tell Grandpapa that my ankle's hurting a lot, and you want to take me home. No, don't argue, you don't want to cause a fuss. Just do it. Eckersley can drive us to Wyncrag and then come back to wait for the others. Shut up, Edwin. I'm not going anywhere in this dress, and while I'm changing, you can get your car out.'

Edwin opened his mouth to protest, but she silenced him. 'Wyncrag, and I get some more comfortable clothes on, or I don't come at all.'

Edwin waited in the hall, drumming his fingers on a marble-topped table. 'Hello, Rokeby, are you still up?'

'Yes, Mr Edwin. Eckersley's brought your car around, and asked me to say that he's returned to the Hall. He hoped you didn't mind him getting back, but he doesn't want to keep Sir Henry waiting.'

'No.'

'Is there anything I can do for you, sir?'

'No, no. Yes, wait a minute, bring me up a bottle of champagne.'

'Certainly, Mr Edwin. Would you be wanting a bottle of Sir Henry's special sort?'

'Better not. Just something bright and fizzy and good for the nerves.'

'I'll see to it right away.'

The house was so very quiet. Even the pipes had temporarily given up their gurgles and thumps and the stairs didn't make a single creak as Alix made her way up them, step by step. Nowhere did a door bang or the sound of footsteps echo along the passages. It was as though she were completely alone in the house. Which she wasn't, of course.

She felt as though a spell had been cast over the house, that the stillness was that of a gloomy castle inhabited by creatures of another kind, that she herself might at any moment come face to face with a wicked witch or a devilish form, bent on mischief. She told herself not to be so silly, but was nonetheless relieved to arrive safely at her bedroom door.

The clock above the fireplace ticked softly, the fire whistled and whined to itself, a muted, peaceful sound. Only a single lamp was lit, the one beside her bed. Beyond the small circle of its light the room was dark except for the dim flickering of the flames that sent shadowy tongues dancing across the panelling. If this were a novel, a gothic novel, this was the moment when a headless monk or the shade of a wronged maiden would appear.

The maid had taken the tweed suit she had worn today. She crossed to the wardrobe and was just taking a skirt from its hanger when she heard a noise.

It came from the stairs, surely. Edwin, no doubt, come to chivvy her on. She listened for a moment, the skirt in her hand, but all was silent again. It must have been Lipp creeping about in her usual fashion, fetching a tisane for Grandmama, or one of those nasty-smelling pastilles she loved to burn in a sickroom. Personally, she couldn't imagine anything worse than having Lipp hanging over you if you had a headache, but Grandmama had no doubt got used to it over the years.

Mind you, there was something slightly odd about the migraine. Grandmama had eaten a good lunch, temper notwithstanding. Usually when she was going down with one of her sick headaches, she couldn't face food for hours before the pain began. Nor had her face taken on that chalky look which they all knew so well.

Almost, Alix might have suspected her of faking a headache to get out of going to the Grindleys', but why would she break the habit of a lifetime by inventing an excuse? An invitation once accepted had to be honoured, and that was that.

There was that sound again. Someone was out there, and it wasn't Lipp. Everyone at Wyncrag knew Lipp's stealthy footsteps as she tripped about the house, keen to come unawares upon wrongdoers – or even upon those going about their rightful employment, since the whole household bitterly resented the sensation of being spied on. This person was heavier than Lipp.

If it were Edwin, he would be banging on her door by now. But if not her brother or Lipp, who? One of the other servants? Surely not. She'd recognise Rokeby's steady tread anywhere, and the other male staff would have no business upstairs.

Alix switched the lamp off, and crept to her door. She turned the handle slowly and noiselessly, then pushed the door open a cautious few inches. The wide passage was lit by wall lamps, which gave off little more than a soft glow; Grandmama couldn't abide brightly lit passages.

Was that a shadow at the end, by Grandmama's room, or a figure?

Good God, there was someone there. Her heart thumped uncontrollably. Whatever should she do? Rush out of her room, yelling and screaming to rouse the household? Well, yes, there wasn't much point in her tackling the intruder single-handed. As she hesitated before launching herself into the passage, she heard the sound of a door handle turning.

The figure had moved out of the shadows; it was clearly that of a man. He was dressed in dark clothes and held his shoes in one hand. That was why he'd made so little noise.

Anger was beginning to take over from fear and astonishment, but her shout of alarm died in her throat as Grandmama's door swung open. The room within was brightly lit; Grandmama was clearly visible as she stood in the doorway and drew the intruder into her room. Then the door closed, and a few seconds later the sliver of light beneath the door disappeared. She had put cushions against it, Alix knew it in her bones. Just as she herself had so often done when she hadn't wanted anyone to know that she was reading in bed long after she was supposed to be asleep.

So much for headaches and lying down in darkened rooms. So much for never using illness as an excuse for getting out of something you didn't really want to do, always a big sin in Grandmama's book. So what was she up to? Who on earth was the man? What was he doing here? Why the secrecy? Where was Lipp, always about when anything untoward was going on?

There was Lipp now, Alix could hear her coming up the stairs. In a trice she pulled the door nearly to, holding the handle so as not to make a sound. The footsteps drew nearer, stopped outside her door, paused.

Alix wanted to laugh. It suddenly struck her as funny that she was standing tense and silent on one side of the door, in the dark, and there was Lipp, listening hard, on the other side. She almost flung open the door and shouted Boo! but restrained herself. Did Lipp even know she was back early from the dance? No, it was more likely that Lipp had heard the door opening, and, being naturally suspicious, had stopped to investigate.

Damn it, she was trying the handle. Alix held on to it, and Lipp made a tutting noise as she pulled at the door. Just in time, Alix released the handle and the door shut with a click.

Lipp gave a little sigh of satisfaction and Alix heard her moving away down the passage. Thank goodness, she had assumed the door had simply been left slightly ajar.

Why should she feel so relieved, as though she were back at school and had escaped discovery by some stalking matron or housemother? This was Wyncrag, what reason should she have for not wanting to be known to be in her room?

One thing she felt certain of: neither Grandmama nor Lipp realized that they weren't all still at the dance. It was evident that Grandmama had planned to receive her mysterious visitor while everyone was out of the house.

It was most peculiar.

THIRTY-NINE

'If there are no lights on, we can't just barge in,' Alix said, wishing she hadn't come. All of Lowfell and half the county was probably talking about Edwin and Lidia, so was there any point to this late-night concern for the proprieties? If he installed a young, single and, according to him, beautiful foreign woman in his house, what did he expect? That people would assume he had a maiden aunt visiting? If she were respectable, then why, they would say, wasn't she at Wyncrag for the Christmas season?

Her hopes for a dark house were dashed as they looked up at the curtained windows on the first floor and saw the faint outlines of light. Their knock on the door was answered, although only after Edwin had called out that it was him. 'And Alix, my sister, is with me.'

The door opened.

Edwin was right. Lidia was beautiful.

One glance told Alix just why Edwin had been so captivated by her. But whatever was he thinking of? This was no soft and grateful refugee, remembering better times back home and regretting a life left behind. Edwin had talked as though a dove had landed on his hand, but he had befriended an eagle. Lidia was a sophisticated, cultivated woman, assured, talented and, at this moment, extremely angry.

Angry with herself as much as anything, which was endearing, Alix felt, her hostility diminishing a trifle. Lidia, it was clear, hadn't wanted to draw attention to herself. It had been that frightful man who had attracted the attention, not her.

'There was only a policeman,' Lidia said vehemently, 'and one or two passers-by, who passed by extremely quickly when they saw there was an argument. So how was it that when I went out again, everyone knew?'

Edwin was frowning. 'Has there been any unpleasantness before? From local people? You never said.'

'Not at all. On the contrary, as you would say. And now they are concerned, they think it wrong that a fascist should stand in the street and abuse me.'

'Well, it is wrong,' Alix said firmly. What did Lidia expect? This was England, and the country, not a foreign city like Berlin or Vienna. People in Lowfell might be suspicious of foreigners, but they were even more suspicious of over-muscled, aggressively-clad men who swaggered about the place and made themselves generally disagreeable. 'I can't think what those men are doing here,' she said, following this train of thought. 'I mean, why here of all places? It's hardly their usual hunting ground. There are no disaffected factory workers to work on up here, no chance to rabble rouse.'

'And no Jews to attack?' Lidia's voice was bitter.

'In fact, there are several Jewish families dotted around the lake,' Edwin said. 'Not vulnerable to attack, however, being both rich and long-standing residents. You know how bullies are, they never go for anyone up to their own weight.'

Alix didn't like the tense lines of Lidia's mouth. It was a generous mouth, made for humour and pleasure, not for fear and rage. 'Edwin, why don't you open that bottle of champagne?' To Lidia, she said, 'He was afraid you might have left, finding it impossible to stay in a place where such things happen. He thought you could have gone, at once.'

'Where do I go where such things won't happen?' Lidia said simply. 'If they can happen here, in this quiet and beautiful place, with the lake and the snow and at Christmas, then where am I safe?'

'You aren't,' Edwin said. 'We need glasses.'

Lidia fetched three glasses, and watched as he prised the cork out of the bottle. 'Are we celebrating?'

'Your courage,' Alix said. 'You have got guts, you know.'

For the first time since they had arrived, Lidia smiled. Alix was stunned. This was worse and worse. Lidia was not in the slightest bit like any of Edwin's previous, light-hearted amours. If this all went wrong, which it most likely would, given her and Edwin's circumstances, it wouldn't be a small matter for him. He might never get over a woman like this.

Edwin raised his glass. 'To you, Lidia.'

Alix, too, lifted her glass to Lidia.

'To Christmas,' Lidia said after a little pause.

'This settles it,' Edwin said. 'Alix, I don't want to make a secret of it, especially not from you.'

Alix felt cold inside. She knew what Edwin was going to say. Of course Edwin and she had secrets from each other as they'd grown up, but never anything really important. And his feelings for Lidia were very different from the past pains and pleasures they had so often shared. What Edwin was doing signalled the end of their lifelong attachment; an empathy normal for twins, magnified by the fact that they were orphans. One of the pillars of her existence was going to be superseded by his relationship with another woman.

She didn't like the prospect, not one little bit.

You're mean-spirited, she told herself. Couldn't she be happy for Edwin, be pleased that he had found a woman to love as he did Lidia?

'I want to marry Lidia,' Edwin was saying. 'I'm in love

with her and want her to be my wife. I want to put an end to her living in lodgings and being the object of gossip and, most of all, I want to give her a name and status that will make it difficult for what happened today to happen again.'

Lidia was shaking her head.

Didn't she want to marry Edwin? How dare this woman shake her head like that. Clearly, she and Edwin were lovers. Why should she turn down his offer of marriage? She must know Edwin well enough to realize that this wasn't a casual or spur of the moment proposal.

'Marriage is too difficult for me at this time. Besides, Edwin feels sorry for me.'

'That's not true,' said Edwin, stung. 'Pity doesn't come into it.'

Alix didn't need the inner certainty that came of being a twin to know that Edwin was telling the truth. There was sympathy in his feelings for Lidia, but not pity. Any pity had been swept aside when he'd fallen so deeply in love with her. Of Lidia's feelings, she was much less sure. At the moment, of course, she was hurt and angry; well, she had a right to be that after what had happened. But beneath the fear and fury, was there any love for her twin? After all, she hardly knew him. How long had they known one another? They'd met only a few weeks ago, that was all.

Long enough ago for Edwin to be sure of how he felt about Lidia.

Alix's baser self was glad that Lidia wasn't close enough to Edwin to realize that he wasn't offering to marry her out of pity. Let her go on thinking that. She didn't want Edwin to marry Lidia, or rather, to be honest with herself, she didn't want Edwin to be in love with her.

She wasn't going to plead Edwin's case, and she didn't want to hear him pleading for himself. Lidia didn't realize her luck, having a man like Edwin at her feet. 'I think we'd better go,' she said, getting up and putting her glass, still half-full of champagne, on the table. 'It's late, and I'm tired.'

Lidia was on her feet, too. 'Of course. I also am tired. It was so kind of you to come and enquire about me.'

Edwin exploded. 'Kind! It's late, you're tired, what is this? We aren't discussing next year's church fête, you know. I want Lidia to come back with us now, as your friend, Alix, and as my future wife, to Wyncrag, where she belongs.'

'I don't belong at Wyncrag. I belong nowhere,' Lidia said.

The voice was proud, but Alix caught the wretchedness underlying the words. 'You damn well do belong,' she said crossly. 'You've come to this country, you're going to make your home here, with Edwin or not with Edwin, of course you belong. And I'm sorry that lout was so horrible to you, and I'm ashamed that an Englishman could behave like that, but it's your country now, and if people like you – or love you – it's because they just do, it's not pity or contempt or anything shabby.'

Lidia was looking at her with huge, surprised eyes. Edwin was laughing. 'Good for you, Alix.'

'Mind you,' Alix said, suddenly subdued. 'I'm not sure Wyncrag right now is an enjoyable place for any visitor. Grandmama's up to something, Edwin, I'm sure she is.'

But Edwin wasn't listening; he had eyes and ears for no one and nothing but Lidia.

FORTY

Saul asked Rokeby to bring him a glass of brandy and took it with him up to the bedroom. Their room was tidy, warm, comfortable and empty. The wide, high bed was turned down on both sides, his pyjamas laid out on the left, Jane's silk nightdress on the right.

A grey silk nightdress, why did she wear so much grey? It wasn't that she looked dowdy or dreary in grey, her clothes weren't the depressing grey of school uniform and English skies; they were subtle, elegant expensive greys, but grey. When she wasn't in grey, she'd wear the palest blue, or what was that shade called? Eau-de-Nil. Washed out, distant colours. To go with her pale face and pale hair.

He changed out of his evening clothes, hanging them up with the creases in the right place, just as he had done ever since he was a boy. He put on a velvet dressing gown, a present from Jane, only mercifully not grey. He'd liked it, and thanked her warmly for choosing the rich dark green.

'I didn't choose the colour, as it happens. I telephoned Harrods and asked them to send something suitable.'

He pulled one of the two buttoned armchairs closer to the fire and sat, sipping his brandy and gazing into the flames. Christmas Eve tomorrow. He looked at his watch. Today, now, it was gone midnight. If he and Jane had children, she wouldn't be out at a dance, happy to see him go. She'd be at home, wrapping up presents, decorating a tree. That evening, there'd be stockings hung up over the fireplace, a sense of expectation and excitement filling the house, happy voices, laughter.

Christmas without children was a sterile affair.

He looked into the dancing flames. Outside, an owl hooted, and another. He didn't hear them. His mind was elsewhere, remembering the childhood agony of waiting for the last hours of Christmas Eve to pass, wanting to go to bed, knowing that once there the quickest way to make Christmas come was to go to sleep, but longing to stay awake to see Father Christmas come down the chimney. Falling asleep well before midnight. Waking up long before dawn to feel the inviting shapes in the full stocking laid at the end of his bed. Nurse calling to him from the night nursery, telling him to go back to sleep, that it wasn't morning yet. Envying Neville the fine railway set he'd been given, and having his own presents taken away or broken by Jack. Trudie's face alight with joy as she saw the tree. Dodie's contented shrieks when she discovered a pink sugar pig in her stocking.

He stirred, drummed the arms of his chair with his fingers, angry with himself for summoning these poignant memories. Would the town brass band still come and play carols on the lawn outside the drawing room on Christmas morning? Did Mama still hand out cloth for uniforms and a modest sum of money, while Papa slipped each servant a more generous offering? He supposed none of that would change until his parents died. Here he was, a man in his forties with a wife who hated him, a mistress he could never marry, and a tedious junior job in the government, a job from which he knew he would never be promoted.

Season of goodwill and cheer? Damn Christmas, he thought.

There was Neville, his body lying in a grave on the other

side of the world, and Jack, whose body lay God knew where, and Trudie a spinster still and not likely ever to marry, and Dodie who had sworn never to set foot in the house after her mother had been so rude to her more youthful husband.

Even sixteen years ago, when the lake had lain in its icy splendour as it did tonight, and the frost had the countryside in an iron grip, and snow had fallen deep and drifting on the fells, even then he had been able to feel some of the spirit of Christmas. He'd been twenty-seven that year. Jane had been twenty-one, and he'd been so much in love with her. He'd bought her a bracelet, gold with sapphires to match the colour of her eyes. He wondered where it was, she hadn't worn it for years.

She'd probably still been mourning Jack then, even though he'd been dead for four years. He had no illusions, he knew that Jack was the brother Jane had loved, not him. Had she married him because she could trace some faint remembrance of his younger brother in his face, eyes, mouth? They weren't at all alike, Jack was the tall, rangy one; he himself had inherited his father's strong, wide frame and high forehead.

His own hair was receding now. Jack had had a thick, dark thatch of hair, the cause of endless conflict between him and school matrons, who had never quite managed to quell its spring, however busy they got with the clippers. Would he have gone bald? No, he would have kept his hair, and probably wouldn't have had a speck of grey among the black. His own hair, fair in youth, long since turned to an undistinguished mid-brown, was speckled with grey hairs. Neville had been beginning to go grey when he went off to Chile. Beginning? Saul would have sworn his brother's hair was turning white before their eyes those last few weeks before he left.

God, how he missed Neville. He knew his mother felt the loss of Jack more than any of her other griefs, but Neville had been the world to him. And lovely, laughing Helena, so beautiful and funny and kind. Dead now, together with their daughter Isabel, who had been such an enchantress as a child, and such a fat flapper in adolescence. How would she have grown up if she'd lived? To be a beauty like her mother? Perhaps.

What a waste, what a terrible waste it all was. And now another war was coming. They were killing each other in Spain, and the Germans were trying out their monstrous bombs, and soon the canker would spread across Europe and there would be more killing, more grief, more waste.

Saul felt a tear on his cheek. He was getting maudlin, that was what Christmas did for you when you reached his age and nobody gave a damn whether you were there or not. Not even his mother. Lipp had seen him off pretty sharply when he'd gone up to enquire how Mama was. How could she put up with such a disagreeable maid? Nobody else could stand the woman. It'd be a good thing if she went back to France *tout de suite*. Especially if the Germans overran her country, they were welcome to Lipp as far as he was concerned.

He got wearily up from the chair, gave the fire a desultory poke, took off his dressing gown and got into bed. Jane would be home soon, he supposed. He'd better leave a light on. No, damn it, she could manage by the light of the fire. One could never get to sleep properly with a light on.

FORTY-ONE

Hal awoke to a silent Grindley Hall on the morning after the dance. Peter had retreated to his study, to work, the maid said. Nursing a hangover, thought Hal. Mrs Grindley and Mrs Wolf were taking breakfast in bed, Mr and Mrs Roger had gone out for a walk, and the young ladies and gentlemen were all still asleep.

Hal ate a leisurely breakfast alone in the dining room with the papers. He'd go to Wyncrag, he decided, and see if Alix was up, perhaps he could challenge her to a game of billiards.

'Miss Alix is in the Herb Room, Mr Hal, helping Miss Trudie with the flowers, there's a lot to do, seeing as it's Christmas Eve.'

Hal followed Rokeby's directions through the labyrinth of rooms on the staff side of Wyncrag's ground floor. The wide passages had mysterious doors leading to pantries and boot rooms and ironing rooms and still rooms and all the other offices necessary in former times for the smooth running of a great Victorian country house, now silent and empty.

Life returned as he neared the Herb Room: voices, clattering sounds from the kitchen, the baker's boy being ticked off by an irate Cook for bringing his muddy boots indoors and bringing an order short by two loaves, a sudden flurry of barks, laughter.

The scent of flowers wafted out to greet him, and he found the Herb Room a bower of flowers and greenery. Trudie was holding a silver rose bowl in the air to give it an all round critical inspection. 'Good morning, Hal,' she said. 'Alix, I'll just take this into the library, we need more space in here.'

'Can I take that for you?' Hal asked.

'Thank you, Hal, but it isn't heavy. Alix, those glads are for the church, not for here.' She went out as a gardener came in with armfuls of silvery leaves. 'On the table, Miss Trudie?' he asked.

'In the buckets underneath, please.'

Alone with Alix, Hal pushed a bowl of hyacinths to one side and hitched himself on to the table. 'I never saw so many flowers in all my life.'

'Some are for the house; most of them are going up to the church. Trudie always does the church flowers at Christmas.'

'Are you going up to the church to help?'

'I am,' said Alix, running a glass vase under the tap at the sink in the corner.

'Can I lend a hand?'

'Do. Perdy and Ursula are helping. Ursula's staying with us, did you know? She came back last night after the dance. One suspects she's very happy to be away from Grindley Hall for a while; I think she finds Rosalind hard to put up with. Goodness, that girl is lovely.'

'She looked as though she'd been dipped in icing sugar last night, but yes, she's a pretty girl.'

Whereas you, Hal said to himself as he watched Alix sorting out a pile of gladioli, her green apron tied in a work-manlike way around her waist, her hair sleek and pushed back behind one ear, are not in the least pretty. Her eyes narrowed with concentration as she wrestled with a tough stalk. He was more than happy just to sit and look at her.

'There's something green on your nose,' he said.

She brushed the back of her hand across her nose. 'A greenfly,' she said in surprise. 'Though why in December, I can't think.'

'Hello, Mr Grindley,' said Perdita, bursting through the door with Ursula close on her heels. 'Are you going to help finish the Christmas tree? We always do it on Christmas Eve, and since Grandmama's laid up, we can string the electric lanterns on it before she can tell us not to. Once all the rest of the decs are on the tree, we can hardly swap the lights for candles.'

'Don't look so confused, Uncle Hal,' said Ursula, as one speaking to someone slightly lacking, he noticed with amusement. 'Lady Richardson doesn't approve of electric lights, she prefers candles. Only these lights are very special ones, Sir Henry brought them back from America.'

'Candles are pretty,' said Hal.

'Pretty dangerous, too,' said Perdita. 'The tree caught fire one year, long before I was born. Do you remember that, Alix? Rokeby was telling me and Ursula about it.'

'Uncle Jack went mad with the taper,' Alix said. 'It was deliberate, I mean he tried to set the tree on fire, it wasn't just a candle tipping up.'

'Rokeby says he could have burned the house down.'

'I bet your uncle got an earful from Lady Richardson,' Ursula said.

'I bet he didn't,' Perdita said with certainty. 'She never got cross with him, not about anything, that's what everyone says.'

'Youngest son,' Ursula said gravely. 'It's not unusual. Wish it applied to daughters, that's all, I'd like to be spoilt for once.'

'Oh, Freud and all that rot, who cares? I expect if she tried to tick him off, he was nasty back to her and so she didn't dare. It doesn't matter, he's been dead for years and she makes up for it by being angry with everyone else.'

'Now, Perdita,' said Trudie, coming into the room with a cream vase in each hand.

'I hate it when people say, "Now, Perdita". I was telling Hal about the tree. Grandpapa and Sanders cut it down themselves,' Perdita said. 'Jolly hard work, but Grandpapa says it's bad joss for anyone but the head of the house to do it. Aunt Trudie, Sanders said he's brought the trailer around to the yard for whenever you're ready. There's a pile of holly in it, you never saw so many red berries. Ursula and I are going to walk up to the church and then we can whizz back down on the sledge. It would be awfully good if you could put the sledge in the trailer, under the flowers, I mean.'

Alix sighed. 'And I shall have to go in the tractor like the farmer's wife. No, don't ask, my ankle is actually much better, but uphill on an icy path is beyond me.'

'Let Hal drive you and bring the trailer,' Trudie suggested. 'I'll walk up with the girls.'

'Good God,' said Hal, as he surveyed the aged tractor out in the yard. 'I haven't driven a tractor since I was twenty. Mind you, that looks just like the one I drove then.'

'It's probably the very same one,' said Alix. 'Give me a hand with the trailer, you wouldn't think you'd need two firm feet to do something with one's hands, but you do. Grandpapa bought the tractor from your brother way back, just to use around the estate.'

'Does Sir Henry drive this?'

'Oh, yes.'

'Well, if he can, I can,' said Hal. 'I'm afraid it's going to have to be an ungenteel shove to get you up there.'

Alix settled herself on the box beside the driver's seat, and shouted helpful instructions as Hal wrestled to start the tractor and then fought with the gears. He was damned if he was going to let it get the better of him, he had no wish to make a fool of himself in front of Alix, not to mention Trudie and the girls, together with Cook and two of the maids who had come out to watch. Citified he might have become, but he could still drive a tractor. He just prayed he wouldn't do anything stupid, such as overturning it on the icy, rutted track that was the short cut to the church from Wyncrag.

He wasn't helped by the dogs bounding along in front of him and playing chicken with the tractor's wheels, and he was heartily glad when Trudie called them off and left the track to take the walker's path up the hill.

Alix was pleased to have Hal to herself, she was dying to talk to someone about the strange happenings of the night before. She had tried to tell Edwin as they drove back from Lowfell, but his head was so full of Lidia and Lidia's troubles, and Lidia's refusal to marry him, that he didn't hear a word she said. When she did finally get through to him that Grandmama, far from being laid low with a migraine had been having late-night visitors, he merely said impatiently that he didn't care what she was up to, what mattered was Lidia.

And today he'd gone off to Lowfell long before she was up, Aunt Trudie had told her. She still felt numb at the thought of Edwin not only being in love with Lidia, but actually intending to marry her. She had known that Edwin would marry one day, but she'd always thought it would be to someone she knew, a friend, 'one of us', as Uncle Saul would put it. Nor had she imagined that the close ties of twin and twin could be severed so abruptly. Edwin wasn't interested in her or her concerns or even whether she liked Lidia. Nor did he have any time to spare for his family, he clearly found her questions about their mother a bore, a pointless harking back to the past.

'He isn't coming up with us today,' she said out loud.

'Who?' said Hal, too involved with driving the tractor to want to talk much.

'Edwin.'

'Are flowers in church his kind of thing?'

'It's our father's birthday today. We usually take flowers up in his memory.'

'You can't have done so for the last few years, if you haven't been home. Damn this thing!'

It was true, Edwin had taken flowers the last three years, Aunt Trudie had told her so. So why shouldn't he miss this year, when she was here to do it?

'Grandmama isn't really ill,' she shouted to him, keen to return to the other subject that was uppermost in her mind. 'She was up and about last night when I got back and went up to my room. There was a strange man visiting her.'

'What?' said Hal, manoeuvring the tractor around a nasty bend.

'Watch out for the ditch.'

'Strange as in peculiar or as in unknown?' he asked once the bend had been safely negotiated.

'Unknown.'

'Perhaps she's lost a fortune at cards and he's come to buy her jewels,' Hal suggested.

'You aren't taking this seriously.'

'Why should I? You can hardly know all your grandmother's acquaintances, can you? I expect there was a perfectly good reason for his coming then, whoever he was. Did you think he was a ghost, stalking the dim corridors of Wyncrag? Or perhaps it was an early visit from Santa.'

This morning, in the crisp, bright air with the snow dazzling their eyes as it lay on the great hills all around them, the fancies of the night before did seem ridiculous.

'It was all a bit creepy, with no one up in that part of the house except me.'

'What, no Lipp?'

'Oh, she appeared, snooping as usual, checking doors.'

'Perhaps the man had an assignation with her.'

So absurd an idea set them both laughing and Hal nearly stalled the tractor.

'Now shut up and let me concentrate,' he said. 'We can return to Gothic Tales of the Night and Hamlet's ghost later.'

Alix caught her breath as she stepped into the stone-smelling church. Two paraffin stoves gave off another kind of smell, but despite them, the church was icy. She clenched her teeth to stop them chattering.

The vicar stood talking to Trudie. He was looking suspiciously bulky; however many extra layers had he put on beneath that thick black cloak to ward off the cold? He had probably come from a soft southern parish; their last vicar had been completely inured to the cold, cycling to call on his parishioners in the most freezing weather, clad in no more than his shabby clerical suit.

Alix strolled around the church, her breath forming little clouds as she leaned forward to read the familiar inscriptions on the stone floor.

Hal, after a brief fight with an armful of holly, was standing in front of a polished oblong of black marble set into the wall beneath one of the windows.

Alix knew the words by heart:

IN LOVING MEMORY OF NEVILLE HENRY RICHARDSON
BORN 24TH DECEMBER 1876, DIED 2ND APRIL 1921.

Beneath that had been added:

AND OF HIS WIFE, HELENA ALEXANDRA
AND DAUGHTER ISABEL CAROLINE,
DIED 1921.

The words always brought a lump to Alix's throat. She busied herself with fetching one of the big vases and placing it on the floor beneath the tablet. She worked without speaking, knowing that Hal was watching her, and grateful for his silence. She used cream and red blooms interwoven with strands of ivy and branches of holly leaves. It was gay and fresh and Christmassy, and anger suddenly rose in her, that this should be all that she had of her mother and father and sister.

She got awkwardly up from her knees.

'It's a bit sparse,' Hal remarked.

'The flowers?'

'No, the words.'

'What can you say, in stone?' Alix said bitterly. 'It's not even as though they're buried here. Mummy and Isabel were buried in America, and Daddy in Chile.'

'Does Sir Henry ever come up here?'

'Never. He insisted on the memorial, quite some time afterwards. Grandmama was very against it, but he had his way. That was the only time he came, Aunt Trudie says, when the stone was first put up. It wouldn't be a happy place for him, would it, with this, and the window to Uncle Jack?'

'I hadn't noticed that,' said Hal, staring with horror at a stained-glass window on the other side of the church. 'That's since my time.'

'I think Grandmama thought that if there were something here in memory of Neville, then there had to be for Jack as well.'

The window, done mostly in shades of brown and sludge green, was in a neo-realistic style. It depicted a young man in army uniform, MC ribbon up, balanced on a large tuft of bright green grass and gazing into the distance, a gun in one hand, the other hand shading his eyes beneath his peaked officer's cap. At his feet sat an upturned German helmet.

'That,' said Hal, 'is hideous. From an aesthetic point of view, it shouldn't have been allowed. Didn't the churchwardens make a fuss?'

333

'I expect so,' Alix said indifferently. 'They usually do, but no doubt Grandmama gave a large donation to church funds to buy them off.'

'Jack isn't buried here, is he?' Hal asked, as he helped Alix and Perdita to twist strands of wire.

'They never found his body. He might be the Unknown Warrior, except that I think he came from a different part of France from where Uncle Jack was. Grandpapa went to Westminster Abbey when they brought the Unknown Warrior to be buried, but Grandmama didn't.'

'No flowers for him today?'

'No,' said Trudie, handing the obliging vicar a heap of ivy and a pair of secateurs.

She said no more, and Alix told Hal in a whisper that she'd always rather thought that Trudie and Jack didn't get on; neither of the sisters had liked Jack much. 'Aunt Trudie never so much as glances at the painted window.'

FORTY-TWO

Lidia had seen the church in the distance from the lake, but had never thought of visiting it.

They sat down to take off their skates. Tina had walking boots slung around her neck by the laces, and she pulled them over her head, unfastened them and began to put them on. Her companion took his skates off and put on a pair of gumboots. Lidia had rubber-soled shoes. Progress from the lake up the hill to the church was slow.

'There are people there,' Lidia said thankfully. 'It will not be a good time to go in.'

'Christmas Eve, there are bound to be people here, decorating the church and things like that,' Tina said. 'Look, they're leaving.'

She had insisted on Lidia coming out for some air. 'Outsiders together,' she said. 'I'm sure I have the most terrible reputation, staying with Newman here, so you're taking a big risk being seen with us.'

'I told Edwin I was going to practise. He will be back later.'

'So will you. Listen, this Edwin doesn't own you. He lent you his house, he's sweet on you, fine, but he doesn't own you, honey. I bet you've hardly set foot outside since that brute shouted at you – am I right?'

Lidia had to admit she was.

'Right, so you come out with us. I've a yen to visit the little church up there. Oh, is that it? You being Jewish, maybe you don't care to go into a Christian church.'

Lidia assured her that she had no scruples on that front. 'My family are not religious at all. We have frequently been to concerts in churches in Vienna, and to weddings of my friends.'

'And as for the plug-uglies, Newman will come with us, he's a pretty tough guy, played football for Yale, no one's going to abuse you while he's about.'

Newman smiled at her. 'Fresh air would do you good, Miss Weiss. You're looking peaky, if you don't mind my mentioning it. We can skate across the lake, and then it's just a short walk up the hill. We can do our spot of sightseeing, then skate back before your friend arrives.'

They stood in the churchyard, shielded by an ancient yew.

Lidia let out an exclamation when she saw Alix.

'You know these people?' Tina asked.

'The woman in the fur jacket is Edwin's sister. Her name is Alix.'

'You don't say.' Tina looked at the group with renewed interest.

'Edwin has another sister, also. Perdita. Perhaps she is one of the two girls.'

'The one in the beret or the one in the woolly hat, do you suppose?'

'Neither of them looks like Edwin.'

'Who's the tall man with Edwin's sister?'

Lidia didn't know. Edwin talked a lot about Alix, and she knew she wasn't married or engaged, that was all. A close friend, it must be, the way they were talking together.

Trudie came into view, deep in conversation with the vicar.

'Now that,' Newman said appreciatively, 'is what I'd call a typecast English lady. My, where do they buy their hats?

It's like my mother's friends in Boston, they have some secret supplier, and wearing the hat tells others in the gang that they belong.'

Lidia was intrigued by Newman, and by Tina. What was an American, a glamorous American judging by what she could see behind the dark glasses and the glimpse of fine blonde hair she had seen tucked up into the hat Tina always wore, doing here at the lake? And why should she have a secretary? Lidia longed to know, but was too polite to ask.

He was a pleasant young man, with a sense of humour, and he was also an educated man. Tina's mention of Yale confirmed what she had seen for herself when he had picked up the Scarlatti and made some observations about Spain in the eighteenth century. 'I majored in European history,' he explained. 'Not all Americans are ignorant.'

Lidia had cried out at that, horrified that she might have been thought to make such a crass assumption. 'My father had the greatest respect for American writers and scholars, he corresponded with many, many people in American universities, and they would come and stay in Vienna, at our apartment, when they came to Europe.'

Tina had mystified her still further by telling her that, despite what the gossips might say, there was nothing between her and Newman of a romantic nature. 'That's why I employ him, it makes life much simpler. He only likes men, you see.'

That had startled but not shocked Lidia, there were such men in her father's circle, writers and musicians were often inclined that way, but a muscular, clean-cut American young man? It was very strange.

'In England, they don't mention these things,' she told Tina.

'In England, it's illegal. And in Hitler's Germany, they throw you into a camp for it, isn't that so? Although they say all the Brownshirts are queers.' Then she'd pulled herself up, apologizing for mentioning Hitler to Lidia after her recent encounter with an English fascist.

'Not talking about him does not unfortunately make him disappear,' Lidia said.

They watched the tractor bump away, with Alix clinging on for dear life and laughing at something the driver was saying.

The red-haired girl called to the other one, 'Come on, Perdy, buck up with the sledge there.'

'There you are,' said Tina. 'The tall girl is the one called Perdita.'

'You OK?' Newman asked, as she searched in a pocket for her handkerchief.

'It's the moss on the tree, it makes me want to sneeze,' she said, and blew her nose. 'I think it's time Edwin introduced you to his family, Lidia. Or doesn't he dare?'

'I think he likes to keep the peace. I think he is afraid of his grandmother.'

'If she's anything like my grandma, then he's right to be afraid,' Newman told her. 'Tina, are we going in, or are we going to stand here until we turn into ice statues?'

Tina pushed open the heavy church door, which swung back with a protesting squeak.

Lidia followed her into the dimness, her eyes taking time to adjust after the bright snow light outside. Gradually the interior became clear.

'Pew boxes,' said Newman. 'I didn't know they still had them in England.'

'Does each family have a particular place?' Lidia asked, bending down to read the worn brass plates attached to the end of some of the pews.

'They used to, I don't suppose many do these days,' Tina said.

Newman had picked up a leaflet from a pile left on the cope chest. He felt in his pocket and posted a threepenny bit into the money box on the wall above the chest. 'It says here the church is fifteenth-century. Built in the reign of Edward

IV, tower finished in the reign of Henry VII, choir added in the time of Elizabeth. Five hundred years of history. Do you reckon it's been this cold in here for all that time? How long do the ministers in this place get to live, I wonder? I should think they keel over in the pulpit, they must get pneumonia after a decade or so of standing in here with freezing feet.'

'Hot-water bottles,' said Tina practically. 'And hand warmers in the pews.'

Lidia shivered.

'Do we have to stay and freeze?' Newman asked. 'Or if you want to look around some more, I could try and find the light switch. Not that I can see a light switch anywhere.'

'There probably isn't one,' Tina said. 'I doubt if there's electricity up here; it'll be lit by candles and oil lamps for services.'

'Are you serious?'

Tina ran a hand along the back of the pew, the cold, polished wood smooth beneath her fingers. On the ledge in front of each place were the two small books of worship, the *Book of Common Prayer*, dark blue, and *Hymns Ancient and Modern*, in a red binding. She leaned forward and picked up a copy of the prayer book. It opened at the 'Order for Evening Prayer', and she began to read the words out loud.

How well she reads, Lidia thought. Of course, if she's an actress, then she would.

'What's that you're saying?' called Newman, who was strolling along on the other side of the church, studying the epitaphs.

'I'm reading a prayer. The Nunc Dimittis, if you want particulars.'

'Lettest now thy servant depart in peace according to thy word,' Newman chanted, in a pleasant baritone.

'I'm impressed.'

'I sang in the chapel choir at college. Tenor. Solos, even.' He had halted beside the black marble plaque. 'Look at this,

339

isn't it the saddest thing? Dad, Mom and kid, all dead in one year. An automobile accident, it must have been.'

Tina came over to stand beside him. 'Don't be obvious, Newman. Families, and family deaths, aren't always what they seem.'

'Oh, sure, there are endless possibilities. Dad could have run amok and murdered his loving spouse and daughter. Or Mom tipped arsenic in his soup, and the daughter got some as well. Or the kid might have been the Lizzie Borden type, slaying her parents then topping herself from remorse.'

'You have a vulgar mentality.'

Lidia was beside the Richardsons' pew. 'It says, Sir Henry Richardson. Is he an aristocrat?' The thought alarmed her. She had seen Wyncrag, from a distance, knew that Edwin, despite his profession, was a wealthy man. Was his family noble, as well?

'Not really,' Tina said. 'The guy's a baronet, it's kind of minor.'

'Do his sons get to be Sirs?' Newman asked.

'The eldest son will inherit the title,' Tina told him. She laid the prayer book back in its place and stood up. 'Coming, Lidia?'

Lidia was more than glad to leave. She found this cold stone church alien, and she was filled with a wave of terrible homesickness for Vienna, so far away from here, not only in miles, but even more in atmosphere and memories.

'Are you planning to attend the service here tomorrow?' Newman asked as he pulled the door open, letting in a gust of colder but fresher air.

'I gave up going to church a long while back when I found God wasn't at home,' said Tina.

FORTY-THREE

Wyncrag had a different feeling to it, that Christmas Eve. Hal had to conclude this was entirely due to the absence of Lady Richardson, still closeted in her room with Lipp in attendance. Sir Henry assured them she would be well by the next day, ready to preside over the Christmas Day celebrations. Hal felt, looking at Alix and Perdita, that his grandchildren took no comfort from this.

How was it possible for there to be such a change, such a lightening of the atmosphere? He had stayed on to lunch and to help decorate the Christmas tree. Drawing-room tea, in the absence of Lady Richardson, was abandoned, and Cook sent up delicious mince pies and melt-in-the-mouth miniature sausage rolls in exquisitely light pastry. Sir Henry came out of his study to superintend the mulling of wine: 'Terrible waste of good wine and tastes like cough mixture if you use cheap wine, but the girls will like it, and it's right for the time of year.'

Hal's height was put to good use when it came to the higher reaches of the tree, and when Perdita grew bored with stringing lanterns on the spiteful pine branches, she went into the drawing room, leaving the door open, and played Christmas carols on the piano.

For the first time since he'd come back to Westmoreland, Hal felt completely at ease and perfectly happy. At this moment, there was nowhere he would rather be, and no one he would rather be with. With a jolt, he realized that it had been days since he'd given Margo a thought. She'd be in New England for Christmas, as he had been for the last two years. Much smarter than this, and not half so much fun, he thought, as he pricked his finger on a broken bauble and cursed.

He slid down the stepladder to survey his handiwork. 'Looks good,' he said. 'We could do with a few more glass balls on the cantoris side, but that's all.'

Alix had silver strips ready to toss on to the branches for the finishing touch. 'Any more will be gilding the lily,' she said.

They sat side by side on the big sofa by the fireplace as Trudie wandered about, picking up needles and bits of tinsel, her mind clearly on other matters as it so often was. Fretting about her mother, most likely. Well, he'd be the fool and rush in where the proverbial angels . . . 'Trudie,' he called across the room. 'Where in America was Helena from? I never asked her. In those days, America was America as far as I was concerned.'

Alix looked up, suddenly attentive. She picked up his cue. 'Yes, I don't know that either, Aunt Trudie. When we were doing the flowers for the memorial this morning, I said to Hal about her and Isabel being buried in America, and I thought, one day, I'll go there and visit their graves, and then I thought, but I don't know where they are.'

Trudie started. 'Go to America? You want to visit their graves? Oh, Alix, that would never do, believe me, no.'

'Why ever not?'

'Much better not to. Morbid. It's the living that count.' Then, with one of her flashes of coherence, 'Besides, I don't know. Idaho, perhaps she came from Idaho. Or was it Oregon? Or, no, maybe Ohio. I know it had an O in it.'

'Aunt Trudie, if you don't know, who does? No, don't tell me. Grandmama, of course, much joy I'd get out of asking her. Doesn't Uncle Saul know, or Aunt Jane?'

'Well, you can ask them. Perhaps Jane, for she was such a close friend. America is a very large place.'

'Grandpapa,' Alix asked as Sir Henry came into the hall to see how they were getting on. 'Whereabouts in America did Mummy come from?'

'It was somewhere in the midwest, I believe. Or do I mean the West Coast? You see, Helena met your father when she was staying with friends in the mountains, and Neville was climbing there. Then, after they were married, her father retired, and her parents moved back to his home state. I can't quite recall where it was. Your grandmother is sure to know.'

Hal could see the disappointment in Alix's face. It wasn't only that she wanted to know, keen as she was to find out everything she could about her mother, but also he sensed she minded that Sir Henry didn't remember and didn't seem to think it important.

'What was Helena's maiden name?' he asked.

'Browne,' said Alix. 'With an e.'

Which wasn't helpful. The Brownes of Idaho, Oregon, Ohio and the West Coast would, he felt sure, turn out to be a numerous breed.

'Didn't you ever meet your American grandparents?' he asked Alix. 'Don't you have uncles and aunts and cousins, don't they keep in touch?'

She shook her head. 'Mummy was an only child, so no uncles and aunts. And both her parents are dead now.'

'You were going to go to America that summer,' Trudie said unexpectedly. 'The whole family. As it turned out, with Neville away in South America, and Isabel ... Isabel not being very well, Helena only took her.'

'Edwin and me? Going to go to America?' Alix sounded incredulous.

'Yes,' Trudie said.

'No one ever said anything about that before.'

'Your mother wouldn't have told you until nearer the time. You were all booked on the *Queen Mary*. As it was, it didn't happen like that. She and Isabel sailed on the *Normandie*, a French vessel.'

'And Edwin and I stayed at home and never met our family over there.'

'No, such a shame.'

'Are you absolutely positive you don't know where Mummy and Isabel are buried?'

'It will come back to me, the place with an O in it. Ontario? No, that's in Canada, how stupid of me. And, of course, a state is a big place, American states are large, aren't they, Hal? It was a small town. Helena used to say she was a small-town girl. She liked Lowfell for that reason.'

Another thought occurred to Alix. She had a strand of tinsel in her hands and Hal watched her twisting it around in a series of savage knots. 'How did Perdita get back to England? Who brought her?'

'It was so long ago. She was such a wee mite. No, I'm out there, she never was a wee anything, she was a big baby, only one felt so sorry for her.'

The tinsel snapped between Alix's fingers and a shower of silvery fragments fell to the floor. Trudie gazed at them, as though puzzled as to how they had got there. 'Do excuse me for a moment, Hal. I don't want the dogs getting that in their paws.'

Rokeby summoned a maid to sweep up the remains of the tinsel. He gave a little cough as he stood by the sofa, directing operations. He spoke in an undertone. 'You were asking about Miss Perdita, and her coming home when she was a baby. It was my sister who brought her to England, my sister Mavis.'

FORTY-FOUR

Alix's heart sank as she came down to breakfast on Christmas morning and saw Grandmama in her usual place at table. She gave her a dutiful kiss and a more enthusiastic one to Grandpapa before fetching a bowl of porridge. Perdita and Ursula came in, tousled and bright-eyed and happy, carrying gaily wrapped parcels.

'Breakfast before presents,' said Grandmama, but Ursula was already handing a package to Grandpapa, and Perdita, after a swift glance at Grandmama, was reaching out for one of her own.

Grandpapa had given Alix a white owl, tipped in gold, from the Herend works. He knew she had a fondness for owls. 'And I sent a donation to that orphanage place of yours, I knew you wouldn't want a cheque from me.'

Alix got up from her place to give him a swift hug. The orphanage was a small one, in East London, where the children were mostly the offspring of visiting sailors and dockland girls. A charitably-minded friend had roped Alix in to help with a jumble sale to raise money for the orphanage, and Alix, feeling a fellow sympathy for all orphans and struck by the disparity in circumstances between these waifs and herself, visited them as frequently as she could, sent money and clothing and bullied friends and family into sending their own contributions.

Perdita presented her with another owl, in the shape of a woolly hot-water bottle cover. 'I knitted it myself, in handicrafts,' she said, with pride.

Aunt Trudie had also sent money to the orphanage, and had found her an eighteenth-century edition of George Herbert's poems, bound in faded leather; she knew how keen Alix was on the metaphysical poets.

Edwin had made her an album of photographs of the frozen lake, bound in a striking modern cover. Aunt Jane came in with an exquisitely wrapped parcel containing some heavenly scented bath salts. 'I shall smell delicious, what with these and the lovely ones Perdy put in my stocking,' Alix said.

She'd had a fit of cowardice over her present for Grandmama, and had given her a biography of a very dull scientist whom she admired.

Grandmama gave her a silver letter knife. 'You still tear open your envelopes, I have noticed,' she said.

'Thank you very much, Grandmama,' Alix said dutifully, and then, under her breath, You aren't supposed to give knives as presents.

Grandpapa always gave Grandmama a jewel for Christmas. This year it was a single, glowing ruby pendant.

What had happened to all the jewels he had given her over the years? Alix couldn't remember her ever wearing them after Christmas Day. On grand occasions she always wore the same set of diamonds, never any of these annual gifts. Did Grandpapa notice? Did he mind?

Later, after church, Edwin and Hal both went out on the ice, with all the other yachts, red sails gay against a brilliant Christmas sky and the snow-covered fells, white sails blending in with the icy landscape. The yachts tacked to the head of the lake, then flew back, the ice hissing beneath their blades.

Alix and Cecy watched from the boatbuilders' yard at Lowfell, drinking milky coffee and eating hot pies which Cecy skated out to buy from Watkins' striped stall out on the lake. Lunch at Wyncrag would be a cold buffet, served by themselves; lunch was when the servants had their Christmas meal.

'Then, they work off the effect of plum pudding and Grandpapa's second-best port cooking our dinner,' Perdita told Ursula. 'You'll need that chocolate I gave you, for dinner's always late on Christmas Day.'

Edwin's present to Lidia had caused him a lot of heart-searching. He longed to buy her something lovely and individual – and expensive – but he knew she wouldn't accept such a gift. In the end he settled for a book of Elizabethan music for the virginal and a silk scarf from Liberty.

'I shall love to play these,' she said, looking through the music with real enthusiasm. 'Very simple, at first sight, but there is more to them than that. It is a pity you don't sing.'

'My father used to. Only amateur, he sang in a choir in Manchester. Perdy sings at school. I just don't have any kind of a voice, so that's that. Nor does Alix, she can't carry a tune to save her life. Lord knows how Perdy's turned out so musical.'

Lidia was pleased with the silk scarf, which she at once tied around her neck in an elegant twist. Edwin could never work out how Lidia, who had so few clothes, and no money to spend on them, always dressed with a sense of style, when most Englishwomen of his acquaintance spent a fortune on their clothes and still looked frumps.

She gave him his present, laying it down awkwardly on the table in front of him. Laughing, he pulled aside the layers of tissue paper, and the laughter died in his throat as he saw the exquisite piece of translucent glass, decorated with bands of red.

'Lidia!'

'You like it? I brought it with me from Vienna. I could bring so little. It was in our house there.'

'Lidia, you can't give me this. It must mean so much to you, and I know something about glass. This is a Hoffman piece. Only think what it's worth!'

Lidia flamed into words. 'You think, because I'm a refugee and scrub steps I am not allowed to give you something beautiful? I don't care if it is valuable or not. It has no price, no money could buy that from me. You have given me my music back, and I may not give you a vase, a lifeless object?'

Edwin went cold. He felt wrong-footed by the disparity in their giving. He'd been thoughtful and spent money; she'd given from the heart. Then he'd rejected her offering, spurned it, on the grounds that it was valuable. How could he be so stupid and insensitive?

'Lidia, my love, I'm sorry,' he said, in anguish because he had hurt her feelings, but his own heart sang, surely – surely? – such a present wasn't only given in gratitude. He cherished her words, hardly daring to hope that the affection he knew she felt for him was at last beginning to grow into something deeper.

They quarrelled again, later, about Lidia spending Christmas night by herself.

'We were together on Christmas Eve, and that is the special part of Christmas in Austria. You should have had your present then, but it's the custom in England to give them on Christmas Day and since we're in England, I shall be English about it.'

Edwin had wondered whether Lidia, from a Jewish family, kept Christmas, but yes, 'My father was happy to celebrate any festival, he loved to have a good time. He had a generous spirit.'

Like her.

At five o'clock, when he knew he would soon have to go back to Wyncrag and change for dinner, he came to a decision. He wasn't going to leave Lidia here, alone, at Christmas. So Grandmama would be furious? To hell with Grandmama.

'Where's Edwin?' Trudie asked Alix. 'Surely he isn't going to be late on Christmas night?'

'I can't think what he's doing. He was dressed before any of us, he came in, changed and rushed out again.'

Alix had her suspicions, and hoped she wasn't right. She'd asked Edwin, half jokingly, if he'd invited Lidia after all. They were going to be a large party, if he asked Grandpapa, he'd say yes; of course he would, the more the merrier as far as he was concerned.

Edwin had pulled a face. 'He might say, ask your grandmother. Besides, Lidia won't come, you know she won't.'

Alix couldn't help being relieved. She wanted Edwin to herself, at least on Christmas Day. She didn't care for the idea of Lidia being drawn into the family circle, the focus of all Edwin's attention.

Michael was talking to Sir Henry about his work, although his eyes kept going over to the door. Watching for Rosalind? Alix wondered. She hoped not, he was much too nice a man to be ensnared by that little madam. Freddie was beside her, and was looking around the room. 'Where's Perdita?'

'Ursula's staying with us, you know how they are at that age, they talk so much, they forget to get changed.' She heard a familiar crashing sound on the stairs. 'Here's Perdy now.'

The door opened and Perdita and Ursula came in, laughing at something one of them had said.

Perdita was wearing her red velvet dress.

Up went Grandmama's *face-à-main*.

Up went Perdy's chin as the cold eyes bored into her.

'What *have* you got on, Perdita?' Grandmama's voice cut like steel across the room. 'Go upstairs and change this instant.'

'Really, Caroline,' Jane protested, as Perdita flushed to the roots of her hair.

Alix flushed, too, annoyed and upset; how could Grandmama speak like that to Perdy, and at Christmas, in front of all the others? 'Grandmama, don't!'

Grandmama rounded on her. 'You're responsible for this.'

'Why?' said Perdita, starting forward. 'What's wrong with my dress? I wore it to the Grindleys', and nobody thought it looked out of place.'

'You wore it to the Grindleys'? Without my permission?'

'You were ill, Grandmama,' Alix said. 'And there's nothing wrong with the dress. It isn't low-cut or tight, it's perfectly seemly.'

'It's the colour. It's far too old for her. Go and take it off, Perdita. At once.'

Alix watched as tears and temper fought in Perdita's face. Temper won.

'If I take it off, I'll have to come down in my trousers or old tweed skirt, for I've no other clothes to wear.'

'You can put on the dress you've worn on previous evenings.'

'I can't. I tore it taking it off, and no, I wasn't clumsy, it's just too small for me.'

'Then you'll have a tray upstairs in your room.'

Ursula put an arm around her. 'I'll eat with you.'

'Rubbish,' said Sir Henry. He'd been so deep in aeroplane talk with Michael that he hadn't paid much attention to the scene being acted out in front of him. Michael had tried to keep his mind on revs and lubrication while distracted by the cold horror of Lady Richardson's abuse.

'Don't make such a fuss, my dear. Perdita can't eat upstairs on Christmas Day. I think she looks splendid, and if she doesn't have any other frocks to change into, that settles it. Now, what's happened to Edwin?'

Grandmama would rebuke Perdita at any time and in any place, however public, thought Alix, but her code forbade her arguing with Sir Henry in front of the others. Thank God.

'More champagne, Rokeby,' said Sir Henry, quite unnecessarily, since Rokeby was already refilling glasses.

'I think that's Mr Edwin now, sir,' Rokeby murmured to Sir Henry.

Alix knew she would remember that room at that moment for as long as she lived. It was a tableau frozen into her mind. The flames of the fire. The soft lights, the silk coverings and velvet curtains, the rich, plush colours and lights of the drawing room. The men, hair smoothed back in gleaming perfection, keynotes of black and white in their tails and starched white ties. Perdita's red velvet. Aunt Jane a slim shimmer of grey silk, Daphne in purple, Grandmama in darkest blue with her habitual collar of lace about her neck. Rokeby, a statue with a silver tray, the bubbles in the champagne flutes the only other movement in the room.

'Good evening,' said Edwin. 'Grandmama, I'd like you to meet Miss Weiss.'

FORTY-FIVE

Jane was first to break the silence. 'Happy Christmas, Miss Weiss,' she said with real kindness in her voice. 'Have you come far? I can see you've been out in the cold. Come and sit here beside me, near the fire.'

The tension eased. Edwin took Lidia over to his grandmother. Alix watched them, her heart in her mouth as she saw Grandmama's hard, unforgiving eyes rake Lidia from head to toe. 'You're a foreigner, by your accent.'

'Yes, Lady Richardson. From Vienna.'

'From Vienna? One need not ask why you have left your native land.'

'I came to England as a refugee.'

'We have too many refugees in this country. If I had my way, they'd all be sent back.'

Perdita and Ursula ran upstairs after dinner to Perdy's room. They stared at each other for a moment, and then collapsed in giggles on to the bed.

'Well, I must say, you Richardsons know how to give a party,' Ursula exclaimed when she could talk again.

'Wasn't it simply awful?'

'Yes, except that Michael and Freddie were marvellous,

352

carrying on as though nothing had happened. What on earth got into your grandmother?'

'Oh, she hates Jews.'

'One doesn't have to hate Jews to have a fit when your grandson and heir to the baronetcy trips in with a Jewish refugee on his arm.'

'Ursula! What a thing to say.'

'I don't mind about Jews, although I have to say that Daddy isn't frightfully keen on them, except for the Rothschilds and people like that. It's only all right to be Jewish in this country if you're fabulously rich, you know that's true. Uncle Roger says they're in league with the Bolsheviks to destroy Europe.'

'How stupid,' Perdita said. 'I never heard such rubbish.'

'It is ghastly,' agreed Ursula. 'Great Aunt Daphne's different, of course. She's so frightfully cosmopolitan that she doesn't mind what people are, as long as they're entertaining or clever or famous. Besides, her husband was a Jew.'

'Lidia's a musician. Lots of brilliant musicians are Jewish.'

'Oh, that's bound to endear her to your grandmother, I can see that.'

'Well, I liked Lidia. I liked her a lot. I think she'd be a far nicer Lady Richardson than Grandmama is.'

'Forget it,' said Ursula, worldly wise. 'Your brother can have an affair with her, but they'll never let him marry her.'

'How can they stop him?'

'Perdy, do talk sense. How do families always stop their young doing what they want? Isn't that what families are all about?'

'Your stepmother was rather horrid to Lidia, wasn't she?'

'She was, jolly rude in fact. I'm surprised Rosalind didn't wade into her, though, the way she goes on about how marvellous all the Nazis were in Munich. She's going down with a cold, so that's probably why she kept stumm.'

'Come on,' said Perdita, smoothing her velvet skirt, creased

353

where she'd been sitting with her legs tucked under her. 'We'd better go down and face the lively throng once more.'

'Must we?'

'*Noblesse oblige* and all that. Let's hope Grandmama's shot her bolt for this evening.'

Edwin was in the hall with Lidia. She didn't look very happy, thought Perdita; hardly surprising in the circumstances.

'Tell Lidia she can't go yet,' said Edwin.

'Of course not,' said Perdita.

Sir Henry appeared from the billiard room, smoking a large cigar and dangling a gaudy parcel from one large finger. 'Come along, come along, we'll have some carols. Caroline's gone up to her room, another touch of migraine, I fancy. Nothing to worry about. Now, whose is this?' He held up the parcel. 'I found it in the clock, of all extraordinary places.'

Alix caught sight of Uncle Saul's face. Goodness, whatever was the matter? He seemed in an agony of embarrassment. Was it something he'd forgotten to give to Aunt Jane?

Rokeby stepped forward. 'I believe it's mine, sir. I can't think how it came to be in the clock.'

'Yours? Here you are, then,' said Grandpapa, amused.

It was something to do with Uncle Saul, Alix realized with astonishment, as her uncle's face returned to an approximation of its usual colour.

They drifted into the drawing room to gather around the piano. 'Awful, awful Grandmama,' Alix whispered to Edwin, as Perdita crashed into the opening chords of *The First Noel*. 'I feel so sorry for Lidia. Still, it could have been worse.'

'Really? Worse than rude questions over the soup about Lidia's people, where are your people now, who are your people, what is your father? Then aggressive remarks about refugees and what a sensible attitude the Germans are taking to cleansing their country of undesirables, while we tried to eat the roast turkey and chestnuts.'

'Grandpapa did shut her up on that one.'

'It didn't stop her, did it? We had eugenics all the time we were eating the plum pudding, all about how inbreeding and racial mixes caused degenerates to be born, thus introducing weakness in the race. Where does she pick up these extraordinary ideas? If that's what coming from a scientific background has done for her, thank goodness none of us had any inclination that way.'

'The tirade about eugenics seemed to upset Aunt Jane.'

'Freddie did try to argue with Grandmama.'

'He won't be asked again.'

Alix gave her twin's arm a squeeze. 'I must say, your Lidia's got terrific courage. I think she behaved beautifully. It must have cheered her that Hal and Daphne Wolf both knew her father's writing.'

'Daphne's a good sort, and she understands what it's like for Lidia, I bet there was a tremendous fuss when she wanted to marry Daniel Wolf.'

They both knew that the difference was that Daphne's husband had been an extremely wealthy and well-connected man, not a penniless refugee. The fact that Lidia's father had been a distinguished man of letters would cut no ice with Grandmama.

'Do you have any idea why she's gone up to her room? Even if she's angry about Lidia, it's something she never does.'

'I don't think it's anything to do with Lidia.'

'Is she ill?'

'No, but she has something on her mind. I keep trying to tell you. Haven't you noticed how odd she is these days? More than usually so, I mean.'

'Perhaps she's slipped away to meet a secret visitor, a lost love.'

Edwin laughed, and Perdita turned around to shut him up. 'Even if you can't sing, you don't have to make a noise.'

Alix, remembering the dark figure she had seen on the night of the dance, didn't laugh.

FORTY-SIX

Inspector Pritchard was an incongruous figure in his dark overcoat and trilby. Despite that, he felt at home amid the great hills and the icy lake. They reminded him of Welsh hills, and were a great deal better than cold and mucky London with its piles of grey snow heaped by the side of the road. He had a sense almost of offence that a man such as Jago Roberts, essentially a product of the city, should sully this serene, beautiful countryside with his presence.

He crunched across the shingle and looked back along the shore. 'You'll know all about the residences beside the lake,' he said to PC Ogilvy.

'I do that, sir. All local people, well known to myself. Except for those putting up at the inn, and Mr Dixon runs a respectable hostelry, he won't have any doubtful types staying there. Why, he turned these men you're enquiring after away from his door, didn't want that sort under his roof, and I reckon he had the right of it.'

Inspector Pritchard had been pleased to find PC Ogilvy the chatty sort of village policeman. On too many investigations he'd been hampered by a tongue-tied local bobby who could be brought to utter little more than a strangled 'Yes, sir; no, sir,' and couldn't be persuaded to give an intelligible account of the facts instead of reading verbatim the gobbledygook recorded in his official notebook.

'That's interesting,' was all the inspector said. He took out his pipe from his pocket, and bent over to tap it on a rock. He pulled out a tobacco pouch and began to fill the bowl, tamping the shreds of tobacco down with a firm finger. He looked up at the sky. More threads of white cloud were floating innocuously above the highest of the hills around the lake.

'Weather going to break?' he asked.

'Likely will, sir. In a day or two.'

The constable was driving them in a police Riley that Pritchard borrowed from the nearest main police station. The inspector was doing what he called getting the feel of the place, driving along the slippery, winding roads beside the lake while the constable pointed out various landmarks.

PC Ogilvy opened his mouth, thought better of it, shut it, saw the look in the inspector's eye and hastily opened it again. 'Are we going to call on Mrs McKechnie, sir? See if this Mr Roberts is at home? Her house is over t'other side.'

'No reason to suppose he's left the area, is there?'

'No, sir. I saw him this morning, skating on the lake with his friend. A right bully he is, too, crashing through a group of youngsters like a bulldozer, and never a look back to see if those he'd knocked over were all right.'

'I see no point in letting him know we're on to him. I want to find out why he's here, for one thing.'

'For the skating, sir?'

Pritchard gave him a cold look.

'Sorry, sir.'

'He's with a friend, you say. Another man who looks as though he's a Mosleyite.'

'With the short hair and all that. And he wears a black shirt, mostly, like Mr Roberts does.'

'And Mr Roberts spends his time skating and abusing the locals, does he?'

'Miss Weiss isn't exactly a local. More a visitor.'

'Makes it worse. You don't want to put the trippers off, do you, Constable?'

'No, sir,' said PC Ogilvy fervently. His parents ran a bed and breakfast establishment in Lowfell and were doing very well out of the frozen lake.

'So no ideas about what either of them is doing here?'

'I have heard that the other man goes by the name of Shackleton, and he's here on business.'

'What business?'

'He's been up to see Mr Grindley, at Grindley Hall, more than once.'

'What is Mr Grindley's line of business?'

PC Ogilvy was shocked. 'Why, he's Jowetts, sir. One of the biggest factories in these parts, his is. They make basins, and . . . well, fittings. For bathrooms and that.'

Pritchard puffed at his pipe and blew out a cloud of smoke. 'Strange time of year to do business. And at a man's house, rather than at his place of work.'

'You have to get up early to catch Mr Grindley out. If there's a profit to be had, he'd work all through Christmas, at the Hall or at the factory.'

'It sounds innocuous. There's nothing suspicious about bathroom fittings, is there now?'

'No, sir.'

Pritchard was consulting his Ordnance Survey map. 'Would that be Grindley Hall over there? The extraordinary house on the hill?'

'No, that's Wyncrag. There's nothing extraordinary about it, as far as I know, very well thought of, the Richardsons are. A wealthy family, lived here for more than a hundred years.'

'I meant the architecture, Constable, not the establishment. All God's children for anything I know. So where is Grindley Hall?'

'You can't see it from here, sir. I can show you on the way back, you can get a glimpse of it from the road.'

'We'd better get a move on, then,' Pritchard said. 'It'll be getting too dark soon to get a glimpse of anything.'

The constable directed the inspector back to Lowfell, with a quick halt to see Grindley Hall.

'Do you think there's anything in this Mr Shackleton visiting at the Hall?' said Ogilvy as he showed Pritchard into the office he'd cleared for him when the call came through from Scotland Yard. 'The Grindleys are important people up here, I shouldn't like to . . .'

Pritchard hung his hat on the hatstand that Mrs Ogilvy had provided and took off his coat. He sat down at the desk and opened his black, official briefcase.

'No one, however important, is above the law. I dare say there's nothing in it. I dare say that even if Mr Shackleton has a smell of fish about him, Mr Grindley is quite unaware of it. This Jago Roberts is no ordinary Mosleyite, and any scrap of information about him could prove to be valuable. So it behoves us to take an interest in any and all of his acquaintances and contacts.'

'I see, sir.'

'Do you talk about your work at home at all, Constable?'

PC Ogilvy reddened.

'I ask because I know your father used to be on the force. He made sergeant, didn't he?'

'He did that, sir,' PC Ogilvy said, not without pride.

'Because what I tell you about Jago Roberts is not to go any further. Your father will understand why you can't discuss the case. It's not like dealing with local policing.'

'I know that, sir.'

'Let me tell you what we know about Jago Roberts.' The inspector pushed the papers in front of him into a neat pile. Then he sat back in his seat, looking up at the beamed ceiling.

'To begin with, that isn't his real name. We don't know

what his name is, but there's no record of any Jago Roberts until three years ago. We've looked at dozens of James Roberts and all kinds of J. Roberts, but no, there's no trace of him. Ergo, it's a false name. So, three years ago, he pops up among the Mosley crowd. Fits in with the toffs in the movement, public school accent, one of them, made welcome.'

The inspector had been lighting his pipe as he spoke. He shook out his match and took a long draw, making the little puffing noises of the expert pipe-smoker.

'Mr Roberts turns out to have a startling gift for rabble-rousing, organising rallies, marches, having a go at the opposition. It worries us at Special Branch, because there's a touch of the expert in what he's doing that we haven't met before among that bunch, and we don't much like the look of it. So where did he learn his skills, eh?'

'I don't know, sir,' PC Ogilvy said, not sure if an answer was expected of him.

'Use your wits, Constable. Where are they good at uniformed nastiness?'

'At the Police Training School, sir?'

'No, no. Not us. Roberts. Where might he have learned these techniques he uses to such effect?'

PC Ogilvy thought hard. 'I don't know, sir.'

'Think, man. Just think about it. You have heard of Herr Hitler, I hope?'

Ogilvy thought again. 'Germany, sir?'

'Bull's-eye. Germany. Now, what would this well-spoken gent of a fascist have been doing in Germany? Did he live there? Was he a German educated in England? Or an Englishman who'd chosen to make his home in Germany and had been taken in by Hitler's pretty words?'

'Couldn't you arrest him and interrogate him, sir?'

'Oh, we did that. More than once. When we said we could find no trace of him previous to three years ago he laughed in our faces and gave us a list of names, places, references.'

'Were they false, sir?'

'Not that we could detect. All pukka as can be. Colonels, an ex-nanny, school record, all impeccable.'

'Wouldn't he have been in the army, sir? He's about forty, he'd have been in the war.'

'Medical exemption. Heart murmur, and a doctor's certificate to prove it. A Harley Street doctor.'

'Seeing him out on the ice, doesn't look like a man with a heart problem to me. But if everything's in order, doesn't that settle the matter?'

The inspector brought the flat of his hand down on the table, making the constable jump. 'It does not. It makes me even more suspicious. For if our friend is not what he seems, then someone is going to great trouble and expense, enormous trouble and expense in fact, to pull the wool over our eyes. Now, no foreign power is going to do that for any Tom, Dick or Harry, is it?'

'No, sir.'

'So, we can assume this Jago Roberts is a big fish. If there's a war, as I personally am sure there will be, men like Jago Roberts may have quite other work to do than organising a few dunderheads dressed up in black shirts and boots.'

'Not boots now, sir,' PC Ogilvy said, mindful of the government's prohibition against the wearing of uniforms by members of movements such as the British Fascists.

'Forget the boots. Concentrate on the mind; razor sharp, by the way, and on the man's ability to blend perfectly into the background. English upper class, beyond suspicion, what could be more useful for any nefarious plans the Germans might have for him?'

'Hardly that, sir. Not if you've pulled him for questioning and have his name on file.'

'He may assume a new persona.'

PC Ogilvy was puzzled for a moment. Then comprehension flooded his face. 'Oh, I see, sir. He'd take on another identity.'

'Exactly. So what is so interesting is why he has chosen to come to this place of all others. Skating, you say? Merely here on business with Mr Shackleton? I doubt it, there's nothing we know about that suggests he has anything to do with business. No, what I'm hoping is that somewhere here, amid these majestic hills, lives a person, or persons, who knows him, who knows who he is, and what he's doing. I have a hunch that he has some connection with this part of the country. It is my task to find out what that connection is.'

Inspector Pritchard leant forward and tapped his pipe on the grate.

PC Ogilvy cleared his throat and ran a finger around the neck of his uniform. 'I don't think I've ever set eyes on that man Roberts before, and when I asked around after that spot of trouble in Lowfell, I didn't find a soul who could say they had seen him before. Except for old Foreby, and he doesn't count, being half blind and a bit weak in the head what with the ale and increasing years. I thought maybe the unaccountable feeling I had of knowing his face was his taking after one of his kin, a brother, or a father maybe. Only I never heard of a Roberts around these parts, barring old Reuben Roberts, that lived over at Bray Beck, and he never married. He's been dead these ten years, besides.'

Inspector Pritchard relit his pipe and sat back in his chair as PC Ogilvy went on in his slow and measured voice. A clock ticked on the shelf above the fire. Someone went past outside, heels ringing out on the frosty ground.

'It's a resemblance, that's all. Like I said, there was this recognition when I saw the photo and it's just come to me who it reminds me of. My mum used to work up at Wyncrag, in old Sir James Richardson's day. She's got a snapshot of him in her album. Well, there is a likeness, that's all.'

'Was this Sir James the type to leave his likeness about the place?'

PC Ogilvy looked blank.

'I mean,' Pritchard said, spelling it out, 'was he the kind of man to have had illicit liaisons with local women?' The distaste in the inspector's voice revealed a puritanical Welsh soul. 'Or his son, the present baronet, what kind of a reputation does he have?'

'Sir Henry's as good a gentleman as ever lived,' PC Ogilvy said, shocked. 'And so everyone will say.'

'I dare say you're right,' the inspector said placidly. 'But it does no harm to make a few enquiries.' He got slowly to his feet. 'You can put a call through for me to the Yard. I'll speak to the Duty Officer. Let's see if we can find out anything more about these Grindleys and Richardsons.'

FORTY-SEVEN

Alix looked at Mavis and marvelled. When she had last seen her, fifteen years ago, Mavis had been a shy laundry maid, deputed to look after the nursery linen and kept very much in her place by Nanny. She remembered a slim girl, and in front of her was an opulent woman in her late thirties, with sparkling eyes and a generous smile.

Rokeby had told Alix where she would find his sister, which left her with the problem of getting there. Eckersley would take her, but Eckersley would talk, and then Grandpapa would get to hear about it and perhaps ask Alix why she'd gone to Askrigg, out of interest, not nosiness, and then Grandmama would pick up the information and she'd be in for one of Grandmama's dreadful interrogations.

Instead, she rang up Hal, with a faint feeling of surprise as she asked the operator for the Grindley Hall number. Hal was the sophisticate that she had determined not to like, but that was only when she met him as a stranger. Now she regarded him as a friend, a man she could trust. And, face it, she told herself, a man whose company she enjoyed. He was clever and witty, if worldly, and kind with it.

She hadn't heard his voice on the phone before, and, even distorted by the line, she liked the sound of it. That was being an actor, she supposed. You had to have a good voice. 'I can't drive, and Edwin won't come, he's in a let-sleeping-dogs-lie frame of mind. Could you borrow a car?'

Hal could, by the simple method of slipping a ten bob note to Parsons, and he had driven Alix over Fiend's Fell to Askrigg, nestling in the next valley. Mavis was staying at the Queen's Head, where, she told them, she'd once worked as a barmaid.

Hal took to Mavis at once, which didn't surprise Alix. She was sure a lot of men would respond to Mavis's charms.

'Well, Miss Alix, it's nice to see you again, it's been a long time. And Mr Edwin, is he well?'

'He is.'

'Got a young lady, so I hear, although not the sort to appeal to Lady Richardson. He won't let that bother him, he's got a mind of his own, has Mr Edwin. So have you, I always said, those twins won't let themselves be pushed around.'

'I wish that were true, Mavis.'

'And Miss Perdita. I wouldn't recognise her if I passed her in the street, and that's the truth, for I only ever saw her when she was a baby. Mind you, Albert says she's the spitting image of her Uncle Jack, so maybe I would. He was a good-looking man, my word he was. Not safe in cupboards, though.'

'What?' said Alix, startled into rudeness.

'It's what we maids used to say. We never had any real trouble at Wyncrag, not after Sir Henry's father passed away, my word, he was a naughty one in his youth they said, and not so well-behaved in his old age, neither. But there was never a spot of trouble from the other boys, not from your dad, Mr Neville, nor from Mr Saul. It was only Mr Jack we had to watch out for. We used to warn the new girls, because he went for the young ones. Thought they'd be too nervous to say anything, I dare say; well, a girl of fourteen or so in her first job, how can she stand up for herself against a son of the household like Mr Jack? But I don't want to speak ill of the dead, and your uncle died for his country, which wipes all that out to my way of thinking.'

'It's Perdita I wanted to ask you about,' said Alix quickly, seizing her chance to flow the stream of reminiscence. 'You brought her back from America, didn't you, when she was a baby?'

'I did.'

'Did you go there just to fetch her? Did Lady Richardson send you?'

'God bless you, no. I was there, in America, that was the whole point.' She paused, looking intently at Alix. 'You know that Lady Richardson gave me the heave-ho?'

'Did she?' Alix was embarrassed, was she touching old sores? 'No, I didn't know that.'

'Yes, she more or less cleared the household out. So, when I was given my marching orders, I decided to go out to Canada. We've got family out in Nova Scotia, and I had a notion I might settle there. I had the money her ladyship gave me, for I will say that for her, she did pay us off generously. Only I didn't take to Canada, and Albert knew I wasn't happy and would be glad of a chance to come back, so when poor Mrs Neville died, leaving the baby, he fixed it with Sir Henry and Lady Richardson that I'd travel across to America and bring the child back with me. I was glad to help, what a tragedy that was, your Ma and Miss Isabel, and after your dad being killed and everything.'

'Where did you collect Perdita?' Alix asked, holding her breath. 'Was it in Oregon, somewhere like that?'

'Was that where they lived? No, I collected her in New York, where the boat sailed from. They had a nurse who brought her there, from an agency she was. She'd looked after the baby well enough, mind you, and Miss Perdita was a happy little thing, no trouble at all.'

'So you didn't meet my American grandparents?'

'No, I never did. I dare say they were upset, losing their

daughter and granddaughter the way they did, you wouldn't expect them to travel at a time like that.'

Alix was disappointed, she had so much hoped that Mavis could tell her where her mother had been staying in America.

Hal intervened. 'Miss Rokeby,' he began.

She laughed at him. 'Call me Mavis, everyone does.'

'Mavis, then. Why did Lady Richardson give you and all the others the heave-ho, as you put it?'

'Well, Mr Hal, that's a question I've often asked myself, and I don't rightly know the answer. Albert says it was as how she was determined not to have anyone to remind her of the days when Mr and Mrs Neville and Isabel were there, but that makes no sense. She still had the twins, you and Mr Edwin, Miss Alix, and then baby Perdita, too.'

'Aunt Trudie says that Grandmama felt it would be easier for Edwin and me not to be encouraged to think about our parents. Maybe that's why she did it,' said Alix.

'Maybe.'

'How many servants left?' Hal asked.

'All of them, at least all the indoors staff, and there were a lot of us back then. Every last one, saving Albert, and why he was kept on is a mystery to me and always has been. He said Sir Henry put his foot down, but I'm not so sure. He's a dark one is Albert, always knew how to keep his mouth shut. Still, I'm the last person to grudge him his place. He's done very well by your family, Miss Alix, with a nice pension to look forward to and a mention in Sir Henry's will, so Sir Henry has told him, although it's to be hoped that's a long way in the future.'

'And the family have done very well by him,' Alix said warmly. 'We couldn't have had a more loyal servant.'

'Well, that's Albert for you. I think it was hard on you and Mr Edwin, though, to be sent off to school the way you were, and your nanny turned off. How she did cry when she had to go.'

'Grandmama told me that she'd wanted to go, that she had a chance of a position in Australia, and she'd always longed to go there.'

'That's what her ladyship told you? No, Nanny no more wanted to go to Australia than she wanted to fly to the moon. She was that fond of you and Mr Edwin and so close to Miss Isabel, I can't tell you. She was wiped out when she died like that. Only it was made clear to her that there would be trouble with references and all that if she stayed in England, so she made the best of it, and it turned out all right in the end, for she married an Australian and settled down, happy as anything. Got three kids, she writes to me every year.'

'She promised to write to us, but she never did.'

'Like you said, I dare say your grandmother didn't want you reminded of that time.'

And with that Alix had to be content, unsatisfactory though it was. Mavis had raised more questions than she had answered. They had a cup of tea, and Mavis told them that she was quitting London and coming back north to marry Joseph Harkness, the landlord of the Queen's Head. 'He was my sweetheart all those years ago, but we went our different ways. Then he came to London and looked me up, and well, there you are.'

Alix said how pleased she was, and Hal went off to say hello to Joe, whom he knew from the old days. Then they took their leave and set off.

'It's one dead end after another,' Alix said dispiritedly, as they made their slow way over the frozen roads.

'Be practical,' Hal said. 'If Sir Henry and your grandmother won't help, and Trudie's clammed up, you should try those trustees of yours, they must have details of your mother's family.'

'They're all in Grandpapa's pocket,' Alix said gloomily. 'They'd hum and haw and say to ask him. He'll say, ask Grandmama. I tell you, it's just round and round in circles.

I'm not giving up, though. I'm going to find out what went wrong that year, whether Grandmama likes it or not.'

'Good for you. Well, the first thing to do is contact your solicitors when you get back to London. No, don't tell me, they're the family firm. Go to another one, I'll find a name for you, a firm quite unconnected with your family, or with anyone up here. You can ask them to trace your mother, they'll do that for you, although it may take a while. It will be expensive, so it's lucky you have the money to pay for it. If they don't have any joy, or it's taking too long, then when I'm back in New York, I'll get my lawyers to look into it for you. It's easier for them, being on the spot. They can hire a firm that specialises in tracing people.'

'Pinkertons?'

'Very likely. Then you'll have the details you want, and you can take unpaid leave from your job if they'll let you, and book yourself on the first boat to America, so that you can visit your mother's hometown and see her and your sister's grave.'

'I should like to do that,' said Alix. 'Thank you, Hal. One is so cocooned in family when one's in Westmoreland that one tends to forget what goes on outside it.'

Then, after a pause, 'Have you noticed Cecy and Michael?'

Hal laughed at her. 'Are you matchmaking?'

'Not at all. I like Michael. He seems troubled, I hope it isn't the Grindleys putting him off.'

'The Grindleys don't seem to have paid him any attention. Since he isn't rich or well-born or well-connected, and has nothing to do with sanitary ware, you wouldn't expect them to.'

They drove on in silence, as the sun went down, sending waves of red across the western sky and turning the frozen lake into a fiery mirage.

'It must have been very hard for you to lose your nanny on top of everything else,' Hal said presently.

'It was, only we were a bit bewildered all round, so it was just one more thing. Grandmama said that big boys and girls didn't need a nanny, and that a new nurse would be coming for Perdita who wouldn't have time to look after us. Edwin had been going to start at school anyhow, after Christmas. She sent me off, as well.'

'Bitter about that?'

'Not really. It wasn't a bad school, in fact I liked it a lot better than my next school, which was ghastly. You see, if I was going to be separated from Edwin in any case, I didn't think it much mattered if I were at Wyncrag or away at my own school. At least I had company there. And I regret to say that I was terribly jealous of Perdita; with her being a baby and an orphan, she did get rather a lot of attention. Not from Grandmama, who's always treated her as though she were a pariah, or at least lacking in any sense or virtues, but Grandpapa and Aunt Trudie. And all the servants thought it was frightfully tragic, like something out of a fairy tale, and made a great fuss of her. So I was better off at school.'

'In America, very few families send their young away to school when they're eight or nine. They tend to like having them about the place.'

'I can't imagine it.'

'They think we English are cruel the way we pack our children off to boarding school.'

'Did you mind?'

'I loathed it, but there was no point in saying so.'

'If I marry and have children, I shan't let them go to boarding school,' Alix said.

'Your husband might insist.'

'I wouldn't marry a man like that.' She laughed. 'It isn't likely to arise; I don't think I'll ever marry, let alone have children. What I've seen of family life has been enough to put me off the whole idea.'

FORTY-EIGHT

'Where's Perdita?' Alix asked Ursula, who was in the hall putting on a pair of boots.

'Up in the nursery, playing the piano. She said all those carols and festive tunes made her want to get back to Beethoven. Actually, what she's doing is scales, with a copy of *Emma* propped up in front of her. Catch me practising in the hols, but then I'm not serious about music.'

Alix wondered if Ursula minded being abandoned like this. She was a guest, Perdita had invited her.

'I'm used to her,' Ursula assured her cheerfully. 'Once she gets a music fit on her, nothing else counts. I doubt if even Lady Richardson would be able to drag her away from the piano. Anyhow, I've got something I want to do, so I don't mind, honestly I don't, Alix.'

She thinks I'm fussing, Alix thought. To her, I'm a grown-up, concerned only with manners and appearances and what one should and shouldn't do. In other words, a bore.

'Going skating?' she asked Ursula, who had put on her coat.

'Not this morning, no.'

Now she was a prying grown-up. 'What a lovely hat and scarf.'

Ursula grinned. 'Not as nice as the hat you gave me, but that's upstairs, it's too nice for this morning. These belong to dear Rosalind, who left them behind on Christmas night. I'm to take them back with me when I go home, but meanwhile, I shall wear them. They're made of angora or mohair or something, with silk, Rosalind got them in Paris. I'm not sure red's my colour, it clashes with my hair, rather, but they're warm.'

Funny girl, Alix said to herself. She wondered what Ursula was up to, what the mysterious something she had to do might be. An assignation? Hardly. And the girl hadn't seemed very enthusiastic about her mission, whatever it was. Well, it was none of her business.

And all thoughts of Ursula were swept away by the phone call that came through only minutes later. It was Mavis.

'I was thinking about you asking questions about Mrs Neville, and I know how her ladyship was that particular about every trace of your mother being removed. It seemed a strange carry-on to me, but it wasn't my place to say anything. Well, Miss Trudie and I went through all her things, and sent clothes away for charity and so on. Only there were some more personal things, not letters, Lady Richardson had seen to all that herself. Just the everyday things she used, no one would have wanted them, and it seemed wrong to throw them away.'

Alix was holding her breath. 'Weren't they thrown away?'

Mavis's voice came tinnily down the line. 'No. Miss Trudie said to do so, but I have to confess, and I've never told a soul about this, that I couldn't bring myself to do so.'

'What did you do with them?'

'I took them up to the attics. There are a lot of cupboards there, and no reason for anyone to go snooping about, not even that old Lipp. Now, what I stashed away isn't going to be much use to you, except to bring back some memories perhaps, but there was a kind of folder, like you get in an office. I think her ladyship had forgotten it, or put papers that didn't matter in there to be thrown out with everything else. Only I did take a peek, and there were one or two photos. The kind of thing you might like to have. Personal. If the folder's still there, that's the thing, for it was a long time ago, and you never know.'

'Do you remember which attic?'

'I do that, which is funny after all this time. They're all numbered up there, the rooms, they used to be servants' rooms. I tucked it away in number five.'

Alix waited, sensing Mavis had something else to say.

'There's a big cupboard, and a small one by the fireplace. The folder's in that small one.'

Photos, of her mother. In the house, all the time.

'Hello? Are you still there?'

'Sorry, Mavis. Yes, I'm still here. I can't thank you enough. I'm going to go up and look right away.'

'You do that, only take my advice and be discreet, go up when that Lipp isn't about. It may all have happened a long time ago, like I said, but I'd bet my best Sunday bonnet Lady Richardson doesn't want anything from that time coming to light. And you didn't hear about that cupboard from me.'

Alix laughed, and said no, if anyone found out or asked, she'd say it was simple curiosity.

Perdita slid into the drawing room, clearly hoping to avoid attention. She had been wrapped up in her music, Alix guessed, and lost all sense of time. She could see that her sister hadn't stopped to wash her hands or brush her hair, no doubt thinking it was better to be untidy than late.

Perdita's efforts were to no avail, Grandmama's eagle eyes were on her. 'Where have you been, Perdita? What have you been doing? You haven't tidied your hair, and I dare say you haven't washed your hands. How many times must I tell you to allow sufficient time to get yourself ready before meals? Where is Ursula?'

'I don't know,' Perdita said. 'I haven't really seen her since breakfast.'

'Perdita, it's your duty to look after your guest. If you aren't prepared to do that, then I don't think we can allow any more of your friends to stay.'

'Grandmama, that isn't fair,' she burst out.

Alix winced. It was a mistake ever to answer back, and she could see that Perdita regretted it as soon as the words were out of her mouth. 'I mean, Ursula doesn't want to be with me every minute of the day.' Inspiration struck. 'I think she said something about writing thank-you letters.'

That was cunning. Grandmama would have to approve of that, although she'd always insisted on her own family writing them on Boxing Day.

'She may have missed the gong, shall I run up to her room and see?'

'Yes, although unless she's suddenly been afflicted with deafness, I fail to see how she can possibly not have heard the gong. It is designed to be heard.'

Perdita escaped, and thundered up the stairs. 'Sorry, Aunt Jane,' she said as she met her on the landing.

Jane raised her eyebrows and stood aside to let her niece pass. 'Aren't you going the wrong way? Shouldn't you be downstairs?'

'I've come up to get Ursula, I think she must be in her room.'

'She went out with a sledge earlier on,' Alix said, coming out into the hall as Perdita and Jane, but no Ursula, came down the stairs.

'When?' asked Jane.

'An hour or so ago. I told her to make sure and be in time for lunch. She knows what a stickler Grandmama is for punctuality, or if she doesn't, she must be unusually thick.'

'Oh, Lord,' Jane said wearily. 'We'll never hear the end of it.'

Despite Grandpapa's attempts to play down Ursula's non-appearance: she was probably having a good time in the snow, had no doubt met up with some friends out on the ice, and it was, after all, the holidays, Grandmama was not impressed. It was a grim meal.

Perdita gloomily pursued a stewed plum around her plate.

'Perdita, don't play with your food.'

'Sorry, Grandmama.' In went the plum. Silence returned.

'After you have left the table, Perdita, you will put on your outdoor clothes and go and find Ursula. I would like an explanation of why she has missed lunch.'

'It had better be a good one,' Alix murmured. Perdita suppressed a giggle, swallowed the plum stone, and choked. Alix thumped her on the back, Grandmama glared at both of them, laid down her napkin and rose from the table. There was a scrape of chairs as everyone hastily got to their feet, and then, at last, the uncomfortable meal was over.

'Ursula is a nuisance,' Perdita grumbled as she pulled on her boots. 'She might have said where she was going.'

'Rokeby saw her heading up the slope at the back,' Alix said.

'It's a fat lot of good telling me that. There are dozens of ways she could have gone once she reached the top.'

'Where does she like to go sledging?'

'Oh, I don't know. The field that runs down to the lake, I suppose. Only you'd have thought she'd have had enough of that if she's been out all this time. I mean, once you've toiled up that hill four or five times, you begin to think it isn't worth it any more.'

'Maybe she took her skates, after all. Or she could have come back for them, and gone out on the ice. She might have skated over to the other side.'

'She didn't take her skates. Look.'

Perdita stood upright, her face red from bending over to see to her laces, and pointed to Ursula's skates. 'Those are hers, and no, she can't have taken anyone else's, she's got normal-sized feet, and she'd be swimming in any of ours.'

Uncle Saul appeared at the door. 'Mama wants me to come with you, Perdita. She doesn't want you to be out alone.'

'Oh, for heaven's sake, why does she have to be such an awful old fusspot? I'm perfectly all right on my own, I'm not a baby.'

'Don't speak of your grandmother like that, Perdita.'

'Sorry, Uncle Saul, but honestly, it's so stupid, don't go out on your own, where are you going, how long are you going to be? What does she think can possibly happen to me here at the lake? I know everybody and everybody knows me.'

Alix wasn't surprised at the tone of suppressed rage in Perdita's voice. She, at that age, had chafed just as much under Grandmama's endless dos and don'ts.

Saul's voice took on a didactic note. 'There are a lot of strangers around, now that the lake's frozen.'

'Not here, there aren't. You know they don't come as far as this. Anyway, it doesn't make any difference, it's exactly the same when it isn't snow and ice everywhere. "If you're going out for a ride, make sure Mungo goes with you." I ask you, no other girl of my age has to have a groom with her when she's out riding in the country. I can't walk by myself, I can't ride, and I can't skate or go sledging alone, either, or there's all this commotion. What am I allowed to do? Answer, nothing!'

She did up the final button of her coat and pulled a woolly hat firmly down over her unruly hair. 'Come on, then, Uncle Saul, I don't suppose you want to come in the least bit, you find it all just as tiresome as I do.'

'Do you feel like a walk, my dear?' Saul asked Jane.

'No. I'm rather tired, I shall rest for a while. I expect you'll meet the child at the bottom of the drive, in any case.'

'Exactly,' Perdita said, bearing her uncle away towards the front door.

Rokeby was there before them. He was just about to open the door for them when he stopped, listening. 'I hear a car approaching.'

'Callers,' Uncle Saul said irritably. 'All we need. Who is it, Rokeby?'

Rokeby had opened the door and was out on the step. 'It's not a car I know, Mr Saul.'

Perdita came out behind him. 'It's the one the American woman and her paramour have rented. I wonder why they're here.'

'Her what?' Uncle Saul said in horrified tones.

'Never mind that. Look, I'm right, it is the para . . . I mean the man at Grindley Cottage.'

A second later, Perdita was flying down the steps to the car.

Alix followed, moving as fast as her ankle would allow. What was Ursula doing in that car, with a strange man?

Uncle Saul ran past her. 'The girl's hurt.'

Alix and Perdita took charge of Ursula, who was pale and shaking. Alix looked with horror at the smears of blood across her face.

'Ursula,' Perdita cried. 'Ursula, what's happened?'

'Can't you see she's too shocked to speak? Bring her inside.'

'Take her into the drawing room, lay her down on a sofa,' Uncle Saul said.

Ursula shook her head.

'Upstairs, then,' Alix said quickly. 'To her room. Lean on Perdy, Ursula, just lean on her.'

Saul led the way into the drawing room. 'Who are you? Would you care to explain what Miss Grindley was doing in your car and in such a state?'

'My name's Newman. I didn't hurt the young lady, if

that's what you're thinking. I was driving back to Grindley Cottage when she stumbled out of the woods, right in front of me. She was obviously in a bad way, although she didn't seem to be injured. So I stopped, put her in the car and brought her here, as it's the nearest place. She needs to see a doctor.'

'Not injured? What about the blood? Did she say what the matter was? Had she had an accident? I believe she'd taken a sledge out.'

'I didn't see a sledge. I guess it's more serious than that. She told me, fairly incoherently, but there was no mistaking what she said, that she'd been accosted by a man in the wood. I think maybe she'd been knocked unconscious, although she seems OK now, says she hasn't got a headache. The blood is a nosebleed, and she's got a split lip.'

'Where exactly was this?'

'You know the place where the woods go down to a little patch of shingle? Next to a fancy boathouse?'

'Yes, of course, that's the Wyncrag boathouse. Although why she should be in there if she'd gone out with a sledge . . . Did you see anyone else there?'

'No. Once I was sure she was OK, I left her in the car for a moment and ran into the wood to look. Not a sign of anyone. I went right through the trees and out on to the shore, however, and I did see skate marks on the ice. That could be anyone, though, and made at any time. No one comes sweeping the ice over on this side, do they?'

'No, no, only around the town and the landing stages on that side.' Saul shook his head. 'It's incredible. To attack a girl in broad daylight. I suppose she might have had an assignation. She could have struck up a friendship with a local lad, led him on and then taken fright.'

'It didn't sound like she'd encountered anyone she knew, not unless she's a damned good actress. Nor, from what she managed to say, was it a lad. Definitely a man. You'll get a better description out of her when she's calmed down some-what. She's had a hell of a shock.'

'Yes, yes, she would have done. A terrifying experience. To think of it, a guest of ours . . . Whatever will my mother say?'

'Look, I'll leave you, you don't want me around at a time like this. Anything I can do, just let me know. Would you like me to call in at the police station and tell them to get an officer up here? Or would you prefer to telephone?'

'No, please don't. That will be perfectly all right, we'll see to all that.' He hesitated. 'It would be unfortunate if, well, if word of this got around.'

'You got some guy in the woods jumping out on young girls, you sure aren't going to be able to keep it under wraps. Besides, word needs to get around, until this maniac is caught, all the women about the place are going to have to be very careful.'

'Careful? Oh, surely he wouldn't attack again.'

'No?' Newman looked surprised. 'I'd have thought he might well do just that. Maybe your English criminals don't operate like they do back in the States.'

'You don't understand. The press, you see. It's the kind of story the gutter press would love to get hold of. What would her family think, if they saw her name all over the news-papers? Publicity is not what our kind of people seek, Mr Newman.'

'I don't think you'd find me too keen on any publicity, Mr Richardson.'

'The cases are different. I venture to say that reporters would not be in the least interested in dragging you and your companion's, Mrs . . . um, Mrs Newman's name into print.'

'You think not?'

'I'm an MP, a minister of the Crown. An American might not appreciate how essential it is that no breath of scandal . . .'

'Politicians are the same the other side of the Atlantic,

380

believe me. Do what you like, as long as discretion is preserved. If you're giving me a warning, I'll just mention that I have no desire to have the press involved – for our own as well as for Miss Ursula's sake. Now, I'll go, but I think you need to call a physician. I'm sure you've got a local man who's known every member of the family since they were in diapers, the sort of man you can trust not to let you down by a word out of place. I'll bid you good day.'

Upstairs, Perdita sat beside Ursula while Alix ran a bath for her.

Perdita had been going to ring for Phoebe, but Alix stopped her. 'I don't think Ursula needs to have too many people around,' was all she said. 'Ursula, your bath's ready. Have a really hot soak.'

Ursula wasn't shaking any more, but she was still dreadfully pale. 'Shouldn't she have something for the shock?' Perdita asked. 'Sweet tea, or a brandy? I don't have to ring, I can go down and get some for her.'

'Brandy, then.'

There was a knock on the door, and Alix opened it to find Phoebe standing there, her face full of concern and interest. 'Mr Saul said Miss Ursula had had a bit of an accident, and I was to bring her up a cup of hot, sweet tea. Mr Rokeby said brandy as well, so I've brought the decanter and a glass. Is there anything I can do?'

'Thank you, Phoebe,' Alix said. 'Since you're here, please bring up a hot-water bottle, Miss Ursula is chilled after being outside for so long.'

She took the tray of tea and brandy and closed the door.

'We could have given her Ursula's clothes to clean,' Perdita said. 'Did you see them, all dirty and her sleeve torn? Whatever happened to her?'

'Wait until Ursula's had her bath and see if she can tell us about it.' She went over to the bathroom door and knocked.

'Ursula, would you like tea or brandy? Brandy? I'll bring it in, if I may.'

Ursula came out ten minutes later, wrapped in a dressing gown, but shivering.

'Into bed with you,' Alix said. 'No argument, I know you aren't ill, but you need to keep warm. Phoebe brought up a bottle, it's in the bed, very hot, so take care not to burn your feet.'

Ursula managed to smile, despite chattering teeth. 'That's just what Nanny would say.'

Alix pulled the covers up for her, and sat down on the end of the bed. Perdita planted herself in the chair beside the fire, her elbows on her knees, her chin in her cupped hands.

'Did you fall on the ice, Ursula? Or have an accident with the sledge?'

Ursula shook her head. 'Nothing like that.' She spoke as though her mouth hurt, and her lip was starting to swell in an alarming way. 'You could do with some ice for that,' Alix said. 'Perdita, ring the bell, would you?' And to Ursula, 'Go on.'

'It was a man,' Ursula said. The words tumbled out as though she was glad to tell someone. 'I was in the woody part, along by the lake, you know, where it's all forest on the hill above, and then there's the road, and a bit of a clearing, and then trees all the way down to the lake. I'd got fed up with the sledge, so I left it by the stile. Oh, it must still be there.'

'Don't worry, I'll get one of the men to go and fetch it,' Alix said. 'You went into the wood.'

'Yes. There's the pebbly bit along the shore there, I walked through to it. I could have sworn there was no one else about. It just goes to show you can't trust your instincts, for when I'd had enough of looking across the lake and seeing if I could spot a perfectly round stone, you know the way one does.' She touched her lip gingerly. 'I'm perfectly all right, really. It was only . . .'

'Don't talk if it distresses you,' Alix said.

'No, it's all right. So I came back, I was going to walk along the road and pick up the sledge. I'd rather lost track of the time, and when I looked at my watch, I saw I was already late for lunch, so I'd better buck up and get back as quickly as I could. I wasn't paying much attention to anything except hurrying, and I didn't expect there to be anyone in the wood. Then he came out from behind the trees in front of me. Quite suddenly.' Her voice trailed away.

'Who, Ursula?' Perdita said. 'Who gave you such a fright? What a stupid thing to do, alarming you like that.'

'Shut up, Perdy,' Alix said, but without rancour. 'Did you know him, Ursula? Had you ever seen him before?'

'He had a hat on, pulled low over his face, and a scarf wrapped around his chin and mouth, but I didn't recognise him.' Her eyes met Perdita's for a fleeting moment. 'He was tall . . . and dark. I mean, I never got a good look at him. He stood there, in my way, and I tried to get past, and then he grabbed me.' She shivered. 'It was awful. He was so strong, and he whacked me across the mouth when I shouted out.' She put a finger up to her lip. 'That's how I got this.'

'Have some more brandy,' suggested Alix, getting up from the bed. She was worried by how pale Ursula was looking, her pallor enhancing the freckles around her nose and making her look much younger, a mere child.

'I'd rather have tea now, if I can drink it with this mouth.' She pulled herself up, hunching the bedclothes around her, and sipped awkwardly at the tea that Alix had poured for her. 'I'm so cold, I can't think why.'

'Shock,' Alix said. 'Perfectly normal. If I were you, I'd be having the screaming ab-dabs by now. You're awfully brave.'

'I didn't feel brave,' Ursula said shakily. 'I thought he was going to kill me. I knew he wanted to hurt me, he was in such a rage. His eyes were horrible, I don't think he was mad or not knowing what he was doing; he was enjoying himself, and he liked watching me being so afraid. I think that was the worst thing.' She swallowed, and two tears rolled unnoticed down her cheeks. 'I am sorry. It was so awful, and now there'll be a dreadful fuss, and police and everything. Oh dear.'

There was another knock on the door, but before anyone could answer it, the door opened, and Lady Richardson came in.

Despite the fire, the room felt cold. Perdita looked at her grandmother and wrapped her arms around herself.

One of the damask curtains drawn across the windows was caught up. Lady Richardson moved swiftly across the room to twitch it into place.

Then, she turned away from the curtains and looked at the girl lying there in the bed, and, to her amazement, Alix saw that Grandmama's face was taut with fury.

Ursula seemed to sense the anger and she pulled herself up on the pillows, dragging the covers up to her chin, reducing herself to a halo of damp red hair, a white face and a pair of frightened eyes.

'You've brought disgrace on yourself and your family. What kind of behaviour is this?'

FORTY-NINE

Alix couldn't believe what she was hearing. What had Grandmama been told? Had Uncle Saul poured some distorted version of events into her ears?

Perdita jumped up from her chair. 'Grandmama, Ursula's done nothing wrong!'

'Be quiet, Perdita. We'll come to your part in this wretched affair in a minute.'

Grandmama was so certain of herself, so dreadfully intimidating as she stood beside the bed. 'Now, Ursula, tell me the truth. You are, fortunately, not one of my family and not my responsibility. Whatever faults in your upbringing that have led you to behave like this can't be laid at my door.'

Ursula was too astonished, or perhaps too distressed, to say a word.

The fire had dwindled to a mere glow. Alix picked up the shovel and mechanically slid coal into the grate. It hissed, and let out a belch of sullen black smoke, acrid enough to make her eyes smart. It would leave a sooty film in the room, but Grandmama took absolutely no notice. Her fists were clenched like claws, bony knuckles white and strained.

'I know about young women like you. You are a fool, to go into the wood alone. No doubt you were meeting some

385

young man. No doubt you thought you were in charge of the situation. When you found you weren't, you cried wolf, and screamed for help.'

Alix felt no warmth from the smoking fire. She was feeling colder by the minute, and Grandmama's words hammered on her frozen nerves. She wanted to jump up, yell at her to stop.

'Don't play the innocent. This man in the wood wasn't there by chance, was he?'

Help and compassion from a concerned hostess? If Ursula had any hope of that, she knew better now. Alix had hardly expected it; Grandmama hadn't an ounce of compassion in her make-up. But this wasn't merely lack of compassion, nothing so negative. This was sheer hostility.

And, yes, fear.

Fear of what, for heaven's sake? What was there that Grandmama could possibly be afraid of? That Ursula's attacker would come to Wyncrag? Hardly. That it would cause talk? The Richardsons had never been involved in any scandal, their good name alone could carry off far more trouble than this without it causing any kind of a stir. The outside world, villagers and neighbours alike, would react with shock and revulsion. They would feel pity for Ursula, and sympathy for Lady Richardson as well as for the Grindleys, for the distress of having a young guest suffer such an attack while staying at her house. Where was the reason for fear in that?

Yet there was fear in this room, and it was Grandmama's fear, not Ursula's.

'You had an assignation with him, admit it.'

'You're wrong,' Ursula cried. 'Completely wrong. You're making it all up.'

Alix was appalled, but even so, she now caught the false note in Ursula's voice.

'You are making things up, not I. You met him out skating,

did you? Flirted with him on the ice, I have seen the way you young girls behave out there.'

This venomous attack had a purpose, Alix realized. It was confusing the issue, trying to make them doubt what had actually happened. Grandmama was blowing a smoke-screen.

'So you gave him all the signals: that you were interested, you were available for a little more private fun.'

This was too much for Perdita. 'Grandmama, you mustn't say such things!' she cried.

'I told you to be quiet. I dare say you played your part, too, Perdita, going on the ice, without an escort, careless of your upbringing and your reputation. How fortunate that you aren't the sort to catch any man's eye.'

'I'm not to blame for being attacked, I'm not,' Ursula was shouting now. 'It's the man you should blame, not me.'

Lady Richardson pounced. 'Nonsense. No one attacked you, why don't you admit it? You met a man in the woods, by appointment, lured him on. When you found that he was after more than mere dalliance, you took fright.'

'I did not lure him on!' Tears were running down Ursula's cheeks.

'Look at her face, Grandmama. He hit her.'

Lady Richardson swung around. 'If she roused him to violence, she has no one but herself to blame. She led him on, and there isn't a judge in the land who would not agree with me.'

'Ursula needs a doctor, not you going on at her.' Perdita was shouting now. 'Just wait until the police come. They'll believe her. They'll go and find this man, and then you'll have to take it all back.'

'There is no question of the police being involved.'

The calm certainty of the words took Alix's breath away. She dug her nails into her palms, counted breaths to calm her jangling nerves. Don't sound desperate. Don't plead. Be reasonable. 'You must tell the police, Grandmama. This man is dangerous. He might attack someone else.'

'The police would no more believe this story than I do. They won't make any attempt to find a man who attacks girls in the woods for the good reason that they very well know there is no such person. Do you think your friend is the first young girl to make up stories of this kind? Don't you understand that every police officer in the land knows you never trust girls of this age? That what they say is fantasy and invention?'

'If you won't go to the police, then Ursula must.'

Lady Richardson changed tack. Her voice was low and controlled now. 'I'm sure Ursula realizes that once it is a police matter, the press will get to hear of it, and her name will be all over the newspapers. Again. They will rake up all the stories about her mother's disgraceful behaviour and the divorce.'

'No, they won't.' Alix had raised her voice now. 'Ursula's the victim, they can't tell anyone her name.'

'They will,' Ursula said despairingly.

Did Grandmama in some contorted way believe that Ursula was embarking young on the kind of amorous career that her mother, Delia, had been accused of? Or did she seriously suppose that Ursula had been victim not of a man, but of an over-active imagination?

She deliberately lowered her voice. 'Grandmama, stop being so horrible to Ursula. She's hurt, look, can't you see?'

'I have some questions for you, Perdita, also. Now, tell me please, why Ursula was out on her own? Against my absolute instructions? Where were you? Also out, alone, without saying a word to anyone?'

Alix was stunned at the viciousness of her grandmother's words. So was Perdita, judging by the way she simply stood and stared at her.

'I'm waiting for an explanation.'

388

Perdita's answer dropped into the waiting silence. 'I was playing the piano.'

'Playing the piano! What nonsense, don't try to lie to me, Perdita. Lipp was downstairs, she would have told me if you had been playing the piano.'

'I was in the nursery.'

'In the nursery! What were you doing there?'

'Playing on the old piano in the day nursery.'

Alix winced. This was not the time for Perdita to confess to playing the piano.

'The old piano in . . . Is this a habit of yours? To sneak off, leaving your guest on her own, without an enquiry as to whether anybody wants you for anything?'

'Nobody ever does want me, and I need to practise.'

'You need to mind your manners. I find it incredible that you can stand there and calmly tell me you were strumming at the piano while your friend wandered off on her own.'

Alix's fists were clenched so hard that they hurt. She was willing Perdita not to answer, not to defend herself. Yet she admired her. Could she, at that age, have stood up to Grandmama for a single moment? No.

'I wasn't strumming. Besides, Ursula doesn't have to be with me every moment of the day.'

'No, she has assignations to make, men to meet.'

'You can't have it both ways,' Perdita flashed back. 'She can't have met a man and have invented the whole thing.'

'She met a man, things didn't go as she had planned, and so she fabricated the story of her attack. That is quite clear.'

'You know all this stuff about Ursula leading a man on isn't true. She was in the most awful state when she came in, you didn't see her, you can't know.'

'Do you imagine I haven't been through all this before? Do you suppose that I go to any lengths to ensure that you are safe and protected at all times just on a whim? Young girls on their own get into trouble, and also manage to get others into trouble. Ursula has brought trouble on you and, if I weren't wise enough to keep the matter quiet, she would cause a great deal of trouble for the unfortunate man as well as for herself.'

'You're the one who's making the trouble, by not believing her.'

'I have nothing more to say. The subject is closed. Ursula, you will oblige me by not coming down to dinner this evening. Lipp will tell the servants you have caught a chill, through inconsiderately and stupidly staying out of doors too long. She will bring you up a tray.'

The door closed behind her with a sharp click.

'Ursula, I'm so sorry,' Perdita began.

'Go away! Just go away. Leave me alone.' Ursula flung herself over and buried her face in the pillows.

Alix found Perdita an hour later, sitting on the piano stool in the nursery, tears pouring down her face.

'Perdita, don't. Ursula's upset, of course she is, but she'll be all right when she's had a sleep. Grandmama's old, she doesn't mean . . . Oh, Christ!'

Perdita gestured speechlessly to the top of the piano. Alix stared, unable to believe what she saw: books of music torn in half, sheets of music lying in shreds.

'All my music,' Perdita said in a flat voice.

Alix stared at the sheets of music ripped and screwed up, stuffed into the waste-paper basket, forlorn fragments strewn over the polished floorboards.

'Oh, Perdy. Oh, no, how could she?' She took Perdita in her arms, holding her sister's tense body tightly against her.

Over her shoulder, her eyes met Edwin's. He was standing at the door, looking around the room with amazement. 'I heard about Ursula. Rokeby told me, he said you were up here. The servants are all in a state, thinking there's a monster on the loose. Lipp says it's all a story. What is going on?' He looked round the room in horrified amazement. 'Who did this?'

'Grandmama,' Alix said.

'Grandmama? I don't believe it. Why ever should she do such a thing? It's not like her, Lexy, it's madness.'

And hatred. 'I don't believe we have the least idea what Grandmama's really like, or what she's capable of.'

'Do you think she's ill? Had some kind of a fit? I mean, if you're right, what on earth could bring on this kind of behaviour?'

'Hatred. Hatred, pure and simple. We must get Perdy away from here. Do you think Lidia . . .?'

'Of course. I've got the car out at the front.' He hesitated. 'I'll tell Rokeby, shall I? About the mess in here. I'd rather none of the other servants –'

Servants? What did servants matter? 'See if you can find Grandpapa. He'll have to know what's happened, sooner or later.'

Alix watched Edwin's car speed away down the drive and around the curve towards the gates. She turned to go back inside, then heard another, more powerful engine coming up the drive.

'I passed Edwin going at the devil of a lick,' Michael said, climbing out of Freddie's Bentley. 'Was that Perdita with him?'

Alix stared at him blankly, her mind miles away. 'I'm sorry, I wasn't paying attention. Have you come to have tea?'

'Bad time is it?' said Michael, eyeing her shrewdly. 'I arranged to drop over and spend a little time with your grandfather.'

'Oh, I see. In that case –' Alix was looking fixedly at the Bentley. 'Is Freddie hidden in the back there, or have you just stolen his car?'

'Freddie's putting in an afternoon with his medical tomes.'

'Studying?' Alix was momentarily distracted.

'Lord, yes, these medics go on for ever, you know. Orthopaedics means surgery, and that means a whole heap more examinations for his FRCS. So I said, would he mind if I take the Bentley for a run, and he said, help yourself, and here I am.'

Alix tried to pull herself together. 'I'm sorry, I must seem so unwelcoming. Things are rather fraught here at the moment.'

'Of course. I understand. Shall I make my apologies to Sir Henry and buzz off? Or is there anything I can do to help?'

Could she trust him? Should she tell any outsider what had happened today? Damn it, Grandmama could think what she liked, what mattered was making sure Ursula was all right. Michael didn't seem a blabby sort of man. 'Perhaps you can. Ursula was attacked today, down by the lake. No, don't look about for a police car, the police haven't been called in. Grandmama is determined to keep it all under wraps. Only I think Ursula really should see a doctor, and it's just occurred to me –'

Michael cut in. 'When you say attacked, what do you mean?'

'A man jumped out on her. She was alone, and, well, it could have been pretty nasty if that American who's staying with the mystery woman at Grindley Cottage hadn't come along. She got knocked about a bit, but she's not seriously hurt.' She paused. 'Her lip's puffed up, and I think she may have other bruises. From what she said, it was no worse than that. She wasn't raped,' she added bluntly. 'But I would feel much happier if she saw a doctor, that's all. To make sure nothing's broken and that she doesn't need stitches.'

'So you wondered if we might wheel Freddie along? Can we do that? From an ethical point of view, if she has a doctor here, shouldn't she see him?'

Alix was impatient. 'It isn't a time for scruples, it really

392

isn't. Freddie looked at my ankle, for heaven's sake. I'm not asking him to operate, just to say if he thinks she should be taken for medical attention, whatever Grandmama says.'

'Does her father know?'

'Grandmama will deal with that. She'll say Ursula had an accident out skating or some such story. Her father won't be worried, why should he be? He doesn't have any great fondness for her.'

'I had noticed.'

'Please.'

Michael, thank God, wasn't going to argue. 'Right, Freddie it is. Shall I run back and fetch him?'

'That's the problem. He can't come here, Grandmama wouldn't let him near her. She's keeping Ursula under guard.'

'What for? Good Lord, she doesn't think there's a chance of the attacker having another go, does she?'

'No, nothing like that, it's all in the name of discretion.'

'I can see someone of her generation would be ultra careful about a girl's good name.'

Let him think that, it would save explanations for the moment. 'The guard is Lipp, a truly appalling person who's my grandmother's maid.'

'It could be tricky, in that case. What do you suggest?'

Alix thought about it. 'It would be much the best thing if we could get Ursula away from Wyncrag. Grandmama flew into a temper with her and I don't suppose Ursula's feeling awfully comfortable being here just now.'

Alix could almost read Michael's thoughts. Curiosity was prodding him to ask just what was going on; good manners held him back.

'I'll have to ask Grandpapa to get Lipp called off. He'll think of a way. Then I can slip Ursula out.'

'Ursula's a guest, won't Sir Henry have doubts about her going elsewhere?'

'I think we're rather beyond those sorts of niceties.'

'At your command, then,' Michael said, sweeping a gesture towards the car. 'Hop indoors and kidnap Ursula. I'll fetch Freddie and then we can drive into Lowfell.' He got back into the car. 'After that,' he said in a voice that allowed no argument, 'I shall go and get Cecy. Someone from her family should be with Ursula.'

'Oh, yes, please do, I was going to telephone her, and ask if she could get into Lowfell. If you can go and get her, that would be much the best thing. Only don't alarm her – and for heaven's sake be discreet if anyone else is around.'

'I shall be the soul of tact.'

As Alix turned to go back into the house, a smile came to her lips. She liked Michael, and she felt he might – almost – be good enough for Cecy.

FIFTY

The stone house in South Street was a sanctuary for Lidia, a place where she might push to the back of her mind the horror of the man who had abused her in the street. In comparison to what was happening in the dark European world she had left behind, it was a nothingness, however greatly it had disturbed her. She had been helped by Tina's New World openness and casual sympathy and Edwin's outraged fury at the very un-Englishness of the incident. Between them, they had quelled her fears of staying where she was and persuaded her not to follow her first instincts and flee back to the south.

'London town isn't a good place to be, honey. It's a grim old city at the best of times, and that's where most of these Blackshirt types hang out, I guess.'

'Where would you go?' Edwin said, reasonably enough. 'You could stay with your sister and brother-in-law, but they don't have much room in their cottage, you told me that yourself.'

She had to admit that they were right. This small town set beside the lake didn't hold the threat of a Berlin or a Vienna, not now, not ever. A little while after the attack, the large policeman had arrived, helmet in hand as he stood pink-faced and uncomfortable in her sitting room. He expressed his concern, said that he would have a sharp word or two with the visitors. If they hadn't fled into the night, leaving the account for their lodgings unpaid. He hadn't said so, but she could see he thought it would serve Mrs McKechnie right for allowing such unsavoury visitors to stay at her house.

She and the policeman came from worlds so different that there would seem to be no point of contact. Yet there was the same sense of affront in both of them, that the stranger should transgress the bounds of good behaviour and trespass on the rights of all peaceable inhabitants and visitors, however dark-haired and foreign, to a quiet life.

'I don't hold with these fascist types, miss, and that's a fact,' he'd said as he paused on the doorstep on his way out. 'If they show their noses in here again, I'll run them in on a charge of breach of the peace. Or affray, even.'

Lidia was often lonely when Edwin was at Wyncrag. She had been used, in that other life in Vienna, to living in a house always abuzz with family, visitors, activity.

So she was pleased to have those two oh-so English girls in the house and Edwin, dark and furious again, and not looking so very much English after all in his temper at the red-haired girl's attacker. He seemed angry with his grand-mother, as well. That wouldn't last. Lidia knew all about the ways of families. And here was Ursula talking to the young doctor with the pleasant voice and kind smile, who complained that he was disappointed that there were no broken bones in the case.

'I need some practice,' he was telling Ursula. 'A decent sort of fracture, and I'd have been at your service.' While he jested and tweaked a wrist with friendly fingers, his eyes were searching for other signs of injury and trauma. 'You'll do. Take aspirin when you go to bed. That'll help any soreness from the bruising as well.' He looked down at her hands and turned them over to observe her knuckles. 'You landed a few good ones, so maybe you won't be the only one with bruises.'

Lidia had made up beds for Perdita and Ursula in a bedroom on the top floor, under the sloping eaves. She thought they would appreciate each other's company, although there did seem to be some constraint between them.

Alix could have told her the full story, but she felt too exhausted to go in for any explanations, and Lidia, with her practical, calm acceptance of her visitors, asked for none. Besides, Perdita at least wasn't worrying about Ursula now; she had other things on her mind. As soon as she'd seen the harpsichord, she forgot everything else. She pinged some keys, announced that it was out of tune, and asked what music Lidia had that she could play.

'I think that you have absolute pitch, which is useful for a musician,' Lidia said, showing her how to tune the strings, and bringing over a box of music.

Alix wondered for a moment whether a recollection of the destruction of her own music might come back to Perdita and cast a shadow over her pleasure in the new instrument, but not a bit of it.

'Goodness,' Perdita said. 'It's as bad as a harp, there's a girl at school who plays the harp, and she's always fiddling around with the strings. Not that it makes much difference, since she never plays in tune in any case.' Then she'd settled down to get to grips with the strange instrument, laughing at her attempts to shade the notes with the pedal, but exclaiming at how Scarlatti sounded quite, quite different on a harpsichord.

A knock on the door. Lidia looked up, suddenly extra alert.

'I'll see who it is,' Edwin said, to return minutes later with Michael and Cecy.

Cecy sank down beside Ursula. 'Are you all right?'

Explanations. Meaningful looks from Alix. Assurances from Freddie. Soothing words from Michael.

'Could someone lay the table?' Lidia said, taking a tablecloth from the drawer of the small dresser and spreading it over the round table in the corner of the room. 'I think we'll all fit around.'

She was a restful person, Alix decided. Despite her elegance and what Edwin assured her was a remarkable artistic talent, Lidia was easy in her domestic role, ignoring Michael and Freddie's protests that they mustn't impose, that they should go and leave the others in peace, and merely handing them a basket of knives and forks with one of her ravishing smiles. 'Edwin may telephone the inn to say that you are dining out.'

'Delicious smells,' Freddie said. 'It'll make a change from hotpot. Mrs Dixon's a good enough cook, but you can have too much hotpot and shepherd's pie.'

'What about Wyncrag?' Alix said. She was sitting back in a low chair, watching the fire from under drooping eyelids.

Edwin gave her a teasing jab with the blunt end of a corkscrew. 'Wake up, you can't leave us to do all the work. Give Lidia a hand in the kitchen. Don't worry about Wyncrag, I told Rokeby we would none of us dine at home.'

Alix felt the tensions of the day drop away as they squeezed themselves in around the table to eat hot fruit soup followed by chicken cooked, so Lidia told them, in the Hungarian way.

'Where did you learn to cook like this, Lidia?' asked Michael, eyeing the chocolate mousse she had just put down on the table.

'My mother taught me. We had an excellent cook, but my mother said that if you didn't know how to cook food your-self, then you would always be made a fool of in the kitchen. I think now that it will be useful to know how to cook, even a little. Cooks vanish in wartime.'

'Don't mention the war.' Perdita spoke through a mouthful of mousse. 'Everyone goes on and on about it, and it might never happen.'

'It's happening in Spain,' Edwin said.

'A mockery of a war,' Freddie said lazily. 'Civil war, ugh. I don't know why people are rushing out there to fight, when there's a war of our own just around the corner.'

'Can I have some more of this, please, Lidia?' said Perdita. 'Edwin, are you going to marry Lidia? Imagine, you'd have food like this every day.'

'It's tempting,' Edwin said. 'Only she won't have me.'

Lidia got up from the table. 'I make some coffee, now.'

Ursula gave a great yawn, and Cecy put an arm around her. 'Come on, bedtime for you.'

She was back before the others had finished their coffee. 'She went straight to sleep, once I'd promised to find the hat and scarf she was wearing and give them back to Rosalind. I'll go down to the lake tomorrow and look for them.'

'And you might look for the sledge while you're at the lake,' Edwin said as he escorted her and Michael and Freddie downstairs.

Goodbyes, the door shutting, voices outside in the street exclaiming on the severity of the frost, laughter as Cecy perched herself on Michael's lap, the roar of the Bentley's engine as it echoed along the deserted, shining streets and faded into the distance.

Alix went downstairs to help Lidia wash up, while Edwin smoked a cigar and Perdita went back to the harpsichord.

'I'll wash and you dry,' Alix said. 'You know where everything goes.' She put in the plug and ran water into the sink, added some soap flakes and started on the glasses. 'Lidia, why won't you marry Edwin? He's head over heels in love with you, anyone can see that.'

'Can they? Maybe so, but love and marriage do not always go together, whatever the songs say.'

'Don't you love him?'

'Yes, in a way, I do. Too much to marry him.'

Alix rubbed a lipstick mark off the rim of a wineglass. 'That's the kind of awfully clever remark I don't understand.'

'You're his sister, and close to him, I think. A twin is special. Do you want to share him?'

'What I want doesn't come into it. What I do actually want is for him to be happy, and he isn't. Not at the moment.'

Lidia rubbed at a glass, held it up to the light and gave it a final polish before she put it back in the cupboard.

Alix felt her hesitate before she spoke again.

'There is a gulf between us, between you and me, and between Edwin's family and me. You are Edwin's twin, and you're very like him in many ways. When I'm with him, I forget how English he is, but when I see him with you, then I know how big the differences are between us. Love is all very well, but it takes more than love to make a marriage.'

'Well, you're certainly not romantic about it.'

'I do not come from a romantic world. I have learned what danger bonds of love and kinship can bring. Hostages to fortune, I think you call them in English. Yes, I have fallen in love with Edwin, though for me it has happened gradually, and it surprises me, still, because after – because I thought I would never love a man again.'

'Then, if you love him, that's all that matters.'

Alix knew as she spoke the words how crass they were. She wasn't a starry-eyed young girl any more than Lidia was. She knew that falling in love and living happily ever after wasn't the way it went.

'I carry a lot of memories, bad memories, around with me,' Lidia went on. 'That's one thing. Then, when I see Edwin at his family home, in his big family house, all the servants, the silver, the whole tra-la that goes with money, I think, what do I, an immigrant Jewess, from an intellectual family in Vienna, have to do with such a man?'

'We're hardly a grand family,' Alix protested. 'You sound as though it were a case of the nobleman in his castle, and it isn't. Our money is new money, and it comes from industry and business, not from land and great marriages. Besides,

Grandmama comes from an academic family, just like yours. Her father was a Cambridge professor.'

Lidia started on the soup plates. 'Aha, your grandmother. There is one good reason why I should not marry Edwin. Your grandmother hates Jews, as we know. She would be hostile to her grandson bringing home a Jewish bride. In fact, such a thing would not happen, for she would not let me in the house, and would drive Edwin away from his childhood home and his family. I would deprive her of one she loves, and when I learn that she has already lost two sons and a granddaughter, I feel I cannot do this to her.'

'She doesn't really give a button for any of us. She despises Trudie, and I make her cross most of the time; she tolerates Edwin, but she isn't close to him. Or to Uncle Saul, although he lives forever in her shadow, always hoping she'll throw him a crumb of interest or affection. If I were Aunt Jane I'd hate it, the way he hangs on every word Grandmama says.'

She attacked a plate with the brush, making Lidia exclaim at the vigour of her efforts.

'Be careful, or you will break that, or at the least rub the pattern off.'

'I sometimes think Grandmama has a screw loose.'

Lidia paused in the action of putting away a bowl. 'A screw loose?'

'Meaning, she's a bit crazy. Not really sane. I mean, look at the way she flew at Ursula today, it was completely daft. I know she's always been funny about men and sexual matters, that kind of thing, but to behave like that! And what she did to Perdita was unpardonable. Her own granddaughter! She keeps Perdy under iron control, as though she were always about to do something terrible. It wouldn't surprise me at all if Perdy doesn't burst out in the end and do something quite dreadful just because she's expected to.'

'She will,' Lidia said with certainty. 'It won't be so dreadful in the eyes of the world, and it won't be to do with men and sex, but your grandmother will hate it. Perdita is a musician, you only have to listen to hear how gifted, and watching her and talking to her, you see at once that she is serious and dedicated to her music. She will be a professional musician if she can find a way, and this will be distressing to your family.'

'Is she so promising? I know nothing about music.'

'She will need good teachers, and soon, for you have to learn when you are young. She should study abroad, that is best for the piano. Only such training is expensive, and she should have the support of her family.'

Feet sounded on the stairs and Edwin came into the kitchen. Lidia shooed him away from the sink. 'There is no room for you in here.'

'Then I shall loll in the doorway and watch you work,' he said, matching the action to the word.

Alix felt a jolt to her heart at the expression in his eyes, which were fixed on Lidia, and at the sudden glow in the look she gave him in return.

Alix changed the water and lifted another pile of plates into the suds, clattering the china to break the silence. 'Lidia says that Perdita is a real musician. That she could be a professional.'

'Why not?'

'Oh, Edwin, think about it. Grandmama let Perdy go to music college and train? As a professional? Can you imagine it? You saw what she did to Perdy's music.'

'That was just an outburst because of Ursula . . . all right, don't glare at me like that. I know Grandmama isn't musically minded, but we could try to talk Grandpapa around.'

'He'll help if he can without Grandmama noticing, but it's hardly going to amount to much. He won't come out on Perdy's side, you know he won't. Not if it means going against Grandmama.'

'What did she do to the music?' Lidia demanded. 'What music?'

Alix told her.

Lidia was horrified. 'Then she is crazy indeed. To do such a thing! To show such hatred! Why, what had Perdita done to deserve this?'

'Nothing,' Edwin said, 'absolutely damn nothing. Excuse my language, but it makes my blood boil, it really does. Look here, Alix, we've got to do something for Perdita. She can't go on like this, ghastly clothes, jumped on if she speaks or doesn't speak, constantly under suspicion for nameless offences. She's going to grow up warped, never mind the music.'

'You have money of your own, Edwin, and you also, I think, Alix?'

'Yes.'

'From your mother and father?'

'We will, next birthday. It's in trust.'

'Is Perdita not also your parents' daughter? Is there no money for her?'

The twins looked at each other. 'We assume so,' Edwin said. 'It's one of those things people never talk about. She'll get her share of the money when she's twenty-five, the same as us. Grandpapa pays her school fees and so on, just as he did for us, so the capital and income are rolled up. In fact, by the time she comes of age, she'll be very well off.'

'Could she not have some money now? To pay for her music? For her to buy clothes for herself, to go to concerts? It is important for her to listen to music also.'

'We could ask the trustees,' Edwin said doubtfully.

'Forget it,' Alix said. She tipped the knives and forks into the water and, without looking around, said, 'The trustees, Lidia, consist of the family solicitor in Manchester, American lawyers about whom we know nothing, and Uncle Saul. Old Noakes, the solicitor, is in Grandmama's pocket, and as for Uncle Saul –'

'He'd never go against Grandmama's edicts,' Edwin finished for her.

403

'We could pay for her ourselves. I'm quite happy to do that.'

'So am I, but it isn't a matter of pounds, shillings and pence, Lexy, you know it isn't. It's about Perdita being under Grandmama's control, and staying there for the next six years, and then it's another four years before she will have any money.'

'Six years! Ten years! *Du lieber Gott*,' Lidia said, and closed the cutlery drawer with a sharp bang. 'Six years is too long. In six years she will be destroyed.'

FIFTY-ONE

'They're both asleep,' Alix said. She had crept into their room to check on Perdita and Ursula. 'I've left a light on.'

'Very sensible,' said Lidia. 'To keep the bad dreams away.'

'Now,' said Edwin. 'I want the truth about what happened today.'

Alix sighed, tucked her feet up underneath her, and rearranged the cushion behind her back.

'Stop fidgeting, Lexy, and spit it out,' Edwin said.

'Ursula did go to meet someone, and got more than she bargained for. But she didn't want to go and she wasn't there on her own account.'

'A go-between?' said Edwin.

'Exactly. Perdy wasn't keen to sneak on her friend, which is how she saw it, but I did finally manage to get most of the story out of her. Ursula went to meet this man on Rosalind's behalf; she's laid up with a cold, and so couldn't make the assignation they had arranged. It seems that the charming Rosalind has been blackmailing Ursula – she found a letter from Delia that came via Nanny, and threatened to tell Peter if Ursula didn't do what she wanted. I gather this wasn't the first time Rosalind has prevailed on Ursula to do her dirty work, and obviously she has no intention of giving the child her letter back.'

'This Rosalind is not a nice person, I think,' said Lidia.

'I didn't like her from the word go,' Edwin said. 'What a little weasel she's turned out to be. So off tripped Ursula, wrapped up in that hat and scarf, and I suppose the man took her for Rosalind.'

'Yes. He was furious, apparently, when he discovered it wasn't Rosalind, and then he said he'd give her a message to take back to Rosalind, whereupon he grabbed her again and started kissing her. Of course she was horrified and pulled away, she thought it was the most revolting thing that ever happened to her. That's when he got violent.'

'It's outrageous,' said Edwin. 'Who is this man? Just let me get my hands on him, that's all.'

'Perdy says she has no idea. I'm not sure she was telling the truth, but she buttoned up, I couldn't get any more out of her.'

'What is this girl, this Rosalind, doing with such a man?' asked Lidia. 'How old is she?'

'Seventeen, I believe,' said Edwin. 'And it doesn't surprise me that she's been making assignations with unsavoury men in the woods.'

Alix stood up, yawning widely. 'I don't in the least want to go back to Wyncrag, but Grandpapa will be worried about me. If Grandmama turns me out into the snow, I'll come and wake you all up.'

Edwin went to get her coat. 'This was with it,' he said, handing her a manila file.

'Good God, how could I have forgotten that?' she said, stopping and taking the folder from Edwin. 'It was among some of Mummy's things that were stuffed away in a cupboard in one of the attics. I went up there earlier today and rescued it, but the lunch gong went, and it completely slipped my mind, what with all the fuss about Ursula.'

'Oh, Lord, you're not still on about Mummy, are you? As if we didn't have enough to think about now, without delving back into the past.'

406

'There might be some photos, and perhaps a clue as to where in America Mummy and Isabel were when they had the accident, and whereabouts Mummy's family came from. It's all such a mystery, and I don't see why it should be.'

'Well, if you must go digging about in cupboards, you must, but I do think it's best put behind you.'

Lidia disagreed. 'You are wrong, Edwin. Where there are questions and uncertainty, one cannot rest until they are answered and resolved. Alix is right to want to know.'

'Thank you,' Alix said, glad of this unexpected support.

Edwin looked at the rather battered file. 'Go on, then. Open it. Let's have a quick look at what's in there. Then you can come back and have a proper look through tomorrow.'

Alix undid the brown tape that was wound around the folder. Inside was a wodge of papers, not apparently sorted into any order, but looking as though they had been carelessly shoved in.

A folded, yellowing newspaper, of a smaller format than English papers, fell to the floor. Edwin bent to pick it up and unfolded it. '*The Peel Reporter*,' he said, reading from the banner across the front page.

'Peel? Is that a place?'

'I should think so. Hal may know where that is, or we can look it up in the gazetteer.'

Then he saw that Alix's eyes were riveted to the picture on the front page. 'That's Mummy,' she cried, snatching the paper from him.

Edwin leaned over her shoulder and read out the headline. '"Tragic death in automobile accident." It's all here, what you wanted to know, Lexy. Where it happened, ten o'clock at night, poor visibility on a misty road.'

'It doesn't say anything about drink,' said Alix, scanning the text.

'They wouldn't put that in,' Edwin said. 'Sensibility of the family and all that.'

407

There was a sound of a door opening, and a sleepy-looking Perdita came into the room, clad incongruously in a pair of Edwin's striped pyjamas. 'You're making a lot of noise,' she said. 'What are you all gazing at? You look as though you'd seen a ghost.'

She came over and looked at the newspaper. 'Isn't that a picture of Mummy? Oh, look, it's all about the accident.' She began to read it. 'Funny that it doesn't mention Isabel at all.'

'Now you come to mention it, it doesn't,' said Alix. 'I didn't notice that.'

'They probably didn't know she'd been in the car as well, reporters always jump on the first news and don't listen to the rest of the story, you know what they're like,' Edwin said.

'Where did the newspaper come from?' Perdita asked, when she'd finished reading the report.

'It was stashed away in an attic cupboard at Wyncrag,' Alix said.

'I suppose the American relatives sent the newspaper over,' Perdita said. Then she picked up the paper again. 'There's something wrong here.'

'What?' said Alix.

'Look at the date.'

'The twenty-ninth of August,' Edwin said. 'So?'

'August?' Alix said sharply. 'Edwin, Mummy wasn't killed in August. She died in September. Perdita's birthday is September the twenty-third, and Mummy died a few days later.'

'Very soon, after having a baby, to be driving a car,' observed Lidia.

'It's odd,' said Edwin.

'It's a printing error, that's all,' Alix said.

'Newspapers don't get that kind of date wrong,' Edwin said flatly. 'If this is dated the twenty-ninth of August, then that's when it was printed. That means that Mummy died about a month before we thought.'

'And Perdy?'

Edwin and Alix exchanged looks.

'There must have been a muddle about Perdita's date of birth,' Lidia said swiftly. 'This can happen, especially when the birth is in another country. Such a thing happened to a cousin of mine, who was born in France. When his birth was registered in Vienna, they put down the wrong year. Such mistakes occur, and when a family is in crisis, after a death, then it is likely that errors are made.'

'Yes, that'll be it,' Edwin said. 'Don't worry about it, Perdy. Off to bed with you, and we'll talk about it in the morning.'

'But Isabel –'

'First rule, don't believe anything you read in the newspapers.'

Perdita wasn't listening. Frowning, she picked up the newspaper again and looked intently at the front page.

'Mungo's youngest sister is really his niece,' she said.

The others stared at her. 'Mungo, the groom?' Edwin said.

Perdita nodded. 'Janet's his older sister. She took up with a Tommy just before the end of the war. He never came back. He wasn't killed in the trenches or anything like that; Mungo said he was already married. When Janet had the baby, their mother pretended it was hers.'

Silence.

'So I suppose that's what happened when I was born. I expect Grandmama wanted it that way. She probably wished we were living in ancient Greece, when she could have left me on a hillside.'

'Perdy!'

'It's all right. She didn't, and here I am, and I'm an orphan, sort of, one way or the other. It doesn't really matter that much.'

Lidia got up. 'I'll make hot chocolate for you, Perdita, the Viennese way, rich, very delicious, and you'll sleep soundly.'

Yawning wildly, Perdita drank her chocolate, said goodnight for a second time and went back to bed.

'Phew,' Edwin said. 'Alix, give me that newspaper.' He laid it on the table, and the two of them pored over it. 'It's a damned nuisance this is the only newspaper,' he said, rifling through the rest of the papers from the file. 'There'd be a follow-up, accounts of the funeral, details of grieving family, all that kind of thing. This is a local rag, they'd go to town over a story like this. This piece is just the bare bones when the story broke. Oh, hell, Lexy, I wish with all my heart that you'd never found this.'

FIFTY-TWO

Alix woke early after a restless night, and decided to miss breakfast. She didn't want to face Grandmama, or even Grandpapa and Aunt Trudie, but it had to be done. She waited until she heard the sound of Edwin's motor car roaring up the drive, then went down the back stairs, keeping a watchful eye out for Lipp. Edwin would have taken his motor around to the stables, so she walked along the wide, stone-flagged passage that led to the back of the house.

Edwin was looking grim, but he gave Alix a hug. 'Where's Aunt Trudie?'

They found her in the Herb Room, seeing to the flowers before going through the menus with Cook. It was all so normal, Aunt Trudie busy attending to her household duties, her firm hands trimming stems and twisting wire. A pile of winter greenery lay on the wooden table, flowers from the conservatory stood in buckets at her feet. It was chilly in there, even though a stove in one corner gave off stuffy fumes. The setters lying close to the stove on a piece of old rug thumped feathery tails as the twins came in.

'Hello, darlings,' Trudie said. 'I'm just doing fresh flowers, they never last long when the central heating is on all the

411

time. I hadn't expected to see you both so early. How is Ursula? And Perdita?'

Edwin swept aside a pile of stripped leaves and pieces of stalk, brushed the dampness off with his sleeve and laid the newspaper in front of his aunt. 'Stop that for a moment, Aunt Trudie. We need to pick your brains.'

Trudie stood transfixed, secateurs raised aloft in one hand, a branch of Cotoneaster in the other. 'Helena,' she said helplessly. 'Oh, dear.'

'Read it,' Edwin said, removing the secateurs from her grasp.

Her eyes wandered around the room, fixing on anything except the newspaper. 'I know, it is awful to see it written . . . Your poor mother.'

Edwin was ruthless. 'Forget the tragic details. Look at the date.'

'Oh. Oh, dear.'

Alix pulled over a chair and pushed her aunt into it. 'Edwin, you don't have to be so brutal.'

'I? I'm not brutal. The brutality lies with the people who made up all the tarradiddles we've been fed over the years.'

Trudie had collected herself. 'Of course, it's a mistake. About the date. Helena died in September. Or was it October?'

'You're telling us she died after Perdita was born, which was on September the twenty-third, that's her birthday, isn't it?'

Trudie nodded. She was twisting a piece of twine around and around her fingers, pulling it so tight that it bit into her flesh.

'That won't wash,' Edwin said.

'What if the paper isn't wrong?' said Alix. 'If Mummy did die in August, and Perdita was born in September. In that case, Mummy can't have been Perdita's mother. Perdy isn't our sister, is she?'

Trudie looked down at her hands and the twine, but said nothing.

412

Edwin, ignoring Alix's warning looks, wasn't in a mood to be gentle. 'If you read the article, which you don't have to, I'll spare you the trouble, you'll see that there isn't a mention of Isabel. Isabel wasn't with Helena in that car, admit it, Aunt Trudie.'

Trudie sighed. 'No. No, she wasn't.'

'So where was she? Where does Perdita come into the story, although I think we can guess that.'

Alix spoke in a kinder voice. 'Don't mind Edwin's bullying, Aunt, but we have to know. You do see that, don't you?'

'You should have been told years ago. All of you. Lies beget lies, and no good ever comes of them, however well-intentioned they are. Drat this twine.'

As she disentangled the loops of string, they heard quick footsteps approaching. They turned to look at the door as it swung open. Saul stood there, sleek and frowning, with his pale, indifferent wife standing behind him. Jane stepped around her husband.

'I was coming to give you a hand with the flowers, Trudie, only Saul heard raised voices and came running to save you. Perhaps he thought Ursula's attacker had got into the kitchens.'

'It's hardly a subject for levity,' Saul said. 'Alix, Edwin, what are you doing here? What have you said to upset Trudie? She's as white as a sheet, really, it's too bad of you. Jane, call Rokeby, tell him to bring brandy.'

'Thank you, Saul, but the last thing I want at this time of the morning is brandy. Where's Mama?'

'In her room. Fortunately, otherwise she might have heard all the noise coming from here, and she needs to be quiet. After the shock of yesterday.'

'Grandmama needs to be quiet?' Alix said indignantly. 'Why —'

'Shut up,' Edwin said.

Saul had spotted the newspaper. 'What's this, what's this?' He took in the photograph and headline, and his face darkened. 'What is the meaning of this? Where did you get this newspaper? Trudie, is this your doing?'

'Stop it, Saul. Posturing and spluttering won't help. Edwin and Alix found the newspaper, don't ask me where, and brought it to show me. They wanted me to answer some questions.'

'It's none of their business to go asking questions. It's not a matter for them.'

'Just who is it a matter for, if not us?' Alix said. Bother Uncle Saul for turning up at precisely the wrong moment and putting his oar in. She appealed to Aunt Jane. 'Can't you take him away?'

Jane shrugged her elegant shoulders. 'Let him get it out of his system. He'll be off to Caroline shortly, in any case, to tell her all about it.'

'Don't you dare, Uncle Saul,' Edwin said. 'No one says anything to Grandmama until we've got to the bottom of this. And don't pretend it's not our business.' He banged the photograph with the back of his hand. 'Whose business if not ours? This is our mother, for Christ's sake.'

'And my brother's wife,' Saul said stiffly.

'Big deal.' Edwin turned to Trudie, and crouched down beside her chair, so that he was on a level with her. 'Please, Aunt Trudie, get it off your chest.'

'Yes, please, Aunt Trudie,' Alix echoed. 'Now we know this much we'll find out the rest, one way or another, you know we will.'

Trudie sat up very straight. 'As I was saying when we ... I think ... You should have been told the truth. A long time ago.'

Saul loomed over his sister. 'Trudie, I forbid you to say another word.'

Trudie took no notice of her brother, but spoke directly to Edwin in a rush of coherence. 'Helena wasn't Perdita's mother, and Perdita isn't your sister. She's your niece. Isabel was her mother.'

Jane let out a long, low whistle. 'Well, really.' She whipped around to face Saul. 'You've known this all along, haven't you?' She picked up the newspaper and ran her eyes down the column. 'Where was Isabel when Helena died?'

'In a clinic, waiting for the child to be born.'

'That's enough,' Saul was almost howling in his distress. 'For heaven's sake, spare us the sordid details. Mama is going to be so distressed that this has come out, and now, of all times.'

Edwin, Alix, Trudie and Jane all looked at him for a long, silent moment.

Saul took no notice. 'I said at the time the child should be sent for adoption.'

'Adoption?' said Edwin, furious. 'Adoption? My sister?'

'She isn't your sister, that's the point,' Uncle Saul said testily. 'A niece, that's all. An illegitimate niece. I knew the pretence of Helena being the mother wouldn't work. I knew it would all come out, sooner or later, and there'd be a scandal.'

'The scandal is that it was kept quiet for so long,' said Edwin. 'And I don't care whether Perdy's my sister or my niece; she's one of the family and her place is here at Wyncrag, as it always has been.'

'We should have been told,' Alix said. 'So should Perdita. She has a right to know who she is.'

'I'm not so sure about that, Alix,' Edwin said.

'One might say, better a respectable orphan than a bastard,' Trudie said.

Saul winced. 'Trudie, your language.'

'If it's morality you're talking of, what about Mavis? I think you'd do better to keep your mouth shut for once.'

Jane's eyes narrowed.

Alix was amazed at the effect this had on Saul, who collapsed like a deflated balloon. Mavis. Well, now. Could it possibly be that . . .? No, surely not.

Jane gave Saul a glacial look. She twitched her cardigan

further on to her shoulders and fingered the pearls at her neck. 'We know what happened to Perdita. So what became of Isabel?'

'She died,' Saul said bluntly. 'In childbirth. Very sad, but maybe it was for the best.'

The others stared at him once more. 'For the best?' repeated Jane.

'Consider, she was only fourteen when she, er, when she got into trouble. She must have had a naturally bad disposition.'

'Shut up, Saul, you've said enough,' said Trudie. 'I'm ashamed of you. Good gracious, as if Jack weren't enough, we have to have a born fool like you in the family.'

'He's worse than a fool,' Edwin said contemptuously. 'To say that about his own niece, my sister, and yes, Isabel was my sister, even if Perdita isn't. It's for the best that she died? Jesus Christ, Uncle Saul, if the government you serve in shares your perverted sense of morality, then God help this country.'

'It's a moral sense he shares with his mother,' Jane said, in almost conversational tones. 'If you want to know who was behind this cover-up and pretence, look no further. You may be sure that your grandmother arranged the whole thing. And, in my opinion, you haven't got to the bottom of it yet. If I were you, Edwin and Alix, I'd start asking a few more questions about your dead sister.'

FIFTY-THREE

Michael was waiting outside the Post Office as the postbus rumbled to a halt. Cecy got off, together with two women in felt hats, who had shopping baskets over their arms. The driver gave the brake an extra tug, and climbed down. He nodded at Michael, and went into the Post Office to collect the mail bag and have his morning cup of tea.

Michael, tired and distracted though he was, felt his heart lift as he went towards Cecy.

'Hello,' she said. 'I hadn't expected to be met.'

'I woke early and thought I'd walk here and get a paper.'

'Are you usually an early riser?' Then, seeing him hesitate, she rushed to apologize. 'Sorry, forget that. I didn't mean to be nosy.'

'You aren't. I like you to take an interest in my way of life. The truth is, I usually rise at a reasonable hour, neither early nor late, in plenty of time for the usual male potter before breakfast. Only I've not been sleeping too well recently.'

They came out of the village and took the road towards the inn, walking in the middle of the road where traffic had vanquished the ice.

'Mrs Dixon's hotpots? Last night's meal can't be to blame, surely, Lidia's food was delicious.'

417

'I've the toughest of digestions. It isn't food, more an afflic-
tion of the mind.'

'What?'

'No, I'm not a candidate for the lunatic asylum. I merely
suffer from bad dreams.'

'Oh, those. Horrid things. Something on your mind?'

'It's a recurrent nightmare. I begin to wonder whether it's
more than that. Maybe a memory from childhood; forgotten
in the daytime, altogether beyond conscious recall, in fact,
so it comes out at night to stalk my dreams. I had it a lot
when I was younger, and then not for years. Or is it some
kind of glimpse into the future? All these theories about time
not being what it seems, I suppose it's possible. Whatever it
is, it's connected with this place.'

'The village? Have you been here before?'

'Not the village, the lake. Yes, we used to come here for
holidays when I was a boy. Since I've been here, it's come
back with a vengeance. I dream it practically every night.'

Why was he telling her this? Was he turning into some
kind of Ancient Mariner, compelled to force the story of his
dream on to every unwilling acquaintance?

'Bad dreams haunt worse than ghosts,' Cecy said. 'Think
of Hamlet, "king of infinite space were it not that I have
bad dreams". Alix always says that Shakespeare was an
insomniac, all those references to disturbed sleep in the
plays.'

'I don't know much Shakespeare, only what I had to do
at school.'

'Don't you like the theatre?'

Michael considered the question. 'I do, but I haven't had
much opportunity to go since I left university. I haven't been
in the right place, or I've not had the time.'

'You should go more. I love the theatre. And going to the
pictures. They take you out of yourself.'

'I go when I get the chance. I suppose I seem very boring

418

to you,' he added, with sudden irritation. 'Work and more work, that's how I spend my life.'

Cecy thrust her hands into the pockets of her coat. 'Is it colder than it was?'

He was grateful to her for not responding to his outburst. 'Not possible.'

'I have a theory: iciness that is invigorating and exciting before Christmas overwhelms one's system by the new year.'

'How does one recover?'

'By catching a train to London. No, don't laugh.'

'I thought you lake families only felt happy when near the lake and the hills.'

'I used to think that, to say that I was a northerner through and through. I'm not. I'd much rather be in London, I've decided. People are more or less normal there. At least, the ones I know are. Unlike my family and relations. Unlike the Richardsons.'

They had reached the inn. Michael led her into the hall. 'I shan't be a tick,' he said, heading for the wooden stairs.

Mr Dixon came out to bid her good-day. 'It's good to see you again, Miss Cecy. How are Mr and Mrs Roger?' He made minute enquiries about her family, and then told her to make the most of the skating, while she could. 'For I smell wind and a change to the weather on the way. There's snow in the air.'

'How can you say that when the sky is a brilliant blue, and the temperature's way below freezing?'

'Not today, and not tomorrow, neither, but give it a few days and you'll see I'm right.'

Michael and Cecy walked down to the inn's landing stage, which stood barely a foot above the surface of the lake. Cecy sat with her legs over the side, pulling up one foot and then the other to fasten her skates. Then she put her feet on the ice and glided off. Michael followed with more caution.

'It's no good you twirling off in all directions. My skating is not of the dramatic kind.'

419

'We'll stick together and skate up and down like a pair of Dutch burghers on a canal.'

'I suppose you've skated every year since you could walk.'

'Most years, especially when I was little. We all skated. Isabel, Alix's older sister, was the best of us, she could do anything on the ice. She was good at so many things. She rode well, and was a wicked mimic, and a very fine shot. The Richardsons don't shoot much, Sir Henry's more of a fisherman, so Isabel used to come to us for the shooting. Our gamekeeper said she was better with a gun than any of us Grindleys.' She cut a leisurely figure of eight in a smooth patch of ice. 'Poor Isabel.'

'Was she a particular friend?'

'She was a few years older than me, so no.' She gave herself a little shake, and wobbled as she skated an edge. 'Let's not talk about the past.'

'Does anyone own the island?' Michael asked, as Cecy set off on a curving course to take them around it.

'Sir Henry.'

'Hence the landing stage. Let's take advantage of it, and sit and smoke a companionable cigarette.'

'We'll freeze,' Cecy warned. 'Be found forlorn lumps of ice.'

'Not in the time it takes to smoke a cigarette, I feel sure.'

'I've given them up.'

'Not when you're outdoors, and there's never a prospective patient or senior doctor in sight. Allow me.'

Before she could protest, he put his hands to her waist and lifted her on to the landing stage, a higher one than at the inn. Then he swung himself up to sit beside her. He produced a cigarette case, patted his pockets for a box of matches and lit their cigarettes.

'What's up?' he asked. 'Are you worrying about Ursula?'

'No. It's something else.'

'Don't talk about it if you'd rather not.'

'I'd like to. You aren't the gabby sort, and I don't know that you'd be interested enough to spread it around.'

He was silent. He didn't want to be told secrets, but he could see something was bothering Cecy, and he was touched by her wanting to confide in him. 'In my line of business, you know, we have to keep our mouths shut.'

She flashed him a smile. 'I'm sure you do. Oh, well, it's more of a family thing than a state secret. Alix telephoned me this morning. After we left yesterday, she and Edwin were going through some old papers, don't ask me why, and they found out something about their mother's death.'

'She died in America, a good while back, didn't she? In a car accident, with her daughter. Just after she'd had Perdita.'

'Ah, that's the point. It turns out that Helena Richardson died before the baby was born. It was Isabel's baby, not hers.'

Michael thought about that as he drew on his cigarette. 'Isabel was the actual mother, Helena was to be the official one.'

'That's it in a nutshell.'

'How old was Isabel?'

'Fourteen. Fourteen when she had Perdita. Just past her fourteenth birthday nine months before when Perdita would have been conceived. It must have been about this time of year.'

Michael whistled. 'Fourteen! Dear God. Who was the father?'

'Lord knows.' She looked up at the peaks. 'The fells seem to hover over us, today. As though they were closer and bearing down on us. Menacing.'

Michael jumped down from the landing stage, and stood on his skates, one arm propped up on the timbers. He still had his cigarette between his fingers. 'Come on,' he said. 'Let's go and find that hat and scarf. And a sledge, wasn't it?'

Cecy slid down to join him. 'No, Alix said that Sanders went out and retrieved that.'

'Where is this place?'

'Not far. We skate around that little promontory and then you'll see the boathouse. Haven't you been to this part of the lake before?'

'No. We always go the other way, where the sun shines. This part of the lake is mostly in shadow.'

They were skating into the shadow now, cast by the surrounding hills.

'There's the boathouse,' Cecy called, flying away ahead of him. 'Come on.'

Michael didn't come on. Instead, he came to so abrupt a stop that he nearly toppled over on to the ice.

Cecy wasn't looking behind her and she sped on, slowing down to trip neatly on to the patch of shingle. She turned, laughing, and saw Michael still out on the ice.

'Michael, hurry up.' Then she noticed his expression, which took the smile from her own face. 'Why, whatever is it? You look as though you'd seen a ghost.'

FIFTY-FOUR

Daphne buttonholed Hal soon after breakfast. 'This morning, we are going over to Wyncrag to see Henry.'

Hal was wary; what was his aunt up to? 'I'd be delighted to go with you. Is there any particular reason for our visit?'

'I want to pick Henry's brains. I bet he knows a thing or two about the Grindley business, and a lot more about what Germans are buying these days and for what purposes. I don't know why I didn't think of it earlier.'

Hal didn't believe that his godfather would shed any more light on the proposed sale. For himself, he thought the German connection unfortunate, but hardly sinister. However, if Daphne believed that the Reich was going to be benefited by the acquisition of a china factory, then nothing he said would persuade her otherwise. She wouldn't agree to the sale; he might or might not. It was beginning to bore him, as were his brothers. He was inclined to think that he'd sell his shares to them; at least that way they wouldn't bother him again.

'I've told my chauffeur to bring the car around in half an hour.'

'Does Sir Henry know we're coming?'

'He does. At least, I left a message with Rokeby, and, unlike the staff here, he's capable of passing it on.'

The purple Rolls drew up in front of Wyncrag and the purple-liveried chauffeur was out of his driving seat and around to the other side of the car in a trice to open the passenger door for a purple-clad Daphne.

Hal followed her, bestowing a wink on the chauffeur, whose wrinkled left eye flickered in return.

Rokeby was there to greet them. 'Good morning, Mrs Wolf. Good morning, Mr Hal. Miss Alix would appreciate a word with you before you go in to Sir Henry, Mr Hal, if you would be so kind. She is in the New Morning Room. The third door on your left, sir.'

'I'll join you in a minute, Daphne,' Hal said. 'You go ahead and put Sir Henry in the picture.'

'Very well, but don't let Alix keep you. I want you to hear what Henry has to say, I want no remarks afterwards about my misunderstanding him or his not appreciating the finer points.'

Hal retreated to the New Morning Room, characterised by being twice the size of the Old Morning Room and by the fact that Alix's great-grandmother had placed in it all the furniture which her husband had bought while on a visit to China, adding Chinese wallpaper and lighting as the finishing touch. It was overwhelming, but Hal, after an initial intake of breath as the room's full glory came back to him, ignored the décor.

Alix was sitting on the edge of a chair covered in red silk dragons. She was smoking a cigarette as though her life depended on it, and frowning. Her face lightened as she saw Hal.

He came into the room and closed the door. 'Something up?'

'And so you see,' Alix finished, 'that explains what happened in nineteen twenty-one, why Mummy went off with Isabel and everything.'

Not by a long chalk, it didn't, thought Hal. 'What about Isabel? What happened to her?'

'Uncle Saul, who, it turns out, has known all along that Perdy was Isabel's daughter, says she died in childbirth.'

'Do you believe him?'

'It's possible. Likely even, because she was so young, and she must have been in a dreadful state with Mummy being killed, let alone the natural fear of having a baby. I can't bear to think about it.'

Hal's private opinion was that if Saul told him it was Tuesday, he'd glance at the calendar to check.

'Does Lady Richardson know you've found out? Do you think it was her idea for Helena to pretend to be the mother and take Isabel off like that?'

Alix shrugged. 'Who knows? It isn't uncommon, is it, for a grandmother to pass for the mother, to avoid scandal, to preserve the decencies. No wonder Grandmama's always been so horrible to Perdita, she despises bastards, as she so sweetly calls them. Mummy, if what you say is true, would have wanted to protect Isabel and the family's good name. She would have considered illegitimacy a stigma, wouldn't she?'

'Yes. And at fourteen, Isabel could hardly get married.'

'Of course not.'

'Any idea who Perdita's father is?'

'None at all. We've all racked our brains, but no, not a notion. It has to be someone local. I suppose the affair was discovered that Christmas, and that's what all the fuss and the scenes were about. Poor Isabel, it must have been frightful for her.'

Hal had been doing his sums. 'If Perdita was born in September, then no one would have known she was pregnant the previous December or January. I wonder why they shut her away and pretended she was ill?'

'Punishment, for being found out with a man,' said Alix glumly. 'Grandmama probably fed her on bread and water, out of sheer temper. Only Mummy didn't seem cross with Isabel. You could tell when she was cross with someone. She was angry with Grandmama, well, that was nothing unusual, and I know she had arguments with Daddy, which had never happened before. Edwin and I were constantly being shooed away, told to go and skate on the lake, or banished to the nursery with books or tasks – we resented that, because we never had to do schoolwork in the Christmas holiday.'

'Does Perdita know any of this?'

'Supposedly not, but I wouldn't be surprised if she'd worked it out by now. You may have noticed that Perdita has a very clear mind. She takes things in her stride in a way I couldn't have done at her age. A fact is a fact, to her, and there's no point in becoming emotional about it. All her emotion is reserved for her music and her horse.'

Hal thought that if he lived with the Richardsons, he'd learn not to let himself feel emotional.

'Frankly, your family terrifies me.'

'Even me?'

'Even you. You've gone at this like a ferret down a rabbit hole, and look what you've turned up. I don't suppose this will be the end of it, either.'

'Why do you say that?'

'A classical education brings to mind Pandora's box, the parcel of winds and a few family tiffs such as occurred among the Atreus kith and kin. Pentheus also, not to mention Medea.'

'Really, Hal, do you think we Richardsons serve babies up in pies and slay our young out of revenge, or suffer from god-induced craziness?'

'Perdita definitely has a whiff of baby-pie about her.'

FIFTY-FIVE

Daphne was in full flow when Hal came into Sir Henry's study, and his godfather was listening to what she was saying with close attention. He waved to Hal to sit down. He listened some more and then interrupted.

'Yes, yes, Daphne, you don't have to go into details. I know all about Palfrey's, I was the one who advised your brother to buy the company in the first place. I can't see that there's a problem. China, there's nothing special about china.'

'Henry, I've no patience with you. Here's this country selling . . .'

She was interrupted again, this time by Rokeby. 'Excuse me, Mrs Wolf. Sir Henry, Mr Wrexham is here to see you. He says you're expecting him.'

'Tell him . . . No, ask him to come in. Daphne, stop glaring at me. Michael's a sensible young man, and he works in the aircraft industry, he knows something about what the Germans are keen to get their hands on. We were having a chat only a few days ago about foreigners buying into British companies for their own purposes. Let's see what he has to say.'

Momentarily thwarted, Daphne rounded on Hal. 'And don't you just sit there and pretend it's nothing to do with you. It's time you developed a sense of moral responsibility.'

Damn her, thought Hal. Palfrey's was a china firm, goddammit, not a factory turning out shells or guns or parts for tanks. Then he was suddenly reminded of the story in the press, which had caused much amusement in his circle, of the worker in a wheelbarrow factory in the Ruhr, who had stolen the parts to take home and assemble into a wheelbarrow to use in his garden, only to find he'd put together a machine gun. Perhaps Daphne's theories weren't quite so ridiculous after all.

Michael listened attentively to what Sir Henry had to say, thought for a moment, and then spoke. 'The Germans are in the market to buy anything which might be useful to them. You could say they want consumer goods, that a china factory is indicative of their desire for nothing but peace and prosperity. I think you'd be wrong. They have a posse of men trawling through the patents office, I know it for a fact. It's like them saying they're buying aircraft engines to build up a civil fleet. It's rubbish. Chums of mine who've made it their business to go and have a look for themselves over there tell a very different story. China. Let me think.'

He gazed up at the ceiling, and Daphne, quite quelled by his vehemence, gave him an approving look.

'China is a first-class insulator,' Michael said suddenly. 'It's used in telegraph installations, you've seen it for yourself, on the poles, up by the wires.'

Sir Henry was suddenly alert. 'Palfrey's make those.'

'Do they? There you are, then. Lots of fellows I know say that communications are what will win the next war. Radio and code machines and all that. It seems to me that a firm turning out china insulators of various types and sizes –'

Daphne was triumphant. 'I knew it. Hal, we must tax Peter with this.'

'Must we?' said Hal. 'Look, Daphne, why don't I sell my shares to you? Then you've got sixty per cent, and they can't do a thing.'

'You, Hal, are a coward. You want to slide out of this. Instead of standing up to Peter and Roger and saying, no, you won't vote with them, you want me to bear the brunt of their displeasure.'

'It's a simple and easy solution.'

'You're a fence-sitter, and I can't abide men who sit on fences,' Daphne said crossly. 'Why should I spend good money because you won't do your duty?'

Duty? Where did duty come into it?

'I'll give you the shares, Daphne.'

'You'll stand up and be counted, Hal, is what you'll do.'

Oh, to be in London, Hal said to himself. Family life, his own and the highly complicated Richardson variety made *Coriolanus* or even *Measure for Measure* seem the very essence of simplicity. *Oedipus Rex*, now it was a while since *Oedipus* had been performed in New York; maybe he could put on a season of Greek plays.

'Hal, you aren't listening to me.'

'I am, Daphne, I hear every word, I assure you.'

Edwin, still in a temper after his encounter with Uncle Saul, was in the hall, about to put his coat on, when he heard sounds of someone arriving. Rokeby materialised from nowhere to open the front door and bow in stately greeting to Lucy Lambert.

'Good God, Lucy, what are you doing here?'

Lucy shed her furs and kissed her cousin on both cheeks. 'Hello, Edwin. I had to come. I thought of ringing up, but instead I jumped in the car and drove over.'

'We're always delighted to see you, Lucy, but you couldn't have picked a worse time.'

'My dear, what I have to tell you is bound to make everything much worse, whatever's up with you here.' She turned to the butler. 'Rokeby, you are not to announce my arrival to Lady Richardson.'

429

'Very good, madam.'

'Although I feel sure that dreadful maid of hers will be creeping around and will see my car.'

'Actually,' Edwin said, gently pushing Lucy in the direction of the sitting room and privacy, 'I think Grandmama and Lipp are closeted upstairs, brewing what Lipp calls a tisane and anyone else would immediately recognise as a witch's brew. Do you want to see Grandpapa? He's got Daphne Wolf and Hal Grindley in there with him, and another chap you wouldn't know.'

'Daphne? Daphne's in England? In the winter? Edwin, you're having me on.'

'Scout's honour.'

'And Hal, too, divine Hal, everyone in London's talking about him.'

Edwin was wondering why people in London should be talking about Hal, when Lucy's next remark startled him into attention.

'I've come with rather bad news, and I think I'll tell you first. You'll know how best to break it to Henry.'

'Out with it, Lucy.'

'First, you're to swear never to let Rollo know I've been here. He'd be furious, because it's the honour of the regiment and all that.'

'Honour of the regiment?' Edwin was bemused. Lucy's husband was a professional soldier, a full colonel, who lived for his regiment and the army.

'Yes. It'll be in the London evening papers tonight, he says, and splashed all over the national press tomorrow morning. He doesn't know how the reporters got hold of the story, but they always do seem to, don't they? Rollo's known about it for two or three days, ever since a Special Branch man went to see him, and they had to dig all the records out. Rollo was appalled, he didn't know that any of it had happened. He wasn't going to tell me, since it involved my family, he wanted to protect me, he said, the silly man. Only once it was going to be in the papers he thought it better for him to tell me the whole story rather than read a garbled version in the press.'

'Lucy, what are you talking about?'

'I'm just going to tell you, and then we can decide what to do about Henry.'

FIFTY-SIX

That night, Michael's dream moved relentlessly to its end.

Once again, he heard the screams. But this time, he drew nearer to where the sounds were coming from, driven by a curiosity greater than his fear. The screams were strange and unfamiliar and threatening, but an even stranger sight met his eyes.

To the boy, the two people on the ground appeared to be a man and a woman wrestling.

To the grown-up dreamer, there was no mystery about what was happening.

It was no romantic coupling. The man was brutal, the woman frantic and afraid. The boy, and the man who became the boy again in the nightmare, was paralysed once more. With a different kind of fear, fear not of a mythical beast or a wild boar, but of this man who was crouched so horribly over the prone figure.

The man's face was in shadow, he could make out no details of feature or colouring. Then he got to his feet, and spoke brusquely to the girl, for he could now see that it was only a girl. 'Get up.'

She said nothing, but rolled over, burying her head in her arm, her whole body shaking.

'Stay here then, you silly little bitch, you'll die, you know. Not that I give a damn about that.'

The voice was shocking, because it was that of a gentleman. This beastly man wasn't a bogeyman of the woods, an outcast, a tramp or a gypsy falling on unsuspecting prey. This was a man who'd been to the sort of school he himself went to, who came from a civilised home, a place in the world.

'Only then,' the man said, 'there'd be a tremendous fuss, girl found dead in the woods, far too many impertinent questions from our wonderful wooden-headed British police.'

The root on which Michael had been standing suddenly gave way, and he lurched to one side, reaching out for a branch to stop himself falling. At once the man was alert, head up, eyes raking the trees around the clearing.

Michael froze, not moving an eyelid.

It didn't work. Bright, hard eyes came to rest on his patch of undergrowth, and then looked right into his own eyes, holding him in their gaze.

'A spy, is it?' said the man, advancing towards him. 'A peeping Tom, how unfortunate. For me, and for you, whoever you are.'

Michael waited, like an animal dazzled in headlights, for his fate to descend. Then another voice rang through the trees: a high-pitched, urgent, woman's voice. 'Who's there? Is anybody there?'

The man swore, turned, and plunged away across the clearing and into the trees on the other side.

Released from that mesmeric hold, Michael burst out of his hiding place, and ran to the girl, now a mere shadow in a clearing dark once more. 'Are you hurt? Can I help?'

Only to be hauled away by his collar and flung to the ground. A whirling demon of a woman bore down on him, kicking him savagely in the side, a stream of abuse pouring over him. He tried to roll away from the blows, but she dragged him back. 'What have you done to her, you little monster? You animal, you'll pay for this.'

Then there was another woman speaking, with a different, softer, kinder voice. 'Leave him alone, Mother, can't you see he's just a boy? No boy did this. You'd do better to get this child wrapped up in a blanket and home to bed before she catches pneumonia!'

In the distance came the sound of a motorcycle revving, and then the roar of a powerful engine gathering speed.

'It was him,' the girl on the ground said, through the tears that were flowing easily now. 'Not the boy, him.'

'Don't say that. It wasn't him, you're lying, lying, I tell you.'

'She isn't,' said the kinder woman, who had taken off her coat and was folding it around the trembling girl.

'She's lying,' the harsh woman said again.

'Did he hit you?' the kind woman was asking. 'We'll carry you to the car, it isn't far. Don't worry, we'll see to it that he pays for what he's done.'

'Pays for it?' the demon woman said. 'What are you talking about? She'll do nothing about this except keep her mouth shut, if she has any sense at all.' Her eye fell on Michael, biting the side of his hand to stop himself crying out. 'What are we going to do about this one?'

'Find out where he lives and take him home after we've seen to her.'

'We most certainly aren't.' She advanced on him. 'Do you know who I am?'

Of course he didn't. He didn't know any madwomen or witches, which was what these women must be.

'Well?'

'No,' he whispered.

'Just as well for you. Who are you?' She didn't wait for an answer, but carried straight on. 'Some country bumpkin out poaching, I suppose. Listen to me. Not one word of anything you may have seen or heard tonight do you say to anyone,

434

and I mean anyone. Not your parents or brothers and sisters or your best friend. Do you hear? Not tonight, not ever.'

Since she seemed to expect some response, he nodded.

'If you do, I shall hear about it, and it will be much the worse for you. Now get out of here.'

He backed away, eyes wide, heart thumping.

'For goodness sake,' the other woman said, 'must you frighten him more than he is already? You can't keep something like this secret. It's a criminal matter, you have to realize that. He's a witness.'

'Over my dead body – and his, if necessary – is he a witness. This is entirely a family affair.'

He finally found the use of his limbs, and fled.

Michael woke from the dream in a cold sweat, terrified still, his heart pounding. He felt sick. He stumbled out of bed, out of the room, across the passage to the bathroom.

A door opened, he heard footsteps and then Freddie was holding his shoulders as he retched miserably. 'It's all right,' he said. 'Come on, back to bed with you.'

He smoothed the bedclothes, found Michael a pair of clean pyjamas in a drawer, helped him into them and then made him get back into bed. Michael lay there, freezing cold, his teeth chattering.

Mrs Dixon was at the door, wrapped in a red flannel dressing gown, her face concerned. 'He's been taken ill, poor man. Shall I fetch up a hot-water bottle?'

With extra blankets from Freddie's room and the glazed earthenware flask of hot water at his feet, the colour gradually began to come back into Michael's face.

'Something you ate?' asked Freddie.

'No, no. I'm not ill. It was that nightmare. I couldn't wake up.'

Freddie gave him three aspirin, which he took with the cup of milk Mrs Dixon had warmed up for him.

'Thanks, Freddie. I'll be all right now. Leave the light on, there's a good chap. I don't think I want to go back to sleep.'

Cecy arrived bright and early with her skates dangling in one hand and a pair of binoculars in the other. 'We were going bird-watching,' she said to Freddie. 'Only if Michael isn't well, then perhaps we'd better not.'

'I'm perfectly all right,' Michael said as he came down the stairs, ducking to avoid the beam over the door as he came into the snug. 'Only I find I don't care for skating today, Cecy. How about a walk?'

He wanted to tell someone about the terrible end to his nightmare, and the person he wanted to tell, he realized, was Cecy.

She glanced sideways at him as they walked along. 'Did you have a bad night?'

'Is it that obvious?'

'You look rather drawn, and you've heavy shadows under your eyes. Was it that dream again?'

'It was, and this time it went on until the end. It isn't a dream, Cecy. At least it is, in that I dream the scene over and over again, but I'm positive I'm reliving something that happened. Only it gets all mixed up, like dreams do, and the people in it turn into people I know now, or two of them did. I think that was almost worse than what the rest of the dream was about.'

Cecy unwound her scarf and rewound it around her neck to give her ears some protection against the icy wind that had blown up.

'You said that the place where Ursula was attacked was the place you saw in your dream.'

'Yes.'

'And was that where you were again last night? In your dream, I mean.'

'Yes. I think seeing the place again, in the snow, jolted my memory, so that all the details I'd forgotten, or repressed, if

436

you want to be Freudian, suddenly bubbled up to the surface. Only, since it was a dream, in a distorted form.'

'Tell me about it.'

He hesitated, wanting to tell her, but searching for the words in which to do so. 'I was a boy of twelve. I was in that stretch of wood, at night, by moonlight.'

'Why?'

'I don't know. I don't remember anything about it, except the part that came back to me in my dreams, and that's the terrifying part. I know I became ill afterwards, probably as a result of exposure, it was bitterly cold. From the horror of it, too, I should think. When I recovered, I had very little memory of my holiday on the frozen lake, and none at all of the incident in the wood.'

'What was the incident?'

'I saw a girl being raped.'

Cecy stared at him. The cigarette she was holding burned her finger, and she flicked it down on to the frozen grass. 'You saw a girl being raped?'

'In the wood.'

'Why didn't you stop it? Why didn't you help her?'

'I was frozen, shivering with cold and with fear. I wasn't sure exactly what was going on. I was twelve years old, an innocent. What did I know about sex except what the school chaplain had mumbled at us? Let alone a violent, criminal sexual attack.'

Cecy walked on, saying nothing. 'You say you saw this, but then forgot about it? For what, fifteen, sixteen years? In your dream –'

'Not just a dream, Cecy. Believe me, I saw it.'

'Very well. Tell me the whole thing. Go on, get it off your chest. And if it did happen, and here, then it's local. There must be some record of an attack like that. We could look it up, ask around. Would that set your mind at rest?'

* * *

437

When he had told her everything, she stopped and looked at him. 'For heaven's sake,' she said, stretching out a hand.

They walked on in silence, hand in hand, heedless of where they were going. Then they turned down through some trees and came to the lakeside.

'Look,' said Cecy, squinting up into the sky.

'What is it?'

She pointed. 'Up there, over Fiend's Fell.'

Michael looked and saw the palest wisp of white, a mere breath of cloud, hanging motionless above the harsh outline of the crags. 'Much smaller than a man's hand.'

'Mr Dixon said we were in for some rough weather. It tends to break at the full moon.'

'Are we in for a thaw?'

'Snow, I should think, but not for a little while yet. It's still freezing hard.'

There was a shout from the lake, and Michael dropped Cecy's hand as he shaded his eyes to look towards the cluster of dark figures on the ice. 'Something's wrong.'

'Do you suppose someone's gone in?'

Michael began to walk along the shore. 'What's up?' he called out.

One of the people on the ice detached himself from the group and skated towards them 'There's been an accident. We've found a body on the ice. The police are coming, but it would be best if you took the young lady away. Oh, it's you, Miss Cecy.'

'Hello, Mr Jessup. Is it anyone we know?'

'He's not a local. One of those as is staying with Mrs McKechnie. Londoners.'

'Did he fall through the ice?'

'It looks like he tripped when he was skating and hit his head on a rock.'

FIFTY-SEVEN

'It's in all the newspapers, apparently,' Edwin said.

They were in the sitting room at Wyncrag. The light slanting through the windows, so bright and brilliant until now, was muted as clouds drifted across the sun. Alix had switched on several lamps.

Trudie had telephoned Edwin at Lowfell and asked him to come back to Wyncrag. 'At a time like this, it is better the family isn't seen to be at odds. Unanimity, don't you think, should be our watchword? Also, we can keep reporters at bay more easily at Wyncrag than at Lowfell.'

Edwin doubted whether there would be any reporters.

'It's a slack time,' Trudie said, her voice was not quite steady. 'With no new world crises. The press are going to have a field day, I fear.'

Edwin stalled, not wanting to see his grandmother, and much preferring to stay near Lidia. 'I'm not exactly keen to come face to face with Grandmama, to tell you the truth.'

'Mama is in her room,' Trudie told him. 'She isn't intending to come down. And Papa has shut himself away in his study. Saul saw Mama for a few minutes, but he won't talk about it.'

She rang him up again half an hour later. 'Edwin, you must

come, and bring Perdita and Ursula, if she's still there with you. Jimmy Ogilvy has been up here. There's an inspector from London, and he wants to talk to everyone who was at Wyncrag on Christmas Day.'

'Lidia was at Wyncrag on Christmas Day. She won't want to come, and I won't leave her.'

'Edwin, you don't perfectly understand. This Inspector Pritchard isn't like a local constable. It will be much better for him to see Lidia here. Better for her, don't you see? Where she'll be among friends. No, not Mama, I told you, she's in her room and no doubt the inspector will visit her there. On account of her age and so on. But for the rest of us . . . Well, I think we should do as he asks. Please, Edwin.'

'What about the Grindley contingent? Have you summoned them?'

'The Grindleys will be here after lunch, and I sent a message down to Michael and Freddie at the inn.'

It was odd, Alix thought, swapping her newspaper for the one Edwin had just finished, that they seemed more of a family at this time of crisis than they had done since Mummy and Daddy were alive. 'Do you think they knew?' she asked, reading out another headline, much the same as all the rest: "War Hero was Army Deserter." Grandmama and Grandpapa and Aunt Trudie and Uncle Saul?'

'I'm positive Grandmama knew,' Edwin said.

'There's the memorial window in the church. I simply don't understand how she could put that up if she knew he wasn't dead but a cowardly deserter?' said Alix. 'Especially the heroic soldier pose.'

Edwin shrugged. 'We can give her the benefit of the doubt, and assume she only found out about Jack later, after she'd had the window dedicated. She could hardly have it taken out, not without saying why.'

440

'I don't care what you say, Grandpapa must have known about it,' Perdita said.

Edwin disagreed. 'Grandmama could perfectly well have kept it from him, if she knew. If she did know and didn't tell him, how would he have found out? It was all buried away. And Grandmama would be careful, she couldn't be sure how Grandpapa would take that kind of thing. He wouldn't approve of desertion, son or no son.'

'I wish we had more details,' said Alix. 'All it says here is that Uncle Jack didn't die, but deserted and turned up in Germany a few years later, thick as thieves with the Nazi leaders, it seems. There's a picture of him with Hitler; truly, it makes me ashamed.'

Edwin inspected the picture in the *Daily Mail*. 'I wonder where he got the scar from.'

'Heidelberg?' suggested Alix. 'An honourable duelling scar.'

'There doesn't seem to have been much honourable about Uncle Jack. Jago Roberts! What a name to choose. How did the newspapers find out that this man Jago Roberts was Uncle Jack, anyhow?'

'A leak from Special Branch, or someone at the Horseguards,' Edwin said.

Perdita hadn't shown much interest in the story. 'Since I never knew Uncle Jack, sorry, Great Uncle Jack, I don't care whether he died or turned into a Hun or whatever. I'm off all my family, and that's that.'

Ursula took a more sophisticated approach. 'A black sheep, that's all he was. Every family has one. It's awfully shaming, being shown up as a coward, and I suppose to Sir Henry's generation it would seem dreadful and shameful and all that. But the war's been over for years and years. I know if I'd been in the thick of it, I'd probably have run away. Like Mummy's cousin Bill, who shot himself in the foot so that he'd be shipped back to England. Lots of soldiers did that when they couldn't stand it in the trenches any more.'

'Did he pull it off?' Perdita asked, looking up from Lidia's copy of the *Forty-eight Preludes and Fugues*, which she'd brought with her from Lowfell. She'd played them until the others begged her to stop. 'I know you think Bach's wonderful,' Ursula said, 'but honestly, it's like a sewing machine twiddling away.'

'He did, actually. He should have been court-martialled and shot, of course, but there was just enough doubt for him to get away with it. The family never spoke to him again, of course.'

Lidia was sitting pensively by the fire, looking, Alix thought, extraordinarily beautiful with her skin and eyes still glowing from the cold outside. What did she think of them? How would this affect her and Edwin? Could she contemplate marriage with a man whose long-lost uncle came back from the grave a thorough-going fascist with Nazi connections?

Rokeby came in with a tray of drinks. 'The boy has just come back from an errand in Lowfell,' he told Edwin. 'He reports that there has been an incident on the ice. The town is full of policemen and police cars and men with dogs.'

'Incident?' said Alix. 'A fight, or riot or what?'

'I believe they have found a man's body.'

'Anyone we know, Rokeby?'

'I don't believe so.'

'Shall we take our skates and go and have a look, Perdy?' Ursula suggested.

'Oh, Perdita, no,' said Aunt Trudie.

'Definitely not,' Edwin said.

'As it happens, I don't want to go. Ursula's just a ghoul. Anyhow, if there's a body, they'll have taken it away by now.'

'It seems the man was lying on the ice for a while before he was spotted,' Rokeby said. 'Under one of those overhanging branches along from Dixon's inn.'

'It's one of the shadowy places,' Alix said. 'You don't see many skaters around there.'

'I hope it's Uncle Jack,' Perdita said.

There was silence. Rokeby withdrew, wrapped in disapproving dignity.

'You shouldn't say things like that, Perdy,' Edwin said, at last.

'Why not? It's only what everyone's thinking. You can't pretend it would be all sorrow and weeping, since we all thought he was dead anyhow. And it might shut the papers up.'

Lidia looked at Perdita, a faint smile on her lips. 'You are very ruthless.'

'No, I just don't pretend about things. What's the point?'

'Do you suppose that's why the police want us all here?' Alix asked. 'Because a man's been killed?'

'I don't see any logic in that,' Perdita said, flipping over several pages of score and letting out little bursts of humming. 'Unless he died on Christmas Day and they suspect us. In which case it probably is Uncle Jack, although I bet he's made enemies all over the place, people queuing up to do him in, they don't need to come to us.'

Edwin went over and put a protective arm around Lidia. 'You don't like the prospect of police questioning, do you?'

A wave of desolation and loss came over Alix at the gesture. Edwin's concern was only for Lidia, now, not for her or the rest of his family.

Lidia shook her head.

'Don't worry, no Scotland Yard officer is going to give you a gruelling interrogation, not in this house, nor anywhere else.'

'Why should he?' Perdita said. 'Not unless he suspects Lidia of bumping Uncle Jack off on account of him being beastly about Jews.'

'Do shut up about Uncle Jack, who unfortunately seems likely to live for ever,' said Alix sharply.

'I can't remember anything happening on Christmas Day

that could possibly be of interest to the inspector,' Edwin said firmly. 'I vote we just answer any questions as briefly as possible, yes and no if we can, don't volunteer any information, and don't talk about family affairs.'

Hal came into the room and overheard Edwin's last words. 'Family affairs? I hope I don't intrude. Daphne wanted to come over ahead of the others and hold Sir Henry's hand, since word came to the Hall that Lady Richardson isn't anywhere to be seen. So I came with her.'

'Grandmama's shut herself up in her room,' Alix said. 'With Lipp.'

'Is she very upset?' he asked.

'Angry, I should imagine. Edwin thinks she's known all along that Jack deserted and didn't die.'

'So the shock is more at the revelation than the facts?' It wasn't what you'd call a cosy family party, Hal thought, looking around at them. He went over to the sofa where Alix was curled up, rather forlornly it seemed to him. 'May I join you?'

She smiled at him. 'Do. Push those newspapers off. I suppose you've read all the stories?'

'Yes, much excitement at Grindley Hall and papers that aren't normally allowed to cross the threshold ordered up from the village. I think Roger is planning to take the case for the defence and get Jack off any and all charges. Probably on a plea of insanity.'

'Can they charge him with anything after all this time?' Ursula asked. 'I mean, it was nearly twenty years ago.'

'In normal circumstances, I don't think they would, him with an MC and all; the army would fudge and say he went off his rocker. Only with his heading for Germany and then taking up with the Mosleyites, I'm not so sure.' He didn't add that a Special Branch inspector on the case almost certainly meant that Jack had been up to more than political activism and desertion.

'Grandmama will have to give his MC back to the King,' Perdita said. 'She'll hate that.'

'I expect the Germans will fly over in an airship and whisk him back to the Fatherland,' Ursula said. 'When are the others coming over, Uncle Hal?'

'After lunch. Except for Eve, who is prostrate with a dizzy attack, and Rosalind, who says she'll stay to look after her mother.'

'She's up to something,' Ursula said instantly. 'Horrible Eve could pass out at Rosalind's feet and, far from being a loving daughter, she'd just step over the lifeless form and go on with whatever she was doing.'

'What will the inspector say to that?' Alix asked Hal. 'If the police want everyone here?'

'They'll have to go to the Hall and question the two of them there.'

FIFTY-EIGHT

The great drawing room had never seemed so oppressive, the sky outside so full of foreboding, the sound of footsteps on the carpet so muted.

Alix had been startled into an exclamation of surprise when Lipp arrived as Lady Richardson's advance guard, announced that her ladyship would be down shortly and arranged a chair as her mistress liked it, precisely one yard from the fire. Then she had shot a venomous look at Lidia, and departed, leaving behind her a sense of unease.

Perdita had said to Alix, 'Do you suppose I should call her Great-Grandmama?'

How did you change the habit of a lifetime? Alix wondered, as she looked at Grandmama, sitting bolt upright on her chair, her expression unfathomable.

Perdita sat beside Ursula on a red damask sofa under the window, well away from Grandmama. Freddie was over there, too, looking as though he'd rather not be in the room at all, which was probably the case. He sat on a wide, armless chair, his feet apart and his hands on his thighs. He seemed wrapped in his own thoughts, unlike Michael, who was on the other side of the room, sitting on a velvet buttoned sofa beside Cecy and talking to her in a low voice. Edwin lounged against the wall by the door, Lidia had chosen a seat close to him, well back from the others and out of Grandmama's direct line of vision.

Grandmama was tense. Grandpapa, sitting in a winged chair, wasn't. He looked as though someone had punched him and he'd only just managed to get up. He seemed old, and somehow diminished in size and personality. He leaned towards Daphne, as though looking for the support and comfort his wife had no intention of offering.

How could such a big man look so shrivelled? Uncle Saul, another big man, didn't look small. He looked worried, and he had dark smudges under his eyes. Alix would be prepared to bet Aunt Jane had been rubbing his nose in this affair. Aunt Jane herself was as still and expressionless as always. No, she wasn't. She had a cat-got-the-cream lilt to her mouth, that must be because she liked seeing Uncle Saul suffer. And Grandmama, too; she'd always hated Grandmama.

Could one blame her? No.

Aunt Trudie was the only one of them who seemed at her ease. She poured out the tea, and told Rokeby to take a piece of cake to the inspector.

The inspector was the one who should have been out of place in this room, in his Burton suit and his ordinary shoes, but he wasn't. His eyes were watchful, and intelligent, and he was quite at ease in the big armchair that had been placed in the centre of the room. Behind him, the fire burned in the huge fireplace, its logs flickering with gentle flames behind an ornate mesh guard.

The whole scene reminded Alix of a picture she'd seen in a gallery, of a family grouped around a sofa, four generations, every person looking out into the world with wary, wide-open eyes.

The Grindleys came in, Peter and Roger in dark suits, Roger looking every inch the lawyer, Peter in a temper. Nicky and Simon slid into the room behind them and wandered over to perch themselves on an ottoman behind a convenient fern. Angela glanced around the room, then went over to sit by Freddie.

Inspector Pritchard put his cup down. Alix braced herself, this was the moment they had been waiting for.

'Thank you for gathering here to see me,' he said in a mild voice.

He was Welsh. Why should that surprise her? One didn't, somehow, imagine a top London policeman, an officer from Special Branch, being a Welshman. Yet she found it obscurely comforting, perhaps he would understand the ways of her family better than a London man.

'You all know by now that the man who called himself Jago Roberts was in fact, Jack Richardson, a son of this house.'

Grandpapa was the only one of his audience who moved. He passed a hand across his eyes, then dropped it back on to his lap. Alix gave him a quick look, then averted her glance, finding the pain in his face too much to take.

'With Sir Henry's permission, my men are at this moment conducting a search of the house, in case Mr Roberts is in hiding here. We have already searched the grounds. I have no wish to distress you unnecessarily, Sir Henry and Lady Richardson. However, I think it right I should place certain facts before you, so that you see why I need to ask various questions concerning the movements and motivation of Jack Richardson, alias Jago Roberts.'

'Could we call him Roberts, please,' Grandpapa said, some of his old authority creeping back into his voice. 'My son Jack has been dead to me for all these years. I find it simpler to think of this man as Roberts.'

'You do accept he is your son?'

'I am told he is.'

'You have read, no doubt, in the newspapers, that your son was not killed in the war as had been supposed, but was a deserter.'

'Have you come to tell us what we already know, Inspector?' Grandmama's voice was acidic with upper-class contempt for the man sitting there in front of them.

This was no time for her to come the *grande dame*, didn't she realize what was going on?

Inspector Pritchard ignored her. 'Unfortunately, he didn't merely desert. That would have been a crime, of course, and punishable in a military court, but would not have been the concern of my department, then or now. Instead, he crossed over to the German side. He was imprisoned, released at the end of the war, and chose to stay and make his home in Germany. He adopted a false name, and took up residence in Berlin. Later, he became a German citizen.' He paused. 'I don't think all these details have been reported in the newspapers.'

Berlin! That city of night. Images flashed through Alix's mind: lamplit, dangerous streets; men dressed up as women, dancing in nightclubs; menacing men in black uniforms standing beside shiny black cars.

That was Berlin now. Had it been the same after the war? No, the capital city of a defeated country had probably been a wretched place to live, yet that was where Uncle Jack had chosen to go to ground.

The inspector was speaking again, after calmly drinking some more of his tea, seemingly oblivious to the eyes fixed on his every move. 'I believe your son spoke fluent German, Sir Henry?'

'He had a German governess. He often accompanied me on trips to Germany. Before the war.'

'You have an admiration for the country? You have friends there?'

'I have no time whatsoever for National Socialism, or fascism in any form, Inspector, if you are suggesting such a thing. I am anti-communist, but as a businessman and a humane person, I feel nothing but loathing and contempt for

449

Herr Hitler and his crew. Does that answer your question?'

The inspector didn't reply to Sir Henry; instead, he addressed Lady Richardson. 'And you, Lady Richardson, do you disapprove of the present regime in Germany?'

'My political views are my own affair.'

'Do you have fascist sympathies?'

This time, she didn't answer. He gave a little nod, and looked down at his notebook.

Fascist sympathies, indeed, thought Alix. She could give those stupid German Nazis lessons in fascism. She couldn't begin to understand what happened to people like Grandmama. Let it never happen to her. Please God, if there were a God, let her never become like Grandmama.

What was passing in her mind must have shown in her face, for Hal, who had been sitting back as though setting himself slightly apart from the scene, leaned forward and laid a hand on her shoulder.

She found it strangely comforting.

'My department has been keeping a close eye on Jago Roberts. We were informed that he had left his London lodgings, and for a while we lost track of his movements. The next we heard of him was from your police here. We'd put out a general enquiry for him, you see. We were a little puzzled; this was an unlikely place for him to come. Why was he here? Had he come for the skating over the Christmas season, or did he have another reason?'

'Get on with it,' Edwin said under his breath. Alix saw Lidia put up a hand and take his, giving it a squeeze – of affection? of warning?

'We believe that he came to make contact with his parents, with you, Sir Henry and Lady Richardson, and perhaps with his brother and sister. You are a wealthy family, and that was of particular interest to us, since we have been anxious to find out how Mr Roberts was funding his activities while in England. Undoubtedly, he has been paid by the German government to foment unrest and to spy on the people of his own class, reporting back to Berlin with names of those who might be considered likely to support the Germans, especially those with influence and power. However, he lives on a scale beyond what might be expected of a man in his position.'

Grandpapa stirred in his chair, but said nothing. Alix looked at him with helpless concern. He couldn't stand much more of this, he wasn't a young man. Why couldn't this inhuman policeman see what he was doing to him?

Grandmama's voice was icy, thin, remote. 'Are you accusing my son of spying? Has it occurred to you that he felt he was serving his country in what he did?'

'Which country is that, Lady Richardson?'

'I find your questions impertinent.'

'I am an investigating officer, conducting an enquiry into a man whose activities have given cause for alarm in certain quarters. In addition to the questionable nature of those activities, he was also a close companion of one Philip Shackleton. Mr Shackleton has been found dead in suspicious circumstances.'

The name meant nothing to Alix. Beside her, she heard Hal say to himself, 'So that's who it was.'

'Mr Shackleton died, the medical men tell us, on Christmas Day. Since this may turn out to be a murder enquiry, I shall ask the questions I consider important. If you choose not to answer me, I shall make a note of that fact. I did advise Sir Henry that he might care to ask his solicitor to attend this afternoon; he declined to do this.'

Fifteen love to the inspector, thought Alix.

No one told Inspector Pritchard what he wanted to know. Alix said not a word about the man in the passage on the night of the ball, although she now knew that it must have been Jack. Sir Henry didn't speak of the jewels that had passed through his wife's hands, used, he now realized, to

451

fund Jack's treacherous activities. Lady Richardson, whom everyone present was aware knew exactly what Jack had been up to, and probably where he was now, sat in rigid silence.

The inspector consulted his notebook. One Mr Foreby had claimed he'd seen Roberts turn in through the gate to Wyncrag on the evening of December the twenty-third.

'My brother knew the locality, he no doubt took a short cut through the grounds,' Saul said.

'He might have wanted to look at the house where he grew up,' Sir Henry said, speaking for the first time and seeming to find the words an effort. Alix winced at the weariness in his voice. 'Besides, old Foreby is as blind as a bat, and usually drunk as well.'

'Mr Foreby claims also that he saw Roberts in the vicinity of Wyncrag when last the lake was frozen over. That would be sixteen years ago.'

A muscle twitched in Grandmama's eyelid.

'He's making it up,' Grandpapa said with finality.

The searchers found no trace of Jago Roberts at Wyncrag, in the house or grounds.

'Not that I expected to,' the inspector said wearily to PC Ogilvy, as they drove away from the house in the big black police car.

'You reckon his family were sheltering him and giving him money? It doesn't seem like Sir Henry, not like him at all.'

'Blood is thicker than water.'

'Do you think Roberts – Richardson – killed Shackleton?'

'I do. I expect Shackleton started to have doubts about the company he was keeping. Jack Richardson was trained to kill men when he was in the army. This time he's been so clever, I don't think we'll ever be able to prove it was murder.'

'But you said back there . . .'

'I wanted to see how they would react to talk of murder. I tell you, though, that if we could prove it was a case of murder, and we accused Roberts, you'd find that your precious Richardson clan would produce an alibi for him, whatever they said this afternoon about not having seen hide nor hair of him. Lying through their teeth, the whole lot of them.'

He pulled his pipe out of his pocket and let down the window to tap its ash into the snow. 'And the Grindley family aren't much better. Those brothers knew quite well what kind of a man they were dealing with. Mr Shackleton wanted to buy that company for his German masters, and not for any peaceful purpose, and they knew it. Morality goes out of the window with men like that, when it's a matter of turning a profit.'

Aunt Jane took a cigarette from Saul's case, which he'd put down on the table in the drawing room. She flicked her lighter and cupped the flame with her hand to light the cigarette.

Her mother-in-law watched her. She didn't permit smoking in the drawing room.

They were alone together. Jane looked at the indomitable and unreadable face. She felt no pity for this woman whose eldest son had died, and whose efforts to keep her house from scandal had been blown to the four winds. She didn't mind that the shame and opprobrium would fall on her as on the rest of them.

'I'm sorry Jack is still alive,' she said. 'I'm glad that I didn't know he was. I think the world would be a better place for his having departed from it.'

'You never did Jack justice. You have a warped mind and a warped personality. You destroy the men you attract.'

Words like icicles, stab, stab, stab.

'He seduced me when I was only a girl, and beat me and brutalised me. You knew it. You made me marry Saul, and I've regretted it every day of my life since. I have no children, and that's your doing. You controlled and ruled your

453

children, and your grandchildren – yes, and your great-grand-child, let's think about her for a moment – and they can't wait to get away. You want loyalty and devotion, and your reward is fear and hatred.'

'I didn't make you marry Saul. No one ever made me do what I didn't want to, why should you lay your mistakes at my door? Have you no will of your own?'

'I have now. I didn't then. Just as you hadn't, not when it came to Jack. You loved him beyond reason, he could do no wrong, so you helped him in every way you could, you forgave him everything and criticised him for nothing. He made a fool of you, and you came back for more. I'm glad this has all come out, that he's disgraced before the whole world. Glad that his wretched plans to betray his country have failed. And, most of all, I'm glad that Saul will have to resign his seat, and I will no longer have to endure the pompous nothingness of his life as a failed politician.'

'Saul is now the only son left to me. Jack will be back in Germany by now. He won't come here again.'

Jane hoped with all her heart that that was true. 'You're welcome to Saul. You've never had a jot of real affection for him, it's merely amused you to watch him dance to your piping.'

Rokeby came into the room, opening the door with none of his usual softness. 'I've brought the tray of drinks, my lady,' he said.

'I bet Rokeby knows more about it all than any of us,' Jane said. She picked up her handbag and drifted out of the room in a cloud of smoke. 'Oh, happy days.'

Edwin wanted to leave, and to take Lidia back to Lowfell, but Sir Henry asked him to stay. 'You, too, my dear,' he said to Lidia, his eyes tired but kind as they rested on her. 'If you can bear to have anything to do with a family such as we are. We'll just have a quiet meal. I don't suppose Caroline

454

will be down. Daphne is staying for the time being, she'll go back with Hal and Cecy later.'

Lidia put out a hand and touched him on the arm. 'We shall stay.'

'We'd better be off,' Freddie said.

'I think you'd better stay as well,' Alix said, looking at Michael, who was standing protectively beside Cecy.

It seemed the weather seers were wrong. The wind died down, the sky cleared, and one by one the blazing winter stars came out, undimmed by the moon, which had yet to rise.

'It isn't so cold tonight, though,' said Alix, pulling aside one of the heavy drawing-room curtains to look out to the lake. Cold, clear, with an eerie brightness. A world without time or emotion, apart from humanity. A peaceful-looking world.

'There are people skating on the other side, where the lights are,' Edwin said.

'Making the most of their time on the ice, in case there really is snow on the way.' Alix let the curtain drop back into place. 'I'm still glad to be in rather than out.'

'It's strange,' Hal said. 'The drama's over, the police have been, the truth about Jack is out, and yet I feel that this is only the interval between acts.'

'Spare us,' Edwin said, who was sitting in a deep armchair with a brandy in his hand. 'I feel that a funeral's taken place, only to find that there wasn't a body.'

Jane came in. Like the rest of the Richardsons, she had changed for dinner, as though by keeping the social niceties going, normality might return. Her dress was the colour of red grapes; it wasn't a frock they'd seen before. It swirled about her ankles as she came in. She looked around the room, then closed the door behind her with a soft, definite click.

'I've something to tell you that isn't to be broadcast.' She crossed the room, sat down in a wide armchair near the fire and took a gold cigarette case out of her evening bag.

'Shall I go?' Hal said.

'No. You knew Jack. I think you ought to hear this.'

Edwin gave her a startled look, and then hurried forward with his lighter. She offered him a cigarette, and he took one. 'Alix?' she said.

'No, thank you. Not before dinner.' Cigarettes in the drawing room. Had the ice queen been vanquished so that green spring could flourish? She doubted it. Grandmama would have plenty to say if she caught the merest whiff of cigarette smoke.

'I put through a telephone call just now to Lucy,' Jane began. 'She has all the details about Jack's desertion, she finally got everything out of her husband. He had taken the trouble to talk to a previous colonel of the regiment, the one who was in charge in nineteen seventeen when this happened. It seems that Jack didn't desert from funk. He ran away because he was likely to face a court martial.'

'Isn't that what happens to deserters?' Alix said. 'Or do they usually shoot them out of hand?'

'No, Alix, please listen to what I'm saying. The court martial was the reason for his deserting, not the result of it. A local girl, a French girl barely into her teens, had been raped and beaten up. Left for dead, but she survived. She claimed that Jack was the man responsible. He denied it, of course.'

Alix found she had no air left in her lungs, and she had to make a conscious effort to take in a breath and speak. 'Oh, Christ. This is going to kill Grandpapa.'

'No, it isn't,' Jane said. 'Not if he doesn't get to hear about it. It's not the kind of thing anyone's going to tell him, even if they know about it. Lucy's as worried about Henry as you are, and she's going to use what influence she can to keep it hushed up. It was all a long time ago, and in wartime, no one wants to drag that kind of thing out into the open.'

'Ursula,' Perdita said. 'What about Ursula?'

Alix frowned at her sister. Didn't Perdita grasp what Jane was talking about? What had Ursula to do with this?

'Where is Ursula?' Jane looked around. 'Not here, I do hope. This is strictly a family matter, and I believe she writes everything down in a journal.'

'No, I meant the attack on Ursula. By the lake. Do you think . . .?'

Perdita was quicker on the uptake than the rest of them. She dropped this new horror into the discussion with a cool clarity of mind that Alix envied.

They looked at each other. Edwin covered his eyes with his hand for a moment, and then spoke in a bleak voice. 'I fear that Perdita is probably right.'

Alix didn't want to believe it. 'It could be coincidence. I mean, that incident in France, it could have happened out of the blue. An accusation by a young girl against a British officer could have been a put-up job. Or perhaps she slept with him and then her family made a fuss. Just an extraordinary incident. The way things did happen in the war.'

'Was he a violent man?' Edwin asked. 'You knew him, Aunt Jane.'

So did Hal, Alix said inwardly, and, judging by the expression on his face, he was quite ready to accept that Jack had assaulted not just one girl in faraway and long ago wartime France, but another one now, in 1936, here at the lake.

Jane was silent for a minute before she answered. 'Jack was always drawn to young girls. Vulnerable girls.'

'Then we had certainly better keep our mouths shut about our suspicions,' Edwin said. 'It gets worse and worse.'

'Is it fair on Ursula not to say?' said Perdita.

'Don't be foolish.' Aunt Jane's voice was sharp. 'Don't breathe a word, Perdita, or you, Alix. For your grandfather's sake, if for no one else's.'

457

'Have you told Aunt Trudie?' Edwin asked Jane. 'I suppose Uncle Saul has known all along.'

'Saul doesn't know, nor shall I tell him. It would only set him off on another round of blustering justification of his brother's behaviour. He's Caroline's mouthpiece as far as Jack is concerned, and I can't take any more of it. I shan't tell Trudie yet, for at present she's looking quite ill. You three are more distant from Jack; you didn't know him, you don't have the mixed feelings about him that his parents and brother and sister do. Not that it will come as a great surprise to Trudie. Jack was violent from his nursery days.'

Rokeby came into the room with the tray of drinks.

'Cocktails, anyone?' Edwin asked. 'Rokeby, we'll leave it to you to mix them.'

'Certainly sir.'

'Grandpapa's showing Lidia the furnace,' Perdita said, when no one else spoke.

Hal burst out laughing, and a moment later, seeing the absurdity of it, Alix found herself laughing as well. 'What a treat for Lidia!'

'No, thank you, Rokeby,' Perdita said. 'Take that lime juice away. I hate lime juice. Aunt Jane, do you think it would be all right if I had a cocktail?'

Jane turned to Rokeby. 'Pour a cocktail for Miss Perdita.'

The lessening of tension and the soothing effects of cocktails didn't last. Alix was savouring the heady drink that Rokeby had handed her, when the door opened, and Lady Richardson came in.

How could she come down after what they had gone through this afternoon? Alix had assumed, they had all assumed, that she would have a tray in her room. No such thing, here she was, and she, too, was in evening dress.

'Her face set in marble,' Alix whispered to Edwin. She

wished Grandmama had stayed upstairs. 'Marble tombstone,' Edwin said from the corner of his mouth.

Alix saw Perdita look down at the glass in her hand and quickly gulp the last of her drink down. Rokeby whisked the glass discreetly away, placing a lime juice beside her in its place. Grandmama didn't seem to have noticed the cigarette smoke.

Uncle Saul was rubbing his hands together in what Alix considered a particularly idiotic way. He went to the window and looked out. 'My word, the clouds are coming up fast,' he said. 'I thought we'd seen the last of them, but we're in for a regular snowstorm by the look of it.'

'I hope all the skaters have left the ice,' Perdita said.

Saul stiffened. 'They haven't.' He put his face closer to the window. 'I'm sure I can see someone – yes, there are two people out there, on the ice, close to our lake shore.'

Hal joined him at the window and peered out into the darkness. 'The snow's blasting down the lake behind them, it's blowing up into a blizzard.'

Edwin was on his feet.

'Wait, you can't –'

Hal was making for the door, flinging words at Alix over his shoulder. 'Those skaters need rescuing now, they'll never make it to shelter, not with this wind.'

'Come on, Saul,' Edwin said. 'Get a move on.'

Edwin and Saul followed Hal out of the room, where Michael, who had stayed on with Cecy to keep Lidia company, was pulling on his boots. 'Have you seen that couple on the lake? They're in serious trouble if we can't get them off. Cecy, pass me that jacket.'

Grandpapa called to Rokeby to bring torches. 'And brew up a hot punch or whisky and lemon. They'll be cold and wet. My word, listen to that wind!'

The front door burst open, and a gale swept into the hall, bringing a cloud of snow to swirl around the chairs and settle on the polished floor. The men vanished into the darkness as Rokeby and Sir Henry struggled to close the door behind them.

'Draw all the curtains back on this side of the house, Rokeby. Tell the girls to help you. Switch every light on, they're going to have their work cut out to find their way back to the house in this weather.'

It took more than half an hour for the rescue party to cover the short distance from the house to the lake and return with the stranded skaters. Frozen to the skin, they stood shaking the snow off themselves in the hall, while Trudie came running to offer hot baths and drinks.

'It's the mystery woman and her boyfriend, I mean Mr Newman,' Perdita announced as she went back into the drawing room. 'Now we'll find out if she really is a film star.'

'Film star?' Grandmama's voice was thin and cold. 'Why should she be a film star?'

'Because she's a secretive American woman who goes around in dark glasses,' Jane said.

'What nonsense.'

Alix looked into her empty glass, considering whether she wanted another cocktail. Outside, the wind was making a keening sound and, even through the thick heavy curtains, she could hear the snow blown against the windows. It was a wild and terrible night out there.

'It won't last, Miss Alix,' Rokeby said as he reached to take her glass and put it on the tray balanced on his hand. 'Swift come, swift go when it's like this. It will blow itself out before long, and then tomorrow the thaw will begin. It's already warmer out there, though you wouldn't know it, not with this wind.'

The men came back into the drawing room. Saul and Edwin had changed into dry dinner jackets, while Michael and Hal were clad in a strange collection of ill-fitting garments;

460

both of them were taller than the Richardson men. Newman had borrowed a pair of trousers and a jumper from Edwin. 'Please excuse the informality, ma'am,' he said to Lady Richardson.

His companion stood in the doorway, wearing a dress that Alix knew well, a claret silk frock that was one of her favourites. Aunt Trudie must have lent it to the unexpected guest. It could have been made for her, it fitted so well. How odd that they should be so much of a size. The woman standing there looked svelte, elegant and utterly composed, and not at all as though she'd just been rescued from an icy wilderness. Gone were the dark glasses, and her blonde hair fell in a smooth line across one side of her face.

'I'll announce myself, Rokeby,' she said.

Alix froze.

The blonde woman came into the centre of the room, her gaze sweeping around the company. 'What a family gathering we have here. Good evening, Grandmama. Remember me?'

FIFTY-NINE

Alix knew who it was the moment she heard the voice.

Edwin recognised the eyes; it sent a shiver down his spine to see his mother's amber-flecked eyes in that lovely face.

Trudie dropped her head in her hands with a sob.

Saul stood like a well-groomed cod, with his mouth open.

Grandpapa started to his feet. 'What? Who are you? Why should my wife recognise you?'

'Come on, Grandpapa, surely you know who I am.'

His voice wavered. 'It can't be. You can't be Isabel.'

'I was Isabel. These days I call myself Bettina.'

Alix took a step towards her, stopped, and then moved closer. 'It is you, oh, it is. I remember your voice so well. Only I can't believe it when I look at you. It really is you?'

'It really is.' Isabel gave a wide smile, so like Perdita's, and held out her arms. Alix hugged her, enfolding the living person of her sister, flesh and bone, not dead in some distant, unvisited grave.

Edwin, dazed and incredulous, took the hand that Isabel held out to him, then took her other one, gazing down at her. 'Hi, little brother,' she said, with a smile that took Alix back to her childhood.

Then she slid away from Edwin and went over to kiss her

grandfather. He drew her to him, patting her shoulder, unable to speak.

She sat down beside him, clasping his hand and smiling at him. 'Yes, it is me, Grandpapa, really and truly.' She sketched a wave in the direction of Saul. 'Hi, Uncle Saul. Ruling the country, so I hear. And Aunt Trudie, do look up, I don't bite.'

Trudie raised her head to reveal a tragedy mask of a face. 'It's too much. It's all too much.'

'We thought that you were dead,' Alix said.

'Oh, I don't think so,' Isabel said. 'At least one of you knew I was alive and kicking, didn't you, Grandmama? Sent me greetings at Christmas and best wishes for my birthdays? I joke, I never heard a word from you, you'd rather I'd died, wouldn't you?'

Saul had found his voice. 'My dear Isabel, how can you say that? We are, of course, delighted that you are alive. I'm sure that whatever Mama did, it was for the best.'

'Oh, sure. The best for her.'

In all the confusion, nobody had paid any attention to Perdita. She stood a little way away, her limbs turned to stone. Then Isabel got up from the sofa and came over to her.

Perdita backed away, Alix could see that she would have given anything to get away from that exquisite face, those lustrous eyes, the vibrant voice.

'You're Perdita. It's not the name I chose for you, but I guess it suited. The lost one, isn't that what it means?'

'It's out of Shakespeare.'

'I know. I played her once, when I did a summer season in Canada. Do you know who I am? Has anyone ever told you?'

'I found out. Yesterday. You're my mother.'

Newman let out a yelp. 'Her mother, for Christ's sake? Bettina, what is your agent going to say about this?'

'Agent?' said Edwin.

463

'Don't you recognise her?' Jane said. 'She isn't just Bettina nobody. She's Bettina Brand, the film actress.'

Isabel swung around on her companion. 'My agent is going to say nothing, Newman, for the good reason that nobody's going to tell him. Not you, not me, not anybody. I'm not ashamed to have a daughter, and Perdita here's going to grow up looking something special if I'm any judge, but she's going to keep the family that suits her best. You've been brought up as Edwin and Alix's sister, I guess?'

Perdita managed a stifled, 'Yes.'

'That's probably a good thing. We live in a wicked old world, sweetheart, and it helps to have two parents of the usual kind, at least on paper.'

'Who is my father?' Perdita blurted out the words before she could stop herself.

It felt as though everyone in the room was holding their breath. Trudie's fists were clenched tight. Grandmama was granite; unmoved and unmoving.

'We'll talk about that in private.'

'Was he . . . was it . . . Did you love him very much?'

Isobel looked into Perdita's pleading eyes.

'Yes, I loved him,' she lied.

It was the strangest evening, with the snow and the storm rising to a frenzy outside, and the family marooned within. Alix felt as though she were detached from reality, and was watching a play being enacted with the drawing room its stage.

Trudie, glad to have something to do, went off to have beds made up, pyjamas and dressing gowns found. 'Perdita's in your old room,' she told Isabel. 'I'll put you in the big room at the end.'

'Wherever you think best, Aunt Trudie.' She gave her a lovely smile. 'Hey, it's good to call someone aunt again. It's kind of lonely, having no family.'

Rokeby announced dinner. Isabel winked at him as she went out of the drawing room on Grandpapa's arm. 'Surprised to see me?'

'It's very good to have you back among us, Miss Isabel, if I may say so.'

'Did you know it was me staying at the Cottage?'

'I saw you on the ice, when you didn't have your glasses on. I knew then.'

'And didn't say a word? I bet you know everything that's gone on in this house since your first day among the boots, you old fox. I'll call in on the kitchen and say hello to the others in the morning.'

'I'm afraid there's no one left from your time, Miss Isabel.'

Isabel's face kept its perfect composure, but Alix noticed the slightest tightening of her jaw. They were in the dining room now, and Isabel threw a look in Grandmama's direction. 'Did a clear-out, did she?' She sat down at Grandpapa's right, where he was holding the chair for her.

'How it all comes back. I remember this room so well, those terrifying meals when I was allowed downstairs.'

'Not everything was terrifying, I hope,' Grandpapa said.

Alix sat silent, looking at this exotic woman who was her sister; a stranger, yet so familiar. What a day of wonders it had been. Jack back from the grave, bringing nothing but trouble and sorrow, and now, as though in some unreal compensation, the joy of a resurrected sister.

How had Grandmama thought she could get away with it?

Easily, she'd managed it with Jack, so it must have seemed easy enough to pull the same stunt again. Only why had she done it? What a thing to do, merely in the name of morality and saving face. It was out of all proportion, surely, to deprive a family of their sister and niece and granddaughter and to desert Isabel, barely out of childhood, at a time when she most needed help and kindness, whatever she'd done. She'd

465

only had a baby, for Lord's sake, it wasn't as though Isabel had committed some crime.

Although to Grandmama an illegitimate child was a crime. Even so, Alix couldn't quell the suspicion that there was more to this than they yet knew.

Isabel called across the table to her daughter. 'Say, Perdita, Lidia tells me you have a real talent for music. Are you planning to study?'

'Yes,' Perdita said, so loudly that everyone else stopped their conversations and looked at her.

'Perdita will go to college,' Grandmama said.

'I guess Perdita should do what she wants to do.'

Later, when Perdita had gone to bed, exhausted from the emotion of the day, but with an air of determined happiness about her, Aunt Jane asked the question none of the others had dared to.

'Everyone else is too polite to ask, Isabel, but I think untold truths have festered long enough in this family. I fear I know the answer. Who is, or was, Perdita's father?'

With one accord, the visitors rose to their feet.

'You stay right where you are, Newman,' Isabel said. 'When you have the whole story, I reckon you'll be less apt to spill the beans to some reporter you meet back home.'

'Michael should stay,' Cecy said in a bleak voice. 'He knows something about what happened here, sixteen years ago, and I think you all ought to hear it.'

Michael knew something about what? Alix asked herself. Her eyes went over to where Hal was propped up against the fireplace, a reassuring figure. He smiled back at her and drooped an eyelid in a wink.

Grandmama made to get up. 'Ring for Rokeby,' she told Aunt Trudie. 'I want Lipp to prepare me a tisane. I'm going to bed.'

'You feel you might be bored, hearing the old story again?' Isabel asked.

Trudie had raised her hand to the bell; she didn't pull it.

Grandmama's face didn't change, but Alix saw wariness in her eyes.

'In my day, we would have called it washing dirty linen in public,' she said.

'If you don't have dirty linen in the first place, there's no problem about the public bit,' Isabel retorted. She looked at Cecy, and then at Michael. 'What does he know?'

Michael shook his head.

'It was sixteen years ago, the last time the lake froze,' Cecy said.

That caught the attention of both Isabel and Grandmama; she was now regarding Michael with hard, malevolent eyes.

'Michael was only a boy. He was out on the lake, after dark. He saw a girl raped, there in the woods by the shore.'

Alix felt a chill wrap itself around her heart. No. Not that. It wasn't possible.

A gasp from Aunt Jane, an indrawn breath from Edwin, a kind of wail from Aunt Trudie; small sounds of shock and dismay whispering through the almost tangible silence that followed Cecy's abrupt words.

They were all staring at Michael now, except for Lady Richardson, who looked straight ahead into nothingness.

'The man saw Michael, but then some other people came into the wood, and the attacker ran away. The girl's rescuers were two women, one kind, one not.'

'Who were they?' Grandpapa asked Michael, his face bleak. 'Did you recognise them?'

'No, sir, I never saw them before.'

'Have you seen them since?'

Michael hesitated, searching for the right words. 'I'm not sure. It was a long time ago. I was ill afterwards, it played havoc with my memory.'

'It's a fantasy,' Grandmama said. 'Nothing more.'

'Of course it's more,' Isabel said. 'I was there, remember?

So were you, Grandmama, and you, Aunt Trudie.' She turned to Michael. 'Aunt Trudie was the kind woman.'

Sir Henry gave a strangled cry of dismay. 'Raped? Isabel was raped? It's impossible, I would have been told. How could a crime like that be committed without my knowing about it? The police would have been called in.'

'No police were necessary,' Lady Richardson said. 'There was no question of rape. Isabel enticed a young man and then paid the consequences.'

'Just like Ursula,' said Alix under her breath. Good God, Ursula had had a luckier escape than she knew.

'Girls are like that.'

Only in your imagination, Grandmama, Alix thought.

'There you have it,' Isabel said. 'To me, it was rape. To Grandmama, I was a seductress who got what I'd asked for.'

'Hey, wait a moment.' Newman was indignant. 'Bettina, you were only a kid then. How old were you?'

'She was fourteen,' Alix said.

'Fourteen? What kind of an outfit were you running here that she was seducing men, if that's true, and out on her own on a dark night?'

'Young girls are not to be trusted. They are deceitful,' was Grandmama's disdainful reply.

'Who raped you?' Edwin asked his sister.

Alix was sure that he, like her, already knew the answer.

'I met him here, at Wyncrag, once, when I was going to the bathroom in the early hours one morning, but I didn't know who he was. Grandmama swore me to secrecy. He was an old friend of hers, she said. She sent me over to the wood where he was living in the old pele tower, the one that was converted for the gamekeeper to live in. It isn't there any more.'

'It collapsed several years ago,' Sir Henry said in an expressionless voice.

This is going to kill him, Alix thought. Daphne was beside him and she rested her hand on his arm.

'He was hiding out there, I suppose,' Isabel went on. 'I had to take food and newspapers and money to him. I thought it was some kind of a game and I was a go-between, like something in all those spy stories I used to read. I enjoyed having a secret from my parents and nurse and Grandpapa. I was, as Newman said, only a kid.'

'So who was he?' Jane asked the question again.

'I didn't know, then. I only knew for sure when I came back this winter.'

'Why did you come back?' The words burst out of Grandmama, high and angry. 'Why ever did you come back? It's all your fault.'

'I came back because it was time to face a few ghosts. When I read about the lake freezing over, I decided to come back. Apart from the rest of it, I hoped to get a glimpse of Perdita. I longed to see how she'd grown up, once I knew she was here.'

'Where did you think she was?' Edwin asked.

'My grandmother, my other grandmother, told me that she'd been sent for adoption.'

'More lies,' Alix said. It was nothing but a tragic tangle of lies, and all of them originated with Grandmama.

'Then, last year, just before she died, she told me that my daughter hadn't been adopted, but had been taken back to England, to her family at Wyncrag.'

'Helena's mother always was a stupid woman,' Grandmama said.

'I wanted to lay the demons to rest. Instead of which, I found them all alive and twitching. Skating about the lake, in fact. You don't need to ask, Aunt Jane. You've figured it out for yourself. The man who raped me, who is Perdita's father, is Uncle Jack.'

SIXTY

From that point on, it seemed to Alix that she, and all of them, were caught up in a sequence from one of her sister's films. It was partly the drama, partly the extraordinary and unearthly beauty of the night. The snowstorm had vanished as swiftly as it had come, leaving swirls of snow across the gleaming surface of the lake, a glimmering kaleidoscope of white and purple under the full moon. And everything appeared to happen in slow motion.

The silence that fell in the drawing room after that last, terrible revelation was broken by a commotion outside in the hall.

A voice; foreign, indignant and voluble. It was Parsons, the Grindleys' chauffeur, who came into the drawing room, unannounced, brushing a protesting Rokeby aside.

He was pouring out the words in almost unintelligible English, with interspersed invocations to the Virgin in his native Spanish.

It took a little while to make sense of what he was saying, and when they did understand him, Hal summed it up in a few stark words.

'You were in the Lagonda, and you had Miss Rosalind in the back.'

'That is right. That is what I have told you.'

470

'Out in a night like this?'

'It was lunacy, and so I told the miss, but she insisted. She said I would lose my place if I didn't do what she said. In such a storm, I have never driven in such terrible weather, never.'

'And then a madman jumped out at you?'

'That is exactly what he did. In the headlamps I saw him, I did not think I could stop. But I did, and he came to the door and opened it and pulled me out.'

'And you were left on the side of the road in all the snow and dirt, while this maniac drove off with Miss Rosalind still in the car?'

For the second time that evening, they were spilling out into the hall, calling for coats and boots and torches. This time, Alix had no intention of being left behind, and she bundled herself into the first coat that came to hand and thrust her feet into a pair of gum boots that were too big for her, before plunging out into the darkness.

Hal was there, holding her hand as they slipped and slithered down to the lake. Strength flowed into her from that simple contact. She saw shadowy figures, moving in the woods and down the slope of the fell, heard the sharp barking of the dogs. Isabel was ahead of them, racing along the shore as though trying to outpace the big car screeching along the silver thread of road beside the lake. She was wearing an overlarge shooting jacket that she had snatched from the Gun Room, and it flapped as she ran.

An official voice rang out, saying that the road was blocked, the car wouldn't get away. Shouts, sounding across the lake.

The Lagonda veered from the road and bucketed down to the very edge of the lake. A moment's hesitation, and Alix yelled as a figure was flung out, landing like a rag doll on the ice. The roar of the powerful engine sounded across the lake as the driver drove on to the ice and set a course for the opposite shore.

Nearby, one of the pursuers was cursing.

'Will the ice bear?' someone called out.

'That it will,' came a shouted reply. 'And that villain knows every inch of the lake and the shore, he'll know where to bring her up yar side, and no one to stop him, he'll be away south long before we get around the lake.'

A police car, its bell still clanging, had driven cautiously down to the edge of the lake. Two men got out and were consulting with others, pointing across the ice.

From nowhere came a crash like thunder, followed by an eerie moment's silence, then a terrible hissing sound as a black line snaked faster than the eye could follow, right down the centre of the lake.

A great sigh, as though the lake had breathed. A series of immense cracks echoing around the fells, as the ice split and fell apart into gigantic pieces.

Half-way across to freedom, the Lagonda was sent flying into the air. A wheel spun above gaping blackness, then the car was no longer there.

The ice shifted and moved as the dark water ebbed to and fro.

Further along the lakeside, where the land dropped sheer into the lake, Alix saw a shelf of ice, attached to the shore, suspended above the surface of the water. She was still holding Hal's hand, and she laid her other hand on his arm.

'Hal, the man in the car. Was it Jack?'

'I think so. He didn't have a chance. The level of the lake has been dropping all this time,' Hal said, his arm tightening around her. 'Of course. The becks feeding the lake froze, but the river flowing out of the lake didn't. So the water level fell, leaving a gap between the water and the ice.'

Alix, numb, watched Rosalind picked up from the ice and carried back to the police car. Her face was white, with streaks of blood on it. Her eyes were closed.

She saw Isabel standing by the lake looking strangely serene.

It was over.

SIXTY-ONE

Ursula was writing in her journal, sitting up in bed with an eiderdown hunched around her shoulders.

'Eve's with Rosalind, who's been given a sedative, thank goodness. I never heard such a fit of hysterics. I think they were more about her being found out than the fact she was thrown out of the car and that Jack or Jago or whoever he was had drowned. Nanny put a stop to her wailings by slapping her face, so of course Eve had a go at Nanny; not that she got any change out of her, and she's a bit stuck, because where can you get a hospital nurse at new year? And Rosalind has to have someone to look after her cuts and bruises.

'Anyhow, that's enough about boring Rosalind. The real excitement was much later, when we were all back at Grindley Hall. Great Aunt Daphne, who was in a real temper, simply took charge. She ignored Eve entirely, and said that she wanted to talk to Daddy and Uncle Roger and Uncle Hal in the library. Then she looked at Simon and said, "Yes, and you, too, and Nicky and Ursula as well." Of course, Eve was consumed with curiosity and was determined to tag along, but Great Aunt Daphne just shut the door in her face. I could see Daddy didn't like it, but even he didn't dare to cross the great aunt in that kind of mood. Besides, even I could see she held all the cards.

'Well, she lammed into Daddy and Uncle Roger for a bit, all about how disgracefully they had behaved, knowing just what nasty types they were preparing to do business with. Daddy looked as though he'd like to defend himself, but I suppose he saw there wasn't any point, and Uncle Roger looked daggers at him, so he sort of subsided, except for a few splutters. Uncle Hal just looked as if he wished he was back in America. Anyway, Great Aunt Daphne made a kind of announcement. Hal was making over his shares to her – I could see that Daddy and Uncle Roger were dying to know how much she'd paid for them – and so she was now in charge of the firm. She would leave Daddy to carry on with the main business, but she was going to buy Palfrey's Porcelain, and run it with the help of an experienced manager, part of whose job would be to teach Nicky the business; Nicky was going to be a full-time, salaried employee.

'Nicky couldn't say a word, he was so amazed. However, if looks could kill, there'd have been infanticide, if that's the right word for a father slaying his nearly grown-up son. Goodness, Daddy was furious. He yelled at Great Aunt Daphne, about how Nicky was going to university, and no one was going to make decisions about the company over his head, and so on and so forth. She let him rant and rage for a bit, and then said, "Sixty per cent, Peter," which shut him up all right. Then he started on about Nicky not being of age, and it being up to him to decide what he was going to do. Nonsense, said the great aunt, Nicky was quite old enough to make up his own mind. Children weren't chesspieces to be controlled and moved about as though they didn't have any wishes or opinions of their own. Any more from Daddy, she went on, and she'd withdraw her offer for Palfrey's.

'You could see that Daddy was really torn. Uncle Roger was standing beside him now, muttering in his ear; of course he doesn't care a jot about Nicky, he just wants to get his hands on the money. Honestly, I was quite ashamed of them both, and I didn't feel a bit sorry for Daddy.

'Great Aunt Daphne is wonderful. She's wrung all kinds of concessions out of Daddy and Uncle Roger in return for bailing them out, as she puts it. It's so marvellous that I almost don't want to write it down, in case it makes it not happen. She's forcing Daddy to allow me and Nicky access to Mummy! Oh, how he did hate that, almost more than Nicky and Palfrey's, I think. He looked so sour, and Great Aunt Daphne told him to pull himself together, "I can't abide a man in the sulks," she said. And then she rounded on Uncle Roger: "You may take that disagreeable look off your face, Roger. In case you're tempted to thwart Cecy's desire to become a doctor by keeping too tight a hold on the purse strings, I shall pay for the rest of her training myself." Uncle Roger is being made to give her a good allowance, so he doesn't get off scot-free, which he probably thought he had.

'As if all that weren't enough, she then set her beady eyes on Uncle Hal and told him it was time to come clean about his profession. I can't believe it: he isn't a failed actor after all, but a frightfully important and famous theatrical director with plays on Broadway. He's made a lot of money by backing successful shows; that was another blow to Daddy and Uncle Roger. Great Aunt Daphne told them that if they weren't such philistines, they would have heard of Henry Ivison and no doubt realized who he was.

'Daddy was livid. He turned on Hal and said, "You've made fools of us, pretending to be a third-rate actor when you were no such thing."

'Uncle Hal was looking a bit pale, but he just shrugged his shoulders. Which was wise, because you can't argue with Daddy when he gets like that.

'Great Aunt Daphne has told me privately that she'll see to it that I stay on at school and go to college if I want to, that she'll do the same for me as she's doing for Cecy. That's just the icing on the cake. I can't believe that I'm going to see Mummy again, and that I can write to her and ring her up and talk on the telephone whenever I want. At least, not as much as I want on the telephone, for Eve is always in agonies if anyone keeps talking after the pips have gone.

'I'll go over to Wyncrag tomorrow, I can't wait to tell Perdy my news. I bet things are a bit fraught there, too; fancy her sister being her mother instead, and being alive all this time, I couldn't believe it when Uncle Hal told me about the skating film star being Isabel Richardson come back to life.'

SIXTY-TWO

Alix was astonished by how Grandpapa rallied once the full enormity of his wife's actions had become clear to him.

He and Grandmama sat face to face, oblivious of the rest of the family grouped around them in the drawing room.

'You've been giving Jack money, all this time, I assume. Money that has gone to finance his political activities, not simply to keep him alive, which might have been forgiven.'

'Forgiven?' Grandmama made an insult of the word. 'I would have given him more, if I had been able. I used my money, and I gave him my jewels to sell.'

So that was why only Grandpapa's most recent Christmas present to his wife had ever been worn. Alix had thought she'd squirreled the jewels away, but no, Jack had had them.

'And my mother's jewels?' she asked.

Grandmama was unrepentant. 'They came from Neville, and Jack was his brother. Pearls and diamonds around your neck, what was that in comparison to the cause that Jack served?'

The jewellery seemed to be the last straw for Grandpapa. Rising from his chair, an old man, but an indomitable one, he said that Grandmama was to leave Wyncrag. He would provide a generous allowance, she might go wherever she

477

chose, with or without Lipp, provided she didn't stay in England.

'Pa, you can't,' Saul said.

'It's time you stopped clinging to your mother's apron strings,' Sir Henry said wearily. 'I can't prevent you going to see your mother, nor should I want to. I dare say she will decide to live in Germany and it would do you good to go over there and see what her kind of politics can lead to.'

It was clear to Alix that Aunt Jane, a new Jane, wouldn't allow him to do any such thing.

'I always knew this bad inheritance business was nonsense,' she said. 'After all, it wasn't on my side of the family that the real trouble lay. And Perdita is all right, and only think of her heredity.'

That was the real worry, what to tell Perdita.

Grandpapa thought Perdita should be told the truth. 'She has a clear mind, free of cant, and is full of courage. She prefers to face up to the facts.'

Alix disagreed with him, her heart freezing at the prospect. Was he really prepared to tell the girl, who was both his granddaughter and his great-granddaughter, that her conception had been the result of rape and incest?

'It's monstrous,' she said. 'I don't see how Perdita could cope with that.'

'Of course she can't, and she shouldn't be expected to,' Saul said, testily. 'Legally, everything must remain as it is, unless Isabel plans to claim her share of her parents' inheritance, which is presently held in trust for Perdita.'

'Leave it there,' Isabel said. 'I'm a rich woman in my own right. I'd like Perdita to have it.'

Alix could see that Aunt Trudie didn't agree. Had she kept the terrible secret for so long that its revelation was the only thing that could bring her peace?

'We should tell her,' Trudie said. 'Young people are resilient, her life is ahead of her, she needn't dwell on the past.'

Jane agreed. 'Concealed truths have a way of coming out, as we've all seen. Perdita may find out the truth at a time when it is more difficult for her.'

'Leave her be,' Isabel said. 'I'm her mother, I'm the closest relation she has, and I say we keep it quiet. I never want to hear the name of Jack again, and I don't want her to have to carry it as a burden for the rest of her life.'

'Burden!' Grandmama spat the word back at Isabel. 'Jack wasn't a burden. He was the only one of you worth anything. He was the only person I ever loved, and because of you, Isabel, he's been destroyed.'

'Grandmama, he brought destruction wherever he went, and he finally destroyed himself.' Edwin sounded as though he were about to lose his temper.

Alix quickly intervened. 'You can think what you like, Grandmama. None of us agrees with you; why, I don't suppose even Uncle Saul can swallow what Uncle Jack did. Not only to Isabel, remember that, but –' she was about to add, 'to Ursula, and others, too,' but caught sight of her grandfather's stricken face and stopped.

Saul had reddened, and was glowering in her direction. Well, pretty silly his kowtowing to Grandmama had made him look.

'Tell her, don't tell her,' Grandmama said. 'As you choose. I may decide to tell her myself. I pity her for having a slut for a mother, a woman who shares a house with a man who isn't her husband, who reveals herself in her underwear to millions of people. Her father was a fine man, and could have been a great one, with a role to play in the new order he believed in so strongly. Perdita is all I have left of Jack. I shall say whether or not she is told.'

'You shan't,' Sir Henry said with finality. 'You are not having any further contact with her at all. Haven't you done enough? Does it occur to you that Neville knew what had happened, and that's why he went to the Andes? Unhappy enough to want to die? Saul's career is finished, he'll have to apply for the Chiltern Hundreds and resign his seat in Parliament. There's no way he can continue to sit as a Member now the truth is out about Jack's desertion. Do you think I'm going to let you do any more damage to our children and grandchildren and great-grandchild than you already have?'

Without a word, Grandmama rose from her chair and went out of the room. Erect, unyielding, unmoved.

Edwin made as though to go after her. 'She may go to find Perdita. She's quite capable of telling her out of sheer spite, you know she is.'

'She won't see her,' Grandpapa said. 'Rokeby knows that they mustn't meet.'

'So what's going to happen to Perdita now?' Alix said.

Perdita came into the room as if on cue. 'I heard my name. What are you all doing closeted in here? Not more secrets?'

Her voice was light, her eyes anxious.

Isabel took her hand. 'Listen, honey, we're deciding what's going to be best for you. This music you want to study, where do you do that? Can you do it right away, or does it have to wait until you're older?'

'You can go to music college in London when you're fifteen, only it's a bit young.'

'Tell us what you'd like to do, Perdy,' Edwin said. 'If you could choose to do exactly what you wanted.'

Perdita was silent.

'I'll tell you,' Alix said. 'I know what she wants to do. She wants to go back to school until the summer, and work with her piano teacher there. Properly, all above board, parents', well, guardian's permission, special case at school, that kind of thing. Then she can start in London in the autumn.'

'Don't say it,' Perdita said quickly. 'I know, it's impossible. I've got to finish my education, Grandmama wants me to go to university. She'd never, ever let me leave school next year, and especially not to study music. She'd not like the idea of London, either, it's a big, bad city. She wants me shut away in some old women's college where the doors are locked every night at nine.'

'Your grandmother isn't well, Perdy,' Grandpapa said. 'She's been very difficult these holidays, and she's having what the doctors call a nervous breakdown. She'll have to go away, perhaps to another country, for a long time. So it's for you, and your mother, and Uncle Saul, who is one of your trustees, to come to a decision about what you want to do.'

Perdita was a girl transformed. A light came into her eyes that Alix had never seen before.

'Do you think it's possible for someone to be so happy they faint?' she asked.

'You aren't going to faint,' Jane said. 'Sit down, for we have to talk about where you'd live in London. You would be welcome to come and live with Saul and me, but Saul has to give up his seat in Parliament and we're going to live in the country. Dorset, I think. We'll love having you to stay in the holidays – you do get holidays at music college? Yes. Close your mouth, Saul, don't look more foolish than the good Lord made you.'

Alix couldn't hide her astonishment. Heavens, Aunt Jane had certainly got the upper hand. She was sure now that in no time at all the house in Dorset would ring with the sound of children's voices and running feet.

Alix didn't know about the gaudy Christmas parcel, that, when Rokeby passed it on to Saul and he finally opened it, proved to contain all the presents of jewellery he had given Mavis over the years he had been with her. 'Except for the last brooch, dearie,' Mavis had written. 'Which I'll keep for old times' sake.'

'Darling Perdy, you can stay with me, heaps of room in my flat, only I work, and it could be lonely for you,' she said.

481

'Perdita, would you care to come back to the States with me? Lidia tells me there are some world-class teachers there,' Isabel said.

'You live in Hollywood. There aren't teachers there.'

'No, I guess she means New York. You could go to college there, and come to California when school's out.'

'Suddenly everybody wants me,' Perdita said.

'It's for you to decide, Perdita,' her grandfather said. 'And I'll make sure that the trustees don't put any obstacles in your way. Your home is here at Wyncrag, and always will be, that won't change. Study in London, or Paris and New York, and come back here in the holidays. I assume pianists have holidays. You'll need a really first-class grand piano, I'll see to that.'

Perdita flung her arms around Sir Henry's neck. 'Grandpapa, thank you. Alix is right. I'd like to go to music college in London, at least for a while. Then I can go abroad, in a year or two, if I want to.'

'That's settled, then.'

'What about Polly? You won't sell Polly?'

Isabel looked perplexed. 'Who's Polly?'

'Polly,' Edwin informed her, 'is Perdita's horse.'

'Polly can't go to London with you, she'd pine for her hills. She'll stay here, and Mungo will exercise her, and you can ride her whenever you're at home, just as you do now.'

SIXTY-THREE

It was a wild, grey whirling world of snow beyond the train windows. Alix and Hal had the first-class compartment to themselves, the four lamps, one above each of the four wide, comfortable seats, gave out a soft glow. Hal had tipped the guard to keep anyone else out of the compartment.

'Not that there's many travelling, sir, not on New Year's Day in weather like this.'

'Will we make it to Euston?'

'Aye, but I doubt she'll run on time.'

The dining-car steward came down the corridor, ringing a peal on his little gong to announce that dinner was about to be served.

Alix and Hal got up.

She relished the feeling of being cocooned in a little world protected from the harsh outside. The white crispness of the table linen, the flower in a vase, the slight rattle of the silver, the waiters' easy movement with the sway of the train, the rhythmic tuppence three-farthings as the wheels clicked over the joins in the rails, the whine and clang of signals, the clatter as the train went over points: it was familiar, ordinary, reassuring.

They spoke about the less ordinary world they had left

behind in the north, further away from them with every passing mile.

'Will Daphne leave her shares to Nicky, do you think?'

'If he does as well in the company as I think he will. Otherwise, no. Daphne has a ruthless streak in her when it comes to business.'

'Did you want to sell her your twenty per cent?'

'For her to give to Nicky? Yes, certainly. It gives him a solid place in the firm, and although Peter won't ever forgive Daphne, he'll be glad enough of Nicky's help when the country comes out of recession.'

Yes, thought Alix, as she ate her salmon. Daphne had been ruthless. A fairy godmother, indeed, but a tough one.

'I'll always be a third-rater to Peter,' Hal said with a trace of bitterness in his voice.

Alix put her hand out to touch his. 'Never third-rate, not you.'

The fish was removed, and the meat course was served by a deft waiter.

'I suppose Grandmama and Lipp will be in France by now.'

They ate in silence again. The waiter brought the cheese board, and Alix dragged her mind from the chilly whiteness of Wynwater to the soft comfort of the dining car.

'Do you think Lidia will agree to marry Edwin?'

'Now that she feels she has the moral advantage, yes, I dare say she will.'

'Moral advantage?'

'It was all King Cophetua and the Beggar Maid, before. Now Edwin has a nicely tarnished name to offer her, she'll be more inclined to take him.'

'You are a cynic.'

'And you're displaying an Emma-like tendency to play matchmaker. I dare say Edwin and Lidia will live at Wyncrag and keep Sir Henry company.'

'I'd be glad if they did. Grandpapa likes Lidia.'

'What about Michael and Cecy?'

'Cecy won't marry him, she can't, without giving up medical school, and she won't do that for anyone. But I should think they'll work out a *modus vivendi*.'

'I like Michael.'

'So do I, and Freddie, too. Grandpapa's going to pay a visit to Michael's chief, he's keen to invest in aircraft.'

'Cunning old devil.'

'I don't think Isabel will ever marry. I suppose that's another legacy left by Uncle Jack. I did wonder about her and this Newman, but he's just what she says he is, her secretary, and not keen on women at all. Isn't it extraordinary, her turning out to be a film star?'

'She has the looks, she has the talent, she has the guts and she has the Richardson determination that sweeps all obstacles aside. It isn't extraordinary at all.'

Alix looked at Hal intently. 'Do you see me like that?'

'I see you as a chip off the old block.'

'If I'd dreamed, when I decided to go north for Christmas and skate on the frozen lake, that any of this would happen, I'd have booked myself into a genteel hotel in Torquay for the festive season.'

'Liar. You're incapable of letting skeletons moulder peacefully in their wardrobes. Will you dine with me tomorrow? We can go on somewhere and dance afterwards if you like.'

Dine, and go on to dance. How normal that sounded, like her life before she came north again. No, on reflection, not like that at all. Dining and dancing with an agreeable man – a more than agreeable man – hadn't formed any part of her life. Ever. At Wyncrag, every move she made as a young woman had been scrutinised and controlled. When she came to London, she had been enthralled by John, and he had never cared for such frivolous activities. They went to the play and, more rarely, to the cinema, to see serious works, often by foreign writers and directors. After John had come her giddy time, living mindlessly as one of a crowd, a hectic, restless, unsatisfied life.

How easy it was to sit here and talk to Hal. There was such a network of threads connecting them, ties of family and friendship, the strong emotional bond formed by common experience and, not least, their shared roots among the fells and lakes of the north.

They had both escaped from their northern homeland, herself to London and Hal, much more adventurously, to America. Where he had made a considerable name for himself. Why had he chosen to keep that side of his life hidden from his family? She might have done the same in his place, when you considered what Peter was like. Hal's brothers were conventional to the bottom of their souls; he was a sport, a strolling player, a Bohemian.

That wasn't quite the right term for him. He might have a streak of Bohemian in his nature, but he was an urbane man, at ease in good tailoring, a man of the world. An attractive man, attractive to many women, she would guess. A humorous mouth and a relaxed air had misled her at first, so that she denied the vigour and the intelligence. She had some to realize that, beneath the elegant exterior, he was a passionate man with a core of steel.

A man you could trust, as he had proved. Yet it was impossible to predict what he might think or say or do in any situation, and that made him fascinating.

Even as these thoughts ran through her head, she knew she was deceiving herself. She could analyse him to shreds, only to what purpose? Her heart was telling her a different story. She wanted to see a lot of Hal, she wanted to let herself be purged of the unhappiness and turmoil of her past by the pleasure she felt being with him. He was half a stranger she longed to know better, half a part of herself. He shared her secrets – which would have to remain secrets to the rest of the world for as long as she lived.

She gave Hal a quick, delighted smile, acknowledging to herself, and to him, that they were setting off on an entirely new adventure together.

'I'd love to.' She paused, swirling the brandy round in its glass. 'Hal, can I ask you something?'

'Anything.'

'When Rosalind was brought back to Wyncrag, she had a broken arm, but no cuts, nothing that might have bled.'

'No?'

'Yet she had blood on her face and clothes.'

'Yes.'

'Just before the ice went, with that noise like thunder, did you hear another sound?'

'What kind of sound?'

'The sound of a gun going off.'

Hal considered before he answered. 'Isabel always was a fine shot.'

Alix let her breath out. 'I'm so glad. Because I keep thinking that although the car vanished, they haven't found a body, and I wonder whether it's possible . . .'

'That your Uncle Jack sold his soul to the devil and is indestructible? No, Alix, I think that he is finally dead, and will lie for ever at the bottom of the frozen lake.'

Tatiana and Alexander
Paullina Simons

Tatiana and Alexander is a powerful story of grief and hope – a passionate and epic love story from the Russian-born author of *The Bronze Horseman*. Tatiana is eighteen years old and pregnant when she miraculously escapes war-torn Leningrad to the West, believing herself to be a widow. Her husband, Major Alexander Belov, a decorated hero of the Soviet Union, has been arrested by Stalin's infamous secret police and is awaiting imminent death as a traitor and a spy.

Tatiana begins her new life in America. In wartime New York City she finds work, friends and a life beyond her dreams. However, her grief is inescapable and she keeps hearing Alexander calling out to her.

Meanwhile, Alexander faces the greatest danger he's ever known. An American trapped in Russia since adolescence, he has been serving in the Red Army and posing as a Soviet citizen to protect himself. For him, Russia's war is not over, and both victory and defeat will mean certain death.

As the Second World War moves into its horrific close, Tatiana and Alexander are surrounded by the ghosts of their past and each other. They must struggle against destiny and despair as they find themselves in the fight of their lives. A master of the historical epic, Paullina Simons takes us on a journey across continents, time, and the entire breadth of human emotion, to create a heartrendingly beautiful love story that will live on long after the final page is turned.

ISBN 0 00 711889 9